Also by R.W Peake

Marching with Caesar-Conquest of Gaul

Marching with Caesar-Civil War

Critical praise for the Marching With Caesar series:

"Fans of the author will be delighted that Peake's writing has gone from strength to strength in this, the second volume...Peake manages to portray Pullus and all his fellow soldiers with a marvelous feeling of reality quite apart from the star historical name... There's history here, and character, and action enough for three novels, and all of it can be enjoyed even if readers haven't seen the first volume yet. Very highly recommended."

~The Historical Novel Society

"The hinge of history pivoted on the career of Julius Caesar, as Rome's Republic became an Empire, but the muscle to swing that gateway came from soldiers like Titus Pullus. What an amazing story from a student now become the master of historical fiction at its best."

~Professor Frank Holt, University of Houston

LEG
X

ANT AVG

Marching with Caesar

Antony and Cleopatra

Part 2 Cleopatra

By R.W. Peake

Marching with Caesar -Antony and Cleopatra by R.W. Peake

Cover Artwork by Marina Shipova

Map of Actium reprinted from "The Roman Republic and The Founder of The Empire" by T. Rice-Holmes
Oxford University Press; London, 1923
Maps of Armenia reprinted with permission from "The Barrington Atlas of the Greek and Roman World"; Richard J.A. Talbert (Editor); © 2000 Princeton University Press
Photographs of Legio X Coin issued by Triumvir Marcus Antonius are from the author's private collection

Printed in the United States of America
First Printing, 2013

Foreword

Since this is just a continuation of what is essentially the third book in the Marching With Caesar series, I don't feel my normal compulsion to say something especially wordy or attempt to be profound, other than the normal thanks to my editor Beth Lynne, my artist Marina Shipova, and to my beta readers that I mentioned in Part I.

I will just say that, as of this writing here in late March, the response to Part I has been so positive and overwhelming that it's hard for me to put it in perspective. Just two days after release, Part I took the #1 spot in the genre of Ancient Rome on Amazon in the U.S., and held that spot for more than 3 weeks, before falling to the second spot.

Normally, this would not be something that thrilled me; I am extremely competitive (as my daughter will attest, as I never let her win at anything, until she was able to do so on her own merit), but this time it's somewhat different watching my third book fall a spot.

That's because what replaced it was my first book Marching With Caesar-Conquest of Gaul, now just two weeks short of its first anniversary of release. I can only attribute this to you, my readers, who have proven to be the most effective marketing tool of everything I've tried.

So I would like to take this space to thank all of you, the readers who took a risk on a story by a completely unknown, unpublished author, and most importantly took to heart what I asked of the first 150 people who liked my Facebook page for Marching With Caesar. (Which you can find at http://facebook.com/rwpeake)

"If you like it, tell somebody" is what I asked of you, and you have done that, and then some.

Thank you.

R.W. Peake
March, 2013

Chapter 1-Damascus

No Roman in Antonius' camp had forgotten that while Antonius was clearly besotted with the queen of Egypt, he was still married to Octavia, who had stayed in Rome and, from all accounts, was the model of what a highborn Roman wife was expected to be. Now she was about to be used as another piece in the great game going on between the two remaining players. Much has been made of what Antonius did to Octavia, and it is inexcusable. Nevertheless, it was Octavian who sent her, though I suppose the winner escapes the blame. She left Rome to go to Athens bearing supplies, 70 ships, and 2,000 more troops in the style of the Brundisium Cohorts, which I personally thought were useless. It was from the Greek city that Octavia sent word to Antonius she would be sailing with all of these goods as soon as the weather permitted. I must admit that it was a very clever ploy on the part of Octavian, even if it was not particularly admirable, putting Antonius in the fork of a cleft stick as it did. Many a watch has been spent in the intervening years with men sitting around fires, or at a table in some roadside inn arguing about what course Antonius should have taken. Naturally, each man is certain that he knows what Antonius should have done, but I do not count myself among those men. For I do not know that Antonius made the wrong decision, nor do I know that he made the right one, because in truth, I think that the gods had decreed that matters among us mortals had gone on long enough without a resolution, thereby moving Octavian to put Antonius in a dilemma that ultimately had only one outcome. If Antonius had not done as he did, telling Octavia that she was to send on the men, ships, and supplies, but for Octavia herself to return to Rome, he undoubtedly would have offended Cleopatra, and he needed the queen of Egypt for the money to fund his campaign. Also, it would have been a sign to the East that he still counted himself as Roman and not the Eastern monarch he had set himself up to be. While I understand why he did it, that does not mean it was a decision that I could follow, for I am and always will be a man of Rome. Therefore, when he turned his back on Octavia, and by extension Rome, it sealed my decision that when the moment came, I would do as Octavian bid me to do. I do think that Octavia did not deserve the treatment she received, from either of the men in her life. I am not alone in that by any means, and it was his abrupt and heartless repudiation of her that turned the lower classes against Antonius once and for all. This, of course, was exactly what Octavian had hoped to accomplish. The sum total of this event meant Octavian had little opposition in enacting any of his deeds from this point forward, no matter how injurious they may have been to Antonius. One other event occurred that, while it did not have a huge impact on our world, did finally close a chapter, and that was the fate of Sextus Pompey.

Sextus, as I have described, escaped from the naval battle over Sicily, which occurred at roughly the same time as our arrival at Phraaspa. For months, nobody knew his whereabouts, until he showed up on this side of Our Sea, where he immediately began to make mischief, and in fact was one of the causes of our difficulties in finding men to fill our ranks. When he landed in Africa, he began recruiting from his father Pompey's veterans, raising three Legions of men before proceeding to try to sell their services to the highest bidder, with Sextus as their commander, of course. While he did approach

Antonius, the Triumvir learned that young Sextus had also approached Phraates with the same offer and, in doing so, sealed his fate. This despite the fact that Sextus had supported Antonius, while according to some, he had been in a secret alliance against Octavian, which if true would explain why Antonius refused to lift a finger to help his colleague for years as the younger man struggled to break Sextus' grip on Rome's food supply. Personally, I think that is the real reason Antonius sent word to Titius, who Antonius had appointed to govern in Africa and who was the man in contact with Sextus, acting as the intermediary between the two, commanding Titius to lure Sextus to meet him. Telling Sextus that Antonius accepted in principle, but wanted Titius to work out the details with Pompey's sole surviving son, Antonius' quartermaster convinced him to meet. However, when Sextus arrived, his bodyguard was overpowered, with Sextus' head summarily removed from his shoulders to be sent to Antonius. With the death of Sextus, the line of Pompey Magnus came to an end and along with it any chance of Sextus possibly embarrassing Antonius with details of the bargain they made to starve Rome and cause Octavian difficulty.

There was one unexpected bonus for us in the army; with the death of their commander, suddenly there were a number of men who had expected to march again. A good number of them had flocked to the standard because of who Sextus was, and some of these men returned to their homes. However, others were still bored and looking for the opportunity for loot, so these men, hearing that there was a *dilectus* being held by a number of Legions, found their way to the nearest party. Sometimes they became men of the 10th, sometimes not, but in the space of two or three weeks, I received word from Scribonius that he was returning with the full complement of men that we needed. It had become clear to all of us that there would be no campaign that year, so I sent a message to Scribonius to march overland to condition the men and get a feel for their abilities instead of securing shipping to transport them.

Meanwhile, I spent more time with young Gaius, working with him on his sword and shield skills, both as a way to help him and to help myself. I worked harder that spring than I had in many years, finally coming to terms with the fact that the things that came naturally just a few years before I now had to work to achieve. The conditioning and muscle strength that never seemed to leave me now required a level of effort I had never had to exert before this. I cannot say that I was happy about it, and I am afraid I was not very good company at the end of the day when I would limp back to Miriam's apartment, but slowly I saw progress. By the time of my forty-third birthday, I finally felt close to my old self, but I recognized that I would never be the same Titus Pullus I had been when I marched with Vibius in Gaul.

Scribonius and the rest of the *dilectus* came marching in with the men he had recruited for the 10th Legion a bit short of three weeks later, just in time for us to pack up to march to Damascus, where we would spend the rest of the campaign season to winter, as Antonius sent word confirming that we would not march that year. Despite the men being sorely disappointed, none of the Centurions were, because we had not been keen on marching with essentially new men in our ranks, no matter how experienced they may have been in other Legions. It takes time for a Centurion to learn the character, strengths, and weaknesses of every man in his Century; for example, who are the shirkers and who are the men that might be troublemakers, for it is very unlikely that a man essentially asking for a job is going to tell the *dilectus* that he is lazy, a coward or likely to cause trouble. If one were to go by what men claimed when presenting themselves, we would never be defeated, while roads would be built in a matter of days instead of weeks or months, since every man had the fighting skill of Achilles, along with the strength of Hercules. Now we would have a whole year to train and evaluate these new men. They were not particularly happy to be told almost as soon as they came off a three-week march that they would only be in camp for a matter of two or three days before setting out again, and the decision was made by all the Primi Pili receiving new men to wait to issue armor, weapons, and equipment until we got to Damascus, so it was not the most martial-looking bunch that departed Leuke Kome.

We were leaving what had been a small, sleepy town that in the space of months had become a good-sized place with several more streets added to accommodate the wineshops, whorehouses, smiths, grain merchants, and the residences that accompanied such explosive growth. The original inhabitants of the town were no doubt happy to see us go, while the newer residents lined the streets and wailed, some of them tearing at their clothes and hair at the departure of their future earnings. As is so often the case a fair number of people, most of them whores who had latched onto one of the men, along with merchants whose goods and services were more portable, tagged along behind us as we marched, giving us a tail that would be with us all the way to Damascus. Every night, they settled down in their own makeshift hovels and patchwork tents a short distance away from our own camp and since we were not marching in enemy territory or expecting enemy contact, the men were allowed to go visit their women after our camp was completed and the evening formation was held. The pace was easy, as we were in no hurry so we did not have many stragglers, and I was very happy to see that none of them were the new men.

We had been so busy preparing for the move that it was not until the first night on the march that I had the chance to sit down with Scribonius to get his initial impressions of the new men. We were sitting in my tent as I cursed the absence of Diocles, for I now had to rely on Agis, who was in effect Diocles' servant and a very slow-witted boy. I had sent Diocles ahead with Miriam to secure accommodations near the winter camp, detaching Gaius to go with them as security, the road to Damascus being rife with bandits looking for easy prey. I cuffed Agis about the head, something that I would not normally do, but it was the second time he had stumbled and spilled the cups of wine he was bringing to us in as many tries. I despised masters who took advantage of a slave or servant's position because it reminded me of Lucius, my father, and his treatment of Phocas and Gaia, but there are limits. Still, I was cursing myself at my display of ill temper and I had to force myself back to the subject at hand. I had asked Scribonius for his report on the new men, yet he was forced to wait while I raged and now was sitting patiently, looking at me with a raised eyebrow and a sardonic smile.

"Well?" I snapped.

"I was just waiting for you to get over your fit," he replied, knowing full well that he was the only man who could speak to me in such a manner and not get his own cuffing.

His words had the effect he desired, as I laughed. Waving at him to go ahead, he pursed his lips as he referred to the wax tablet he had brought with him. Scribonius was the only Centurion I knew who actually took notes on matters he considered important, and it was such a good idea that I had tried to get the other Centurions to adopt it, but with limited success.

He looked up, then said, "Overall, it's a good bunch, but I'm concerned that we have a few too many former Centurions and Optios."

With those words, Scribonius touched on one of the biggest problems with enlisting veterans from other Legions into your own. While it would seem that it could only strengthen a Legion to have former Centurions and Optios in the ranks, I had observed that other Legions who had done so did it to their detriment. As I have said before, every Centurion runs his Century, every Pilus Prior runs his Cohort and every Primus Pilus runs his Legion in slightly different ways, while in each of their minds, the way they do it is the right way. Of course, their thinking is shaped by their superior Centurion, as a Pilus Prior has his Centurions run their Centuries to his standards, while all the Pili Priores must conform to what the Primus Pilus wants. After years of doing things a certain way, it becomes ingrained in a Centurion that this is the proper way of doing things, which is why the first preference when promoting Centurions is to do so from within the Legion, so there is less of a ripple of confusion when he takes over his new command. Having men who had gotten accustomed to command, then finding them doing things their way while marching in the ranks had shown to be problematic in other Legions, and in fact, Scribonius and I had discussed it before he left. I did not voice the question that popped into my mind at Scribonius' words, knowing that if he had allowed it to happen there was a good reason for it.

"How many, do you figure?"

He shook his head. "It's hard to say, because a number of them claimed to be rankers, but you know it's impossible for a man who was a Centurion or even an Optio to hide it for long. Maybe 50 altogether."

I whistled. That would be almost one such man in every Century, so depending on their intentions and attitude, it could cause a number of problems. Most concerning was the Tenth Cohort, which still was the weakest in numbers if not quality, so I made the decision that we would not put any of those men who had either claimed the Centurionate or who we suspected of being such into the Tenth Cohort. Frontinus was doing an adequate job of running the Cohort, but this would be the first big test of his leadership with the influx of men from outside the 10th.

"Otherwise how are they?"

He shrugged. "They're mostly old-timers who are long in the tooth for a full enlistment, but we promised them that they'd only be marching for the rest of this enlistment, which suits us anyway. We do have a few youngsters, maybe twenty percent of the men."

"Any troublemakers?"

He looked chagrined, but I did not hold his answer against him.

"More than I'd like. It seems as if some of our Centurions aren't the best judges of character, Decimus Ovidius in particular," he replied, naming the Princeps Prior of the Fifth Century. "I was tempted to throw out half the men he signed up, and of the problems we had on the march, most of them came from his group. Numerius Cossus wasn't much better, but I think he's a scoundrel at heart himself."

I sighed, shaking my head at Scribonius' words, not just because of the implication of them concerning the number of men who might cause problems, but I also knew that his assessment of Cossus was dead accurate. Cossus was the Hastatus Posterior of the Seventh Cohort, and was proving to be one of those Centurions I so despised, using his Century as a source of income by inflicting or withholding punishment depending on how much a man was willing to pay. His Century was one of the unhappiest in the Legion, but to that point, I had been unable to catch him in anything egregious enough to relieve him.

"Anyone stand out? Someone who might be worthy of being restored to the Centurionate or as Optio?"

"Quintus Albinus," he responded instantly. "He was a Pilus Prior in Pompey's First Legion, or so he claimed, and I believe him. He's about our age. Or, my age," he amended hastily, "but he's fit. And he's a leader; you can tell just by looking at the way he goes about his business and the way he was helping the raw youngsters."

My brow furrowed, trying to remember where I had heard that name before.

"Is he about this tall?" I held my hand up to just above my shoulder.

Scribonius laughed. "Yes, but isn't everyone compared to you?"

I shook my head in irritation, the memory of a man in Dyrrhachium slowly returning.

"Very fair?"

"Yes, hence the name 'Albinus,'" Scribonius replied dryly.

The final piece of what had become a puzzle clicked into place as my mind's eye recalled more details from that day and the man of whom I was thinking.

"Did he have a long, jagged scar up his arm?"

Now Scribonius was surprised, which made me feel a bit smug, I can tell you.

"Yes! You do know him! But how? From where?"

I explained the circumstances of my meeting with then-Decimus Princeps Prior Quintus Albinus, when I had led the Second Cohort to take a redoubt that Pompey constructed in the lines surrounding our positions, when Scribonius was my Optio. As I recounted what I remembered, my old friend's eyes lit up, then he snapped his fingers.

"Yes! I remember now! I should have recognized him myself, but that was so long ago. Titus, you have the memory of Perseus himself. I didn't speak to him that day. I was taking care of the wounded as I remember, but I certainly saw him closely enough."

Once we had established his identity, I decided to renew our acquaintance, and I knew just how to do it. I called for Agis, and was about to send him to find Albinus. Then, realizing that he would disappear and never come back, I gave him the simpler task of finding Lutatius, who arrived shortly. If he was surprised at my order to go find a ranker out of the new men, he did not show it. Since we had not made the assignments of the men to their respective Cohorts and Centuries, they were in their own part of our area, meaning Lutatius had to parade up and down the streets calling out Albinus' name before he was found.

Quintus Albinus, new Legionary Gregarius of the 10th Legion was escorted into my presence by Lutatius, who I dismissed to return to whatever it was that Optios did in their spare time. Scribonius and I sat silently, surveying the man standing at *intente*¸ his eyes locked at the spot above our heads as they were supposed to be. He had not had the chance to look at my face, as I made sure that it was turned from him when he entered, pretending to be absorbed in some paperwork.

Since I was seated, my unusual height did not give me away either, so the surprise on his face was unfeigned when I asked him, "So, Albinus, did you ever give Labienus that message I asked you to relay?"

Along with the surprise came confusion, his eyes shifting nervously in my direction, but being the good Legionary that he was, his eye contact with me was only fleeting before he looked back at the original spot.

"Sir?"

His voice was hesitant, but I thought I heard the first glimmering of realization.

"I didn't think I stuttered. As I remember it, I was very specific in telling you that as part of the condition of your surrender at Dyrrhachium that you were to convey to that bastard that Titus Pullus was going to cut his balls off."

Now the flood of conflicting emotions was plain to read on his face as the memory of that day came back to him. There was the dawning of recognition, then his eyes moved back to my face, which I now made no attempt to hide from him, widening as he realized that sitting before him was an old enemy. Then I saw the unmistakable look of shame in his eyes as the memory came back to him of the day when he was forced to surrender the redoubt that he commanded, or at least had been the only surviving Centurion, so commanded by default. I suddenly felt a similar sense of, if not shame, unease at rousing what had to be undoubtedly unpleasant memories of a day when the fighting had been fierce and bloody. To counter this, I stood and walked over to the man, offering my hand. He hesitated for a moment, then clasped my forearm as we looked each other in the eye for a silent moment, both of us reliving that day of blood and chaos. Finally, he gave a hesitant smile, revealing surprisingly good teeth, which I returned, then turned to point to a seat next to Scribonius, who was also standing.

"I don't have to tell you that this is unusual, as you're technically a ranker, but when I heard your name, I thought it was right to renew our acquaintance."

"Frankly, Primus Pilus, I've spent most of these years hoping that I never saw you again."

Scribonius' smile froze on his face, and I admit that I was taken aback. However, his tone was more rueful than defiant, and I found myself laughing at his candor.

"Fair enough," I conceded, then offered him some wine, which he accepted.

We spent the rest of the evening chatting, Albinus admitting that he had never given Labienus the message, which I had truly not expected him to do, nor did it matter because he was long dead, getting what was coming to him for many years. Albinus talked of Pharsalus and I complimented him on the performance of the 1st Legion that day, as they had proven themselves to be worthy opponents and had been one of the only Legions to leave the battlefield in good order.

"Life as a farmer just didn't suit me," he admitted, a common complaint heard by more old Legionaries than any of us could count. "It's hard work, every day, and you can do everything right, you can make the right sacrifices to Ceres, and to all the different gods that control the weather, and one drought can ruin you." He took a deep swallow of wine then shook his head. "Truth be known, I would rather lead men anyway."

"Well, that's not going to happen right away." I wanted to make sure that he had the proper expectations, and while it was plain that he did not like it, he nodded in understanding.

"But," I said carefully, "that doesn't mean that you can't exhibit leadership in other ways."

He looked at me sharply, his face a mix of interest and caution, and he was right to be wary.

"What are you asking of me, Primus Pilus?" Before I could say anything, he shook his head. "Because I won't be a spy for you."

"I don't want you to be a spy," I said a bit more sharply than I intended, for he had unwittingly touched on another sore subject with me, the practice of some Primi Pili and lower grade Centurions to pay men to inform on their comrades.

While I certainly appreciated the need and usefulness of a carefully cultivated network of men like Vellusius who would alert their Centurions to possible trouble, I refused to pay men, having seen firsthand the corrosive effect it had when it inevitably becomes known that a man marching next to you is spying.

"What I need is your leadership skills in the Tenth Cohort," I said as I proceeded to explain to him what had happened to the Tenth during the last campaign.

"I wasn't going to put any former Centurions, or Optios for that matter, in the Cohort because I don't want that kind of tension with the officially appointed officers," I said, and he nodded his head at the sense of this. "But I know that I can count on you not to be disruptive, and to provide the new men with help and guidance, because it will be the rawest of the Cohorts in terms of experience within the 10th." Now it was time to dangle the promise of reward. "And if you perform as I expect you will, I'll put you on the list to be promoted at the earliest opportunity."

I felt Scribonius' eyes on me, but he said nothing. At least not until after Albinus had left.

"That's not going to go over well with the veterans already on the list," he said quietly.

"No, it isn't," I agreed. "But if Albinus is the leader I think he is, I'm willing to risk it."

Arriving in Damascus, we moved into the winter quarters, which are maintained by a staff of men who have been invalided out for injuries, but who are fit enough to keep up the various winter camps spread throughout the Republic in proper working order. All that needed to be done were sweeping the huts out and taking the shutters off the windows, as it was not winter and Damascus can get hot. There was a mad scramble, men with women and families who had not planned ahead running into town at the earliest opportunity to secure some sort of lodgings for them, paying exorbitant prices in the process. Not that I expected to pay that much less; moving an army of our size is not a secret and, as is usual, the citizens of the city knew well before we did that we would be arriving.

As soon as we were settled in, Diocles came to camp with Gaius, but instead of just giving me directions, both of them insisted on escorting me to where Miriam was waiting, refusing to say any more. Intrigued and irritated in equal portions, I followed them through the streets of Damascus, past the district that I would have expected to be suitable for our circumstances. Still they refused to answer my questions, both of them looking very much like cats that had gotten into the cream. Reaching the outskirts of the city just outside the main walls, I saw it was in the area where the wealthier merchants obviously lived, with wide paved streets that were swept daily from the looks of it. My confusion deepened when they both stopped outside a Roman-style villa, with a wall enclosing it that bordered right to the edge of the street. There was a wooden door set in the whitewashed wall, with a peephole protected by an iron grille in the middle of the door. Without saying anything, Diocles went and knocked on it. He was clearly expected, because the peephole door opened immediately and I could see an eye set in wrinkled folds of skin peering out, looking up and down at the three of us, the sound of the latch as it lifted making a jarring sound. The door opened to reveal an old man, the rest of his face as wrinkled as the eye that had surveyed us before allowing entry. However, it was what he was wearing that gave me a shock, because the wizened old man was wearing a full Roman toga, folded perfectly and draped over his left arm in the appropriate manner. His skin tone was akin to a darkened walnut, but he addressed us in flawless, native Latin.

"*Salve,* Primus Pilus Titus Pullus, hero of the 10th Legion."

He laughed at my obvious confusion before stepping aside to beckon us into the confines of the villa as he did so. Both Diocles and Gaius were beaming at me in the same manner as this little Roman, but before I could say anything, the man I assumed to be our host spoke again, offering his hand in a thoroughly Roman manner.

"My name is Tiberius Flavius Laevinus, Primus Pilus, and I must say that it is a great pleasure meeting you." The man was positively bubbling over, pumping my forearm enthusiastically. "When I heard that one of the stalwarts of Rome, a man who chastised the Parthian and Median scum and his lady were looking for accommodations, I absolutely insisted to your servant here that it would not do for you to stay anywhere else but with me. And please, I insist that you call me 'Uncle Tiberius.'"

My head was positively whirling and Diocles, seeing how confused I was, stepped forward, grabbing my elbow.

"Master," he insisted on using a formal title in front of others, no matter how much I insisted that he could call me by my given name or my family name, if he preferred. "When Gaius and I were searching for accommodations, I ran into Master Laevinus, er, I mean Uncle Tiberius," he grinned at the older Roman, who was beaming back at him, "and when he heard that it was you that was looking for lodging for yourself and the Lady Miriam, he insisted that you be his guest."

"But that's too much to ask," I protested, mainly to be polite, but also because I had no wish to share a house with anyone, no matter how much of a kindly uncle he may have been. However, he seemed to read my true thoughts because he gave a laugh, which sounded remarkably like the braying of a goaded mule.

"My boy, clearly you don't understand. This is my second home. I live just over there." He pointed over my shoulder at some point across the street. "So this villa would be entirely your own, for as long as you wish. It's the least I can do." Without waiting for an answer, he turned, beckoning to us to follow. "Please, come. I want to show you where you'll be living."

I looked over at my nephew and servant, who were grinning at me, as Gaius whispered, "Uncle, I wouldn't argue. Believe me, you're going to want to see this."

I entered a residence that could have been ripped from the streets of Rome and magically transported to this spot outside of Damascus. Walking through the main entrance, we passed around the atrium, in which a number of plants and small trees were growing, clearly attended to with much care and love. Ringing the atrium was a number of rooms, while on the left side was the *oecium*, in which there were a number of couches and chairs, the floor covered in rich carpets, with marvelous frescoes decorating the walls. Seated on one of them, and astonishingly dressed in a Roman gown, with her hair swept up in the Roman style, sat Miriam, looking more beautiful and radiant than I had ever seen her. Her smile washed over me, making me feel warm and loved, my desire for her never greater than it was at that moment. Seated next to her was an older woman, dressed in the same manner as Miriam, except her hair was as gray as iron, but I could clearly see that in her day she had been a great beauty herself. Nevertheless, I only had eyes for Miriam at that moment, and I barely heard our host speaking.

"This is my wife, Pompeia. She absolutely insisted on being here to meet you, for she is as much an admirer of you as I am. Judging from the way she's mooning at you, I daresay she's an even bigger one."

He chuckled, and I was astonished to see the older woman blush.

"Tibi," she chided the man I was even beginning to think of as Uncle Tiberius, "you really shouldn't say such things! People will get the wrong idea!"

"What people? It's only us here," he boomed, sweeping his arm in an expansive gesture. "Besides, you know it's true. I can tell by the way you're blushing.

"So, as Diocles here, a good man, a great fellow I can tell you, says, when I heard that it was the Primus Pilus of the 10th Legion, of *Caesar's* 10th who was looking for some hovel in which to shelter this lovely, lovely creature! Well, I just wouldn't hear of it! I told Mother that since we had this great huge house sitting vacant, it would be absolutely silly for you to stay anywhere else!"

He turned his wrinkled, bald head towards me, the gaps in his teeth not detracting from the dazzling smile he gave me.

I realized that all eyes were turned on me, and I found myself stammering, "Sir, I mean, Uncle Tiberius, that is most, most generous of you. But a house like this," I swept my arm at the wonderful carpets on the floor and the equally impressive frescoes on the wall, "I simply can't afford something this grand."

I was worried that I would offend the man, but he threw his head back with that braying sound of a laugh again. "My boy," he gasped, after he had recovered from his spell of mirth, "this trifle of a house won't cost you one brass obol. As I said, it's my second house. Mother forced me," he grinned at her squawk of protest, "to build something a bit more suited to the style to which she aspires, and because of you and the Legions, business has been good enough that I could indulge her." He gave me a wink then continued in a loud whisper that he clearly meant for his wife to hear, "Though why I don't know. My mistress is much less demanding."

Despite his wife spluttering in protest, it was clear that this was all done in fun and love. I felt myself relaxing as my mind started to accept what was taking place.

I believe it was the sight of Miriam's face, aglow with happiness as she sat on the couch that clinched the decision for me, so I sighed and in the same playful tone, "Well, sir, I know when I've been outflanked. I surrender, and I thank you for your kindness and generosity." I winked at Uncle Tiberius. "Besides, I know if I refused, I'd be sleeping by myself."

"Yes, you would," Miriam said sweetly, causing all of us to laugh.

The villa was the largest house I had ever lived in, despite the apologies of our host for its small size. Uncle Tiberius was Roman, a native of Campania who had come to the East some 20 years before to import, among other things, olive oil and wine, obviously making a fortune in the process. He was one of the most powerful and influential Romans in Syria, though you would not know it to look at him. He took us on a tour, passing through the atrium where a host of plants and small trees grew, every name of which he knew, pointing them out while giving a brief explanation of their origin. Surprisingly, very few of them were native to the region, but had been brought from Italia, an expense that I did not even want to consider.

"It reminds me of home," he sighed. "Whenever I miss Campania, I'll just come here and sit and drink it all in, then I feel better."

"If you miss Italia, surely you have done enough to go home, have you not?"

Miriam never ceased to surprise me, for underneath her meek exterior and seeming submission there was a soul that seemed to be unafraid of asking someone from any station any question. I marveled at how graceful she was in doing so, never arousing anyone's ire or making them uncomfortable. Uncle Tiberius gave her an appreciative smile, clearly enjoying being asked something other than polite questions.

"I have, I have indeed, young lady!" He heaved a sigh, affecting an air of melancholy that was so theatrical that it made all of us laugh. "But you see, I talk a great deal, as you undoubtedly have learned by now, about all manner of things that I never do, because ultimately I'm perfectly happy here. It's just bad form not to profess to miss your homeland, particularly if you're a Roman, so I whine and wring my hands and shed a tear for dear old home."

Moving through the atrium back into the first wing of the house, he took us into the *triclinium,* where a massive low table inlaid with citrus wood arranged in a series of geometric patterns was lined with couches covered in some sort of rich fabric and was the central feature of the room. Completing this wing of the house was the *oecium*, where Uncle Tiberius entertained other rich merchants, and where we had first met our benevolent host and his wife. Moving back through the atrium, he ushered us into the main bedroom, and I had to suppress a gasp of astonishment. The walls were plastered in frescoes of an erotic nature, where satyrs were cavorting about doing all manner of sexual things with nymphs in woodland settings, while in others Bacchus was holding court at what was obviously an orgy. Located in each corner of the room were statues of men and women coupling in a variety of positions, the floor decorated with a colorful mosaic of a surprisingly detailed scene of the sun rising over the seven hills of Rome. Prominent landmarks like Pompey's Theater and the Forum Julii were plainly visible, along with the Circus Maximus. As I studied it more closely, it did not appear that the creator of the mosaic had ever been to Rome, or perhaps he just had to stick the landmarks in places where they would appear. Against one wall was the largest bed I had ever seen and Miriam was standing by it, which I reached out to touch with a hesitant finger.

"It's not straw," she marveled. "I have been sleeping on it now for several days and I still do not know exactly what it is made of."

She turned to Uncle Tiberius with a questioning glance.

"Straw! Straw? Well goodness no, my dear! There's nothing better than goose feathers. I trust you and the Primus Pilus will no doubt put this to good use, neh?"

He turned to give me a lewd wink, but his manner was so jovial that it was impossible to take any offense, and I found myself laughing. Even Miriam, whose people do not have the same open attitudes about sexual relations as we do, was smiling shyly, shooting me a glance through lowered lashes that told me that Uncle

Tiberius was correct in his prediction. On each side of the bed, there were carpets of the type that abounded here in Syria, with deep, rich reds and golds, so striking that even I, who never took notice of such things, had to stop to admire the handiwork, recognizing that they were smaller versions of the much larger one on the floor of the *oecium*. There were two wooden chests, while on top of each were a set of cupboards where our clothes and personal items would be stored, and I assumed Miriam's were already in one of them. Adjoining the bedroom through a short passageway was the bathing area, where a steaming bath was already ready for us, complete with a set of slaves to attend to our needs. There were a number of smaller bedrooms arranged around the bath, each with their own access. This was where Diocles would stay instead of the servants' quarters, which was in a separate building, though I did not tell him that yet. Uncle Tiberius led us back out past the atrium to the far side of the house, where we passed through another hallway and into the kitchen area and storerooms. There were perhaps a half-dozen people, men and women, bustling about obviously preparing a meal.

"I hope you don't mind, but I took the liberty of having the cooks prepare a dinner that I hope you will allow Pompeia and me to attend before we leave you two to make yourselves at home."

Even if I were inclined to disagree, I did not see how I could refuse without appearing to be completely ungrateful, so I naturally said that we would be absolutely delighted, which had the added benefit of being the truth. In the short time I had known the man, I had grown to like him immensely, and I could tell that Miriam felt the same way, as did Gaius and Diocles. With the tour of the house complete, we returned to the *oecium* to sit on the couches, as I fumbled with the words I wanted to say. Despite being extremely grateful for the kindness being shown to us, there was still a nagging buzzing inside my brain that told me that such things just did not happen; rich people are not kind to poorer people as a general rule, so I struggled to find a way to properly frame the question I wanted to ask. Fortunately, Uncle Tiberius was an astute judge of character, or at least was able to divine what was on a man's mind, because he turned serious.

"So, Titus Pullus, hero of the 10th Legion. You're sitting there trying to come up with a polite way to ask me why in the name of Hades am I doing you and your lady this kindness, neh?"

I had to laugh as I nodded. "Yes, Uncle Tiberius, that's exactly what's going through my head right now. I mean no disrespect….."

He waved me to silence, shaking his head as he said, "I would be more concerned if you didn't have doubt about my motives. But please allow me to defer answering your question until dinner. Is that acceptable?"

I of course agreed, whereupon Uncle Tiberius and Pompeia excused themselves, saying that they needed to go to their home to take care of some things, all of us agreeing to have our dinner in two parts of a watch.

Uncle Tiberius turned to Miriam, telling her, "Prepare yourself for a truly Roman banquet, dear lady. The wine will be unwatered, and there will be more food than you have ever seen in your life."

"I am looking forward to it," she replied, and I could see that she was truly excited.

After the older couple left, I turned to see all three of the conspirators beaming at me with smiles from ear to ear.

"I told you that you'd be surprised," Gaius said smugly, and I had to laugh in agreement.

I sent Diocles back to camp to arrange the transfer of my baggage while I enjoyed a bath, trying to fight the feeling of unreality as I let the hot water soak my doubts away. Miriam and Gaius were off somewhere exploring the grounds, as I had been forced to promise Miriam that Gaius could attend the dinner before returning to camp for the night. When the time came for the dinner to be served, I went to find Miriam and my nephew. With a man on each arm, she was as beautiful as any of the highborn women I had seen in Rome, at least in my eyes. Our manner of women's dress showed off what I had learned to be an exquisite figure, the upswept hair emphasizing the long line of her neck, slender and graceful. I could not have been prouder if it was Cleopatra on my arm. Uncle Tiberius and Pompeia were already there, reclining side by side in the second position, leaving the *Lectus Summus* vacant. Remembering the occasion of my one previous formal Roman upper class experience, I guided Miriam to the middle of the couch to my right, pointing Gaius to the third couch. Then, I turned to Diocles, who was hovering just outside the dining room, again pointing to the third couch. One would have thought I had let out a tremendous fart, as everyone in the room froze, even the two slaves bringing in the food. In retrospect, I suppose that it is unusual for a master to insist that a slave recline at a table with freeborn company, yet I had stopped thinking of Diocles as a slave so many years before that it just seemed a natural thing to do. Diocles looked horrified; even Uncle Tiberius looked uncomfortable, while Gaius sat there surveying the dishes being laid on the table, almost drooling and paying no attention to what was going on around him. Then I saw Miriam out of the corner of my eye, smiling up at me proudly, so any thought I had of reversing myself vanished like smoke before a strong wind. I pointed again, and Diocles, visibly gulping in nervousness, came in to lie gingerly on the couch, as if expecting the thing to suddenly sprout wings and fly away.

I refused to make any comment about Diocles' place at the table, turning instead to Uncle Tiberius and saying, "So Uncle Tiberius, you promised to tell us what was behind your extraordinary act of kindness." Before he could answer, I continued, "But first I would like to raise my glass in a toast to you, Tiberius Flavius Laevina, and to your lovely wife Pompeia. Thank you for making my life here much easier, in more ways than you can imagine."

I grinned as I shot a sidelong glance at Miriam, who blushed prettily. As I lifted the vessel into which a slave had poured the wine, I saw that it was indeed a glass, an incredibly fragile thing that I was afraid I would crush in my rough hand. I had only seen such finery once before, not surprisingly in Egypt and I had been twice as petrified then that I would break something. Holding it carefully, I lifted the glass then drained it, as did the others, Miriam and Gaius looking similarly apprehensive as they tentatively touched the rim of the glass to their lips. Fortunately for everyone, nothing bad happened, then with the toast finished, I turned back to Uncle Tiberius, who was smacking his lips, his glass already empty and already reaching for the pitcher. Sensing eyes on him, he looked up guiltily, giving a chuckle as he shrugged.

"I do like my wine, yes I do. What was your question, Pullus? May I call you 'Pullus,' or do you prefer to be referred to by your rank as well?"

"Seeing as we're practically family, you can call me 'Titus,' or 'Pullus' if you prefer and I don't require being addressed as 'Primus Pilus.'"

"Except when we're around other men," Gaius mumbled, his mouth full of the tiny shrimps that had been soaked in brine from the taste of them.

"That's different and you know it, Nephew, or do I have to send you home early without supper?"

"Sorry, Uncle." He sounded anything but as he continued munching, while Diocles was trying to hide his own grin without much success.

"Very well, 'Titus' it is. Well, Titus, my boy, I wasn't always the picture of the successful merchant that you see before you now." He shot his wife a sly grin, which she returned in kind. "In fact, you and I have much more in common than you would think. You see, when I was much, much younger, and much spryer, I marched under the standard, as you do now."

I had been reclining partially on my stomach, but I pulled myself to more of a sitting position to stare at the older man.

"I know, I know; hard to believe looking at me now, but a bit more than 50 years ago, I was a *Hastatus* in the 3rd Legion of Lucius Cornelius Sulla when we defeated Mithridates at Chaeronea."

Now he had everyone's attention, for the name of Sulla was almost as well known throughout the world as that of Caesar, albeit for far different reasons. His reign of terror was both bloody and had lasted much longer than the brief reign of Gaius Marius after he went insane during his last Consulship. It was Sulla who started the practice of proscriptions, offering rewards for the heads of proscribed citizens. I looked at Uncle Tiberius through new eyes then, not as a smiling, somewhat silly old man, but a veteran and I raised my glass to him again in a salute, which he returned with his own glass. Gaius had stopped eating altogether, and I suspect his reaction was much the same as mine, as I saw him staring at the old man with undisguised interest.

"So, was Sulla as terrifying as they say?"

I distinctly remember when I had been a *tiro,* the older men had spoken of Sulla as we sat around the fire, and they still shuddered at the mere mention of his name.

"Oh, he wasn't so bad, as long as you stayed on his good side, if you know what I mean." He gave me a wink. "In fact, you could say that it was the Dictator, that's what he wanted to be called, you know, who staked me when I left the Legion and started out on my own, though it was in a, shall we say, a roundabout fashion."

He chuckled at his own wit, but I felt a shiver run up my spine, the full import of what he had just said hitting me. The veterans had always claimed that there were men who had gotten rich from informing on men who were proscribed, and here was a man sitting next to me essentially saying that he was one of those men, at least if I read him correctly.

"He had a fearsome temper, that's true," he continued. "But it was more of an icy, controlled kind of thing that I can see men finding absolutely terrifying, though I never worried about it much. I just did what he wanted me to do and I never felt his wrath. But you marched with Gaius Julius Caesar, and the gods know that he had his own temper, didn't he? I've heard tales of it."

While I had suddenly become reluctant to share much with Uncle Tiberius I saw no harm in speaking of my dead general, chiding myself for being so suspicious, but immediately I countered that with the reminder that these were suspicious times, where it was impossible to know who to trust.

Still, I was not willing to be rude, so I answered honestly. "He did have quite a temper," I acknowledged. "But he never lost it without cause. And he wasn't one to be vindictive."

"That's certainly true," Uncle Tiberius countered. "Much to his detriment, I would add. He showed mercy to his enemies, and look where it got him. Sulla, on the other hand, never forgot a wrong done him and would always exact vengeance, even if he had to wait 20 years to do it."

"Where it got him," I said quietly, feeling the first flickering of anger at what I took to be a criticism of my general, "was to be considered a god by his people, and what Rome got was more new territory and people at one time than it's ever conquered before. Your general," I pointed out, "was so full of putrescence that the gods wouldn't accept his body being purified in fire when he died."

Oh, that made him angry; I could see the flashing in his eyes as his liver-colored lips thinned. Yet, after the space of a breath, he gave a harsh chuckle, and as quickly as it had fled, the jolly old man came rushing back.

"*Pax*, Titus Pullus, *pax*. I didn't mean to offend the memory of your general, as I hold it in the greatest respect. It's just that no matter how noble Caesar's motives may have been in staying his hand and exacting retribution against his enemies, the end result was exactly the same as it was under Sulla, and that was civil war."

I could not disagree with him on that, as the end result of Caesar's clemency, which I privately had always thought was a mistake, was more than ten years of civil war in which thousands of Romans lost their lives. There were times when I thought of all the Legions of men that were lost with whom we could have subdued the Parthians several times over, but that was smoke that had blown away many years before, so there was no point in dwelling on it. The main course of the meal had come, the next few moments occupied with the dishing out and consumption of the food, allowing tempers to cool so that when the conversation resumed, the tension had eased considerably.

"Titus, tell me as one old soldier to the other, what happened in Parthia?"

Uncle Tiberius asked this question between smacks as he chomped noisily on his leg of chicken, the grease running down his chin.

"I wouldn't know," I answered evasively, "since we never made it to Parthia."

He laughed, nodding in salute at my attempt to avoid the question, but he was not so easily put off.

"Very well, Media was it? What happened in Media?"

"Bad luck mostly," I answered, pausing as I thought about it. "Of course, looking back you can always see the mistakes, but in the moment it's not so easy. Leaving the baggage train was a mistake, and ultimately it cost us the campaign, but I think it goes deeper than that. I think we left too late. We got to Zeugma later than we should have, then we stayed there almost three weeks. I think if I were to trace the cause of our setback," I refused to use the word "failure," "it would be there."

"Ah yes, the Queen of Egypt that holds our Triumvir's heart captive," Uncle Tiberius chortled. I should not have been surprised that he knew, but I was, and he must have caught the look on my face. "I heard about him mooning about her in the camp for weeks. Pregnant, wasn't she?" He gave a look of surprise that I suspect was completely feigned. "What? You don't believe that this is a secret do you, Titus? The spell that Cleopatra has put on Antonius is all people in these parts talk about, and I can assure you that if what I read from my correspondents in Italia is accurate, it's the subject of much of the talk in Italia in general, and Rome in particular. Octavian is using Antonius' behavior against him, I can assure you of that, and he's whipping up the mob by portraying Cleopatra as an evil temptress who's duped your general."

While his description of Antonius as my general was technically accurate, I still did not like hearing it put so baldly.

"Cleopatra is many things, but I don't believe she is evil." I tried to keep my tone cool and dispassionate, yet I could feel Miriam's eyes turn on me.

When I glanced over, I saw her giving me an appraising look, something Uncle Tiberius did not miss.

"Oh my boy, you have stepped in it now," he chuckled, but he turned the conversation back to the subject. "She may not be evil, but I can assure you that she has some sort of hold on Marcus Antonius, and Octavian is using that to his advantage."

I could only shrug at that, having no reason to doubt what he was saying was true. "Whatever the cause, I think that delay is what cost us dearly. Losing the baggage train was the second mortal blow, and the third was not turning back sooner, before the weather turned bad. We lost most of our men due to weather and not battle."

I looked over at Gaius. Just like I suspected, his eyes had taken on a faraway look as he relived his ordeal in the snow trying to save Vulso. I wish I could have told him that those memories would go away, but all they do is fade and never completely disappear, while you find yourself almost paralyzed by them at the oddest times.

"It must have been truly horrible." Pompeia spoke for the first time, and I saw she had noticed Gaius' stricken expression.

"It was, my lady," Gaius said suddenly, though he was still staring off into space, his voice hollow with pain. "It was truly, truly horrible."

"But you survived, and that's what counts," Uncle Tiberius was suddenly uncharacteristically fierce, leaning across the table to put one spotted hand out, resting it on top of Gaius', who returned to the present with a startled look at the touch. "Remember that, boy, that you survived. And your survival is what counts in this world. Nothing else."

I was not so sure about that, and I still am not, but I did not say anything, content to let the old man comfort the young one.

"That begs the next question. Will Marcus Antonius succeed this time around?" Uncle Tiberius asked the question lightly.

However, I could sense that the old man was probing, giving me a strong sense of unease. Still, I answered the question truthfully, or at least with enough truth in it that it made it easier to say and not ring false in my own ears.

"I don't believe that Antonius will make the same mistakes twice," I replied, which was my honest hope, though not necessarily my belief, for I was always conscious of Antonius' impulsive nature and how it seemed to govern him at the worst possible moments. "Further, I believe that we'll have the help of forces similarly composed to those that we'll be facing, the lack of which was yet another part of the challenges facing us."

I made the statement deliberately vague, not willing to divulge the details of the agreement made between Artavasdes the Median and Antonius, but the old man was not so easily thrown off the scent.

"So you'll have cataphracts and horse archers this time? Or at least ones that won't run away?"

"We will," I answered.

No matter how much he pressed, I refused to give any more details, and he finally gave up. Seeing that the other guests were openly fidgeting and picking at their food, by unspoken consent Uncle Tiberius and I moved onto safer, more acceptable topics for mixed company. The rest of the evening passed very pleasantly, and it was very late when Pompeia stifled a yawn behind her hand, which Uncle Tiberius immediately saw and I took to be a signal, rising to help Pompeia to her feet.

"Well, young people, I must say that neither Mother nor I have been up this late in some time, but I'm afraid that we must say good night now."

The rest of us rose, though Gaius managed to snag the last of the brine shrimps to stuff in his mouth, earning a cuff on the back of the head from me as we all made our way to the main entrance of the house while the women hugged each other. I felt a hand grab at my arm, Uncle Tiberius making a clear signal to drop back and let the others continue, so I gave my own signal to Diocles and Gaius to keep moving.

Once they were out of earshot, Uncle Tiberius said quietly, "Titus, I have a confession to make."

"Oh, what's that? You lust after my woman," I joked, then saw that he was very serious.

"While this is my house, and everything I told you was true, my motives are not quite as pure as I would lead you to believe."

Ah, here it is, I thought, glad at least that my instinct was correct, but I was still disappointed. However, I was not prepared for what came out of his mouth.

"I send greetings from Gaius Octavianus Divi Filius, who insisted that should the opportunity arise this house be offered to you for your use as a token of his esteem and admiration for all that you've done for Rome." His tone was quiet, making the words all the more chilling. I almost took a staggering step backward, but managed to stop myself. Uncle Tiberius' face was grave, and the anger I had felt earlier began to flare up again as I cursed a bit louder than I intended, causing both Diocles and Gaius' heads to turn. "He knew that this is my second villa, and asked me to make it available to you, which I'm happy to do."

"So you're one of Octavian's agents?" I asked incredulously, and while he refused to answer, the look on his face gave me all the answer that I needed.

We stood there for the space of several heartbeats, me glaring down at the wizened little man, he looking back with a defiant expression on his face, and when the silence was broken, it was by him. His face changed before my eyes, his lips pulling back over his rotten teeth in a sneer.

"We all work for someone, Titus Pullus, and I will not apologize for doing what I must do in order to survive. It's no secret that I'm a very, very wealthy man, and I would have been proscribed by the Triumvirs, but I'm more valuable with what and who I know to the truly powerful men like Octavian, who you're foolish to think will not win between him and Antonius." He grabbed my arm, his tone turning placating and wheedling at the same time. "You and I are but pieces in the game played by patricians, and each of us must do whatever we can to make sure that we're a piece that's not sacrificed. Don't blame me for doing the same thing you did."

I pulled my arm from his grasp, looking at him coldly, but there was an equal pit of ice in my stomach at his words, fearing what they meant.

"What are you talking about, old man? I don't spy for Octavian."

"No, you don't," he admitted. "Not yet. But I was given specific instructions that should you show the kind of hostility and attitude you're displaying now to remind you of your agreement with Octavian and how dangerous reneging on that agreement would be."

Now it was his turn to stare at me, his eyes boring up into mine as he sent an unmistakable message, reminding me of that thing, that reptilian coldness I had seen in the young Caesar's eyes, and I knew that he was right. I had been ensnared and whether it happened willingly, as it seemed to be with Uncle Tiberius, or I had been forced by circumstances did not really matter at this point. I could feel my shoulders slump, the anger and the fight draining from me, while I was almost overwhelmed at the feeling of tiredness and hopelessness that washed over me like a cold flood. I had tried so hard to avoid becoming one of those pieces that Uncle Tiberius was talking about, yet it was clear that it was a hopeless struggle.

Uncle Tiberius' face, I suppose on seeing my capitulation, softened as he whispered to me, "There's no shame in doing what you must do to survive, Titus Pullus."

"There is for me," I said bitterly.

Nevertheless, when he offered his hand, cutting his eyes to the others, who were now watching in open curiosity, I took it, shaking it warmly while loudly thanking him for all that he had done for us.

After the old couple left the house, the other three gathered around me, clearly intent on finding out what the whispered conversation between me and Uncle Tiberius was about, since it clearly had disturbed me. Surveying their faces, I made the decision right at that moment to say nothing about the true nature of the words spoken between us, just making something up on the spot, and I do not remember what it was. If the others had their doubts, they did not voice them, though their faces told me their probable feelings on the matter. I pushed Gaius out the door after handing him the pass that I had written for him to get him back into camp and excuse his absence, warning him that I was not willing to make this a habit. With that, we retired for the evening, and as tired as I was and with my mind occupied elsewhere, I suspected that there would be more conversation that night with Miriam. I was lying in the bed, watching as she brushed her hair by the light of the single lamp still lit, reveling in the quiet beauty of these moments when I believe a woman is at her most desirable, and I felt my pulse quicken with a surge of new energy. Finished, she came to the bed, pushing her back against me in her favorite position for sleeping, meaning her face was turned away from me. Her tone was playful and teasing as she asked the question I had known was coming since my defense of Cleopatra earlier that evening.

"So is the queen of Egypt as lovely as some say she is?"

Despite myself, I let out a laugh.

"Gods, no. She's homely, and thin as a stick. If you stood next to her and she weren't dressed with all that claptrap and finery, no man would cast a second glance her way."

I smugly congratulated myself at both deflecting and complimenting with one stroke, however Miriam was not so easily put off.

"But she must have some appeal for a man like Marcus Antonius to fall so madly in love with her," she insisted.

"How about her money?" I suggested, earning an elbow in the ribs.

"More than that. She must have something."

I should have known that a trap was being baited, but I was too tired to see it, so I actually answered honestly, "She's unlike any woman I ever met in the way she can be so many different things. One moment she can curse worse than any Centurion I ever met, and I've seen her make men blush with her language. Then she can tell a joke that you'd expect to hear sitting about the fire in camp that makes you laugh until you cry. Just when you think you have her figured out, she starts to speak of art and music in perfectly accented Attic Greek, or so Diocles informs me. That's how she beguiles men, by being so many things to a man."

The words were barely out of my mouth when she whirled about, her eyes wide and mouth open, as she exclaimed, "So you DO love her!"

"What? What are you talking about? I didn't say that." I knew I was babbling, but she spun back around.

Scooting to the edge of the bed, she shot back, "You did not have to; it's obvious. You are completely in love with her."

"How did you reach that conclusion?" I was completely mystified, thinking for perhaps the thousandth time in my life that I would never understand women, remembering all the way back to Juno and Vibius.

Miriam gave me a derisive snort, tossing her head, her hair now that it was unbound whipping across my head.

"Conclusion," she scoffed. "What is this word 'conclusion'? I know what I know, and you are in love with Cleopatra, the queen who beguiles men of all classes!"

This launched a tirade in her native tongue as she mumbled to herself, her body rigid, sending a clear signal that there would be nothing happening in our bed that night except fitful sleep.

"Fine," I snapped, still trying to understand where it had all gone so wrong. "I was tired anyway!"

With that, I rolled to my edge of the bed, both of us spending the next few moments angrily talking to ourselves until we fell asleep.

Fortunately for me, Miriam was not the type to stay angry long and in the morning all was forgiven. While I still did not know what I did wrong, I had become experienced enough with women to just apologize and accept her forgiveness. In truth, I did not need the distraction of fighting with Miriam, because my head was still swimming from my conversation with Uncle Tiberius, the implications continuing to mount as I peeled each layer back. How had Octavian known so quickly that we were headed back to Damascus?

By this time of year, the prevailing winds had shifted, blowing from here in the East in the general direction of Italia, which makes sailing this direction usually more difficult. I remembered hearing talk that the winds had been extremely mild for this time of year but still, it seemed to me that Octavian had to have some sort of advance information for him to react so quickly or perhaps, I thought, he truly is guided by the gods. More specifically, perhaps it was Caesar, who really was a god as people said, who was giving Octavian the gift of second sight. I shook my head, chiding myself for letting my mind run to places that would not actually provide any value to thinking through my dilemma. Aside from divine intervention, the next most likely possibility was that Octavian's network of agents was much more extensive than I, or anyone for that matter, knew; that he had men on almost every ship crisscrossing Our Sea carrying messages and information back and forth. This meant that the possibility that I would run into more men like Uncle Tiberius was very high, so I resolved to guard my tongue as much as I was capable. The only men I trusted enough to discuss the matter with were back in camp, and I decided that it would be better to talk with them away from slaves and servants who worked for Uncle Tiberius.

On my walk back to camp, I pondered whether it would be possible to remove them from the villa while we stayed there. Thinking it through, I did not see any way where it could be done gracefully and not be insulting to Uncle Tiberius, not to mention that it would signal to him that I suspected that there were spies among the slaves. I would just have to watch what I said, and as soon as I could think of a way, I would warn Miriam, though she very rarely discussed politics and never talked about our private conversations, or so I believed. The morning formation was held, then I made my way to the small house that served as the Legion office and my private quarters when I was in camp. Now it held only a cot, table, and chairs, along with the rack to hang my armor, helmet and baldric, the rest of my possessions already transferred to the villa.

Diocles, as was his habit, had risen earlier than I and was already sitting at his desk in the Legion office, with

Argus and Eumenis in their places, copying out ration reports, and I sent Eumenis to fetch Scribonius and Balbus. They arrived in moments, and I motioned for them to follow me into my quarters. When they were seated, I recounted all that had happened the night before, leaving nothing out. Once I was finished, they sat silently, Scribonius with his frown while Balbus stared at the floor, which I knew was a sign that he was also lost in thought.

Finally, the scarred face turned upwards and he said flatly, "Get out. Go find something else."

"No," Scribonius said sharply. "He can't do that. Weren't you listening? This Uncle Tiberius character specifically warned him that refusing Octavian would be suicide."

Balbus' face reddened, for it was very unlike Scribonius to speak harshly to any of his friends, and it was a sure sign to me that he was extremely worried about this development.

"I heard, I heard. I just can't think of anything else he can do," Balbus protested.

Scribonius took a deep breath, my heart sinking as he shook his head.

"Neither can I," he admitted. He looked at me, his face grave.

"You're trapped, and I have to say that it was neatly sprung. This old bugger sounds like a crafty one and you're going to have to step very lightly. But I don't see any way out of it now. You already accepted his offer."

"I didn't know at the time that he was working for Octavian!"

"Which is why I say he's as straight as a snake. He waited until you stepped into the snare before he yanked it closed. Titus," he said in a firm, almost harsh voice.

"You're going to have to guard your tongue more than you normally do."

"I will," I assured him. "I hardly ever talk about Octavian anyway."

He shook his head, surprising me. "I'm not talking about Octavian. You mustn't say anything about Antonius either."

I did not understand why he believed this was important. "But that's what Octavian wants, I'm sure of it. He wants information about Antonius."

"I'm sure he does, but you can't be the one who gives it to him."

"Why not?"

Balbus was clearly as surprised as I was, for it was he who asked the question.

"Because if this Uncle Tiberius is as slippery as I think he is, I'm willing to bet you a thousand sesterces that he's working for Antonius as well."

That had not occurred to me and the doubt must have shown on my face, because Scribonius patiently explained how he had come to this conclusion.

"No matter how many agents Octavian may have, the East is Antonius' and has been for some time. And Antonius has been squeezing everyone he thinks has a few sesterces rattling in his purse, yet this Uncle Tiberius is doing so well that he can build a lavish second villa? Didn't he himself say that he's managed to avoid being proscribed by the Triumvirs? That would indicate to me that he's managed to escape Antonius' depredations as well as Octavian's, and I seriously doubt that it's because Antonius has a soft spot for an old man who marched for Sulla." He shook his head again to emphasize the point. "I would say that it's because he's working both sides of this game. Antonius probably lets him report to Octavian because Uncle Tiberius will feed Octavian information that Antonius wants him to have. And on the other side, Octavian probably does the same."

I was impressed, and did not bother to hide it. Nonetheless, a problem occurred to me, which I pointed out. "That's a really, really dangerous game for an old man to play."

"You said it yourself. He was a Sullan, so he learned to play it very well. The fact that he's made it to his age is proof that he's very good at it. That makes him dangerous, Titus, and you must never forget it. I think your best and only course is to steer right down the middle. Say nothing that you wouldn't want either Octavian or Antonius to hear coming from your lips."

I could not deny the sense of this, although I saw another problem.

"What if the old man gets impatient that I'm not providing him with grist for either mill and decides to make something up?"

For there was one conclusion I had reached sometime during the night, and that was that Uncle Tiberius was not one to worry about such niceties as whether something was actually true if it meant that it kept him from getting what he wanted. I had little doubt that back when he was working for Sulla in the proscriptions more than one man he turned in had done nothing wrong, but still had been condemned by the kindly old Uncle Tiberius.

"Then," Scribonius said grimly. "You kill him, slowly and painfully." He paused, peering intently into my eyes. "And you need to make sure that he understands that. Remind him that both Octavian and Antonius are far away, and before either of them could lift a finger to help him, you'd flay him."

"And turn his shriveled ball sac into a coin purse," Balbus added gleefully. "Make sure you tell him that."

"What is it with you and your fascination with ball sacs?" Scribonius asked in mock annoyance. "You always talk about doing that."

Balbus' scarred face took on a hurt expression, looking incongruous to say the least.

"I just think it would be a good idea. I know it would scare the *cac* out of me."

I did exactly as Scribonius suggested, inviting Uncle Tiberius to dinner that very night, asking that he come alone, giving the excuse that Miriam was feeling ill and would not be joining us so there was no need for Pompeia to endure the drudgery of men's talk. When I told Miriam that I needed her to absent herself from the dinner, she started to protest, then quickly stopped when she saw the look on my face. Diocles was back at camp, also on my orders, but Scribonius and Balbus were with me, for after discussing it with my friends, they both insisted that there would be strength in numbers when confronting Uncle Tiberius.

"He needs to know that if anything were to happen to you that you have friends who will avenge you," was how Scribonius put it.

"I can do that myself," I protested. "I can tell him that without him laying eyes on you. You're putting yourself in danger for no reason."

"It wouldn't have the same impact," he said, with a firm shake of his head. "For all Uncle Tiberius knows, you could be just making these friends up." He shook his head again. "No, it will be a much stronger message if Balbus and I are sitting at the table with you."

"Couches," I interjected. "You won't be sitting. You'll be lying on couches."

"*Gerrae,*" Balbus exclaimed, his face alight. "I've never had a dinner reclining on a couch like a patrician."

"And you're not going to tonight," Scribonius snapped, grabbing my arm as he spoke. "Titus, you have to change that arrangement. You're not exactly your most intimidating if you're lying on a couch. Have the slaves move the couches and put some chairs about the table."

"It's too low for chairs," I replied, thinking about it for a moment. "But I'll either have the table brought from the servants' dining area and covered with something, or I'll figure out a way to elevate the table. Are you sure about this?" I directed this question to both Scribonius and Balbus, still worried about putting my friends in harm's way, yet they were both adamant that they wanted to come.

"Besides," Balbus grinned, "I want to hear you tell that old bastard you're going to cut off his ball sac and turn it into a purse."

I did as Scribonius suggested, ending up having the table raised rather than have the one from the slaves dining area brought in, and the three of us were waiting when Uncle Tiberius was announced. I met him in the *oecium* alone, forcing myself to be affable as we chatted a moment before I ushered him into the dining area, where Scribonius and Balbus were already seated. The old man immediately stopped short at the sight of my two friends, his wrinkled old face flashing a look of equal parts suspicion and surprise, and I found myself mentally saluting the old bastard for his quick grasp that something was amiss.

"I hope you don't mind that I asked two of my oldest friends to eat with us. You haven't met them, and I thought you'd enjoy their company as much as you seem to have enjoyed mine."

I made a signal and both men rose, each of them introducing themselves in turn to Uncle Tiberius, who had managed to recover his equilibrium nicely, I was forced to admit, becoming the jolly old man once again. We all seated ourselves and the first course of the meal arrived, which I had ordered to be ready immediately so we could begin eating without having to fill the space of time with conversation. My goal was to unsettle Uncle Tiberius as much as possible now that I had seen him become suspicious at the presence of my friends. I wanted their presence to rattle around in his head as he tried to think of all the reasons they could be seated next to him. He was also unsettled by the use of chairs, as it completely disrupted the normal way that Romans of his class were used to dining, and he paused, clearly unsure where he was to sit, but I pointed to the spot to my right, the place of honor.

"You'll have to forgive us, Uncle Tiberius, but we've been in the army so long that neither Balbus nor I are used to reclining while we eat. I hope you don't mind."

To anyone who did not know him, Scribonius' smile was genuine and warm, though both Balbus and I saw the cold glint in his eyes. Nonetheless, his soothing words had the desired effect, Uncle Tiberius giving a chuckle and wave of his hand.

"No apology necessary, young man. I admit that I've gotten lazy by lolling around on a couch. It will be good for my old bones to remember how real men eat their food again."

With that, we tucked into our meal, making only desultory conversation about mundane topics like the weather and gossip about the sexual escapades of some of the leading Romans of the region. If it had not been for the real underlying reason we were all sitting there, it would have been pleasant. We ate our way through each of the three courses, pausing as we three Legionaries loosened our belts to accommodate the large amount of food in our bellies. Like all good soldiers, we had learned that when there was plenty of food that was our signal to stuff ourselves. Finally, Uncle Tiberius broke the silence.

"So, Titus, my boy, I assume there's a reason you invited me to dinner. Aside from the pleasure of my company, I mean."

I nodded. "You're right, Uncle Tiberius, there was something I wanted to discuss with you."

We had carefully rehearsed what I was going to say, but I was not to be the only one with a part in this play. I leaned forward so that my superior height, even seated, came into play, and I was pleased to see Uncle Tiberius shrink back a bit.

I paused a moment, just to build the tension more, before I continued. "I've been thinking a great deal about our discussion last night, and I wanted to make sure that you and I understand each other clearly. After all, you were frank with me, so I feel that it's only fair that I be the same with you."

Now the old man was clearly nervous, his eyes darting over to Scribonius and Balbus, both of whom had shifted in their seats to face him, their faces set as if made of stone, their eyes equally cold.

"You threatened me last night, old man." My tone hardened, letting just a trace of anger show as I pinned him with my gaze.

"Titus, my boy, you misunderstood. I wasn't threatening you, at least that wasn't my intent." He held his hands up to me in a placating gesture, but I was having none of it.

"Silence." I did not yell. I have been told that when I speak quietly I am even more menacing than when I raise my voice. "We both know that's a lie. You used Octavian's name because you thought it would intimidate me. What I wanted to tell you tonight is simply this." Now I leaned even closer so that we were at eye level. "Octavian is far, far away, and while I don't deny that you can do me a great deal of damage with one message, you need to remember that you're here, and he's there. Italia is on the other side of the world. By the time whatever happens to me happens because of whatever message you might send, your bones will be white from the sun bleaching them."

"I say we just go ahead and kill him now," growled Balbus, standing up out of his chair, taking a step forward while reaching for his dagger, right on cue.

Uncle Tiberius gave out a frightened yelp, almost tipping his chair over. Equally on cue, Scribonius reached out to grab Balbus by the arm, seeming to restrain him.

He turned to Uncle Tiberius, then said soothingly, "Nobody is going to kill anyone. At least, not tonight."

He gave Uncle Tiberius a smile to ease his obvious fear further while Balbus sat back down with a great show of reluctance. When we had come up with our plan to confront Uncle Tiberius, it was Scribonius who had assigned the roles, there being little question between the two who would be the snarling Cerberus, if only for Balbus' scarred visage. Scribonius now began to play his role as the only one sympathetic to Uncle Tiberius, which, speaking honestly, I had not believed would be effective.

"Not normally, no it wouldn't," Scribonius had admitted. "Which is why Balbus needs to scare him out of his wits first. Then he won't be able to think clearly and he'll reach for whatever kindness comes his way, and I'll be the one to show it. You'll see it works."

Now Scribonius turned towards me, giving me a reproving look.

"Titus, I think you might be a bit harsh with this dear old man."

I almost burst out laughing because I could see how false Scribonius was being, but when I glanced over at Uncle Tiberius, my jaw almost dropped. He was sitting looking at Scribonius with a pathetically grateful gaze, just as a drowning man would at the rope that had just landed within arm's reach.

"You're right, Scribonius, was it? I meant no harm, truly I didn't! Please, tell Titus this so that he believes you, because he clearly doesn't believe me!"

He turned towards me, clearly checking to see if this was having an effect, which I answered with a shake of my head. Scribonius peered into the rheumy old eyes of Uncle Tiberius as if he could see into the very depths of his soul before looking over at me, shaking his head.

"Titus, I must say that I truly believe Uncle Tiberius. I think it was all a misunderstanding."

I acted as if I was considering this, then shrugged doubtfully.

"Maybe," I said finally. "But what about the other thing?"

Uncle Tiberius' head was whipping back and forth between Scribonius and me as we talked, his face displaying a range of emotions while trying to keep track of the conversation.

"Ah, yes. That. The . . . other thing." Scribonius sounded almost regretful, turning back to Uncle Tiberius. "Unfortunately, Titus is right. There is one other thing that we need to clear up."

"What? What other thing are you talking about?"

It was plain to see that Uncle Tiberius' confusion was genuine, which was exactly as Scribonius had predicted.

"It's just that as we discussed it, well, it's very clear that you serve two masters. Isn't that right, Uncle?"

He did try to keep his face from revealing the truth, yet the flash of guilt was plain on his face. "I don't know what you mean, Centurion Scribonius!"

"I think you do, Uncle," Scribonius said, his tone dripping with sympathy. "It must be difficult, as if you were walking on the edge of a sword with a slavering wolf on either side and truly we don't wish you any ill. But what we need you to understand is that what Titus here is saying about Octavian goes for Antonius."

Uncle Tiberius' expression suddenly turned cagy. "While I don't know what you're talking about, I can assure you that I would never speak an ill word to Antonius about Titus here." To my astonishment, when he looked at me I could see the glint of tears in his eyes. The man was as changeable as the most experienced whore I had ever seen. "He's like the son I never had, and I couldn't bear to see anything bad happen to him. From either Octavian or Antonius." There was no mistaking the meaning in his tone as he looked at each of us in turn.

Nothing more was said for several moments. Finally, when I looked at Scribonius, he gave a faint nod, while Balbus just looked disgusted, I presumed because we had not killed the old man outright.

"Very well," I relented. The relief was clear to see on the old man's face, then it was as if a great breath of air was released from the walls of the room itself. "I think we understand each other now."

For some reason, Uncle Tiberius did not seem eager to continue our evening, claiming that his age required him to retire early, and it was true he had been up late the night before, so he was allowed to leave in peace and in one piece, if somewhat shaken. After he left, we retired to the *oecium,* draping ourselves on the couches to discuss the evening's events.

"Overall, I think it went well," Scribonius opined, and I had to agree.

"I definitely think he got the message," I agreed. "Now we'll see if he forgets."

"Oh, I doubt it." Scribonius shook his head, seeming very sure. "That old man hasn't survived all these years by forgetting nights like tonight." He sat up, turning to me, his face intent and serious. "But you still must guard your tongue, Titus. I think we won't have to worry about Uncle Tiberius overmuch, but there's no sense in taking chances."

I agreed that I would in fact heed his advice, telling myself that I was at a point in my life where it was high time to learn discretion. After that was settled, we began talking of other matters, and as the time passed, I could not help noticing that Balbus was sitting silently, not saying a word. I heaved a sigh, knowing the answer before I asked the question.

"And what has suddenly struck you dumb, Balbus?"

He looked away from his careful study of the fresco on the wall. "I wanted to tell him I was going to cut off his ball sac, but you cut me off before I could," he grumbled.

Both Scribonius and I started roaring with laughter, and soon Balbus was joining in.

With that matter settled, I was able to turn my full attention back to the Legion and the integration of the new men into the ranks. Unlike my customary practice of allowing each Centurion to train those among the new arrivals that were raw *tiros,* I took an active role in their training, much to the irritation of the Centurions. I am sure some would have argued that I was doing much more than taking part, that I was taking it over altogether. Looking back, I suppose there is truth in that, but I needed something to infuse me with the enthusiasm and fire that had been such an integral part of my career in the Legions to that point, because I had noticed that it was fading. I was finding it hard to rouse myself from the warmth of my bed with Miriam to make my way to camp in time for the morning formations, and I was quick to find an excuse to go home early if I could. However, when I asked Scribonius what was wrong with me, he just gave me a strange look before he burst out laughing.

"Why, Titus, you're in love, that's all."

That caught me by surprise, I can tell you, yet when I opened my mouth to protest, nothing came out. I snapped my mouth shut and shook my head.

Finally, I said, "I suppose I am."

It had not been anything for which I had prepared myself. For more than a year, I told myself that I liked Miriam well enough, it was just that there was no future in a relationship with her, since I would be leaving again at some point, or I would be dead. Now, Scribonius was looking at me with undisguised amusement, irritating me that he had seen something so clearly to which I was blind until he had pointed it out.

"What about you?" I snapped. "You've never been in love, so how would you know?"

As soon as the words were out of my mouth I regretted saying them, for Scribonius was my best friend and did not deserve such treatment.

His face clouded, and I could see that my words had wounded him, but his tone was even as he replied, "That's not true Titus. I have been in love. In fact, I still am."

It was my second surprise in as many moments. Now I turned to examine Scribonius more closely, my friend looking off into the distance. I continued staring at him, and he sighed.

"Fine, I'll tell you about her."

Now, I was expecting to hear him speak of some married woman here in Damascus, for if it had been a maiden I saw no reason for them not to be together, and Scribonius rarely left the camp, always coming to my villa when he did. I was not prepared for what he was about to reveal.

"Her name is Aurelia. I've loved her for as long as I can remember. She lives in Rome, and the last I heard she is still married."

I looked at him in surprise, letting out a low whistle.

"You're in love with a married woman? You dog." I must admit that I was pleased with myself for having guessed that she was married, but Scribonius was looking anything but pleased.

"It's not just that she's married, it's who she's married to that makes it difficult."

"And? Who's that?"

He shot me a guilty sidelong glance, refusing to meet my eyes.

Turning his head to stare off into space, he answered, "My brother."

The story came out as we sat in my bare quarters in camp. When Scribonius chose to follow his older brother in the Catiline conspiracy, he had been forced to flee when it all went bad. At the time, he was betrothed to Aurelia, the daughter of a close family friend and despite Aurelia being six years younger than Scribonius; they had always been in love with each other, at least for as long as Scribonius could remember. Scribonius said it was the happiest day of his life when his father informed him that his friend had been delighted to give consent to the marriage and they were waiting for Aurelia to become old enough before the marriage was consummated. Then, the Catiline conspiracy boiled over and Scribonius was forced to flee. He was sure that Aurelia would then be promised to the son of a family whose name had not been sullied by the events with Catiline. That was why he had been shocked to learn, albeit several years later, that Aurelia ended up wedding the third brother, Quintus.

"I thought at first that it would make me feel better," he said sadly. "You know, that she was still allied with my family, but the truth is, I can't stand it. I never liked Quintus much; he's always been the slippery one of all of us, always thinking of his own skin before anything else."

"Sounds like she made the wrong choice," I commiserated, but he shook his head.

"No, she did the right thing. If she had waited for me, what good would that have done? We couldn't be legally married."

Personally, I had never seen what the fuss was about the niceties of a legal marriage, despite knowing that women put much store in the idea that their union with a man is somehow sanctified, not just by the gods, but by whatever authority they live under. I cannot say I understand it, I just know that it is there.

"Then what are you moping for?" I demanded, mainly because I could think of nothing constructive to say. "If you say she did the right thing, then you should be happy for her and leave it at that."

He looked at me as if I was perhaps the most stupid man in the Republic, which I must admit is a possibility when it comes to matters of the heart.

"The heart wants what the heart wants," he replied quietly.

That was, and is certainly true, and I could think of nothing to add to that. Then I thought of something else.

"Do you realize," I asked, "that I've learned more about you in the last few weeks than I did in the previous 25 years?"

He gave a short laugh. "I didn't feel like talking about it before now."

"Well, I'm glad you finally changed your mind," was all I could think to say.

I spent several thirds of a watch a day working with groups of *Tirones* on the stakes, smiling inwardly when I heard the countless groans and muttered curses as I forced the new men to bash the poles with their wooden swords, over and over and over, never satisfied. Just as I had hoped, I did feed off their youthful energy, feeling rejuvenated by their exuberance and enthusiasm, despite being tempered as it was by their frustrations. Like countless other generations of Legionary before them, they carped and complained about being forced to use the heavy wooden sword instead of being able to immediately start hacking away with a real blade. And just as all the Centurions who came before me, my colleagues and I were unmoved by their plight. The new men had learned how to at least march in a manner somewhat resembling Legionaries on their travel from their respective recruiting grounds. Now we had to integrate them into the Legion and go out into the countryside, which we began to do three times a week. The older veterans like Albinus fell easily back into the rhythm and routine of a Legion in winter camp. Still, it was easy to see that some of the older men were struggling. I was determined that there would be no alteration or diminishment of the training cycle to accommodate the older men, so inevitably we lost a fair number of them who had to be sent back to their homes because they were found unfit for further duty. There was also quite a bit of grumbling from these older men, who seemed to think that their status as veterans should exempt them from the harshest of the training that I had devised. These malcontents were quickly silenced, not by me or the other Centurions, but by the men themselves, who understood what I was doing and why. The horrors and deprivation of the campaign in Media were still fresh in every man's mind; the memory of the seemingly endless miles of harsh terrain with the wind howling in the ears with every step, the towering mountains covered in ice that had to be traversed could still rise up and haunt a man's dreams, causing him to cry out the names of friends as he relived seeing them fall to their deaths or die of exposure. The veterans in the ranks who had survived their ordeal knew that I was doing my best to prepare the Legion for the moment when we would find ourselves once again in those barren wastes, so when the new arrivals began to complain, there was a bit of unofficial chastisement dealt out to them, and the complaining soon stopped.

The men were not the only ones haunted by what we had endured, although my sleep was not interrupted by dreams of seeing men plunging down icy slopes. I had lost almost half my Legion to a foe who never drew a sword or fired an arrow to cut them down, and I was determined to do what I could to avoid a repeat of the same fate. The other Primi Pili were similarly involved, making it a very busy time in camp for every man. After we trained the new men up to a basic level where I was reasonably sure that they wouldn't stab themselves to death, only then did we begin training with real weapons, which is always a day of great moment to a new Legionary. I enjoyed the look of wonder that men had when they hefted the real weapon for the first time, realizing how much lighter it was than the wooden sword. Then when they were given their shields, they had the same reaction as they whipped them about in delight. Scribonius and I were watching, and I imagine we had the amused expression of a father when his child has a new toy.

I turned to him and said, "I think it's time we have a few mock battles, don't you?"

He grinned. "I was wondering how long it was going to take you."

This was the manner in which we passed the time as the army rebuilt itself, preparing for the day that Antonius would return to lead us back into Media. Our general had other matters on his mind, however, the most controversial being his marriage to Cleopatra. When Antonius sent Octavia back to Rome, according to her brother he had not properly divorced her, so he was now an adulterer. And who he was committing adultery with made matters worse, because Octavian always hated Cleopatra; it was he who coined the term Queen of Beasts to describe her. Octavian continually declared that he would never attack Marcus Antonius, that he would not make war on a fellow Roman, yet there are more ways of waging war than picking up a sword, and it was in these more subtle ways in which Octavian has no equal. Antonius made no attempt to reply to Octavian's charges directly, though I have no doubt that he had his own creatures hard at work behind the scenes in Rome trying to refute the various accusations. It was clear to everyone in our world that these two men were on a collision course, the only question being when and how it happened, which not surprisingly was the topic of conversation most nights in the huts of the men. The only place where it was never discussed was at Uncle Tiberius' villa, where all guests who came to visit were strictly warned that the subject was off-limits. Uncle Tiberius and his wife were frequent guests and I must say that, even knowing how dangerous he was, I enjoyed his company, as did Miriam. For the sake of peace in the house, I did not tell Miriam any details about Uncle Tiberius' true nature or who he worked for, just making her promise that she would not venture any opinion about Roman politics in his presence. She agreed and thankfully did not ask any questions, though I could see she was curious.

The months marched by, and now the Primi Pili were faced with the problem that always come from a prolonged period of peace, which has two prongs. The first is that without an opportunity for fighting and plunder, men become restless for action, and it is always the civilians or their comrades who bear the brunt of their boredom. This is an issue that can be controlled with a few floggings and perhaps an execution or two to keep the men in line. It is the second prong that is actually more of a challenge. Like a blade that is finely honed, an army that is not allowed to fulfill its true purpose will become dull and worn down from constant sharpening without any cutting to go with it. We had trained the army back up to a level that every Primi Pili believed was sufficient to sweep any enemy we faced from the field, but now we had to go into the field before that edge was completely lost.

As Spurius, the Primus Pilus of the 3rd Gallica put it, "If Antonius waits another year to put us in the field, we're going to have start over with another training cycle, and these men aren't getting any younger. Neither are we, for that matter."

None of us wanted that, so with that in mind, all the Primi Pili put their names to a message to Antonius where we outlined the situation and asked if we could expect to march soon. We received a curt reply from Antonius telling us that he would indeed be marching, and that he was sending Canidius to begin preparations for our march into Armenia. With the pact between Artavasdes the Median and Antonius, our focus now became Artavasdes the Armenian, which was perfectly fine with every man in the army who had survived his treachery. About a week less than a month after we received our reply from Antonius, Canidius arrived in Damascus from his post in Antioch, and we began our preparations for the invasion of Armenia.

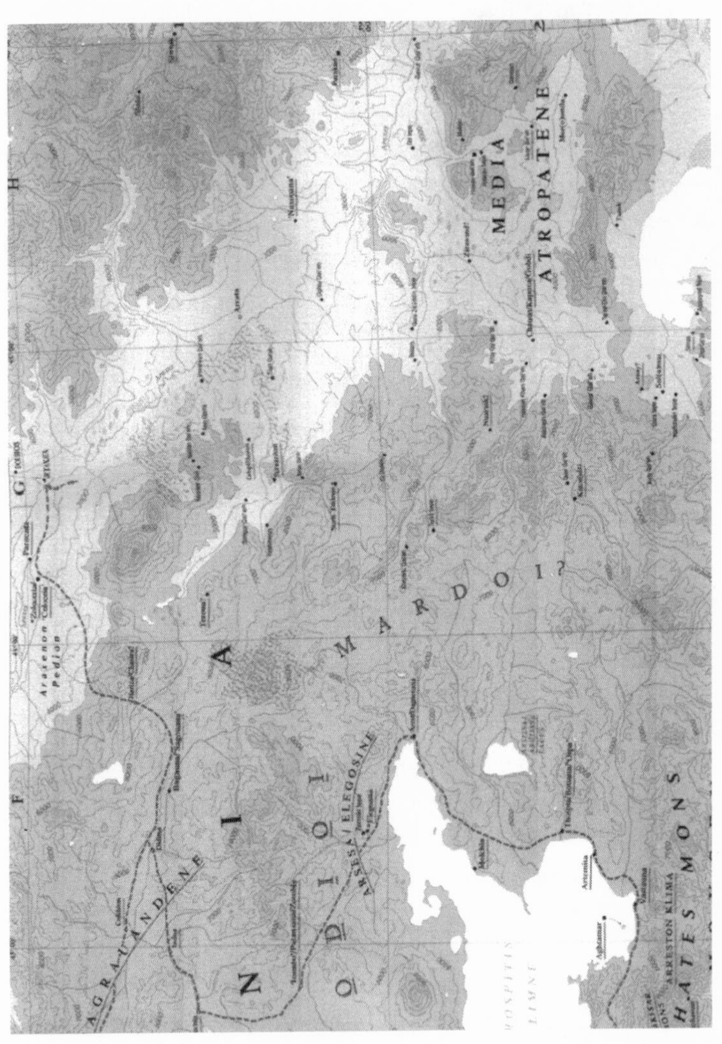
MEDIA
ATROPATENE
M A R D O I ?
ARRESTON KLIMA

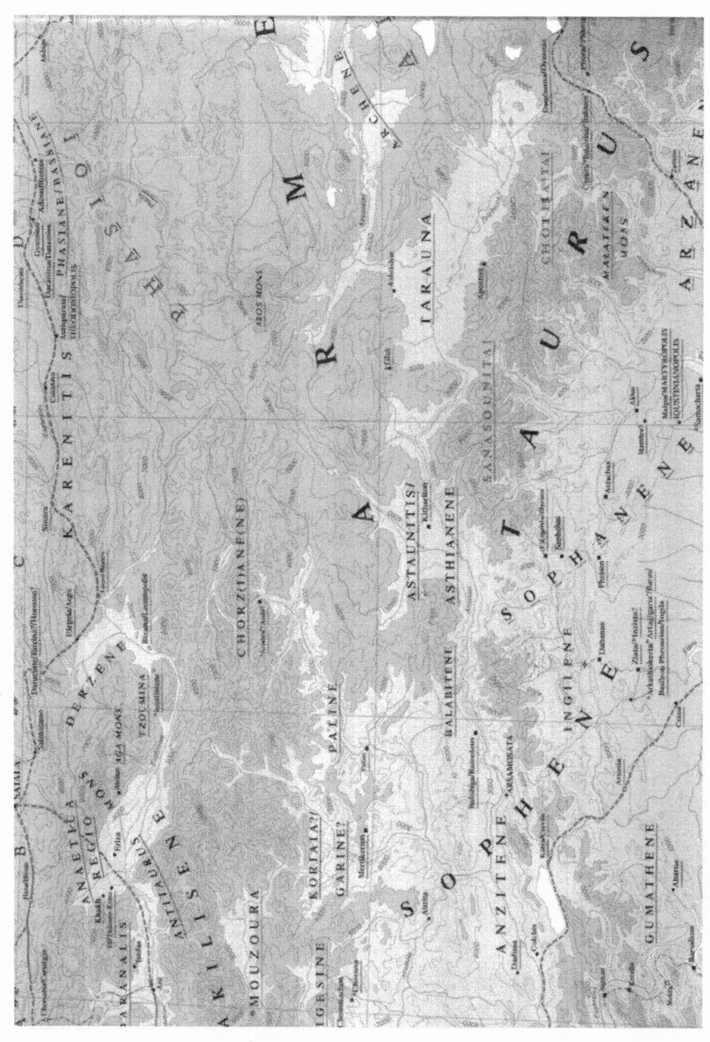
KARENITIS
PHASIANE/BASIANE
DERZENE
TZOUMINA
PALINE
ASTAUNITIS/
ASTHIANENE
BALABITENE
TARAUNA
SANASOUNITAI
INGILENE
ANZITENE
GUMATHENE
MOUZOURA
T A U R U S
S O P H A N E N E
S O P H E N E

Chapter 2- Armenia

"We'll be marching with an even larger army than before," announced Canidius when the Centurions met him in the *praetorium* shortly after his arrival. "Antonius has summoned the Macedonian Legions, along with those in Egypt to join us. We'll march with sixteen Legions."

We all listened impassively, more concerned with other matters, which Canidius went on to address.

"And this time we'll march with the baggage train no matter how slowly it marches."

"Well, that's a relief," I heard a voice say quietly, and there were a few snickers, but if Canidius heard, he chose to ignore them.

"We're going to begin marching to Zeugma in Januarius, which we'll use as a jumping off point. This time we're not going to Parthia, at least at first. We're going to subdue Artavasdes first, and I know I don't have to tell you why. Depending on how long that takes, we'll either continue on to Parthia to bring back Phraates, or we'll spend the winter in Artaxata before renewing the campaign the next season."

This was a sound plan for a campaign, and ambitious to say the least. If we prepared ourselves properly, it was a challenging but attainable goal. Canidius went on with some other details, but if the other Primi Pili were anything like me, they stopped listening as soon as he uttered the information that was pertinent to us. Seeing that we were no longer paying attention, Canidius dismissed us, and we hurried off to our respective Legions to make preparations. He had joined us on the Kalends of December, giving us a month in which to prepare, precious little time, given everything there was to do. That is always how it seems to be in the army; you either have nothing but time, or not enough of it. Fortunately, the core of the Legions were still veterans who had done this before, so the work went smoothly, although there were a few sleepless nights, mostly on the part of the Centurions on whose shoulders fell the ultimate responsibility to make sure that every man's equipment was in first rate order and they were ready to march. The myriad details to make that happen are positively dizzying; everything from inspecting that the blades of the turf cutters are still serviceable to making sure that the wicker baskets are still tightly woven and will not break or leak depending on what they carry. Each of these items had to be attended to, and there was no detail too small, because it is precisely those small details that can spell the difference between a campaign that sees men marching in a Triumph through the streets of Rome at its conclusion, or trying to survive a death march as we had been forced to, and none of us wanted the latter. This preparation period was notable in the lack of persuasion that the Centurions had to administer with the *vitus* to get the men to perform all of their various tasks, a clear sign that the men understood the importance of all that they were doing.

Whenever I could, I continued working with Gaius, and I was pleased to see how much he had progressed, making me confident that he would come out victorious against all but the most experienced and skilled warrior we might face. I barely had enough time to go to the villa to see Miriam, though I did manage to squeeze in a few visits. She did not complain, but her worry was plain to see on her face. Meanwhile, I had gotten to an age where I was no longer so blithely confident that I would return alive or even unscathed. Still, I tried to make light of our impending parting, making the evenings pass pleasantly without argument or too much sadness.

Finally, the day came that all was deemed ready, the baggage train fully loaded and arrayed in a huge park just outside the camp under heavy guard. There was no huge battering ram this time, as that had been the most significant impediment that contributed to the slow pace of the train, although there were raw materials to assemble at least four rams of a standard size. Most significantly, every man was equipped with warm gear, with spare fur-lined socks for the hands as well, and the men treated these items as if they were made of gold, which of course in a sense they were. In recognition of their hard work, the men were given two days to debauch and spend what money they had left on the whores of Damascus. Naturally, I chose to spend it with Miriam, and the last evening I invited Uncle Tiberius, Scribonius, Balbus, Macrianus, and Gaius to dinner. Gaius declined the invitation, having developed a romantic relationship with a young lady in the city and wished to spend it with her, for which I could not rightly blame him.

I put Diocles in charge of making the dinner a memorable one, but unfortunately it was more tense than enjoyable, each of us occupied with our own thoughts. Scribonius and Balbus still viewed Uncle Tiberius with barely disguised hostility, understanding but disagreeing with my desire to keep him close so that I could keep an eye on him. Therefore, it was not surprising that the conversation between these parties was stilted. Miriam and Pompeia did their best to keep the talk on neutral subjects, but it was like a weak swimmer trying to fight an outrushing tide, since it seemed that no matter how hard they tried the talk turned political.

"Antonius has forgotten what it is to be Roman," Uncle Tiberius declared, after quaffing his third cup of unwatered wine. "He's setting himself up to have his own kingdom, but the only way he can do so is to take the Eastern provinces from Rome."

Now, I happened to know that both Scribonius and Balbus were essentially in agreement with Uncle Tiberius, as was I for the most part. It did seem to me that he was shedding the skin of the Roman patrician, becoming more of an Eastern potentate with each passing day. However, I also knew that Uncle Tiberius' role as an agent for both Octavian and Antonius made anything he said against either man suspect, making it just as likely to be an attempt to bait one of us into saying something impolitic as it was an expression of his honest opinion. I shot a warning glance at Scribonius, despite believing he was the last person likely to forget this, but he either chose to ignore me or missed my signal.

"It's interesting that you should say that," my friend said coolly, setting his cup down to turn his full attention to the old man. "Antonius is, after all, still a Triumvir and has been legally appointed the entire East to *govern*," Scribonius emphasized the word "govern," clearly intent on making a distinction, "not rule. Kings rule, and he was extremely clear not to give himself such a title."

Uncle Tiberius snorted in derision. "No, he just gave his children the titles, and they're minor children, so who's making the decisions?" He gave his braying laugh. "Perhaps you're right. I'm sure that it's Cleopatra, now that I think of it."

"So you're saying that Marcus Antonius is not actually governing the provinces?" Scribonius asked in an idle manner, but I knew there was nothing idle about the question at all.

I sat wondering where he was headed. Clearly, Uncle Tiberius did not see that, because he did not seem to be wary in the least, waving his hand in a dismissive gesture.

"Isn't it obvious? You've seen how he moons over Cleopatra. Absolutely disgusting for a Roman man to behave in such a manner, especially over a foreign queen."

"She's hardly foreign in her own lands," Miriam spoke up, and while her tone was mild, I could see she was angered by Uncle Tiberius' words.

I was suddenly reminded of how Gisela felt about what we had done in Gaul, the bitterness and sadness that would spill out at odd times, causing harsh words between us.

Uncle Tiberius peered over at her in surprise before reaching out to pat her hand as he said, "Yes, that may have been true at one time. But they're Roman lands now, my dear. Her father Ptolemy Chickpea," he cackled at the derogative nickname that had been given to Cleopatra's father, "gave Egypt to Rome."

"Just because they occupy it does not make it theirs," she said tightly. "And one day Rome will be gone, and the people will still be there, as they always have."

"Rome's not going anywhere," I said in what I hoped was a tone gentle enough not to make her angrier, but ensured she knew there was no point in arguing.

"Rome is forever," Scribonius agreed, while Balbus raised a cup at Scribonius' words.

Seeing that she was at least outnumbered if nothing else, she fell silent, yet I could see by the set of her jaw that this was likely to come back up later in private.

Turning back to the original topic, Scribonius picked up where he had left off. "So Antonius loves Cleopatra," he continued. "What does that have to do with how he governs the East?"

"Look at how he gave the balsam rights of Judaea to Cleopatra," Uncle Tiberius argued. "Those are in Herod's kingdom, yet she wheedled and cajoled Antonius, and he gave her lands that aren't even adjacent to her own kingdom!"

Scribonius nodded thoughtfully, as if seeing the point, then gave one of his frowns.

"But didn't she also pay for the bonuses for the army? Couldn't that be argued to be a payment for those rights?"

"That's what Antonius claims," Uncle Tiberius grudgingly agreed. "But do we really know where that money came from?"

To be fair to Uncle Tiberius, he was not saying anything that had not been a matter of some conjecture, the rumor certainly going around that Antonius actually borrowed the money from the plutocrats in his camp, making the payment of the bonus from those funds while claiming that it came from Cleopatra in order to make her more popular with the army.

"So you think he might be lying about that?"

"I think it's certainly a possibility."

Almost as quickly as the words came out of Uncle Tiberius' mouth, he seemed to realize that he had gone too far, but it was too late, Scribonius giving me a long and meaningful look before turning back to Uncle Tiberius.

"That's certainly good to know," my friend said quietly, and Uncle Tiberius immediately raised his hands in protest.

"I'm not saying that he is," he sputtered. "I just said that it's . . ."

Scribonius cut him off. "I know, a possibility. You're saying that it's possible that Antonius lied about the source of funds to the army."

There was no way that Uncle Tiberius could dispute this, because that was exactly what he said. It just sounded much different when Scribonius repeated it back to him, which of course was exactly what Scribonius intended. The old man began looking wildly at me, then Balbus, but there were no friendly faces looking back at him, though I imagine I was looking a bit triumphant.

"It's good that we're just speaking here, in private, among friends," Scribonius said with a smile. "Because that kind of talk could be dangerous. If it were to get back to the Triumvir, of course."

The silence that fell over the table was uncomfortable even for me, who was the primary beneficiary of Uncle Tiberius' misstep, so I imagine it was excruciating to the old man and his wife. I felt a pang of sympathy for Pompeia, who had been nothing but kind to Miriam and had proven to be a good friend to her. My feelings towards Uncle Tiberius were not so tender, however, especially now that we had a sword with a very sharp point to dangle above his head. I had no idea whether or not the three of us would be believed if we were to go to Antonius and claim that Uncle Tiberius was one of the sources spreading the idea that he had made the bonus payment in Cleopatra's name, but that was not important. That Uncle Tiberius believed Antonius would accept our version of events was all that mattered, and he clearly thought that very thing, for he said barely a word the rest of the evening, instead looking down at his plate, picking at his food while muttering to himself. The only sound was the smacking of lips as food or wine was consumed, and it was becoming more oppressive by the moment when Miriam, clearly desperate to reignite some sort of conversation, chose that moment to make an announcement.

"I'm pregnant."

It felt as if all the air was sucked out of the room, as I suddenly found it difficult to take a breath, my eyes fixed on her face. She was looking directly at me, calmly but with just a hint of defiance, her chin tilted upward.

"By the gods, that's wonderful!" Pompeia had leaped off the couch to run over to where Miriam was seated to my right, embracing her tightly.

The older woman beamed over at me. "Isn't that wonderful, Titus? You're going to be a father!"

I felt my mouth opening and closing, but nothing seemed to come out, my eyes fixed on the face of the woman sitting next to me.

"It's certainly . . . interesting," was what came out, and I winced at the sound of the words, knowing that I had just said perhaps the worst possible thing.

"Interesting?" Pompeia's face showed undisguised horror. "That's all you can think to say?"

She turned back to Miriam, whose eyes had filled with tears, the older woman patting her hand.

"Don't worry about the things that come out of a man's mouth at moments like these, my dear. They're worthless when it comes to expressing proper emotion."

She turned to glare at me with a severity that I imagined my own mother or sister would display at my callousness, and I immediately felt ashamed. I looked over at Scribonius and Balbus, both of whom looked as if they would rather be standing in the arena facing a hungry lion than where they were at that moment, and truthfully, I wished I could have joined them. Reaching for Miriam's hand, I patted it awkwardly, though I was heartened to see that she did not jerk away immediately.

"I'm sorry, Miriam," I said. "It's just that you caught me by surprise."

The face she turned towards me almost rent my heart in two, so full of anxiety and sorrow as her eyes searched my face.

"Are you angry with me? I know that you did not want children, and I was careful, but . . ." she shrugged, then gave a self-conscious laugh. "These things happen, no matter how careful you are."

"These things do happen," I echoed, my mind still whirling from the import of her words.

I had not wanted children for purely selfish reasons; I remembered the pain of losing my family all too well, to the point where it still haunted my dreams at times, and I did not want to relive that pain. But as I sat there, I was suddenly reminded of all the other moments, the joyful ones, few and far between as they were because of my long absences, of seeing my son walking and talking, of the smell of my daughter's hair when I held her. Who says that it has to happen again? This was the question that kept crowding into the front of my mind as I struggled with the unexpected news.

Moved by impulse, I reached out to embrace her, whispering in her ear, "I'm truly, truly happy at this news."

She pulled back, again searching my face, her own clearly imploring me to assure her that it was true, and it was. I wanted this child, and I held her tightly, whispering this truth to her, over and over.

The dinner ended and as I reflected on it later, it had been a momentous night and worthy of the event that it was marking. I was marching off to war again, but this time I had something more to come back for; the start of a new family, so I suppose it was a natural thing that my thoughts then turned back to the idea that it was time to retire. I would be 43 in April, and I had served in the Legions since I was sixteen. I had been frugal, so that between the money I made in Gaul and the resulting increase in investments in certain businesses that were made in my name by the plutocrats that had worked for Caesar, along with the bounties and plunder I accrued during the civil wars, even with my expenditures, I had more than enough money to purchase my way into the equestrian class, along with enough to live on in a decent style. When I talked to Scribonius about it, for the first time, he did not laugh as he had every other time I brought it up, instead giving me his thoughtful look.

"Maybe it's time," he said. "But let me know, because when you do, I will as well."

I looked at him, not trying to hide my astonishment. "But you'd be Primus Pilus if I did. I've made it clear with everyone, and they agree. Besides, you have more than enough money to sway Antonius."

For this is the flaw in our system of promotion. Scribonius was the most qualified, but even if there were no other contenders for the position the ultimate decision was up to Antonius, who was so strapped for cash at this point that it was not a stretch of the imagination to think that Antonius would simply auction off the post.

Now, Scribonius laughed, shaking his head at me. "Titus, I am not, nor have I ever been as ambitious as you. In fact, I think you could give Caesar a run for his money when it comes to that. Also," he pointed out, "I'm older than you, and I'm just as tired, if not more so, as you are. No," he concluded. "If you retire, I will as well."

I did not know what to say. Never before had any man made such a clear and open declaration of loyalty to me and to my horror, I felt tears pricking my eyes at the thought, forcing me to fall back on the defense of a gruff exterior.

"You're right, you probably aren't up to the job," was all I could think to say.

Fortunately, he saw through my words and just laughed.

"Probably not," he said. "So it's a good thing that we'll never find out."

"You are truly not angry with me?"

I looked over at Miriam lying next to me then shook my head. "No, I'm not. I thought I would be, but the truth is, I'm happy that you're pregnant."

She searched my face, but I was being honest. I was leaving in the morning, so this would be our last time together for the gods only knew how long and I forced myself to discuss the possibility that I would be gone for the entire pregnancy and the first months of the child's life. The corners of Miriam's mouth turned downwards, the sign that she was about to start crying again, which made me miserable, so I stopped talking and just held her until she fell asleep. The next morning I arose a few thirds of a watch before dawn, dressing myself in the darkness and wondering how long it had been since I had done so without the help of Diocles or Agis. I had already packed the belongings that I would not be carrying on my mule and had them taken to the baggage train, while everything that I would carry was already stowed and ready. Miriam got up to sit on the edge of the bed, neither of us talking much, then it was time for me to leave. I stood looking down at her, not sure what to say, remembering that I had done this before.

"Take care of yourself," I said, sounding awkward even to my own ears.

To my surprise, she laughed at that. "I am not the one marching off to war. You take care of yourself, Titus Pullus."

"All right. Take care of the baby then," I amended, reaching down to pat her belly, which was still flat, though she insisted it was not.

I took her in my arms, we kissed, and then I picked up my gear, leaving the villa.

The camp was a swarm of activity, men racing about attending to all the last-minute tasks their Centurions could think of, the mules loaded with the freshly made tents and stakes, the braying of the animals competing with the shouted orders of the officers. The baggage train was assembled outside the main gate, waiting for the rest of the army to march out so that it could fall in behind us. Antonius was not yet with us and would be joining us somewhere along the way to Zeugma, so Canidius was in command. He still clearly remembered our conflict in the last campaign because he barely had two words for me and those were always sarcastic or biting in some way. Finally, a third of a watch after dawn we were ready to depart, the front gates swinging open as the vanguard stepped out to a waiting crowd of people, composed in seemingly equal parts of well-wishers, gawkers, camp followers and army wives seeing their men off. Like the last campaign, Antonius had imposed a strict rule that camp followers and army wives would not be allowed to tag along with the army, but unlike last time, there was very little argument.

After the deprivation and hardship that we had suffered and after hearing the tales of the barren wastes we would be marching through, it did not take much to dissuade anyone from following us this time. Consequently, the men would be leaving their women and children behind. It was the families who wailed the loudest at our parting, children running alongside their fathers, begging them to stay. It was a wrenching sight, the tears of the children softening even the hardest hearts in the Legions, and no man chastised or mocked the fathers of the children for matching their emotions. Women called out men's names as they marched by, wishing them luck and that the gods watch out for their men, while for a moment I regretted making Miriam stay at the villa instead of coming to see me off, though I reckoned that it was best that way. We marched through the streets of Damascus, the tramping of our feet echoing off the stone walls of the buildings as even more people lined the roofs and side streets, all 16 Legions taking more than a full watch to march past a given point, the baggage train following us taking at least that long by itself. We would not post a rear guard on the baggage train while we were in Syria, then only when we left Zeugma would we march in the *quadratum*, with the train in the middle. Since we were determined not to leave the train behind, we were prepared to move at perhaps a third of our normal pace, which was why we were leaving at the beginning of the year.

It was the year of Antonius' second Consulship, ironic considering he had not set foot in Rome in at least two years, and the junior Consul was Lucius Scribonius Libo, a distant relative of my friend and Secundus Pilus Prior, though it was something he did not want known. I was fitter than I had been in years, thanks to the work I did with the new *tiros* that we had drafted to replace the men lost more than a year before. The Legion had more than a year in which to get the new men trained and integrated into the ranks. While they were not completely raw, a little more than a third of the Legion was still unblooded and until we faced battle, there was no way really to tell how they would perform. They did well in all the mock battles, including the one Legion on Legion exercise we had conducted, which turned into a bloody brawl that sent hundreds of men across the army to the hospital with broken bones. But that was not the same thing as standing in line, waiting for the thundering cataphracts to slam into you, or holding a shield above you and your comrades for what felt like thirds of a watch as the sky seemed to rain arrows. Only after that happened the first time would I and the other Centurions know what the new men were made of, though with men like Albinus stiffening the ranks, I was cautiously confident that the 10th would acquit itself well. We had been doing conditioning marches as well, but it is never the same as when you are marching off to fight, though I do not know why. Whatever the cause, it seems harder on the body to know that you are marching for real rather than just on what is essentially a pleasure jaunt out in the countryside, knowing that you are at most going to spend one night under leather. Perhaps it is the knowledge that you are not going to be sleeping under a roof, or be in familiar surroundings for the next several months, or even longer, that wears a man down. Whatever the cause, at the end of the first days on the march, men were exhausted, while there was a minimum of horseplay and spirited talk around the fires at night, though I knew that this would not last. The weather was mild, even for winter in this part of the world, which helped, but the farther north and east we marched the colder it got. Still, it was nowhere near the bitterness we would be facing once we crossed the Euphrates.

With the influx of new men, there was the requisite shuffling in the ranks, Scribonius having promoted Gaius to Sergeant, leader of his tent section, which I had mixed feelings about, to say the least. On one hand I was proud that he was viewed as worthy of a leadership position, even if it was the lowest rung of the ladder. On the other, I was justifiably worried about whispers of favoritism shown to my nephew, but when I voiced my concerns to Scribonius, somewhat to my surprise he got angry.

"It sounds like you're questioning my judgment, Titus," he said stiffly.

"You know it's not that," I protested. "I just don't want him to have to face difficulties because he's my nephew."

"You're underestimating the boy," he retorted. "Besides which, so what if he does have to face some questions about how he came to be promoted? Maybe you should let him fight his own battles. I remember there were more than a few questions about how you got promoted."

I bit back a sharp reply, knowing that he was right in every way. I had indeed faced some bitterness and resistance when Calienus was promoted and I had moved into his spot, and I bitterly recalled the troubles I endured at the hands of Spurius Didius. But Gaius was not me, I thought, he does not have my size and while he burned with an ambition similar to mine, I was worried that he did not have the savagery needed to not only achieve but to secure a promotion. Still, I knew that Scribonius was right, so I relented in my questioning, allowing that I would sit back to let him either thrive or fall flat on his face. My fears proved to be unfounded, though what seemed to help Gaius was that he was so likable and earnest that even the most hard-bitten of the men in his section did not want to let him down. He had proven to be a good Legionary, now he had to prove that he could be a good leader, and I offered a prayer to the gods that he would be as happy and successful in the army as I had been. I was struck by how fitting it would be if he began his rise through the ranks at a time when I was seriously thinking of leaving the army to begin a new chapter in my life.

The army plodded towards Zeugma and as expected, the weather turned colder but this time all the men were prepared so there were no complaints or illness because of the weather. We finally reached Zeugma almost three weeks after leaving Damascus, only to find that Antonius, who had supposedly gone by ship from Alexandria up the coast to Antioch, then was coming overland to Zeugma, still had not arrived. Unsurprisingly, almost immediately the grumbling began, the men blaming Cleopatra for the delay without having any evidence to support their belief, which I took as a sign that Octavian's agents had been successful in painting her as the cause of every Roman ill. Fortunately, we were there less than a week before Antonius arrived, thankfully without his queen in tow, causing the complaining to cease. He looked fit, with no signs of the dissipation that had so marked our stay with him at Leuke Kome. We stayed at Zeugma only a day after he arrived and despite it being very early in the season, with the land still in the grip of winter, by setting out immediately, Antonius was making two gambles. One was on the weather, the other on the fact that our slow progress would actually be to our benefit this time. Unlike what was now two years before, the winter of this year had been exceedingly mild and I do not know whether he consulted astrologers or some other soothsayers, but he seemed confident that the trend would continue. Adding to that was the knowledge that we were going to move only as fast as our baggage train, and this time we were not marching with the tail of auxiliaries we had before. This was an almost completely Roman army, with the exception of some 7,000 Galatian cavalry and 2,000 slingers, both of these forces proving themselves useful in fighting the type of enemy we would be facing.

Our slow progress would actually play in our favor, or at least Antonius so believed, since it meant that by the time we reached the higher country it would be late spring, and Antonius had made it clear that we would wait if need be until the passes cleared. As he pointed out, it was a much better proposition to be poised in position to march the relatively short distance left than to wait at Zeugma or even Samosata for it to happen. Artavasdes the Median would supposedly be joining us, which was the one question hanging over our collective heads that would ultimately determine the success or failure of this campaign, none of us having any confidence in the trustworthiness of these allies of convenience.

Accompanying Antonius was Ahenobarbus, who had waited in Antioch for him and, because of his seniority, he took over as second in command from Canidius, who did not like that a bit, I can tell you. Titius was left behind in Africa to govern, along with Plancus and a few others, but Fonteius was in his usual spot tethered to Antonius' side, his nose tilted in the air at its accustomed angle whenever he was forced to deal with the likes of us. Along with the Macedonian Legions came the 23rd Legion, with old Torquatus as Primus Pilus, who I greeted as an old friend. The events that led to his relief as Primus Pilus of the 10th having happened long enough in the past and not being of a personal nature, it seemed to me that whatever rancor there might have been between us had long since faded. Unfortunately, the same could not be said for Torquatus' feelings for Balbus, although I cannot say I was surprised, given the nature of their dispute. The woman over whom they had fallen out died in childbirth many years before and I believe that most of the bitterness was borne by Torquatus, which I suppose is natural since he was the loser in that contest of the heart. They greeted each other politely enough, but the tension between the two men was thick enough that it would require a dagger to cut through it. The feelings between the two were so obvious that even Gaius commented on it the one night that I made the regrettable mistake of inviting both Torquatus and Balbus to dine with me.

"What's the matter with those two?" my nephew asked after the two had practically torn through the wall of the tent to leave without offending me at the first opportunity, albeit in two opposite directions.

"It's a long story, and it goes back a long way."

I did not feel like explaining to Gaius, thinking that he was still too young to understand.

"It's obviously about a woman." I looked at him in surprise, but he just shrugged. "It's the only thing that could keep two men who've known each other most of their lives so angry at each other, though it seems to me that Torquatus is the angrier of the two. So I suppose that means that Balbus took his woman."

I could only shake my head, wondering if it indeed was that obvious, or if Gaius was just particularly observant and wise beyond his years.

"It's nothing for you to be concerned about. Besides, that's not the only thing that can ruin a friendship," I stood, making it clear that the conversation was over as I thought about Vibius and me.

Antonius' gamble was paying off as we marched in the *agmen quadratum* every day, with the baggage train and noncombatants in the middle. Reaching Samosata, Antiochus, clearly mindful of the last time we passed through, stripping his granaries and stock of firewood bare, was waiting with sacks of grain and stacks of wood, which Antonius took with thanks. We spent a few days once again camped outside the black walls of the city before resuming the march. Despite the bitter cold, the fact that the men were prepared made all the difference and it was heartening to see that there were no appendages turning black, the Centurions inspecting the men every morning and night for the telltale signs that signaled the onset of frostbite. Helping the situation was the weather slowly but surely turning the other way, the days growing warmer and longer, keeping morale high as we continued northward, beginning the gradual climb onto the high plateau; headed for Melitene next. It was there that Artavasdes the Median arrived, who as promised, brought a force of almost 12,000 men, roughly even between cataphracts and archers. Although this was good news and was taken as a positive sign for the most part, none of us were willing to put much faith in whether or not the Medians would actually fight. The fact that these were in all likelihood the same men who participated in the massacre of Statianus, the baggage train and the Legion accompanying it was not lost on any man. When they went parading by on their horses we were under strict orders not to say anything that might incite a fight between our two forces, but it was extremely difficult to maintain order, our men growling their hatred at these allies who did not help matters by openly smirking at us, giving mocking salutes or calling out in fractured Latin a variety of insults. Then, making things even worse, one of the men of the 10th spotted a distinctive ring, worn by one of the cataphracts, recognizing it as a piece of booty that had been in his possession and stored in his valuables packet on one of the Legion wagons.

"By the gods, that cocksucker is wearing my ring," I heard the man roar.

Before I or any of the Centurions or Optios could stop him, the man, a veteran named Plautius, made a move to rush the mounted man, who had seen the danger and was even now reaching for his sword.

"Plautius," I roared at the top of my lungs. "If you take another step, I will have you *crucified*!"

Thankfully for everyone, not least Plautius, he stopped, bodily anyway, although it did not stop him from hurling curses and threats at the mounted cataphract. The Median did not help matters, laughing openly at Plautius' impotent fury, and that more than anything incited Plautius' friends to begin edging toward the column riding by. I had to use the *vitus* on more than one man, even striking Vellusius who was speaking in a dangerously loud voice what he would like to do to a Median if he could get his hands on him, while moving out of the formation. I smacked him across the back of the legs, the favorite spot when a man is marching with his pack and shield, his back being protected by the shield while striking him on the arm might cause him to drop his *furca* and his pack, creating a disruption in the march. He yelped in pain, but his manner was anything but apologetic as he continued to glare at the Medians streaming by.

"Primus Pilus, doesn't it bother you to know that we're marching with the bastards who stole our money?"

For that was the nub of the problem; the fact that most of the men's savings were now jingling in the purses of the men riding by, not to mention the personal items that men had accrued over the years, which in some ways was even more important, was a huge insult. Pieces of plunder that had some sort of special significance only to the man who had taken it, a broken dagger that had belonged to a dear comrade, or Plautius' ring, these were the things whose loss made the men truly angry, and I was no different.

"Yes, it does," I answered Vellusius' question. "But they're our allies now, and that's that. There's nothing to be gained other than a flogging. Or worse."

I looked meaningfully at Vellusius, who blanched visibly. I was glad to see his reaction, having deliberately invoked the memory of Atilius in order to impress on the old veteran the need to restrain not only himself, but his comrades.

"Nothing will happen, Primus Pilus," Vellusius said grimly. "You have my word on it. But that doesn't mean I have to like it."

"I would be worried about you if you did," I replied, and I meant it.

From Melitene we continued northward, until we reached the great bend of the Euphrates that turned us eastward, turning toward Calcidava, which would be the last major city before heading into the wastes of Armenia. Despite the men of the 10th restraining themselves from taking some form of revenge on the Medians, men from other Legions were not willing to let matters rest and it was only a matter of a couple of days after the Medians joined us that the first Median body was found, covered in bruises and with his throat cut. At first, not much was made of the murder, but then it started happening with more frequency, until one memorable day, three dead Medians were found in a similar state as the first. Finally, Antonius could ignore matters no longer, calling a meeting of the Primi Pili. His face was set as if made of stone, and his anger seemed unfeigned as he surveyed the 16 of us.

"I called all of you here, but we all know that it's unlikely that the Legions from Macedonia and Egypt are involved in what's going on," he began. "And I know why it's going on, but….It. Will. Stop."

He bit off each word, looking at every one of the Primi Pili whose men were on the first campaign. I was sure that none of the 10th was involved, if only because Vellusius and the other veterans had sworn to me that they would stay their hand in exacting vengeance, and there is no way to keep that kind of thing secret. One murder perhaps, but by the time of this meeting there had been more than a dozen. I found it unlikely that it was the work of anything but one man or a small group from within the same Legion and probably the same Cohort.

"Put the word out to the men that if the murders stop now, nothing more will be said. But if there is one more, I'm going to start drawing lots and one man from each Legion who marched in the last campaign will be put to death, no questions asked."

The gasp was audible, coming from more than one of us.

"That's not fair, Antonius," Spurius burst out, and it was fortunate that it was him, being one of Antonius' favorites as he was.

Antonius' face flushed, that red spark showing in his eyes, but his tone was calm.

"I realize that it's not fair, Spurius, but that's the point. I don't have the time to investigate properly to determine who's behind this. In fact, I suspect that it's one of your Centurions, so this is the best and fastest way to get it to stop. The man or men responsible for this may not care about the political implications and damage they're doing to our alliance with the Medians, but I'm gambling that they'll not want the death of men who are in all likelihood innocent."

It was brutal, but it was logical and hard to argue. He was right; almost as quickly as we made the announcement, the murders stopped, at least on the part of Romans against Medians. Then, one night about a week later, there was a shout from one of our sentries, followed by shouts from other men. It was at a point on the rampart close to our Legion area, so I heard the commotion. It was enough of a racket that I rose to investigate, throwing my *sagum* over my tunic, cursing at the interrupted sleep. Moving in the direction of the noise, I saw a ring of torches held by a group of men, surrounding a prone figure. Moving closer I saw that whoever it was, he was clearly still alive, writhing and groaning in obvious pain. The duty Centurion was standing over him, firing questions at the sentry, who I could see was one of the youngsters, though he was not in the 10th. He was clearly shaken and it was easy to see why, once I finally got close enough to see the shaft of what I assumed to be the sentry's javelin protruding from the man's midsection. I was also close enough to see that the man on the ground was Median, and I bit back a curse. The duty Centurion turned and saw me, obviously recognizing me because he saluted, though I did not recognize him.

"Primus Pilus Pullus, good to see you again," he grinned at me.

I turned to squint at him, still not recognizing the young Centurion. Not wanting to be rude by making it clear that I did not know the man, I grunted, then indicated the Median, who I noticed nobody was attempting to help.

"Is there a reason we're not trying to stop the bleeding?"

The duty Centurion looked down at the man, scorn written all over his face.

"Because we caught this bastard sneaking over the wall into the camp. I don't have to tell you the rules, Primus Pilus. He's dead either way."

He looked over to the youngster who was still shaking, and I walked over to the boy, putting a hand on his shoulder.

"You did your duty, and you did it well, Gregarius," I said quietly, which did seem to calm him.

I looked back at the duty Centurion, who was beginning to look vaguely familiar, despite the fact I still could not recall his name or how I knew him.

"Have you sent a runner to the *Praetorium*?"

He nodded, adding, "I also asked for someone who speaks the Median tongue. We should at least find out why he was trying to sneak into camp, though I can guess."

I could as well, but I felt the need to point out, "Then it doesn't make a whole lot of sense to let him bleed to death before we find out."

The Centurion looked chagrined, then turned to one of the other men, ordering him to do what he could for the Median while sending yet another off to get a *medici*. The Median was laying on his side, curled up with knees near his chest, his breathing becoming more labored. The javelin had pierced his midsection on the opposite side he was lying on, the head protruding out his back more than a hand span. The blood looked black in the guttering torchlight as it pooled around him, and the Legionary had taken his neckerchief off, placing it around the shaft in an attempt to stop the bleeding.

While we waited, I took the opportunity to pull the duty Centurion aside so that the others could not hear me.

"I'm sorry, Centurion," I began. "You obviously know me, but while you look familiar, I don't know your name."

He laughed, clearly amused at my mystification. "There's no reason you should, Primus Pilus Pullus. The last time I saw you I was a boy." He turned to face me, giving me just the glimmer of knowing what he was going to say. "I'm Decimus Hastatus Prior Spurius Torquatus. Primus Pilus Torquatus is my father."

I barely remembered a boy of perhaps eleven or twelve years old who Torquatus had once introduced on some occasion, but I smiled and offered my hand. "It's good to see that you followed your father's path."

He laughed again. "It's not as if I had much choice, but I like it well enough."

By this time both the provosts and the *medici* had arrived, the latter beginning to work on the wounded man, while the provosts brought one of the men assigned as interpreters. His face was impassive as he began questioning the man, who answered in gasps while the orderly worked with practiced ease. Removing the pin that affixed the head to the shaft so that he could withdraw the missile without doing more damage, he extracted it with one swift motion, eliciting a scream of pain from the Median. The interpreter waited for the Median to recover somewhat, before he continued the questioning. After a series of exchanges, he turned to young Torquatus.

"He says that his brother was one of the men killed by the Romans, and he was coming to exact vengeance," he said in heavily accented but understandable Latin.

"Didn't Artavasdes send the same message to his men that Antonius sent to us?" I asked, and the interpreter looked at me in surprise, obviously thinking that I was one of the rankers.

He shot a glance at Torquatus, who nodded his head to indicate that my question should be answered, which he did with a shrug.

"I believe so, but it is his brother and they were very close."

"Well, he must not have put it in strong enough terms," I said angrily, thinking that the last thing we needed was a blood feud between the two forces.

The Median was carried away to the hospital tent.

When I asked the orderly if he thought the man would live, he said, "It's in the hands of the gods now, Primus Pilus. He's lost a lot of blood, but only time will tell if his bowel was pierced."

If that had happened, there was no saving the Median an agonizing death, though by custom and regulation we had the right to execute him. Seeing there was nothing else to be done, I retired to my tent, my mind occupied with a number of different thoughts.

The Median did not die that night and in the morning, he was sent over to the Median camp, with a stern warning from Antonius that this was the only act of mercy he would show to any man who tried to exact vengeance on a Roman. His message was not received well, but there were no more attempts by any Median to sneak over the wall or any other incidents for the remainder of the campaign. Reaching Calcidava, we went into camp for a week as wagons that needed it were overhauled and repaired. It also gave us an extra week to let the weather change for the better, and whereas everything that could have gone wrong during our last campaign into this country did, this time the gods seemed to look on our endeavor with great favor. Few of the wagons were damaged, while what damage there was seemed to be fairly minor, so it did not take long to get them fixed.

The men were holding up well on the march, the weather now mild enough that frostbite was no longer a concern. However, we also knew that the most difficult part of the march was coming, the veterans who had been over this ground before trying to warn the new men what was facing them. We replenished our supplies at Calcidava, most importantly laying in a stock of charcoal that we could use if absolutely necessary, knowing that it was likely that there would be little or no firewood. The march resumed, and despite everything going well to that point, there was still a fair amount of trepidation at what lay ahead. It was hard going, yet not nearly as difficult as it was the first time we passed this way, both because we were marching at the same pace as the baggage train and the weather was turning milder with every passing day. There was still snow on the higher peaks in the distance, while there were patches in the spots where the sun did not strike, though overall the path was clear.

About a week out of Calcidava, our scouts began reporting signs of the Armenian army, sending a flash of excitement through the ranks, the talk around the fires at night turning to what the new men could expect. I was happy to see that the veterans were taking the opportunity to help the new men, despite the fact that there were always those in the ranks who could not resist filling the youngsters' heads with horror stories. Fortunately these were in the vast minority, which I believe was another example of how the experience of the previous campaign had bonded the men more tightly, making them realize how inextricably intertwined were their fates. Once the Armenians were sighted, the men did not need any urging on the part of the Centurions and Optios to remain alert as we marched. It was not long after that men began to shout out, pointing to a nearby hill or bluff where a line of horsemen sat, watching us pass. From that point on, the camp guard was doubled, since we had learned from bitter experience the myth of Eastern armies not fighting at night, but there were no probes to our defenses. The army continued to rattle along towards Artaxata and I will say that the surrounding countryside was not nearly as desolate in the spring as it had been when we passed through in the late autumn and early winter. There would be brief showers during the day, not enough to soak us through but enough to keep the vegetation green, providing fodder for the livestock. After another week, when we were about three days' march from Artaxata, the entire host of the Armenian army was spotted, camped directly athwart our expected line of advance. The *bucina* immediately sounded the signal to make camp, then once the *Praetorium* was set up, we were summoned to meet with Antonius. The entire command staff was there waiting as we filed in, and once we were settled, Antonius began the briefing.

"It appears that Artavasdes wants to give battle." He smiled at us but it was a savage, mocking grin. "So I believe we should oblige him, don't you?"

The walls shook with our roar of approval, lasting several moments. He waited for a moment before continuing, giving us the dispositions of the forces. We would be aligned in our normal three wings of infantry, each wing composed of four Legions, so that we would have three Legions in reserve, posted behind the main body, ready to move to a possible trouble spot, with a Legion left behind to guard the camp. Our slingers were to be evenly divided between the three wings, arrayed in front of each. The Median forces would be posted on our right flank, while the Galatian cavalry would be on the left flank. The 10th was in the right wing, though this time we would not be to the right of the line, but one of the middle Legions, positioned between the 3rd Gallica, which would be on the far right and the 4th to our left. I was not particularly happy about this, knowing that the men would take it as a bit of an insult that we were not in our accustomed spot. I put it down to the actions of the 3rd during the last campaign when Antonius had led them to try to rescue Gallus. Unlike with Caesar, we would not be in an *acies triplex*, but in a *duplex*, Antonius wanting a broader front so that we could overlap the Armenians with our cavalry, freeing them to swing around the flanks of the Armenian army. With our orders complete, we went to prepare the men.

The Armenian camp was about five miles away, the ground in between gently rolling, with a number of gullies and dry streambeds cutting across our line of march. These features served as obstacles, making it difficult to keep our cohesion and alignment and forcing us to stop at regular intervals. While the scouts assured us that the ground ahead was not as broken, it was a worrying prospect, this type of terrain negating our advantage with our own cavalry forces. As we advanced, I walked over to Scribonius' Cohort, marching next to the First Century, to voice my concerns, but he did not seem worried.

"The Armenians aren't likely to choose ground like this, because their entire force is composed of cataphracts and archers," he pointed out. "I wouldn't worry about it."

I could immediately see the logic in this, so I returned to my spot more confident. Of course, Scribonius was right; the Armenians still a dark line on the horizon when the ground began to level out. Drawing closer, the enemy army became more distinct, until we could begin to make out individual men and horses. Once we got to that point, Antonius ordered a halt to allow the men to catch their breath while the Centurions dressed the line, making sure that the men were ready. He came galloping in our direction on Clemency, his *paludamentum* swirling behind him, wearing his golden lion armor, but still with his helmet strapped to his saddle so that his face was clearly visible. The weather was mild enough that he bared his arms, except for his arm braces, made in the same decorative style as his armor, his biceps rippling and defined, again sparking a pang of envy at his physique. Pulling up in front of our wing, he began his pre-battle speech by pointing over at the array of banners and glittering standards that marked the position of the Armenian king.

"There is Artavasdes of Armenia. Our *ally*." His voice dripped with contempt as he spat the last word out. "He left us, he left you, and he left men who are missing from our ranks because of his betrayal."

He paused to let his words sink in, and a low growl of hatred began issuing from the men behind me.

"Now we've come to set matters to rights," he continued, his voice rising in pitch so the words rang out to the last rank of the last line. "We are here to collect a blood debt owed to us by that faithless, gutless bastard. But I need you, each and every one of you to do your duty to me, to Rome and to your friends who are no longer here. And after we've killed every last piece of scum, we will march to Artaxata and take that city, which I will give to you as payment for all that you lost. How does that sound?"

The growl turned into a full-throated roar, men shaking their fists or bashing their javelins against their shields, shouting their approval as Antonius galloped away to deliver the same message to the other two wings of the army. I glanced over to where the Medians sat their horses, watching our demonstration impassively, wondering for perhaps the hundredth time when the moment came what they would do. Neither the other Primi Pili nor I would have been surprised if they refused to fight, while in the back of my mind was the possibility that they might even turn on us, and Spurius, since he commanded the Legion closest to them had gone as far as warning his men to be wary for such treachery.

After a short while, Antonius returned to his spot at the center of the army, where he would signal the advance before moving to his spot behind us on the right wing. Ahenobarbus commanded the left wing, Canidius the center, and I was just happy that I would not have to cross paths with the latter during the battle. Antonius turned to his staff, ordering the *cornicen* to sound the signal to advance, its heavy bass note thumping through each man's chest. In kind, I turned to Valerius, who gave the Legion signal as my *aquilifer,* Aulus Paterculus, dipped the eagle forward. This was then repeated by every *signifer* carrying the Cohort and Century standard. An instant later, the entire army stepped off towards the enemy. Now, I thought, we'll see what the Medians do.

To my cautious relief, the Medians began moving along with us, but I could not spend too much of my attention on what they were doing, instead turning to watch the 10th moving towards the enemy. The ground was level, but was more broken than it appeared to the casual glance, some men stumbling when their foot caught on a rock, causing a sharp reaction from those around the offender and a shouted curse from their Centurion or Optio. Seeing that most of these were new men, I knew that it was a sign of nerves as much as clumsiness. The tramping of our feet began to raise the inevitable film of dust, the thrumming sound of every step accompanied by the clanking of metal bits against each other, the creaking of leather harnesses, all punctuated by the count of the Optios, whose job it is to call out a rhythmic count to keep the men in step. Squinting into the glare of the sun, now low in the sky off our right quarter since we were headed in a northeasterly direction, I watched for any sign that the Armenian host was beginning their own advance. It was inconceivable that they would stand waiting for us to close with them, yet that appeared to be exactly what they intended on doing, their lack of movement forcing Antonius to call a halt to our advance. The three wings came crashing to a stop, dust slowly settling at our feet while Antonius called the commanders of the mounted troops to attend to him. The Galatians and Medians came trotting over as we stood watching idly, giving me the opportunity to walk through the ranks to talk to the new men. This was one of those times when I had to appear to be a father figure, reassuring nervous boys with my presence, joking with one man, while chiding another for some transgression they had committed in the past. I never started by addressing a new man directly, instead choosing to start a conversation with the veteran standing next to him, but I would surreptitiously watch the face of the youngster to measure what effect I was having on him. I knew Centurions, and I had a couple of them in my Legion, who would sneer at any display of nerves by one of these men, openly mocking his fear or threatening him in some way in an attempt to get the man to focus on their duty, or their hatred for their Centurion, instead of their fear. Their logic is sound, as far as it goes; by making the men fear something more than what they are about to face, or by humiliating them, they get the youngster's mind off what lays ahead, even if it is through his anger at his Centurion for ridiculing him in front of his friends and comrades. Personally, I did not see the point in cluttering their mind with yet one more source of worry. Thinking back to my own early experiences, I recognized that I always performed best when my mind was not on other matters. In fact, I did best when I did not think, and I had talked to enough veterans to know that most of them felt the same way. Therefore, I attempted to take the burden off a new man's mind, though I knew approaching them directly in the moments before their first battle would just rattle them further. Instead, I worked indirectly, and this was how I passed the time while Antonius was conferring with his cavalry commanders, until Balbus called to me that something was happening.

Trotting back to the front, I saw both the Medians and Galatians resume the advance, despite no signal sounding for the army to move forward. Instead, the order was sent that the contingent of slingers would now move to the front while shaking out in a loose formation in front of us, prepared to send their lead missiles buzzing at the enemy. The sun had risen to an angle where there was not as much of a glare, allowing us to see the Armenian army more clearly, and I noticed two things that I had missed before. The ground we would have to cross was actually more sloped than it originally appeared, with the Armenians sitting on what now was clearly the crest of a small hill, explaining their reluctance to move. Also, the other item was more one of proximity;

we had not been close enough to distinguish between archers and cataphracts, at least with my old eyes. Now I could see that in fact there were relatively few cataphracts, that it was mostly archers. I was not the only one to recognize the proportion, and there were muttered curses rippling through the ranks at the sight.

"There goes another shield," a man muttered. "By the time they're through, it'll be ruined."

Our cavalry forces were swinging wide out on either flank of the Armenians, forcing Artavasdes to spread his own lines to meet the threat. The black line of men and horses blurred into motion, becoming less dense as we watched, then a few moments later, the signal was given to resume our own advance. Very quickly, the ground tilted upwards and we climbed the gentle slope, each of the Centurions watching very carefully to make sure that our spacing stayed as precise as it was possible to be given the terrain. While it was true that the Armenians had more archers than cataphracts, there was still a formidable number of the heavily armored cavalry, so that a ragged gap in our lines because of a lapse could be just the kind of mistake on which battles turned. I was mindful that if and when the cataphracts charged, they would be coming downhill, whereas in our other battles the situation had been reversed, and I found myself questioning Antonius' decision in choosing battle on this day. However, I did not know whether Antonius had been informed of the lay of the ground by our scouts. Whatever the case, he and the army were committed now so I kept moving my attention from the ranks to the enemy to Antonius as we continued forward. Men were breathing more heavily, the combination of nerves and slope seeming to work together to suck the air from our lungs. Finally, the enemy began moving in our direction, with two prongs containing archers heading down the hill towards us. We were still well out of bow range, but we all knew that it would not take long for them to close the distance. At the sight of the Armenian archers advancing, almost simultaneously a large group of Median archers and Galatian cavalry wheeled about from their respective sides, spurring their mounts into a gallop, converging on the Armenians.

I do not know if the Armenians were expecting this, though they should have, but judging from their reaction they were caught by surprise, each group of Armenians turning to face the nearest oncoming threat, completely ignoring the army marching slowly towards them. Arrows began flying through the air, crisscrossing the sky as the Armenians and Medians began firing at each other as fast as they could pull their bowstrings back. The sky filled with black streaks as the missiles flew, though it was hard to tell which arrows found their target. Men were falling from their horses and, across the distance, the shouts of pain carried to us over the sound of our own advance. The Galatians, not armed with bows, were forced to move at a full gallop to try closing with the archers in order to use their long swords. However, the Armenian horses were too fleet, their riders too skilled, making it almost seem as if they were dancing away. Despite this, the Galatian commander was not through; while he could not close with his group of archers, he could herd them down the hill towards us and most importantly, within range of our slingers. Suddenly veering slightly uphill, he led his force parallel to the Armenian line of battle, between the main force and the archers, who were now isolated. In order to maintain a safe distance, the Armenian archer commander led his force down the hill, not realizing his mistake until our slingers' arms were already in motion, whirling their leather thongs above their heads.

Now the air was filled with the distinctive buzzing sound of the lead missiles, followed by a wet thud as the piece of lead hit flesh, flattening out. In a matter of a few heartbeats, men and horses were down and screaming, the horses' hooves flailing as they fought the pain of their wound. When a horse was hit and lost its footing, throwing its rider, a number of slingers would aim at the archer before he could be snatched up by one his comrades and thrown behind his rescuer's saddle, cutting the man down. Those archers whose mounts fell closer to the Galatians proved to be too tempting a target for our cavalrymen, who would swoop in, chopping down with their long swords, the blades flashing in the sun before sweeping down. While all this was happening, we continued marching up the hill, closing the distance, using the fighting to our front as a screen. The dust churned up by the hooves of the horses helped obscure our actions as well, although it started to fill my nose and mouth. Coughing, I spat out a brown glob of mud, hearing the men behind me doing the same. The slingers were slowly moving forward, but they were now taking casualties, their lack of armor the sacrifice they made for their mobility. The Armenians engaged with the Medians had broken off and since the Median cataphracts had not done as the Galatians to move in between them and their lines, they were able to flee back to safety. In doing so, they exposed our wing, letting Artavasdes see how far we had closed the distance, perhaps 200 paces away from javelin range. Now that we were exposed without the second prong of archers between us, the enemy wasted no time in launching a swarm of arrows.

"Shields up!"

I bellowed the command, as did every Centurion along the front line. The rustling, bumping sound behind me told me that the men had brought them up over their heads, but I could not afford to look back, keeping my eye on the feathered missiles that were now streaking downward from their highest point of flight. You can dodge an arrow if you can track it with your eye, yet when they are coming as thick as they were at that moment, it is mostly a matter of luck.

"Jupiter Optimus Maximus, protect this legion, soldiers all!"

The first wave of arrows began striking, thudding into the upraised shields with that solid, thumping sound as the metal head struck the wooden surface, though occasionally there was a sharp twang as a missile struck the metal boss. Sometimes there would be a yelp of pain, a lucky shot finding an opening between shields, but I was too occupied to see how many men and how badly they were hit. I had just hopped to the side to avoid an arrow, feeling the whisper of air as it passed over my shoulder when I was struck by what felt like a hammer blow to the left side of my helmet. My vision suddenly exploded in a burst of stars, my knees buckling for a moment before I regained the use of my limbs. Reaching up, I felt the crease in my helmet where I had suffered an obviously glancing blow, yet to my relief there was no blood trickling down the side of my head. I would just have a headache for the next week, with occasional spells of blurry vision, though the gods took pity on me and my sight was clear for the rest of the battle. Even as I paused to examine my close call, another arrow whistled down to strike the ground directly between my two feet, so I decided to take the risk of turning around to find a shield from a man who had fallen and been dragged off by the *medici*. The men of the front rank had shields already pierced with several arrows apiece, and it took a few moments for me to find a discarded one that was largely undamaged. Grabbing it, I trotted back to the front, feeling much better about my chances of surviving the battle.

Closing the gap between our two lines, it became apparent that Artavasdes was counting on the massive volleys of arrows to stop us short and pin us in place to allow his cataphracts to break our formation. However, he could not commit his cataphracts without exposing his flanks to his Median counterparts, who continued to patrol to our right, or allow the Galatians to do the same on the left. Additionally, the Galatians could take the opportunity to try to force their way through the remaining force of archers to overwhelm the royal bodyguard and take the king himself. It was possible that the battle could be won without the Legions committing themselves and Artavasdes, had he been a prudent commander, would have recognized this and withdrawn with his forces largely intact. He had picked decent ground, but the impetuous rush of the two prongs of archers, combined with the bold response of both Galatian and Median commanders as ordered by Antonius, had largely negated that advantage. The Legions, sensing there was a possibility that the despised cavalry arm of the army would win the battle without their help, began shouting for the order to be released to finish the advance at the run. I looked over to Spurius to my right, who shrugged helplessly since no order was immediately forthcoming. We were less than a hundred paces from javelin range now before there was finally the signal releasing us, but it came from an unexpected quarter. It was not the command group *cornu*, which is used to signal the whole army, but from one of the

Legions. I looked over to see Spurius shouting the advance to the 3rd Gallica, realizing that he had taken it on himself to give the order, and while I mentally saluted his initiative, I hoped that his status as Antonius' favorite would be enough to let him escape serious retribution. Knowing that we could not allow a single Legion to charge unsupported, especially on the wing that did not have the advantage of the melee still going on to our left, I ordered Valerius to give the same signal, hearing that Corbulo was doing the same at about the same time, as well as Balbinus of the 12th, the Legion at the end of our line. It was a ragged charge, the 3rd gaining several paces on us before we began our own charge, but I quickened the pace at the front to close the gap. That meant we were winded when we stopped even with the 3rd to prepare our launch of javelins, and I wondered if Spurius, Corbulo or Balbinus would pause a few heartbeats between volleys to give the men a chance to catch their breath. With our position in the center of the right wing, I could not afford to give the order to charge unsupported on either side, since I would be vulnerable on both flanks if I moved forward without their help, but neither did I want to lag behind and have them do essentially the same thing. Deciding that I would just follow Spurius' lead, I hoped that Corbulo and Balbinus would do the same.

"Prepare javelins!"

Thousands of arms swept back in a rippling line. I watched Spurius for my cue, then when his arm swept down, I did the same, shouting the order.

"Release!"

The air turned black as the javelins went arcing through the air, slicing down to slash into the ranks of the Armenian horsemen, despite the rain of arrows continuing to head our direction. We knew that there would be a moment when we were vulnerable to the hail of Armenian missiles, there being no way to keep a shield up and throw a javelin at the same time. Inevitably some of the men were struck down, but we inflicted more damage than we sustained, though it was mostly on the archers who, like our slingers, sacrificed armor for greater mobility. Actually, it was the horses who suffered, the archers' mounts not carrying the same heavy armor as their cataphract counterparts, the animals shrieking in pain as the heavier javelin did much more damage than an arrow.

"Prepare javelins!"

The men made ready the second volley, which I tried to time so that the archers fired their last arrow before giving the command that would make the men vulnerable again, but the bowmen of the East can draw and loose arrows faster than any we ever encountered, so there was not much respite.

"Release!"

The second volley was barely out of the men's hands when Spurius, Corbulo, Balbinus, and I almost simultaneously gave the order for which the men had been clamoring.

"*Porro*!"

With a roar, we went charging up the remaining slope, counting on the confusion that always occurred in the moments after a javelin volley. This time was no different as the Armenian horsemen were still milling about trying to pick their way clear of fallen men and horses, or wrenching the spent javelin shafts out of the way where they had lodged in the horse or rider's armor. The only chance the Armenians had at this point was to launch a concentrated countercharge with their cataphracts, but the range closed too quickly so that we were almost in their midst before a signal of any sort was given. Seeing that he had lost whatever opportunity he held, Artavasdes ordered a withdrawal that was clearly meant for only the cataphracts, who wheeled about to begin trotting ponderously away from us. The archers, most of them anyway, remained in place, drawing their own swords as they fought desperately, buying the cataphracts time with their own lives. It was at this moment that the Median cataphracts entered the battle.

We had just gone running into the wall of horseflesh and man, holding shields above our heads as we crouched down, doing what had proved so effective under Ventidius by attacking the horses. Their screams of pain and terror were pitiful but we were remorseless, intent on bringing their riders down to a level where they could be dispatched with relative ease, few of the archers showing much skill with the sword. Meanwhile, the Median cataphracts launched a devastating charge, pounding across the space between themselves and the retreating Armenian cataphracts, so even from where we were fighting the crashing impact could clearly be felt through the ground. There was the sound of another fight added to the din, while the dust was stifling our vision and breathing. Nevertheless, we showed the Armenians no mercy, the men working in teams as they grabbed the enemy from their saddles, dragging them screaming to the ground, where there would be the quick flash of a blade followed by a crunching sound when the point punched into a chest or face. In the space of a few moments, we destroyed the force of archers that had chosen to obey their king and stand, though a good number of them, seeing the futility, turned to flee. Taking advantage of the confusion brought on by the melee between the cataphract forces, the remaining archers made their way either to the center wing, or back to where Artavasdes and his force of bodyguards, numbering about a thousand cataphracts was still stationed. With the archers out of the way, we turned our attention to where the remaining Armenian cataphracts were still engaged with the Medians.

Seeing an opportunity, I ordered the men of the second line forward and into javelin range, while I had the men of the first line wheel to face the Armenian center in the event that they tried to fall on our flank. Spurius and Corbulo, seeing what I had done, quickly ordered the same for their Legions, so I waited for them to get into position. The Armenians still had not seen us approaching, while the din of their fighting was too great to hear the shouted warnings of their comrades from the center that there was a new danger. With the men of the second line in position, we gave the order, the arms swept back, the javelins pointing skyward.

"Release!"

Javelins, particularly when they are a surprise, are a devastating weapon, and even as heavily armored as the cataphracts are, the shock of the sudden attack from an unexpected quarter completely shattered the morale and will of the Armenians. They had been hard pressed, but they were still maintaining their cohesion and discipline. Until, that is, they were struck from behind by our heavy missiles. Although most of the javelins did not penetrate deeply, the blow in the back of the men or hindquarters of the horses had to have at least completely surprised them or in many cases, knocked the wind from the men's lungs. No matter how disciplined a man may be, when the surprise is so complete it is almost impossible to maintain enough discipline to keep facing the most immediate threat, meaning men instinctively turned to face the new one to their rear. This gave the Medians the opportunity to finish their opponents, and in a matter of a few more moments, without any more help from the Legions, the left wing of the Armenian army was destroyed.

With the removal of the Armenian left wing, Artavasdes was in even more trouble, now having an essentially intact four Legions of Roman infantry, along with the Median mounted force on his left flank, ready to roll up his center like a carpet. If he turned his center to face the new threat, that exposed the flank of that group to our center line, not even having begun its charge and still somewhat hampered by the ongoing fighting between the other prong of Armenian archers, which had taken heavy losses but still had not withdrawn. Meanwhile, the Galatians were now protected by our left wing, which was also within javelin range, thereby keeping the right wing of the Armenians from swinging down onto the rear of the Galatians. It was a combination of luck on our part and what I can only describe as timidity, or worse, incompetence on the part of the Armenian king. Artavasdes really had only one option left and that was to attempt to withdraw the rest of his army, but still there was no movement backward.

The sun had climbed in the sky so that it was getting warm and we took the opportunity from the pause in our part of the action to allow the men to drink from their canteen, while I took a quick tally from the Centurions. We had suffered only a handful of men killed, with roughly 30 men suffering wounds, most of them from arrows, and that was in the Cohorts of the first line. The men were catching their breath, in moments eager to get back to the fighting, but we received no orders and I wondered at the reason for the delay this time. Antonius had moved to the center to confer with Canidius, so I assumed they were discussing the best way to launch an attack through the fighting that was still going on, despite it slackening in fury considerably as the Armenians were being whittled down in numbers. After a bit, Antonius came galloping back to his command group, snapped some orders to a Tribune, who then came galloping over to where we were standing. Spurius and I had come together, while Corbulo and Balbinus came trotting over when they saw the Tribune approach. The Tribune pulled up, relaying Antonius' orders.

"The general is sending in the center, and as soon as they're engaged, the 4th and 12th are to attack the flank." Turning to Spurius and me, he finished, "The 3rd and 10th are to head for the Armenian king and his bodyguard, but wait for the Medians to begin their charge. Do you have any javelins left?" We both answered that the men of our second line had one apiece. At the answer, his face was grim. "Hopefully that will be enough. The general wants you to launch your javelins when the Medians are in position to begin their final charge. Judging from the impact the last time you did it, it should be enough to at least distract the Armenians before the Medians hit them."

Saluting and signaling our understanding and acceptance of the orders, we then turned to our respective Legions to give the order to make ready to move. We would wait until Corbulo and Balbinus fell onto the flank of the Armenian center to prevent any attempt they might make to intercept us. The left wing began their attack, their javelins looking like tiny slivers as they fell onto the enemy right wing. The center had not launched their attack yet, so neither Corbulo nor Balbinus moved their Legions into a position that would give away the impending charge, meaning that we could not move either, so for several moments we were nothing but spectators. The Galatians were finally down to the remnants of the Armenian archers and I was struck by how bitter it must be for those men to be fighting for their lives while their comrades watched without lifting a finger to help, no matter how understandable the tactic was given the circumstances. The Galatians had suffered a fair number of losses and once they either killed or drove the survivors from the field, they trotted out of the way of the center, who immediately began their assault. After the second volley, they threw themselves into their charge, their roar carrying across the field. As soon as they struck, Corbulo turned to shout the order for the 4th to begin their own charge, with Balbinus quickly following suit. Immediately after that happened, we began moving towards the Armenian king, the Medians beginning their own advance at the trot. Never in all the battles in which I fought had things seemed to work this smoothly, and while part of me believed that this was a sign that the gods had returned their favor to Antonius, and by extension his army, there was another part of me nervous that whatever bad thing that always seemed to happen to foul things up was about to happen. Whatever occurred, I thought, it will not be because we did not do our jobs. With a wave of my sword, I pointed towards Artavasdes.

"Let's go get him, boys," I called out, then began trotting.

Artavasdes might not have been a good general, but he definitely possessed a healthy sense of self-preservation, because the minute we began our movement towards his position, he wasted no time in turning tail to gallop off, with roughly half his bodyguards surrounding him. The other half, along with the archers who fled earlier, and the remnants of the cataphracts shattered by the Median charge and our javelin volley, were left behind to hold us back long enough for him to escape. Swallowing my disappointment, I turned to shout that the men of the royal bodyguard were all rich men themselves, which I fervently hoped was true. Without waiting for the coordination between us and the Medians, we went hurtling into the ranks of the Armenians. The men, equally frustrated at the sight of Artavasdes escaping, took their anger out on the hapless enemy, who fought with a desperation brought on by the knowledge that they were being sacrificed for their king. I have often heard highborn men expound on the glory and honor that comes from sacrificing oneself for their king, but I can tell you that idea is abhorrent to a Roman Legionary. We much preferred killing, and if absolutely necessary, dying for our city and Republic than for a single man who inherited his position and title, essentially doing nothing to earn it. If we were forced to sacrifice ourselves for a man, at least it would be for a man like Caesar who had done so much for us, both as a class and as soldiers.

But the men of the East think much differently than we do, so those doomed men left behind fought ferociously to buy Artavasdes time. Again, the Legionaries worked in teams, as many as four of them surrounding one cataphract, while it only took at most two to dispatch an archer. The men of Artavasdes' bodyguard who had either been ordered to stay behind or chosen to do so, not surprisingly proved to be the best fighters of the bunch, while the quality of their armor, some of it chased with gold and silver as Gaius Crastinus had so long ago dreamed about, drew the attention of most of the Legionaries. It was getting to the point where it looked as if they would allow a fair number of the other less wealthy Armenians to escape, forcing me to snap out orders to the Centurions to pay equal mind to the impoverished. Small groups of Armenians would be quickly surrounded, whereupon one would be further isolated, hemmed in from all sides by Legionaries, in much the same manner as a pack of wolves surrounds its prey, the doomed and desperate enemy trying to wheel his mount quickly back and forth to stop any attempt to bring him down. Of course, this was futile, just as it is with the animal beset by wolves, and the only chance he had was if his comrades were able to come to his rescue, but they were all similarly occupied. It was brutal work, yet it was also efficient, and the only reason I participated in the fighting would be when a group of combatants would drift in my direction. Then I would use my height and size to end that particular struggle, usually by reaching up to drag the man out of his saddle while he was occupied with one of my Legionaries.

Despite it being difficult to make sense of the overall tide of the battle because of the dust and confusion, I was confident that we were slaughtering the Armenians. I could barely make out through the dust the sight of the Medians giving chase to the fleeing king, but I knew that it was very unlikely that he would be caught. Turning my attention back to the matter at hand, I took my Century on a wide loop around the last knot of Armenians, mostly cataphracts, determined that the men would at least have the satisfaction of killing these last remnants and looting their corpses.

As a first battle for the new men, things could not have gone much better, and they were all doubly flushed with the success of their easy victory along with the relatively low toll taken from among our ranks. Not everyone was happy, however, as we discovered just moments after the last Armenian fell on the field, only a handful escaping to rejoin their king who made good his escape, at least for the time being. While the veterans were teaching the new men the finer points of how to loot a corpse and what they could take and what had to be turned over as spoils for the general, the *bucina* sounded the assembly for the Primi Pili. Balbinus, Corbulo, Spurius, and I made our way to Antonius' standard, under which he and the rest of the generals had already gathered. Corbulo was sporting a slash on his arm, which he bound up with his neckerchief, but it was still bleeding a bit, staining the neckerchief through with his blood. When I asked what happened, he only gave a sour laugh.

"What happened is that I'm too old for this *cac,* that's what happened."

When we reached Antonius' side, I do not believe any of us were prepared for what we were about to face. Fully expecting to be greeted, if not with a smile then a heartfelt "well done," instead the Triumvir sat astride Clemency, his face dark with fury.

"Well, if it isn't the Titans of the field," he snapped. We exchanged surprised looks, which only served to infuriate him further. "Oh don't pretend to be innocent with me! You know perfectly well that you disobeyed orders. I have every right to have each of you brought up before a tribunal." He pointed at me, directing his next words only to me apparently. "And I know that there'd be a vote of 'Condemno' from at least one of my generals in your case, given that he's already experienced your disobedience in the field and wanted me to try you the last time."

I was too astonished to speak. I knew that he was clearly referring to the dispute between Canidius and me at the battle where Gallus fell, but I had a very clear and vivid recollection of a conversation with this very same man where he told me that I had done the right thing.

Fortunately for everyone, he turned his attention to Spurius, who was clearly as shocked as Corbulo and I, judging from the way his mouth was hanging open.

"But I know that you were the main culprit," Antonius said savagely. "I saw you advance your Legion, despite the fact that no such order was given!"

Spurius' face was now as dark as that of Antonius, and I suspected his anger was as much of a match, but his tone was even.

"We were exposed and vulnerable standing there after the Medians pushed the Armenian archers back. We were taking casualties because we weren't moving. I decided that it was better to move and engage than to continue absorbing punishment."

"That's not your decision to make, Primus Pilus," Antonius spat. "I had a perfectly good reason for not ordering you forward at that moment. The center and left couldn't move because of the fighting, but it was moments away from breaking open. The attack should have been coordinated with every wing!"

"Then why didn't you sound the recall?" Spurius asked quietly, and I do not know if it was the words or the tone, but whatever it was, it stopped Antonius cold.

His face gradually returned to a more normal coloring, and his jaw slowly unclenched. Finally, he let out a breath, giving a harsh laugh.

"So this wasn't the perfect battle, on anyone's part."

He wheeled Clemency and without another word galloped off, leaving us standing still in shock. Canidius gave me a look of savage satisfaction, as if Antonius' words validated his opinion of what had taken place between us and it was only through an act of supreme self-discipline that I did not give him a rude gesture when he went trotting after the Triumvir.

"Who stuck a standard up his ass?" Corbulo muttered as we turned about to go back to our Legions, but none of us answered.

Returning to camp, most of the men were in high spirits, though there were always a few who suffered the loss of a friend who did not join in the celebration. The losses throughout the army were laughingly light; in the 10th we suffered a dozen dead and about 50 wounded, only a few of them seriously, most of them being arrow wounds. A few men, mostly new men, were struck down by a cataphract, usually because they had been overeager and too inexperienced to defend themselves successfully, while most of the dead came from that part of the battle. The royal bodyguards' bodies had yielded up quite a bit of loot, men stripping the corpses of their armor to take back and remove the gold and silver leaf, so that along with the contents of their purses, some men made a tidy sum. Not all of the bodyguard were killed or had escaped, and we had about 50 prisoners that Antonius ordered be treated well, announcing that he planned on ransoming them back to Artavasdes, something that did not make the men very happy.

"We already beat them," I heard Vellusius complain to another man. "And now we're going to let them go and have to fight them again?"

The Medians were continuing in their pursuit of Artavasdes. Shortly before dark, a messenger came riding into camp to report that the Armenian king had been joined by another large force, too large for the Medians to fight on their own. Antonius gave orders that we would break camp in the morning to go off in pursuit of Artavasdes, which did not give us much time to honor the dead, care for the wounded, or repair and replace equipment. The camp was a frenzy of motion as men were given a brief period of rest before being sent off to perform whatever tasks their Centurions deemed necessary. We knew that this was the time to pursue Artavasdes, before he could gather any more men and we were thankful that the battle had gone as well as it had, but it was still a strain nonetheless, though it did relieve us of the problem of disposing of the enemy dead, since we would not be staying. Nothing more ever came of Antonius' accusations against Corbulo, Balbinus, Spurius, and me; in fact, he acted as if it never occurred, though I cannot say the same, I for one taking it as another sign of his inconstancy and fickle nature.

With a few thirds of a watch until dawn, we were finally finished, the men allowed to retire for the night to grab a watch's sleep, while the Centurions finished up the administrative tasks that come with men being killed. The urns are collected, and if there is time, the close comrades of the dead man are consulted for the copy of the will that they carry to find out if there are any special bequests concerning their remains. This night the urns were stored in the Legion wagon, then we all tried to get some rest, not knowing exactly what the next day would bring.

Breaking camp quickly, we did not bother to fill in the ditches, Antonius being so eager to resume the pursuit of Artavasdes. Sending the Galatians out as an advance guard the army rumbled out, following the churned earth left behind by Artavasdes' flight and this time we did not have any objection or worry when he ordered the baggage train left behind, since he left three Legions to guard it. This allowed us to travel much faster, despite still being at a disadvantage when chasing a mounted army. Just past midday, we could clearly see where another force, probably twice as large from the size of the trail, joined up with Artavasdes, though it was still much smaller than ours. It was getting close to the end of the day, a time we would normally be heading to the spot selected for that night's camp, when news was brought to Antonius from the Galatians. The Armenians had stopped just on the other side of a river some four miles away, making a fortified camp. Consequently, we continued to march to a spot where the enemy was just visible, the river making a silvery line across the ground. Again, Artavasdes had chosen ground that favored him, the banks rising steeply up from the river, which did not appear to be much of an obstacle, the water running swiftly but with the rocky bottom clearly visible. We began making camp immediately, digging the ditch, throwing up the rampart and pitching the tents before the baggage train and the Legions guarding it arrived. Once the rest of the army arrived, all Primi Pili were summoned to the *Praetorium* to discuss the plans for the coming day. We were all ready to cross the river, even knowing that with archers raining their missiles down on our heads, it would be a grim business, but Antonius had something else in mind.

"I've sent a message to Artavasdes, asking him to come treat with me here in camp."

Antonius clearly expected a reaction for he stopped speaking and sat on the edge of his desk, arms folded as the room buzzed with comment. Once we had absorbed the words then settled back down, he continued.

"I have no desire to waste men in an assault across that river. You all know as well as I do that it would be a bloody mess trying to cross under fire."

"Why don't we wait him out?" someone asked. "We're in a better supply situation than he is. He can't stay there for more than a day or two, then he has to try and make a break for Artaxata. We could pounce on him once he does that."

I do not recall who it was that said this, but it was sound advice as far as I, and judging from the reaction of the other Primi Pili as well, was concerned, but Antonius shook his head.

"No, there are other factors at play that I can't discuss that mean I need to conclude this as quickly as possible. So, we're waiting to hear from Artavasdes."

We were dismissed, as Balbinus, Corbulo and I speculated about what it could be that was now making Antonius so anxious to end this without battle.

"I heard that a courier arrived earlier today, riding hard. I wonder if that has anything to do with it."

This came from Balbinus, although I had heard as much already, through Diocles, of course.

"Who knows with that man?" Corbulo grumbled. "He changes from one day to the next."

I knew that Corbulo was still thinking about the incident the day before, and I confess it still rankled me as well. Returning to our respective Legions, I relayed the orders for the men to prepare for battle, going on to explain that this was not the Triumvir's first choice. I just did not see why Artavasdes would accept an invitation to come into the camp of the man trying to destroy him, surrounded by men who hated him for his actions in the previous campaign, so I wanted the men to be ready for what I considered to be inevitable. It just goes to show why I am not an augur or in the divination business, because I was wrong.

The *bucina* of the guard Cohort at the Porta Praetoria sounded the call that a party approached as Scribonius and I were eating our dinner in my tent.

I shook my head at Scribonius' raised eyebrow, saying flatly, "It's just the messenger from Artavasdes saying that he's declining Antonius' generous invitation to come put his head on the chopping block."

I could always count on Scribonius to argue a point when he did not see things the same way, which is a rare luxury for a Primus Pilus, who is usually surrounded by men who are thinking of their own advancement and want to be in the good graces of their Primus Pilus. However, I was more fortunate than most in that I had several Centurions who liked to argue. Now, he sat back with his frown as he shook his head.

"I wouldn't be so sure, Titus. These are nobility we're talking about. Artavasdes is a king, and I wouldn't be surprised if he's so sure that Antonius will respect that fact that he comes riding in with all the ceremony he thinks he deserves."

"Then he doesn't know Antonius," I retorted, but Scribonius was not moved.

"Oh, I think he does well enough. He also knows that if Antonius does something to him, every client king in the East is going to hear about it, and will always be wary of answering a summons from Antonius. How many client kings are there out here?"

"Too many to count," I grumbled, but I was beginning to see his point. Still, I was not so willing to concede. "Fifty sesterces says that he doesn't show up."

"Taken," he said instantly.

It was a matter of less than a third of a watch passing that I learned I had lost the bet, when one of Diocles' friends from the *Praetorium* came running to find him.

A moment later, Diocles came rushing in where Scribonius and I were still relaxing, his face flushed.

"Artavasdes has been taken prisoner by Antonius."

I sat bolt upright, too shocked to be angry at losing the bet. I looked over at Scribonius, and I took some satisfaction in seeing his mouth hanging open, clearly as surprised as I was. I had been sure that Artavasdes would not show himself, he was sure that he would, but I had insisted that if he did, he would regret it, which Scribonius did not believe would happen. So we were both wrong and right at the same time, though I immediately regretted not wagering that Antonius would do exactly what he had done when Artavasdes did show up. I stood up, directing Diocles to go to the rack and bring my armor, not willing to go see the Armenian king while I was dressed in anything but my proper uniform. I turned to Scribonius, asking if he wanted to come, but he waved off the invitation with a grin.

"No, I think I'll stay here and think about how I'm going to spend your money."

"I should have bet you that Antonius would do something like this," I grumbled, to which he only laughed and nodded.

"You should have, but you didn't."

He dodged the cup I threw at him before I pushed aside the flap to head to the *Praetorium*. The camp was abuzz with men running from one fire to the next, the news leaping through the camp faster than I could walk. The reaction from what I could see was mixed; some of the men were happy at the news, while others cursed bitterly, disappointed that the chance of more fighting and more plunder seemed to have gone.

"Don't get discouraged, boys," I called out to a clearly disconsolate group sitting around their fire. "There's still the Parthians to take care of."

That thought cheered them considerably and they immediately began arguing over how much wealth was awaiting them with the conquest of the Parthians. Reaching the *Praetorium,* I noticed the ground outside the tent was soaked with dark stains immediately outside the entrance, the men of the Brundisium Cohorts still dragging the bodies of what I assumed were Artavasdes' bodyguard off somewhere. There were a number of other Centurions of various rank milling about, but nobody was being allowed into the *Praetorium* by Rhamnus' men, who blocked the entrance.

"You finally bloodied your swords. Too bad it was on unarmed men," I heard someone call out to the guards at the entrance, the faces of all four men darkening at the insult, but they said nothing, which was wise of them.

Pushing my way through the throng, I did not really expect to be let through, but was surprised when the guards stepped aside.

"We have orders for all the Primi Pili to be allowed in, but nobody else," explained the Brundisium Centurion standing just inside the entrance.

I saw a knot of men gathered, recognizing Spurius and a few others and walked over. They were talking in low voices, and even before I got within earshot, it was clear they were not happy.

"It's got to be because of Cleopatra," someone was muttering.

I looked over to Spurius, who was as unhappy as the others. Thinking that he was likely to know more because he had a good relationship with Antonius, I asked him what he knew.

Apparently, I was not the first, since he snapped irritably, "Why does everyone keep asking me that? I know as much as any of you, and that's that Artavasdes answered Antonius' request for a parley, and when he showed up Antonius was waiting with some of his

Brundisium boys. They slaughtered the bodyguard before they even knew what hit them, and they dragged Artavasdes off into Antonius' office."

"I didn't know that much," I replied, which seemed to soothe his temper. "All I heard was that Artavasdes had been taken."

"It's shameful," opined Servius Palma, the Primus Pilus of the 5th Alaudae, one of the Legions who had come over from Macedonia. "There was no honor in what Antonius did."

He shook his head in disgust, sparking an intense debate among the gathered men. From what I saw, it seemed to be evenly divided. Not surprisingly, Spurius was defensive about Antonius' actions.

"He removed not just an enemy king, but the commanding general of an army we would have to fight. I don't see how that's a bad thing."

"What kind of message does it send to the other client kings?" I asked, seeing looks of surprise at this thought, and I was a little ashamed that I was essentially stealing Scribonius' idea, but not enough to credit him. "Do you think any of them are going to be eager to answer a summons from Antonius, knowing that he would go as far as he has?"

"I hadn't thought of it that way," Spurius admitted, then clearly did think of something. "But Artavasdes was an enemy because of his actions against us during the last campaign. Any client king who remains faithful to Antonius has nothing to worry about."

"While I agree that Artavasdes deserves to be treated as an enemy, do you think the other kings see it that way? From their point of view, Artavasdes simply recognized the inevitable when the baggage train was destroyed and took care of his men by taking them home."

Spurius clearly did not like this argument, but I saw other heads nodding up and down.

Normally, I would not have cared whether or not Spurius, or any other of the men gathered there took offense, yet never far from my mind in those days was the political climate in which we were living, the vision of Uncle Tiberius' wrinkled bald head popping into my head, compelling me to say, "I'm not saying that I disagree with what you're saying, or what Antonius did. I'm saying that I think it may cause Antonius difficulties in the future, and any problem for him becomes a problem for us."

Even Spurius seemed to accept this, but Palma was not through with voicing his opinion.

"I still think it's shameful, and I can assure you that Octavian is going to view it in the same light."

There was something smug in his tone, some hint that he was speaking with more than just speculation that caused me to look more carefully at the man, and I saw that I was not the only one. Was this yet another of Octavian's agents, I wondered? I felt a by now familiar churning in my stomach at the thought that here was yet another piece in the game that I, or anyone else for that matter, had to watch carefully. Perhaps it was this thought that colored my thinking, but I suddenly looked at Palma through different eyes, seeing something oily in his demeanor, something devious in the way his eyes shifted from one man to the next, imagining that he was carefully watching the reactions of the others so he would have something to put in his report to Octavian.

Whatever the cause, the conversation came to a standstill, it suddenly seeming that men had run out of things to say, therefore we turned our attention back to Antonius' office, which still had the flap down so we could not see what was taking place inside. Excusing myself from the group, I wandered over nearer to the *praetorium* entrance, as I had seen Corbulo and Balbinus arrive and was more comfortable in their company. I had not forgotten that I was positive that Balbinus ostensibly worked for Octavian, but I sensed that his support was half-hearted, so I suppose I distrusted him less than Palma. As I neared, I heard Ahenobarbus' harsh voice coming from within Antonius' office. I slowed my progress so that I could more clearly hear what was being said by the most outspoken of Antonius' generals.

"Antonius, this is a huge mistake that you're making."

The Triumvir's voice was surprisingly mild at such an unequivocal rebuke. "I heard you the first several times you said it, Ahenobarbus. If you're going to keep repeating yourself, this is going to be even more tedious. I understand. You don't approve my capture of our royal prisoner here."

I do not know if Antonius was going to say something else because Ahenobarbus interrupted. "I don't give a rotten fig about the way you captured this bastard." It was clear that Artavasdes was sitting nearby, but was saying nothing. "It's your plan to withdraw the army from the campaign that I object to. The men aren't going to like this at all, and I can't say that I blame them. This campaign has been blessed so far, and it's clear that the men view how things have gone as a sign that we've been favored by the gods. To throw that away is almost criminal!"

"Be careful, Ahenobarbus," Antonius' voice was still soft, but there was now a distinctly dangerous edge to his tone. "I don't take being called a criminal lightly."

If Ahenobarbus was intimidated, his words and tone did not show it as he retorted, "Then what would you call it? There's no military reason for us to turn back now."

"There's more to this than martial reasons why I've made this decision, Ahenobarbus. Truly, I've accomplished what I set out to do. Artavasdes of Media and I have already concluded a treaty of friendship and I've promised Alexander will marry his daughter as soon as they're of age. Don't you understand? With the capture of this bastard here, and the treaty, I've brought both Media and Armenia under my control." There was a pause that lasted so long I was about to move away, then Antonius continued, and what he said froze my blood. "And you know the contents of this message from Rome and what it means. It's not bad enough that Octavian used his sister to try and shame me, now the cocksucker has the gall to announce to me, ME, Marcus Antonius, that since he had every confidence I would achieve my goal of subduing Media, Armenia, and Parthia that he saw no need to set aside land for my veterans in Italia! He said that I would have more than enough land with the conquest of the East that I could supply my veterans with land here!"

"All the more reason you need to continue the campaign into Parthia," Ahenobarbus retorted. "The men who are retiring next year need this campaign, Antonius. And now that they're not getting land in Italia, they need it even more."

"Who says they're not going to get that land?" Antonius shot back, the fury making his voice throb. "Do you think I'm just going to sit by and let that happen? But I can't do anything about it here in the wastes of Armenia. That's why I have to get back to civilization."

"So you're going to Rome, then?"

There was a catch in Ahenobarbus' voice that gave me the feeling that he already knew the answer and did not like it.

"No. I'm returning to Alexandria. It's only two or three weeks sailing away from Rome at this time of year. I can do what needs to be done through my Senators and allies without having to be there in person."

"I think this is a mistake that will haunt you the rest of your days, Antonius," were Ahenobarbus' final words, and while I do not know if this was the crucial error on which all that followed hinged, it certainly had an impact.

At that moment, I was faced with a dilemma, cursing my insatiable curiosity and need to know what was going on as I made my way, now going very slowly towards Corbulo and Balbinus, trying to think of what to do. I knew that Antonius did not have any desire for the news that the veterans would not be receiving land in Italia to get out, but when he told Ahenobarbus that he was not going to Rome to fight for the veterans and the land that was rightfully theirs, I did not see how he could possibly hope to thwart Octavian's plans. As far as I was concerned, I was with Ahenobarbus in the belief that Antonius had to be in Rome to have any hope of success. While the matter of land for veterans who were retiring the next year would not impact the 10th directly; the men's discharges were still five years away, the 3rd Gallica, the 4th, and a number of other Legions were the ones most affected. There would doubtless be tremors within my own Legion because of the misfortune of others. There was no way that the men of the 3rd and 4th would sit still for being given land in what we essentially viewed as a barren, uninhabitable wilderness. Doubtless, Antonius would choose the most fertile spots, regardless of who was already settled there, which would cause all sorts of trouble for the settling veterans. To be fair, this would be a problem in Italia as well, which is one reason why Octavian did not want to give up land in the territory of the Republic that he was responsible for, particularly for Legionaries of Antonius, except that in Italia, the retiring veterans would have the full force of the Senate and the law behind them to enforce whatever evictions would take place, albeit with the help of a few Cohorts. Here in the East, the men would have just the law, a law with no teeth in it without the strong arm of a Legion, so they would have to rely on themselves and, in all likelihood, would find themselves fighting all over again. This would be foremost in their minds if and when they learned of the development, as I could easily envision a situation in which a good number of the Legions, and the most veteran at that, simply refused to march another step in any direction until Antonius fixed the problem to their satisfaction. Which, of course, he could not do here in the middle of nowhere; it was this that was foremost in my mind when I walked over to Corbulo and Balbinus, both of whom eyed me curiously.

"What were you doing over there? Trying to listen in on what's going on in there?" Corbulo jerked his head in the direction of Antonius' office, where he was still occupied, arguing with Ahenobarbus, I assumed.

"Yes," I admitted, not seeing any point in denying what was obvious.

"And?" Balbinus demanded, and I looked over at him, thankful that I had to lie to him and not to Corbulo, who I respected more.

"Nothing that you probably don't already know," I lied. "Just that Antonius signed a treaty with the Median king, and they have Artavasdes in there, but he's not saying much."

I did not see the harm in divulging that one piece of what I had overheard, and I was thankful to see that they seemed to be satisfied with my response.

"What are we supposed to do now?" Corbulo wondered, which I only answered with a shrug.

We were still standing there talking when finally Antonius emerged from his office, holding what looked like a chain in his hand, but there was something different about it that I could not immediately place. Tethered to the other end was Artavasdes, whose hands were shackled by what appeared to be the same type of chain wrapped around his wrists, though the lock was a plain old lock. The shackles were attached to a chain around his waist, from which a length dangled down to his feet, which were also chained. He still wore his diadem, and his robes of finely brocaded material, while torn, were otherwise intact. Artavasdes was staring at the ground, the shame clearly written on his face, and despite what he had done, I felt a pang of sympathy for the man, though it was clear that everyone else was enjoying the spectacle.

"I thought you would like to see the great king of Armenia," Antonius boomed, the group inside the *Praetorium* letting out a raucous cheer.

Artavasdes refused to look up to acknowledge what was happening around him, men calling out insults to him as I thought that this was just the beginning for him, or at least the beginning of his end. Antonius raised a hand for quiet, and when the excitement had subsided somewhat, he raised the fist in which he clutched the end of the chain, pointing to it.

"Let it not be said that Marcus Antonius doesn't give this royal prisoner the proper respect. I had these chains made of silver just for this occasion!"

This brought on another round of cheers, but it was not quite as loud, and I heard Corbulo murmur, "I wonder when he had those made."

It also explained why they looked different, the sound being quite distinctive as they dragged on the ground, making a more musical noise than iron chains. I doubted that Artavasdes would find it pleasing to the ear as he dragged them around to wherever Antonius was going to take him. The first place he dragged him was predictably out to the forum, after having the assembly called for all the men to gather. I had no real desire to watch, but there was no way that I could not be present for a formation of the entire army, so I stood watching as the men roared their approval at the sight of the Armenian king humiliated. Antonius let the men carry on for a time, then signaled for quiet. Involuntarily, I looked over to where the 3rd and 4th were standing side by side, wondering if Antonius was going to make any mention of the dilemma Octavian had put him in.

"My soldiers," Antonius called out, waiting for his words to be relayed to the Legions farther back. "I give you truly good news! With the capture of this piece of filth who so foully deserted us during the last campaign, and with the agreement that I have just concluded with the Medians whereby they recognize Rome as their master, we have accomplished all that we have set out to do. We can return to Syria, covered with honor and glory. You faced the Armenians in the field, and the defeat was so overwhelming, so convincing that the wretch you see before you begged me for terms. You see the terms I give to traitors to Rome! Now we can return, we can go home!"

He paused, clearly expecting to hear the roar of cheers washing over him. Instead, the silence was absolute, though it only lasted for a moment before a buzzing began rippling through the ranks, slowly growing in volume. Men started with a whispered, "No," but they quickly raised their voices until it was a steady and constant roar of protest, men shouting their dismay at the news. Antonius' face was a picture of shock, clearly not expecting this reaction. He waved his hands, trying to get the men to quiet down so that he could speak.

"We want to make back the money we lost!"

"How are we expected to retire without more money?"

"We're not going home broke again!"

These were the types of things being shouted at Antonius, the men ignoring his plea for them to quiet down, and there were a fair number of them from the 10th who were shouting. This is what it was about, when all was said and done, money, and I remember thinking that of all the people who should appreciate this, it was Antonius, who had been almost single-minded in his pursuit of it for the entire time he was contending with Octavian. He always had a reputation for greed, even when he was a Legate with Caesar, but what he needed to fulfill his ambition of becoming the First Man had to have been a staggering amount. Now he was being accosted from his army, all of them, or most of them clamoring for the same thing he was always after and it was clear that he did not like it. Finally, the men quieted enough for him to be heard, and I was close enough to see the rigid spine and clenched fists as he spoke, though his voice betrayed none of that tension.

"Who told you that you were going to return without money?" he demanded, and it was true, he had made no such statement.

But Antonius was demonstrating a trait I had seen in so many of the upper classes, assuming that because few of the men were educated that they were stupid.

However, I could see by the faces of the men as I glanced around that they were not fooled, though he seemed oblivious as he plowed on.

"You will all receive healthy bonuses, as befits Legionaries who have conducted a successful campaign. I swear to you all now on Jupiter's Stone that none of you will have cause for complaint for the amounts you will receive."

"How much?"

This came from somewhere in the 19th Legion, and I suspected it was a Centurion, but it was quickly picked up throughout the army, and I could see that Antonius was dangerously close to boiling over.

His voice sounded strained as he replied, "I haven't decided on an amount, but I can assure you that I will consult with your Centurions and we will come up with an amount that pleases all of you."

Without waiting for any response, Antonius wheeled to stalk back to the *Praetorium*, snapping an order for Artavasdes to be dragged away to custody with the provosts. Watching his retreating back, I thought that it was highly unlikely that the Triumvir would ever be able to come up with a sum that would satisfy every man as he promised, but that was more due to the greed of some men than anything else. I also wondered where in Hades he was going to get the money.

It became clear that Antonius had no intention of telling the Primi Pili of the retiring Legions of Octavian's declaration that they would not be receiving Italian lands, so I kept what I knew to myself, though it was not the easiest decision to make. We began the march back to Syria with the men still in a surly mood, although there were no overt acts of disobedience. Antonius' mood corresponded with that of the army, making it as if both officers and men were engaged in a giant sulk all the way back to Syria. Leaving the Medes behind now that they were our friends, Antonius also left orders that they should continue to wage war against the Armenians and their new king Artaxes, the son of Artavasdes. Perhaps a week into our return journey, we were caught by a Median courier riding hard, and with one stroke Antonius' dilemma about where the money would come from to come up with a payment for the army seemed to have been solved. The courier carried news of the fall of Artaxata and the plunder of the city, which apparently was fabulously wealthy. I suppose this made sense because it was the Armenian capital. The Median Artavasdes was honoring the newfound friendship and treaty with us by sending a train carrying half of the plunder from the Armenians, and according to the courier's message, just this portion solved Antonius' money problems. Naturally, this improved Antonius' mood considerably, although he did not tell the men of this development, and the only way I heard about it was through Diocles' network of contacts in the *Praetorium*. I wondered why Antonius did not immediately spread this news, before I began to think that he was planning on keeping the money for himself, so I toyed with the idea of putting a quiet word out as a way to force Antonius to use the money to honor his promise. I finally decided that I valued my skin too much, knowing that Antonius would be relentless in his pursuit of whoever leaked word. Gradually, as the weather continued to cooperate and the miles passed, the men slowly recovered from their funk, the prospect of returning to the world of wine, women, and gambling with someone other than the same old faces cheering them up. My thoughts were of one thing; Miriam, and I was in a state of anticipation that seemed composed of equal parts joy and worry. While we had not been gone as long as we thought we would be, it was still enough time when the woman you love is pregnant with your child that there is more than enough reason to worry. Childbirth is a hard business on women, and I had known too many men whose women or children had died, sometimes both, not to worry. We would be arriving back home before the baby was due, and that more than anything gave me reason to want to end the campaign, so unlike the rest of the men, I was actually happy to be returning.

Rolling through Samosata on our way to Antioch, we stopped for a few days to give the stock a chance to rest, at least that was the reason Antonius gave, but I suspected that it was to give the train of plunder a chance to catch up, since every day a courier from the Medes arrived with a report on its progress. To my eyes, while the stock was slightly worn, they were not sufficiently so to warrant a stay of almost a week, and the men certainly did not need the rest. We were all more than ready to go by the time the order came to resume the march, moving next to Antioch, arriving in the capital of the province in mid-June.

We stayed in Antioch for more than two weeks, and ironically, this was the most difficult period of the campaign for the Centurions, since the men took out their anger and frustration at the premature end to their quest for loot on the hapless citizens of the city. I was forced to execute three Legionaries before the 10th got back in hand, while the other Primi Pili were forced to take similar measures before things were under control. Then the train of plunder arrived, whereupon Antonius immediately called an assembly of the army, where we were greeted by the sight of more than a dozen obviously heavily laden wagons, arrayed in a semicircle behind the

Triumvir. The sight of the wagons elicited an excited buzz among the men, despite Antonius keeping the presence of the train a secret, and I had not divulged what I learned to anyone, not even to Scribonius. I was beginning to feel weighed down by all the secrets I was keeping, longing for the days when all I had to worry about was running a Legion. Antonius was beaming, his smile clearly visible to the men in the last rank, and once we had gathered and come to *intente,* he turned to gesture to the wagons behind him with an expansive sweep of his arms. Then he turned back around to face the men, his voice booming across the forum.

"My soldiers, I know that some of you doubted Marcus Antonius. I know that some of you didn't believe me when I said that you would be compensated for this campaign. But in these wagons is just a portion of the spoils given to us by our allies the Medes, courtesy of their conquest of Artaxata that occurred a month ago. It is from this hoard that I will pay every Legionary from a Legion with more than a year on its enlistment 1,000 sesterces!"

The ground shook with the roaring approval of the men, but Antonius was not finished, although it took a few moments for the men to quiet down. Finally, he finished by announcing, "For those Legions who are retiring next year, I will pay every Legionary the sum of 2,000 sesterces. Naturally, Centurions and Optios will be paid more."

There was good-natured grumbling at this, but nothing that was unexpected, and I was curious as to how much we would be receiving. With this good news, and with the cheers of the men ringing in his ears, Antonius dismissed the men to go back to their areas, all of them chattering about what they were going to do with the money.

We had to wait a week for the spoils to be converted into hard cash, Antonius' money people being hard at work melting down the silver ingots then hammering them into money. Finally, the day came when each man received a pouch heavy with coins, carried to each Legion in iron-hooped chests. One of the generals oversaw the disbursal of the money, this being one of the few times when the vast gulf between general and Legionary was not as vast, with even men like Ahenobarbus making jokes, teasing men about what they would do with their earnings. Antonius stopped at each Legion, giving a short speech thanking the men for all they had done, admittedly not that much on this campaign. Nevertheless, each of us knew that this was just as much about the previous campaign as the current one. The Centurions of the lower five grades each received 10,000 sesterces; the Centurions of the next four grades received 15,000, and the Centurions of the first grade received 20,000, while I and the other Primi Pili received 25,000 sesterces. These are all staggering sums, but even after such a massive outlay of cash, it was not lost on any of us that more than half of the wagons that rumbled into Antioch remained. With the men paid, Antonius gave us another week for the men to debauch themselves, the man taking full advantage of the opportunity, some of them not taking a sober breath the whole week. It was a groaning, sour bunch that the Centurions rounded up the day before we were set to march back to Damascus, with part of the army ordered to stay in Antioch to ease the strain of supporting such a large host. For a short time it sounded as if the 10th might be selected to stay in Antioch, something that I could not accept, so 2,000 sesterces of my bonus went to the clerk charged with deciding what Legion went where to ensure that we returned to Damascus.

We left Antioch at the end of June, the sun already broiling the men just a few thirds of a watch after dawn, making us all thankful that we were able to march without wearing armor. The first day the men were in bad shape from the excesses of the previous week, meaning we had more than the normal number of stragglers, something that did not make me happy at all, therefore the next day I made sure the men knew that there were floggings in their future if there was a repeat performance. Fortunately for everyone, they took me at my word, and we more than doubled the mileage from the previous day. I was in a tearing hurry to get to Damascus, and although I refused to reveal why to Scribonius, Balbus, or Gaius, I doubt that I fooled any of them. Antonius was now heading to Alexandria, but he was going overland, not willing to part with the plunder train, and I cannot say that I blamed him. He still had not told the Primi Pili of the retiring Legions of the problem with the Italian lands, and since both Corbulo and Spurius were marching with us, I decided that the best approach would be to avoid the two of them completely for the march to Damascus. It made things awkward, since I repeatedly declined their offer to eat dinner, and they clearly sensed I was hiding something from them, but I did not know what else to do.

Once we arrived in Damascus, I am only slightly ashamed to say that I spent as little time in camp as I could get away with before rushing off to the villa. I had sent Diocles ahead immediately upon marching in to give Miriam proper warning that I was coming, and he was waiting to greet me at the door, the expression on his face causing my stomach to twist in knots.

"What is it?" I demanded. "What's wrong? Is Miriam all right?"

"Yes, master. She is now."

I did not immediately take his meaning, and I could feel my mouth pull down. "Now? What does that mean? By the gods, Diocles, what are you talking about?"

He looked thoroughly miserable as he said, "Master, Miriam lost the baby. I am so sorry."

I felt as if my entire body had been dashed with a bucket of cold water, and I could feel my knees begin to shake, but I forced myself to remain calm. "How is Miriam?"

"She's recovering, master. It happened only a week ago, so she's still in bed. But the physician said she would make an almost complete recovery, that the worst is past."

"Almost? What does that mean?"

Diocles started looking uncomfortable, as if he would rather have been surrounded by a horde of Parthians than standing before me. "I think you need to talk to Miriam, master," he said quietly. "I think she should be the one to tell you exactly what's going on."

I rushed into our bedroom to find Miriam lying on the bed, propped up, looking extremely pale. Her face was puffy with tears shed and unshed, a fresh spate of them starting at the sight of me. Going to her, I sat down gingerly on the edge of the bed, not wanting my weight to jar her, before taking her into my arms as she began sobbing, speaking words in a combination of Syriac and Latin that I could barely understand.

"Hush," I said in the most soothing manner I could, holding her tightly, gently rocking her back and forth.

"Titus, I am so sorry. I lost the baby and I don't know why. I did everything the physician and midwife told me to, but it still happened."

Her body was shaking uncontrollably, while I tried to let her know that it was all right, that I was just happy that she was alive and that she would recover. She did not seem to hear me, continuing to say the same thing over and over, until I finally took her gently but firmly by the shoulders, and held her at arm's length to look directly into her eyes.

"Miriam, it's all right. I don't care that you lost the baby. I care that you're all right. Besides," I gave her what I hoped was my most winning grin, "that just means we can try again."

This had the exact opposite effect that I intended, making her cry even harder, and I felt the first flash of irritation as I struggled, trying to think of something else to say that would stop the crying. She was shaking her head, saying things so rapidly that I could not understand a word, as I looked around helplessly for some hint as to what was going on. Finally, she began to calm down, her crying slowing down until it was a series of hiccupping sobs. Once I judged her to be sufficiently calmed down, I gave her a kiss on the forehead, telling her that I would be back shortly, then went off in search of someone who might know exactly what was going on. Wandering through the house I finally found an old crone sitting at the table in the servants' quarters, talking to one of the kitchen slaves. Seeing me walk in, the slave jumped up and went scurrying off, leaving the old woman behind, who looked as if she hoped a hole would open up in the ground to swallow her up. But she did not run off, looking up at me with a mixture of apprehension and defiance.

"Are you the midwife?" I winced inwardly at the sound of my voice, knowing that my tone was excessively harsh.

"Yes, master." Her voice quivered with fear as she stared up at me.

"What happened?" I made a conscious effort to soften my voice, and she responded, visibly relaxing.

"Your woman went into labor early, master. The babe was not developed enough to survive and was stillborn."

"What caused it?"

She shrugged. "Only the gods know why these things happen, master. I have noticed that women with the frame that yours has seem to run a higher risk of losing the baby as your woman did, but I do not know why that is so. Perhaps it is because of her narrow hips that there is not enough room for a babe, especially one the size of yours."

That froze my blood, I can tell you. "What do you mean?"

The midwife looked down at the table, the uncomfortable look back on her face. "You are a large man, master. And your babe, even as early as it was, was very large."

This did not make sense to me. "If the babe was so large, then why did it die?"

"Its lungs were not developed, master. The babe could not breathe."

I immediately regretted asking the question, the thought of my child suffocating like a dagger in my heart.

Shaking my head to try and clear the image, I asked, "How is Miriam? Was there any permanent damage?"

The midwife hesitated for a moment, then shook her head. "I do not believe so, in fact I am sure she will make a complete recovery. It's just that...." She paused then looked me directly in the eye. "You will undoubtedly produce a babe of similar size. Your woman is unharmed in the body this time, but I cannot make any promise that the next time won't be different. Do you understand?"

I did indeed, it feeling as if my heart were being squeezed by this old woman's hand.

"Yes, I understand," I said coldly, then reached into my purse for a gold denarius, handing it to the woman while thanking her for all that she had done.

I returned to sit with Miriam as I thought about what I had learned.

She looked up at me, her eyes haunted as she searched my face. "What did the midwife say?"

"That you're going to be fine," I told her, but she was not fooled.

"What did she say about having a baby?"

I hesitated, which caused her tears to start anew. I reached out to hold her, but she pulled away, turning her face from me as she wept bitterly.

"I don't care about having a baby, Miriam." I thought to soothe her, but it did not work and indeed, again seemed to have the opposite effect.

"Well, I do," she said fiercely, showing a flash of temper and anger that I had never seen before, telling me how badly this hurt her.

"Then let's talk to another midwife," I replied, though I doubted that the news would be any different, but the thought soothed her.

"That's a good idea," she said, biting her lip. "I did not care for her anyway."

With that decided, I held her until she fell asleep, my mind and heart full thinking about how I could avoid putting Miriam in danger again. As far as I was concerned, this was all my fault; after all, I had killed my mother because of my size when I was born, and I could not bear the thought of the same thing happening to Miriam. These were the thoughts that continued to run through my head as she drifted off to sleep.

Unfortunately I could not afford to spend as much time with Miriam while she recovered as I wished, having to attend to matters with the Legion settling into garrison duty. Not surprisingly, many of the men chose to carry on with their debauching that they started in Antioch. Consequently, the punishment square got a fair amount of business as a number of men had to be flogged for a variety of transgressions, while two men were executed for the rape and murder of a young girl. It was matters like this that kept me occupied, though the problems were no more or less than in the past.

Antonius, plodding along with the train of plunder given to him by the Median Artavasdes, finally arrived in Alexandria in July, which I thought was strangely appropriate. It was about a month after Antonius arrived in Alexandria that word arrived of an event that I believe was the signal of the beginning of the end for the Triumvir of the East. I suppose he decided that if he were going to turn his back on Rome he was not going to leave any doubt that he was doing so. First, he called all the citizens of Alexandria to witness the crowning of Cleopatra as queen of Egypt, Cyprus, Libya, and Coele Syria, with Caesarion, Caesar's son who was now about 14, as co-regent. His own children, the twin boy and girl, along with the infant son that Cleopatra had borne him while we were on campaign, he had seated on gilt thrones at his and Cleopatra's feet, while he and his queen sat on thrones made of solid gold. Although Balbus and Macrianus snorted at this, both Diocles and I had seen the wealth and opulence of Egypt, so neither of us doubted for a moment that they were made entirely of gold. Antonius' older son Alexander Helios was given Armenia, Media and Parthia, the latter of which we still had to conquer, with the infant they had named Ptolemy made king of Phoenicia, Syria and Cilicia. Both boys were dressed in the manner of the kingdoms over which they were supposedly to rule, with Alexander, who was more commonly called Helios, dressed in the Parthian cap and Median robes, the infant wearing the flat hat of the Macedonians, along with the high boots, no doubt both small versions since he was still a babe in arms. Both boys had the ribbon diadem draped around their respective headgear, and I do not know if it was the diadem or the titles that Antonius insisted be bestowed on the children that caused the most trouble, all of us vividly remembering what befell Caesar because of a diadem wrapped around his statue. For along with the diadem came the title of King of Kings for young Caesarion and his half-brothers, and while having significance to the Eastern ear that we Romans could not comprehend, was doubly offensive to the ears of Antonius' countrymen, because no Roman could claim the title of king without arousing much hatred. And as foreign-born as Caesar's and Antonius' children may have been, and raised in the Egyptian style, they were Roman by virtue of their patrimony, and no Roman can be king. Antonius obviously knew this, for he claimed no title of king for himself during this ceremony, yet it did not matter. Adding to the damage was the idea that Antonius was dispensing Roman territories without consulting the Senate, or his colleague Octavian, and I believe that between his actions with Octavia and this public spectacle, Antonius was announcing to the world that he had completely broken with Rome. Finally, to add even more insult to Romans, he held a quasi-Triumph celebrating his conquest of Armenia, which by all rights should have been conducted in the sacred precincts of Rome and not Alexandria. At the end of the Triumphal parade through the streets of Alexandria, the Armenian Artavasdes was executed, though not in the Roman tradition by strangulation in the privacy of the Tullianum, but in the Eastern way of public beheading, a grievous insult to a man who was a king. However traitorous or despicable the actions of Artavasdes were, he did not deserve such a public humiliation. I believe that ultimately Cleopatra was behind this insult, because Artavasdes had refused, even in captivity, to show any deference to the queen of Egypt and as much as I liked Cleopatra in many ways in those days, she was extremely ruthless when she thought she had been belittled.

Compounding Antonius' problems was the reception that Octavia received when she returned to Rome, the people lining the streets to welcome her, shouting their adoration for her all the way from Ostia to the villa she and Antonius had occupied in Rome. Octavian milked the outrage of the lower classes for every drop of political advantage he could squeeze, and he was hugely successful. Octavian addressed the Senate, taking the role of outraged, loving younger brother as well as *paterfamilias*, asking the Senate to pass a decree of *sacrosanctas* for Octavia, giving her the same status as a Vestal Virgin, although to say it was a request by Octavian is charitable. In Antonius' absence, and even with the Senate still loaded with his creatures, Octavian had become the most powerful man in Rome, backed by Agrippa and Maecenas. However, Antonius' actions, both with Octavia but more importantly with his measures dividing what was essentially Roman territory, had forced even his most stalwart supporters to recognize that the Marcus Antonius they knew no longer existed. It was now clear to everyone on both sides of Our Sea that there would be a final reckoning between the two remaining Triumvirs. The only question was when it would happen. Meanwhile, I found my thoughts turning increasingly to the question of what I would do when the moment came when I would receive the message from Octavian calling in his debt.

Miriam recovered quickly, physically at least, though she would still burst into tears at odd moments for weeks afterward. Things between us returned to normal, however, which I believe made both of us happy, and I have to credit Pompeia and Uncle Tiberius for helping us through what could have been a very rough time. They resumed their visits and even with my suspicion of Uncle Tiberius, I appreciated the effect the old couple had on Miriam, before long our dinners becoming the same spirited affairs that they were before we left for Armenia. Scribonius, Balbus, and Macrianus were frequent guests, while Gaius was an occasional one, having developed a romance with a girl in Damascus and spending most of his time with her. I tried to keep the topic of conversation away from politics, but soon found that it was a practical impossibility to keep Romans from discussing the events that would have a huge impact on their future. However, none of us forgot Uncle Tiberius' connection and role with both Triumvirs, so we were all very careful not to give him anything that he could put in a report to either Octavian or Antonius, though if he was disappointed, he did a good job of concealing it. In private, usually back at camp where I could be sure that there was nobody trying to overhear our conversations, Scribonius, Balbus, and I spent many thirds of a watch discussing what seemed to be almost daily developments, trying to formulate a strategy for the day that we all knew would inevitably come.

"You know we'll follow you no matter what you decide," Scribonius said one evening. "At least most of us will, but I think you need to try and feel all the Centurions out so there are no surprises when the moment comes."

Despite seeing the sense in that, I was not sure what I would do if I discovered there were Centurions who might try to betray the rest of us.

"I know," Balbus said, and even before I turned to face him, I knew what he was going to say. "You tell them that you'll make their ball sac into a coin purse."

Scribonius and I just looked at each other, shaking our heads.

"All right, beside that, what do I do?"

Scribonius shrugged. "I don't know, really. But we'll have to think of something."

First the weeks, then months passed uneventfully, at least for us in Damascus. In Rome, as Antonius' pseudo-Triumph in Alexandria was described in ever more lurid detail by a number of correspondents, few if any of whom were on Antonius' side in the matter, the uproar over his actions grew steadily louder. Octavian, in order to continue to honor his oath that he would not go to war on a fellow Roman, lay the blame for all that Antonius did at the feet of Cleopatra, making much use of the Queen of Beasts characterization that he had painted her with years before. However, I do not want to put all the blame, if that is even the right word, for what happened on Octavian's shoulders, because Antonius did not help his cause any. First, he sent a bill of divorce to Octavia, which was bad enough, but along with the bill came a peremptory and curt order for her to vacate his residence in Rome, an act that was loudly decried by all the classes of Rome. Citing this as further proof that Cleopatra had somehow bewitched Antonius, Octavian was relentless in his attack on the queen of Egypt, and indirectly, Antonius.

Meanwhile, Antonius continued to do nothing to help his cause, seeming to immerse himself completely in the role of Eastern potentate and consort of a queen. If half the stories coming from Alexandria were true, then it was increasingly clear that Antonius had either decided to precipitate the long-coming confrontation with Octavian, or had lost his mind. Octavian, on the other hand, was all about calculation and never making a misstep, having been hard at work consolidating his power. One of the most damning accusations against Octavian in those years was his lack of military prowess, the flames of this calumny being fanned by Antonius, much in the same way that Octavian did the same concerning Cleopatra, through the use of agents, although Antonius went even farther in calling Octavian a physical coward. Of all the things said against Octavian, this was given the most credence and was the most damaging to the younger Triumvir's reputation. Octavian quashed this talk by going on campaign in Illyricum, even leading an assault on the town of Promona, a Dalmatian stronghold, where he was wounded. Still, even that was subject to controversy. Some men, undoubtedly working in Antonius' interests, insisted that it was not a wound, but a broken leg, incurred when he jumped down off a siege tower to run away when the action got hot. The official story, and as far as I know the correct one, is that he received a grievous wound from a slinger's missile, shattering his kneecap while leading his men onto the parapet of the town. What I can say is that I saw him limping when the weather turned cold, the stiffness clearly coming from his knee area, which to my eyes does not indicate a broken leg. Whatever the truth, as far as the lower classes were concerned, Octavian redeemed himself with his campaign in Illyricum.

In contrast, Antonius seemingly did everything he could to flaunt the customs and traditions that Romans hold dear. It was somewhere about this point that it came out that Antonius had married Cleopatra before he divorced Octavia, causing even more of an uproar while arousing even more sympathy for Octavia. Some of the reflected warmth from the glow of adoration directed towards Octavia naturally washed over her brother, his stature as a model of upright Roman virtue and decency enhanced when compared to the Eastern debauchery of Antonius. No Roman man in our history had ever been married to two women at once, and of all the things Antonius did, I think this caused the most uproar, while I have little doubt that most of the indignation and outrage expressed emanated from the hearth of every Roman home. Speaking honestly, I do not believe any Roman man really cared whether or not Antonius was married to two women; in fact, I think he would probably be regarded with a great deal of sympathy, but the woman in the average Roman's life was not going to sit still for the example Antonius was setting. I imagine that it was the fear that other Romans would start emulating Antonius that was the real motivating factor in all the expressed outrage as men spoke the words of protest that were put in their mouths the night before by their women. Even Miriam, shy and quiet woman that she was, gave me an earful revealing her true thoughts about Antonius' actions, and they were not charitable.

I do not imagine Antonius cared much about what Miriam, or seemingly anyone else for that matter, thought about his actions, because he certainly did not modify his behavior in any way. In fact, the greater the outcry was, it seemed to spur Antonius to ever greater excess, as if he were trying to prove to the world that he was above the conventions of Roman society. It was becoming increasingly difficult for Antonius' tame Senators back in Rome to continue defending his actions while promoting his interests in the Senate, despite their best efforts. However, Octavian was relentless in his pursuit of enumerating all of Antonius' supposed crimes; Antonius had behaved without honor in his capture of Artavasdes, he overstepped his authority in giving territories away to his children, since they belonged to Rome and not Antonius. Most importantly and most threateningly to Octavian, at least so I believe, was Antonius' recognition of Caesarion as Caesar's legitimate son, and in this Octavian was right to be worried. We veterans of Caesar's army, especially those of us who had seen both Octavian and Caesarion, knew that the younger man was the living image of a young Gaius Julius Caesar. Such a powerful resemblance equates to an equally strong attraction to men who remembered the best years of their lives as those spent marching under the standard when the army was led by Caesar, so it is not idle speculation to say that if Caesarion grew to be a man and snapped his fingers, thousands of men would have come at his beckoning to lay down their lives for him. It is as close to a certainty as it is possible to be, and Octavian was nothing if not a very smart man who immediately saw the danger to his own status represented by Caesarion, so he did everything he could to denigrate the image of Caesarion as Caesar's son. Octavian's resemblance to Caesar was strong, but much of it was artifice, Octavian wearing boots with high soles to make him seem to be as tall as Caesar, while he had perfected Caesar's mannerisms down to the way he tilted his head at certain moments, along with perfecting his way of speaking so that if one closed one's eyes one would swear on Jupiter's Stone that it was Caesar himself. Of course, the factor that worked in Octavian's favor more than any other thing he did was the fact that we old veterans wanted him to be Caesar, that we wanted to believe that he was Divus Julius Caesar. For many years, Octavian was unchallenged in that regard, being accepted as not only Caesar's son but the embodiment of Caesar himself. Then, Caesarion came along and now that he was in his teens, the buzzing amazement surrounding the boy could not be ignored. Where Octavian pretended to be Caesar, Caesarion *was,* in that indefinable but undeniable way where the essence of a man is passed on to his son. Ahenobarbus, Canidius, all of these men who had spent more time around the young man than I, swore that you did not have to close your eyes to know that it was Caesar speaking. In fact, looking back at all that transpired, I think that Cleopatra's great error was in keeping Caesarion out of sight of the Roman people, particularly the army. For, if we had seen and heard him, there is no telling how differently our history would be written.

This was the manner in which the rest of the year passed, with Octavian working methodically and tirelessly to undermine Antonius, while his older counterpart kept handing Octavian tools with which to dig. The matter of the veterans' lands still was not settled, the moment rapidly approaching where Antonius would be forced to admit the truth to his retiring Legionaries, that there was no land to be had in Italia as had been promised. However, instead of concentrating on this matter, Antonius was either forced, or chose, depending on to whom you listened, to answer all the other charges Octavian was laying at his feet. I believe that yet again Octavian outmaneuvered Antonius, knowing his mark as well as any man did, sure that Antonius would be unable to discipline himself to concentrate on matters of larger import than his own pride and honor. By throwing out the variety of charges against Antonius that he did, Octavian kept Antonius so busy sending messages back, hotly contesting each one that Antonius either forgot or ignored the looming problem about to confront him. The end of the year saw the expiration of the Triumvirate, though why it was still referred to in this manner I do not know, since Lepidus was long gone, while neither side showed any real interest in renewing it for another term. This year Octavian was the senior Consul, and as custom dictated, he announced that he would be leaving Rome for the following year, despite having no plans on taking a governorship as would be normal, retiring to his ancestral estate in the country near Rome where he could keep an eye on things.

The incoming Consuls were none other than Gnaeus Domitius Ahenobarbus and Gaius Sosius, so that on the face of things it appeared that now Antonius would have the upper hand, between his tame Senators and Consuls solidly on his side. Sosius I did not know, though Ahenobarbus was well known to me. Despite the fact that I did not particularly like the man, I respected his ability. Most importantly, he was extremely loyal to Marcus Antonius, and was one of the few men who could voice his objections to Antonius without risking the wrath of the Triumvir. His loyalty to Antonius was put to the test almost immediately, when Antonius sent a letter that he wanted the two Consuls to read jointly before the first Senate meeting of the new year. It was a letter that Ahenobarbus refused to read, deeming the missive a further sign that Antonius had lost touch with the people of Rome. I do not believe that the Antonius of Gaul, or even Philippi would have committed such a basic mistake as to believe that a letter defending his awarding of territory to his children would do anything other than further inflame opinion against him. He had been removed from Rome too long, and I will admit under the influence of Cleopatra, to understand fully how much she and her Eastern ways were hated. I learned of these developments indirectly through Scribonius, who had resumed his correspondence with both his father and his brother, the latter of whom now sat in the Senate. According to Scribonius, his brother was what they called a pedarii, or back-bencher, too junior and too poor to have a real voice in what was taking place, meaning that as a result he was more of a spectator than participant, but reading his letters I could see that my friend was not the only member of the Scribonius family with wits about him. His prose was a little flowery for my tastes, especially for a letter to a brother, but his recounting of all that took place was certainly descriptive. Although neither Consul would read Antonius' letter, that did not stop them from going on the offensive against Octavian. Their task was made easier when it finally came out, during open session of the Senate that Octavian refused to give up land in Italia for Antonius' veterans, repeating his claim that since Antonius had supposedly conquered vast new territory that the men should be settled there. There was no way to keep news of this nature quiet, and I could easily imagine men literally running from the Senate meeting to dash off messages to friends or relatives in the retiring Legions to inform them that they would not be coming home to a plot of land after all. As many mistakes as Antonius made, he was not alone, and I believe this was one of Octavian's errors, although it is hard to describe it as such, given how things turned out.

In early Februarius, Gaius Sosius convened the Senate in order to push through a resolution to censure Octavian. According to Sosius, Octavian was the aggressor in this war of wills between him and Antonius. As proof, he listed all the compromises and concessions that Antonius had made over the previous years, and when they were enumerated in writing, as Scribonius' brother did, it was clear that Antonius was making more of an attempt at a peaceful solution than his counterpart. When put the way Sosius had; according to Scribonius' brother, it was one of the most powerful speeches he ever heard while sitting in the Senate, it was enough to sway the lower classes, thereby alarming Octavian into taking action. Even after the defection of a number of Antonius' tame Senators after the news of what had come to be called his Donations in Alexandria, the combination of the remaining Antonians and those men like Scribonius' brother who were trying to remain neutral was enough to pass the resolution of censure. Only a veto by one of Octavian's bought and paid for Tribune of the Plebs Nonius Balbus kept the resolution from passing. Nonetheless, it was a shocking defeat for the younger Triumvir. There is no doubt that it was this resolution that precipitated his reaction and all that followed.

Returning to Rome from his villa, Octavian brought along a Cohort of hard-bitten Caesarian veterans, some of whom I knew from Gaul when Scribonius' brother named them. With these men behind him, Octavian came to the Senate house, despite having no authority whatsoever to do so, calling for another meeting of the Senate. It was a mark of his power and authority, however unofficial it may have been at that moment that every man who was able to attended the meeting. Directing his own ivory curule chair to be set between those belonging to Ahenobarbus and Sosius in a thinly disguised show of his power, he then proceeded to answer the charges brought by Sosius. The fact that arrayed behind him along the wall were what I suspect were the most formidable looking of those followers, all of whom were wearing their daggers in another flaunting of the rules of the Senate, was the most likely reason that after he finished no man was willing to offer a reply. Scribonius' brother wrote that one could have heard a gnat fart when Octavian was through, though he did not put it quite that way. Upon seeing that no Senator was willing to risk their lives in speaking out, the young Caesar got up, leaving the assembly to stew in its juices. The message was clear, but I do not believe Octavian counted on the reaction that followed from his display.

"Ahenobarbus, Sosius, and about 300 Senators left Rome to go to Alexandria. They're probably there by now," was how Scribonius informed me of the next act in the unfolding drama, waving the letter from his brother, which had just arrived from the coast.

"Left?" I exclaimed. "What does that mean?"

He looked down at the letter, reading from it. "Quintus says that they left before Octavian announced that he could produce some sort of documentation of Antonius' crimes that he spoke about at the first meeting. He claimed that he could provide proof of every one of Antonius' crimes, that he had the document to prove it. Apparently Sosius really got under Octavian's skin because our young Caesar was particularly scathing about the junior Consul."

"Probably because Sosius was the one to propose that resolution," I suggested.

"True," Scribonius agreed. "Whatever the case, neither he nor Ahenobarbus stuck around to find out. They and the Senators left just the day before Octavian was to present his supposed evidence."

"Did he?"

Scribonius read some more, then shook his head. "It doesn't appear that he did. Quintus said that between the 300 Senators and the ones who stayed behind, but chose to stay inside their own walls, there wasn't enough of a quorum, so Octavian didn't bother. He's got his hands full, since Ahenobarbus and the others left because they claimed that the Republic is dead and that Octavian was its murderer."

Something else had occurred to me. "What about Quintus? He didn't leave with the others?"

Again, Scribonius shook his head. "It's bad enough that I'm over here and with Antonius. We decided that it was best if Quintus at least appear to be favorable to Octavian."

"We?" I asked.

"My father, brother, and I," he replied, his tone telling me that he invited no more questions on the subject, so I let it drop. Turning my attention back to the letter, I asked Scribonius if there was anything else noteworthy.

"Just that Octavian is trying to put the best face on matters. He's putting it about that he allowed both Consuls and Senators to leave the city, that contrary to what people might hear, it had nothing to do with his actions." He gave a chuckle. "I can imagine that there's a lot of money being thrown about right about now. Octavian on one side, Antonius on the other, both of them claiming to be the injured party and that they alone are the saviors of the Republic."

"And neither of them are any of that," I said sourly, thinking only of my own role in all this, knowing that there was still a reckoning coming.

"Oh, and my brother's wife is pregnant again," Scribonius finished, but he did not sound especially happy about this. I did not comment, not wanting to pick at a scab that he clearly still found painful. Turning the conversation back to the safer ground of politics, I thought of the irony of that as I did so.

"So what now?"

Scribonius considered my question, but could only shrug. "Your guess is as good as mine."

"Then what good are you?" I grumbled.

"What do you think is going to happen?" he shot back. "We're going to be fighting at some point in the future. What else do you need to know?"

I could not dispute the wisdom of that, so I did not try.

I do not want to characterize the flow of upper class Romans as going all one way, although Ahenobarbus, Sosius, and the Senators was the largest bloc by far. All was not going smoothly in Alexandria, Roman men still finding it particularly irksome to take orders from a woman, even if she was a queen. The fact that they were actually in her kingdom did not help matters, so that even under the best of circumstances friction was most likely inevitable. As much as I do not agree with the characterization of Antonius as Cleopatra's puppet, I cannot deny that she had an enormous influence on him, and I think she was the real source of the implacable hostility that most people ascribe to the relations between Antonius and Octavian. She clearly viewed Octavian, and even more importantly, Rome, as her enemy, and it was through Antonius she planned on bringing Egypt into ascendancy. While it would be nice to credit the Romans with whom she had the most contentious relationship with the motive of serving Rome's best interests, I have little doubt that it had much more to do with how she rubbed them the wrong way than any higher calling. She could be overbearing, sarcastic, petty and, most maddeningly of all to a Roman man, superior in her dealings with every other person, no matter their station. For men of the upper classes it was the worst, because they had never been told by anyone what to do, especially by a woman. Therefore, it was not much of a surprise when we heard that our former quartermaster Titius, and Plancus, who was one of Antonius' governors, went sailing out of Alexandria in a fit of temper, both of them angry with Cleopatra, after she took to restricting access to Antonius. They sailed directly to Rome, but it was what they took with them that proved to be the excuse that Octavian needed to declare war, doing so without breaking his vow never to attack a fellow Roman, and I learned of this development from an unlikely source.

Uncle Tiberius came to the villa one evening, and one look at his face had me excusing myself from Miriam's company, motioning the old man to follow me into the small office that I had taken to using for private meetings or when I had reports to complete that I did not want to sit in camp to finish. Motioning him to a seat, I did not immediately offer him refreshment, so he sat looking at me, almost literally drooling until I bit back a curse before calling one of the slaves to bring us some wine.

"Not the good stuff," I commanded, pleased to see the upset look on his wrinkled face.

I indicated he should begin, but he shook his head. "I need something to fortify myself for what I'm about to tell you, and I suspect you'll want the same for what you're about to hear." That was ominous indeed, but he refused to elaborate until he swilled a glass of unwatered wine. He pointed to my cup, then said, "Titus, my boy, you're really going to want that before I tell you."

"Just out with it," I snarled, tired of the mystery.

Instead of answering, he reached for the pitcher to pour another cup until I grabbed his arm to stop him.

Sighing, he said, "Very well. I have news from Rome."

"I gathered as much," I was trying to stay patient.

"You heard that Titius and Plancus left Antonius in Alexandria and went to Rome, did you not?"

This was old news, happening several weeks before, and I told him as much.

He shook his head, the skin on his jowls quivering with the motion. "I doubt you heard this, since I just received word this afternoon when a ship from Ostia arrived. When they went to Rome, they didn't go empty-handed. In fact, they brought something to Caesar that's beyond any value you could imagine."

He stopped, giving a longing look to the pitcher, so I grudgingly relented, pushing it towards him. He poured another cup, drained it, then smacked his lips, a habit of his I found particularly disgusting, although I said nothing.

"What they brought was nothing less than the will of Marcus Antonius."

I sat up, fully intent on the old man now, sensing where this was headed while not fully believing it. There is nothing more inviolate to a Roman than his will, and every citizen with property has a will. Those with enough property to warrant it have their wills stored by the Vestal Virgins, in the temple of Vesta. In fact, that is where a copy of my own will is located. The Vestals guard these wills, not only with their lives but with the power and protection of Vesta, goddess of the hearth and protector of Rome.

Uncle Tiberius continued talking, the wine finally loosening his lips. "More importantly, they knew what the will contained, and they told Caesar about it. It's what's in the will that I believe spells the end for Marcus Antonius, for he not only bequeathed Cleopatra with most of his fortune, but he affirms Caesarion as the true son of Divus Julius and rightful heir. Finally, he directs that on his death he be interred with Cleopatra in the manner of the Egyptians."

He gave an involuntary shudder at the thought of what would happen to Antonius' body when it was prepared in the Egyptian ritual of burial. Sitting back, I was too stunned to speak, the old man giving me a grim smile as he pushed the pitcher close to my hand. I took it, poured myself a full cup, drinking it in one gulp as my mind tried to make sense of what I had just heard, and more importantly, what it meant. Then a thought occurred to me, and I shook my head in dismissal of the dire nature of the news. "Antonius is alive, and even if Titius and Plancus are telling the truth, the contents of a man's will are sacred and won't be known until after he dies. All Antonius has to do is deny it, and there's nothing Octavian can do about it."

Uncle Tiberius gave me a long look, his rheumy eyes viewing me with an undisguised look of sadness, and not a little pity. Shaking his head once more, he heaved a great sigh as he did so. I noticed the tremor in his hand, wondering if it had always been there.

"Everything you say is true, Titus my boy. But you're making a faulty assumption. You're assuming that our young Caesar would stop at anything to achieve his aim of being the First Man in Rome."

He stopped, his expression still grave, watching as the import of his words sunk into my brain.

I heard someone gasp, only realizing it was me as I spoke. "What are you saying? That Octavian somehow got his hands on the will?"

Uncle Tiberius nodded. "That's exactly what I'm saying, dear boy. *Caesar,*" he emphasized the name, and I took this as a reminder that it would be wise of me to refer to him by the name he preferred, "went into the temple of Vesta, or I should say, sent some men and retrieved the will. It's in Caesar's possession now."

I was glad I was seated because my mind was whirling as I tried to think. It is hard to describe just how damaging this news was to Antonius. Seeing it written down, I suppose it is easy to wonder why this was as momentous as it turned out to be. After all, it seems straightforward; Cleopatra was Antonius' wife, even if he was married to Octavia as well for a period of time, so it should not be a controversial decision to give her most of his fortune. The lower classes would not care whether Caesarion or Octavian was considered Caesar's legal son, meaning it could be argued that it was just Octavian's problem. No, what would shake the foundations of our society down to the very bottom was in his insistence on his body being embalmed and interred with Cleopatra. That would horrify most Romans, particularly in the lower classes, who believed that the only way the soul could be released was through the purification of fire. Leaving a man's soul trapped in his body meant that his *numen* would wander the earth forever, causing all sorts of mischief for the living. It would be this fact that Octavian would use to show that Marcus Antonius the Roman no longer existed, that he had been replaced by a minion of Cleopatra. That would be the reason that Octavian would give when he roused the people of Rome against Antonius; the real cause was in the form of a teenage boy who would be legitimized in the eyes of the world, spelling the end of Octavian's status as the only son of Gaius Julius Caesar. This was the real danger that Octavian had to eliminate, and I shivered as I wondered how much blood would be spilled to achieve that aim.

Thanking Uncle Tiberius for the news he brought, for once I was not just being polite, but was truly grateful. Walking with him to show him out, he paused at the entrance, his face a study of conflicting emotions. I must confess that my mind was elsewhere, thinking about the next steps to take, so I was not prepared for what was coming.

"Titus, I just wanted to tell you that over these last months, I've come to think of you as a son."

My thoughts were interrupted by his words as I looked at him sharply, about to remind him that he had said that when we had known each other for just a few thirds of a watch, but there was something in his manner that stilled my tongue.

As if reading my thoughts, he continued hastily, "I know that I said that when we first met, so I understand if you don't believe me, but now that I've gotten to know you and Miriam, I just wanted you to know there's no way that I could ever do anything that would bring any harm to you or her."

Giving him a long, searching look, I tried to find a sign of deceit, but his gaze was steady as he peered up at me.

Finally, I could think of nothing else to say but, "Thank you. That's good to know."

He was clearly pleased by my acceptance of his words, though I did not want to have to put his promise to the test.

"Besides, I can't agree with what Caesar has done," he was saying, then a look of alarm flashed across his face as he searched my eyes. "Not that he needs to know that."

I had to laugh at this sudden reversal; now this old man was worried about what I might say to Octavian.

"Don't worry, Uncle Tiberius. I won't be sending a report to Octav…..I mean Caesar," I amended.

The old man's leathery face flushed even darker. "I'm sorry, Titus. Of course, you wouldn't. You're not that kind of man." He shook his head, giving me a rueful, toothless grin. "It's a sorry day that's come to pass, hasn't it, Titus? That we should worry about guarding our tongues with fellow citizens?"

"Indeed it has," I agreed.

With that, we parted, he back to his villa, me to camp to tell Scribonius, Balbus, and the other Centurions to expect to move.

For once, I had news before Scribonius, who was as surprised as I had been.

He did not say anything for a long moment, the frown firmly in place. "Antonius can't ignore this," he said finally. "I think we'll be marching soon."

"That was my thought," I agreed. "I'm going to alert the Centurions to get the men ready."

"Good idea. But that doesn't address the real question."

"Which is?"

I suspected that I knew what Scribonius was about to say, but for some reason I needed it to be spoken aloud by someone other than me, perhaps because I did not want to tempt the Fates, since I seemed to have had more than my share of good luck.

"What does the 10th Legion do when Antonius commands us to attack fellow Romans?"

The question hung in the air between us. I hesitated in my answer as I thought about it, although I had been thinking of little else lately. It would not be the first time we would be called on to fight fellow Romans; in fact, almost all of the battles we had fought in the last 15 years were against our own countrymen. The ranks of the Legion were full of men who had never lifted a sword against a Helvetii, or Allobroges, and they had never shirked their duty before, cutting down whoever stood before them regardless of their nationality. Somehow, though, this felt different, and I could tell that Scribonius felt the same way. Some of the differences were obvious; we would be fighting against a Caesar this time, albeit his adopted son who seemed to have inherited part of the great man's genius, but not all of it. If we marched for Antonius, we would be on the side of the *mos maiorum*, no matter how much Octavian tried to position himself as the defender of the old values and traditions of Rome, whereas if we marched with Octavian, he posed a threat because he was something new. Antonius, through what I believe was apathy more than anything, represented a return to the way things were before Caesar came. The army that marched with Caesar was composed of veterans from Gaul, while the army of Antonius was more than half full of raw youths or Legions who had only been slightly tested in combat, never facing anything as formidable as another Roman. The 3rd Gallica and 4th Macedonica had just finished their enlistments, so there had been a *dilectus* for each one, but as Antonius was barred from recruiting in Italia, the men of these Legions were from Syria and Judaea. Roman citizens they may have been, but very few of them were what we would consider truly Roman. However, there were other, deeper and more subtle differences that I felt tugging at my gut. At the base of my decision was the simple question; who was going to win? While this last campaign had gone well, it was still cut short, and when I looked at the entire picture, it seemed clear to me that despite Antonius' blustering about it, Caesar's luck had settled squarely on Octavian's shoulders. Also, I could not discount the impact that Cleopatra had on every decision Antonius made. While she was more predictable than Antonius in that everything she did was to advance the fortunes of Egypt, she was still a threat to do something that would put the Legion in needless danger. Perhaps it was this that tipped the scales in my mind. Simply put, Cleopatra wanted to raise Egypt into the spot of the most powerful nation in our world; in order to do that she had to destroy Rome. I had spent almost 30 years in the cause of advancing the glory and power of Rome, or at least so I believe, and if I led my Legion under the banner of Marcus Antonius, it would help to achieve Cleopatra's goal, meaning that my life's work, and that of all the men who marched beside me, would be for nothing. That was something I could not accept. At long last, I turned back to face Scribonius, having thought things through.

"I'm not going to allow this Legion to be used to help Cleopatra destroy Rome," I said slowly, thankful to see Scribonius' face show relief and agreement.

"I don't know what that means right now, exactly," I added.

"This is only the first step, deciding what we're going to do. The moment's not right for you to announce your intentions, because in reality nothing has been said officially."

"That's only a matter of time. We're going to be getting orders in the next few days. I can feel it in my bones."

"That may be, but even when we get orders it will be too soon."

I did not understand or like what Scribonius was saying, since it ran against my grain to not just act then handle the consequences that came up, whatever they may be.

"Why? I say the quicker we announce our intentions, the sooner whatever Antonius is going to do about it will happen, then we'll know."

Scribonius gave a sigh. I knew that sigh and I did not like it one bit, because it told me that he was seeing things in a way that I had not. Of all the men I have known, Scribonius was the one who could make me feel stupid, though I do not believe it was ever his intention to do so. Now he gave me a level look as he thought about his next words.

Finally, he posed a question. "All right. Let's say that we do as you say. As soon as we get our orders, we announce by word or deed that we're not going to march for Antonius. Then what?"

I felt a thrill of something when he put it in this manner, and it took a moment to realize that it was fear. What Scribonius described was a mutiny of a Legion, nothing short of that, and I had never been involved in that, being with the 6th when the 10th had done so under Caesar. Of course, I suppose technically we had mutinied when we had been under the command of Lepidus, but I did not then, nor do I now consider him even worthy of mention as a commander of the Legion, and I have absolutely no regret for the action we, and being honest, every other Legion in his army took. Still, I had heard enough tales around the fire from the men to know that it was a shattering experience for most of them. I thought about it, not liking where my train of thinking took me. Once I took a moment, it became clear that without having to spell it out, Scribonius was right. If the 10th mutinied, I was rolling the dice that a significant number of the other Legions would follow our lead. In fact, without verbalizing or even really thinking it through, it was the key to the success of what I wanted the 10th to do and to his credit Scribonius had immediately seen that. Now he was forcing me to really think about it, and I suddenly did not have any confidence that the other Primi Pili and Centurions would follow so readily. Torquatus had just retired; he was still in the army as one of the Evocati, which I suspected was as much to keep an eye on his son as any love for the army, and I did not have the same close relationship with the new Primus Pilus, Decimus Galerius, who had been the Pilus Posterior. Spurius was still in command of the 3rd Gallica, and while I respected his ability I also believed him to be bought and paid for by Marcus Antonius. Both of these men, even if they were inclined to join with the 10th, had their hands full with a new Legion and new Centurions in at least half the Centuries. Running down the mental checklist, of the nine Legions in the Damascus camp the only one I thought I could rely on was Balbinus' 12th, and I had to admit to myself my only reason for thinking thus was based on my conviction that he was an agent of Octavian, something that he had never admitted. Even if I was right, that would be just one other Legion to face the rest of the army, should it come to a fight. I could easily envision the carnage and slaughter that would ensue, realizing that Antonius would have no choice but to try to destroy the mutiny before word of it spread to the other Legions encamped in Antioch and elsewhere. He could not take the risk of doing anything else.

Although I was proud of my Legion and its capability, an army of this size, even with as many raw youngsters as this one, would be too much to defeat, and we would be overwhelmed. Seeing all this in my mind's eye, I bit back a curse at Scribonius for being so much quicker than I was.

"You're right," I said, if a bit grudgingly. "If we move too soon I'll just end up doing what I'm trying to avoid and get men killed for no reason."

Scribonius was plainly relieved that I had seen his point, but he was not yet through. "That's only part of it. You have to make sure that all the Centurions are of the same mind as we are."

In my view, that was going to be next to impossible, if only for the reason that getting 60 men of any kind to agree on something almost never happens. I decided that since Scribonius seemed to have all the answers, I would ask him. After thinking about it for a moment, he burst out laughing.

"I have no idea," he admitted. "But you're going to have to think of something, and I suggest that you keep quiet about it until the last possible moment."

"So you're saying I should wait until the night before the battle, whenever and wherever that is, then somehow convince all of the Centurions that their best interests and that of their men are served by turning on their commanding general."

"Something like that," Scribonius conceded. We both sat there for several moments, absorbed in our own thoughts, then Scribonius asked, "You know that you can count on me, don't you?"

I do not know why, perhaps it was the way he said it, but I was deeply moved. I opened my mouth to reply, yet somewhat to my surprise, I felt a lump in my throat that threatened to choke any words that came out.

Finally, I just reached out to clasp him on the shoulder, the only thanks I could manage at the moment.

It did not take long for the news of Antonius' will to circulate on both sides of Our Sea, and as I suspected, his desire to be embalmed and entombed with Cleopatra caused a huge uproar among the men. I suppose I should have thanked Antonius, because the contents of his will made the Centurions much more willing to listen when the moment arose, but that is said only with the clarity of looking back over the years. At the moment, the confusion and anger at Antonius' actions was so strong that the men talked of nothing else. Octavian chose to read the will aloud, not only in the Senate but in the forum as well, so that Romans of all classes could witness how the man they thought of as Roman no longer existed. With ships crisscrossing Our Sea, word reached us that Antonius and Cleopatra had relocated to Ephesus, then using the queen's money, were commissioning a huge fleet to be built or commandeered, the first solid sign that Antonius was preparing for war. Orders were sent to shift the army to Ephesus in stages, staggered over a period of a month, in order to give the engineers with Antonius time to construct a large enough camp. The 10th was scheduled to leave in the last group, giving me time to send Diocles ahead with Miriam, along with my baggage and the other slaves to find a place to live. I debated with myself whether to leave Miriam behind, thinking that I could send for her, yet the future was so uncertain that I did not have any confidence that I would be able to do so when the time came.

The men were subdued, for a number of reasons, not least of which that relatively few of them could afford to bring their women along with them, and we had been in Damascus for a few years by this point. That meant children, so yet again it was a pitiful sight, seeing the families lining the street outside camp, women clutching their small children, wailing as their men marched away. The feeling was much different from previous campaigns, with an air of finality and farewell that seemed to drape about our shoulders. Somehow, we knew that we would not be coming back here, the people of Damascus seeming to understand this as well. I am sure that some of them were happy to see the backs of us, though there would be a lot of businesses of all sorts that would suffer, while some of them would shut down operations to follow us to Ephesus.

I had not breathed a word of my plans to anyone other than Scribonius, Balbus, and Diocles, not even telling Gaius because I did not want to burden him with the secret. Still, I caught snatches of whispered conversations that immediately stopped whenever I approached, then saw the long, searching glances out of the corner of my eye as I passed, and I knew that every man in the Legion was waiting for some signal from me. Finally, it was a delegation consisting of the Pili Priores and some of the Centurions who had been with me the longest who approached me one evening just a couple of days outside of Damascus. They waited until I was busy doing my daily exercises shortly after dinner, where I was stripped to the waist and sweating well despite the cool evening air. I had turned 45 a short while before, and my mind was occupied with thoughts of where the time had gone and how I was beginning to have trouble with my teeth, meaning that I was not in the best frame of mind when I saw the small knot of men gather before me. I was under no illusions about why they were there, not needing the warning look Scribonius was trying to give me, though I decided to play dumb anyway.

"Well? What is it? The wine supply already turned to vinegar? The grain's moldy already?"

I did not mean my tone to be so harsh, but as I said, I had been contemplating my continuing degradation at the hands of whatever gods control the passing of time. I saw men glancing at each other as if asking if this was really a good idea. Naturally, all eyes turned to Scribonius, since it was no secret that he was my closest friend, and I do not know if the uncomfortable look on his face was feigned or not, but it looked real to me. He cleared his throat, then using my correct title as he always did in front of others, spoke just loudly enough that those immediately around could hear, but not enough that his voice would carry to the rankers.

"Primus Pilus, we were wondering your thoughts about this current situation."

I furrowed my brow as I pretended not to understand.

"My thoughts?" I rubbed my chin, determined to make this as difficult on the Centurions as possible, since I was angry at the interruption, among other things. "I think that we only made 25 miles today, and that my Centurions need to put their boots up the men's asses if we're going to make 30 tomorrow, as I expect a veteran Legion to do."

Oh, they did not like that one bit, even Scribonius stiffening at the rebuke. He seemed about to argue the point before catching himself, turning back to the topic.

"Yes, sir. Of course, we'll do our best and make sure that we'll do as you direct. But what I," he turned to indicate the other men, "what *we* were referring to is the current situation with General Antonius. Most specifically, the men want to know what we're going to do."

"Do? What we're going to do?" I looked at the assembled men coldly, making sure that my gaze fell on each one of them before I spoke again. "What we're going to do is our duty to Rome, as we've always done."

It was a vague answer, and while I hoped it would be enough I was not surprised when Metellus raised his hand then asked, "Excuse me, Primus Pilus, what exactly does that mean, that we'll do our duty to Rome? Are we going to follow Antonius, or are we going to . . . do something else?" He finished, his voice trailing off, clearly realizing how weak that sounded.

"Something else? What are you suggesting, Metellus? What is the . . . 'something else' you're proposing?"

Metellus' face took on a look of panic as he put his hands up in protest.

"I'm not proposing anything, Primus Pilus, honestly I'm not! I was just asking for your thoughts on the matter."

I heaved a large sigh, making a show of trying to be patient.

"I think I just expressed my thoughts, Metellus. Marcus Antonius is our legally appointed general, and has been for many years, has he not?"

I waited for the men to nod or answer, which they all did, however grudgingly.

"So any order he gives is a legal and binding order, according to the laws and customs of Rome. I think that answers the question."

"But what if it's the wrong order?"

The question came from somewhere in the back, but I recognized the voice of my old Optio and the Pilus Prior of the Ninth, Glaxus.

"When has that ever stopped us from carrying it out?"

I surveyed the faces again, knowing that there was no real answer to that question, since over the years, particularly in the army of Antonius, we had followed more than our share of questionable orders. I knew that this was at the heart of this meeting; the men did not believe in Marcus Antonius, and to a man, they were all convinced now that he was nothing more than a puppet of Cleopatra. This was unacceptable, even to me, although I was not yet ready to reveal that truth to these men. I could see that they were disappointed that they had not gotten what they obviously came for, but I had no more to say on the matter, and to make that clear, I resumed my exercises, cursing the fact that I had cooled off and would have to start over. The men took the hint, dispersing in smaller groups, muttering to themselves. I was just happy that darkness had descended and they could not see my smile.

That evening, Scribonius came to the tent, where I was in an expansive mood.

"I think we have our answer," I told him as we sipped our evening unwatered wine. "It seems clear to me that the men don't want to follow Antonius any more than we do."

Scribonius set down his cup to give me a long look before shaking his head.

"Don't be so sure about that, Titus. I admit that it's a good sign, but I don't think this is a strong enough sign that all of the Centurions are going to follow your lead."

I knew better than to argue the point, instead just asking him why he thought this.

"Because it wasn't unanimous to come to talk to you in the first place. There were at least two Pili Priores that didn't want to approach you. The only reason they did was because they were afraid that if they didn't, you'd start to question their loyalty."

I had not realized this, nor had I even given it any thought.

"Who were the two?"

Scribonius looked away, clearly reluctant to tell me, then said finally, "If I tell you, I'm afraid you won't be able to hide it from them that you know."

Swallowing my irritation, I was forced to recognize that he was right. Hiding my feelings has always been hard for me, but I tried to assure him.

"I know what's at stake," I said. "And I swear to you on Jupiter's Stone that they won't have any idea that I know. After all," I joked, "I can't stand you, and I've been able to hide it pretty well, haven't I?"

This made him laugh, so he relented.

"Nigidius and Gellius," he said. "Neither of them were keen to come, though I can't honestly say why. I don't think it's because they want to follow Antonius, but everyone is being very tight-lipped about this whole thing."

I could only shake my head, thinking that when the climate of fear and suspicion had trickled down so far in the ranks it was as clear a sign as any that it was time for action.

Scribonius seemed to read my thoughts, adding, "I don't think it's ever been this bad, Titus, even in the early days of this current fight between Antonius and Octavian. Even the rankers are watching each other and guarding their words with men outside their own fires."

"Do you think it's time for me to announce my intentions?"

He shook his head.

"It's still too soon. Nothing is going to happen of any note this year, at least I don't think it will. Antonius and

Cleopatra aren't going to move until the fleet is ready, and I suspect that we're going to do whatever Cleopatra decides to do and not Antonius."

I looked at him in some surprise, since he had not talked much about Cleopatra and her role in all that was taking place.

"Not you too? You think that Cleopatra is truly making all the decisions?"

He looked slightly uncomfortable, but he held his ground.

"Titus, I know you have a soft spot in your heart for Cleopatra, but I think that this matter of the will proves that whatever was left of Marcus Antonius the Roman is gone."

I had not thought of Scribonius as being a superstitious type, but when I said as much, he shook his head.

"It has nothing to do with superstition, or even my belief that a woman isn't fit to make military decisions. It has everything to do with how out of touch Antonius has obviously become with how Romans think. The fact that he even put such thoughts down on paper, and that he didn't realize that even men such as Titius and Plancus who've been as loyal as they've been couldn't stomach his pandering to Cleopatra, that's what has me convinced that he's now Cleopatra's to command. Putting it simply, it's clear to me that he fears Cleopatra more than he fears the laws and traditions of Rome."

When put that way, it was impossible to argue.

"So when do I move?" I knew I had asked this question before, but I was still as much in the dark as when I first asked, and Scribonius' answer was not much help.

"Not now. You'll know it when the moment comes."

We arrived in Ephesus to a city bursting at the seams, learning that Antonius had summoned every single Legion from the East, not just those of his that marched into Armenia the year before. Instead of 16 Legions, there would be 30, meaning that even with the army split into three separate camps around Ephesus, the strain on the city was enormous. Consider that the standard ration in camp is a *modius* of grain per man per week, supplemented by three Attic quarts of chickpeas along with a side of bacon. With 30 Legions, most of them near full strength, that is around 150,000 men eating the corresponding amount of food each and every day, which does not take into account the food required for the auxiliaries. There were perhaps 25,000 in their own camp, along with the forage for the livestock, both in draft animals and in cavalry mounts. There were 12,000 cavalry gathered in Ephesus as well, mostly Galatians, although there were still some Gauls that had not gone back home.

Diocles managed to find quarters for Miriam, but it was nowhere near the luxury of the villa, and it cost me a great deal to secure, since the area was crawling with Tribunes and other high-ranking Centurions, each of whom seemed to have a woman they wanted to keep happy.

Antonius called a meeting of all the Primi Pili as soon as the army was assembled, and thanks to Diocles and his network, I was not caught by surprise at the sight of Cleopatra, sitting next to Antonius. What did surprise me was her garb, for she had chosen to dress in her suit of cut-down armor gilt with silver and gold, complete with an Attic helmet, which she placed on the table in front of her. I do not know what reaction she was hoping to elicit, but I doubt it was the open scorn and mocking laughter at the sight of a woman attired for war. The 30

Primi Pili assembled in that room were some of the most hard-bitten soldiers who ever marched for Rome, and none of them were impressed at Cleopatra's display of martial ardor. For her part, she did not take it well. Perhaps this was the cause of what followed, as she turned to whisper something in Antonius' ear. He clearly did not like what she said, a furious argument taking place, though they spoke in low tones so that we could not hear. Making emphatic gestures then stabbing one finger at Antonius, Cleopatra clearly won her point; what it was became clear when she stood to face us, while Antonius sat next to her, looking thoroughly miserable. Looking at us, her head was held high, defiance and anger radiating from her tiny armor-clad body, and I had to stifle a laugh at how ridiculous she looked. I had no doubt she believed that she looked absolutely warlike, and perhaps if she had been a bigger-sized woman it might have worked, but she seemed oblivious to the incongruity she was embodying.

"Marcus Antonius and I called this meeting today," she announced in a surprisingly loud and clear voice. "Both to inform you of our plans for victory and to make it known to each of you that Antonius and I are co-commanders of this venture, equal in every way."

The last of her words were drowned out by the cries of outrage as men jumped to their feet, completely forgetting all military discipline, the Primi Pili calling to Antonius.

"Is this true, Marcus Antonius?"

"A woman? You expect us to obey the commands of a woman?"

"She's a foreigner! A queen! She's not Roman! What right does she have to command a Roman army?"

I had come to my feet with the rest, although I was not yelling, since unlike the others I was not surprised by this, thanks to my warning from Diocles. Spotting Ahenobarbus sitting behind the pair, he was looking grimly amused at what was taking place, while Canidius looked as if he would rather be anywhere else. To her credit, Cleopatra did not wilt under the verbal assault, standing her ground.

"What right? What right?" Her lips curled up, and I was struck by how with her beakish nose at that moment she looked very much like a bird of prey. "I will tell you by what right! It's my silver that you're putting in your purse every payday! It's my gold that's buying the wheat that fills your bellies! It's the wealth of Egypt that has built the greatest fleet ever to float on the seas! That is by what right I claim co-command!"

Oh, that shut them up quickly enough. Nothing will end an argument more quickly than the sound of purse strings drawing shut, despite the fact that clearly not one of the Primi Pili was convinced. All eyes turned to Antonius in mute appeal, but he was as defeated as every other Roman in the room, instead giving a weary wave at her to continue. Her eyes gleamed with the triumph of her victory, but I was sure that it would be short-lived, since I did not see any man willing to capitulate in the long run.

"Now that this question is settled, let me inform you of our general plan of action. We," she deigned to turn to acknowledge Antonius, "have decided that the best course of action is to transfer the army to Greece. The ground there is more favorable, and more importantly, the problem of supply will be solved by access to the grain in Thessaly."

So far, this was hard to argue with, but glancing at the set of men's jaws and their rigid posture, I was sure that there would be objections.

"The fleet is not yet ready, but the last of the transports should be completed by the end of the summer, so we'll be here in Ephesus for two more months. We have sent out ships to Cyprus and to the Euxine Sea to acquire more supplies, but as you all know an army of this size is quite demanding to feed."

"What would she know about feeding anyone but herself?" I heard someone mutter, followed by a low growl that I took to be agreement, though if she heard she ignored it.

"Our other reason for choosing Greece is that after the usurper Octavian is defeated, Greece will serve as our base of operations for the next logical step in liberating Italia."

The effect on all of us was as if Jupiter had hurled a bolt of lightning into our midst, with even Antonius sitting upright in apparent shock, hissing something to Cleopatra that I could not hear. I expected another outcry, but I think the Primi Pili were too shocked to speak. Again all eyes turned to Antonius, who now stood.

"That's premature," he said as much to Cleopatra as to us, her face reddening with the rebuke, her lips pulling back again. Before she could speak, he held up a hand in a clear command of silence. He continued, "That's only one possibility. My hope is that with the defeat of Octavian, the people of Italia will welcome my return and the bloodshed will end. That's the primary aim of this campaign, to settle the question about whose version and vision of Rome should prevail. Once that's decided, we'll put down our swords and not raise them against another Roman." He turned to face Cleopatra directly, adding in a firm tone, "Ever again."

Again moving before she could mount an open challenge to his authority, Antonius dismissed us, and we filed out, an angry buzzing filling the room as we left. Even before we were all out of the room, the sounds of the two voices, one male and one female, arguing ferociously replaced our muttering. If I was wavering before, my mind was now irrevocably set on keeping the 10th out of harm.

While we waited, the men were paid. Normally this is not a noteworthy event, except that for the occasion Antonius had ordered coins struck for each Legion. Ours had the Legion number along the edge, with the original symbol of the bull, but also a figure of a horse directly beneath, on the obverse side, in tribute to that day so long ago when Caesar had a group of us ride horses. I was only one of two men left from that original group, the others either being killed or retiring long before, which men like Vellusius did not let anyone forget. I am not ashamed to say that this enhanced my status as a legend of the Legion, helping me enormously in my leadership of the 10th. There were now less than 200 men of all ranks left from the original *dilectus* held when Caesar was *Praetor* 29 years before, and there was a bond among these men, regardless of rank, that we did not have with our younger comrades. So when the men received their pay, and they were reminded of why the horse was on their coins, I found myself circulating from one hut to the next reliving that day when we went to face Ariovistus and his bodyguard. I made the men laugh by recounting how I had never ridden a horse before that day, how my legs had hung down almost to the ground. And as most stories go, it was slightly different with each retelling, as I added color to what was already a memorable event, not only in my life but in the Legion history.

However, it seemed that for every positive step Antonius took with the army, he took at least one step back, if not more with another action. The problem was the reverse side of the coin, upon which was emblazoned a picture of a trireme, a symbol of Cleopatra's navy, which she had taken great pains to remind everyone she was paying for. We Romans are not seafaring people, and to a man, the rank and file believed that it was the Legions of Rome that would prove to be the difference in the coming struggle. Having this pictorial reminder of the Egyptian influence over our general, and the army in general, guaranteed that there was much furor on payday. As unpopular as the Legion coins were, there was another one that only heightened the hostility, and that was the coin that Antonius used to pay for supplies. I am sure that he did not intend for these coins to be put in circulation among the men. However, it was a futile hope to think that men buying and paying for services in Ephesus would not receive these coins back. As much as men bought things, they also sold them, most commonly items of plunder they had taken on one campaign or another, the civilians always eager to get their hands on something taken off a dead enemy soldier, or so whoever was selling it would claim anyway. Most commonly, it was the men who elected to bring their families that would find themselves in need of cash, prices in the city now exorbitant because of the demand. I was sure that as men ate through their savings they were regretting the decision to bring them along. Nevertheless, I could see how hard a decision it was, making me thankful that I had sufficient funds to allow Miriam to stay nearby. Now these men were returning from trips to the city carrying these new coins, which began circulating among the men, causing much consternation.

It was Balbus who brought it to my attention, bringing one for me to examine one day.

"Have you seen these?" he demanded, tossing the coin onto my desk.

It was a gold *denarius.* I picked it up, hefting its weight in my hand, thinking that was the source of his obvious anger. Shaking his head irritably at my upraised eyebrow, he pointed to it sitting in my palm.

"Read it."

I was afraid he was going to say that, and I cursed my eyes when I squinted at the gleaming coin. It was still new, the edges not worn down as commonly happens with gold coins, meaning the script was plainly visible, even if it was hard for my old eyes to read. The visage of Marcus Antonius stared up at me, his one eye in a fixed stare, his chin lifted, and a garland on his head. Around the edges was the abbreviations of his name and title of Marcus Antonius, Imperator. All in all, it was completely unremarkable, and I said as much.

"Turn it over," Balbus said through gritted teeth, and when I did, I let out a gasp of shock.

It was not the sight of Cleopatra, since I expected that, thinking that whoever had struck this coin was no admirer of the queen, since she looked positively severe and as unfeminine as it was possible to be. It was the script around her head to which I had the reaction, making Balbus' anger immediately clear.

"Cleopatra, Queen of Queens, Her Son King of Kings" was what was written on the coin.

I looked up at Balbus, whose fists were clenched, angry as I had ever seen him.

"First Antonius says that her brat is Caesar's son, making him Roman, then declares that he's King of Kings?"

"That doesn't necessarily mean that Antonius plans on helping Caesarion become King of Rome," I said mildly.

Balbus gave a dismissive snort.

"What else can it mean? Isn't it clear that Antonius means for Caesarion to inherit Caesar's estate and that he plans on having Caesarion succeed him as King of Rome?" Without waiting for me to answer, he went on, "And what about that bit about Queen of Queens? If Antonius wins, she won't suddenly cease being a queen, will she? No, she'll be Queen of both Egypt and Rome! It's bad enough that we'd have a king, but a queen? That will never stand! I don't know of a Roman who wouldn't rather die fighting before allowing that to happen. The Republic will be soaked in blood!"

While I did not necessarily agree with Balbus about every Roman being willing to die to keep from being ruled by a queen, thinking of Gaius' father on his farm and finding it hard to see him worked up enough about something happening so far away, I did agree with Balbus' overall point. And I had never seen him so worked up, so I could only imagine the level of outrage among the rest of the men.

"How many of these are floating around?" I asked.

He shook his head grimly. "I don't know, but enough for everyone in the army to know about it by now."

I put my head in my hands, suddenly developing a headache. If I was not careful, Antonius' actions would force me to declare myself to stay in front of the men, then once that happened my days would be numbered. I had no doubt that Cleopatra could find someone to slide a knife between my ribs, although from what I knew about her and her Egyptian ways, she would probably favor poison, and in all likelihood would have it put into food that Miriam and I shared. It was becoming a race to see what would happen first, the proper moment to declare myself, or actions that would undoubtedly lead to my death.

Chapter 3- Interlude in Ephesus

The moments that I spent with Miriam proved to be some of the most enjoyable of that time in Ephesus, as I was able to put my worries aside for a short time. Since the apartment I found was nowhere near the size or luxury of the villa, we could not entertain guests as easily or in the style to which she had become accustomed, but that turned out not to be a bad thing. We still would have Scribonius, Balbus, or sometimes Gaius as guests, except they would not be all-night affairs like they were in the past. This was due not only to the accommodations; there was also a good deal of training that had to take place in order to keep the men sharp for whatever was to come, and as sullen as the men were, I knew from bitter experience that keeping them busy was the best way to keep the pot from boiling over before I was ready. I felt as if I were balancing on the edge of a dagger, with the prospect of having the men finally mutiny on one side, or being put in a position where I put myself in danger by declaring that the 10th would not be marching for Antonius on the other. As bad as the situation would have been in Damascus facing eight Legions, the idea of facing up to 19 Legions was even more unappealing. Despite being sure that by this point the 10th would not be alone if we chose to revolt, it was still not a risk I was willing to take if it could be avoided.

Scribonius and I spent many thirds of a watch closeted away in my private quarters in camp discussing the situation, both within the Legion and the rest of the army. A fair number of the Primi Pili were as openly against the idea of following Antonius to Greece, yet both Scribonius and I knew that talking and doing were often two separate things. All we were confident of was that if the 10th declared that we would not follow Antonius was that the Legions led by these men would not immediately fall on us. The larger question facing us was exactly what it would mean when I chose the moment for the 10th not to follow Antonius.

"Does this mean that we're Octavian's men?"

Scribonius asked this one day, and I froze at the question, since in all honesty I had not thought of that. In my mind, I had gotten as far as the fact that I would choose a moment to either openly disobey Antonius and Cleopatra, or would do so by not acting when the time came. I had not considered what that meant outside of Antonius' army and his reaction, yet now Scribonius was once again forcing me to consider the deeper aspect of the question.

"I don't know," I said slowly.

"You don't believe that Octavian isn't going to remind you of the debt you owe him, do you?"

"No," I admitted. "In fact, I'm surprised I haven't been reminded about it yet."

"That's because he knows it's too early to act. And I'm about as sure as I can be that you're not the only man who he has a claim on."

"I know that's true," I replied, thinking of Balbinus.

"I wouldn't worry about Octavian reaching out at some point, but you're just going to have to accept that it will be at a time of his choosing and not yours."

Scribonius' words reminded me of how much I and men like me were pieces to be thrown away at some patrician's whim, a bitter draught every time I was forced to swallow. It is bad enough that we are at the mercy of the gods, but to have our fates determined by other men, all in order to further their own aims, still makes me angry when I think about it.

Trying my best to avoid both Cleopatra and Antonius, I used Diocles' contacts in the *Praetorium* to alert me when they would be absent if I needed to do some business there. It helped me personally that they decided to go off to the island of Samos for some sort of festival, although the stories of the excess and debauching that took place did not help matters with the army at all. Both of them seemed oblivious to the impact their actions had on the men, with morale continuing to sink lower with every passing day. One day shortly after their return from Samos, evidently there was a mix-up from Diocles' contact in the *Praetorium*, since I entered the building and ran directly into Cleopatra, who was in the middle of tongue-lashing one of the clerks, using language that made a Centurion envious, all while dressed in her ridiculous suit of armor. I froze for a moment, then thinking to escape unseen, I turned to leave.

"Primus Pilus Pullus!"

The voice seemed to strike me between the shoulder blades like a javelin, and I took a moment to brace myself before turning around, making my face into what I hoped was the mask of a professional soldier. Standing at *intente,* which Cleopatra could not fault, but it also forced her to come to me, a small victory I know, yet it made me feel a bit better. Walking up to me, her diminutive size was made even more apparent when compared to my massive frame, and I could hear snickers as she approached. She clearly heard them as well, as two bright red spots appeared on her olive cheeks. Despite this, she kept her eyes fixed on me, her gaze reminding me of a predatory bird, the image helped by the great beak of a nose. There was nothing warm or familiar in her gaze as she strutted around me, inspecting my uniform while commenting on some smudge on my leathers and a loose strap. I felt a burning resentment growing as I stood enduring her examination, and I realized that she was paying me back for making her come to me. After completing her inspection, she returned to her original spot facing me, looking up at me, while I refused to look down, choosing a spot on the far wall on which to fix my gaze. Not a word was spoken for what seemed like a full watch, but was no more than the space of a few heartbeats, until she finally broke the silence.

"Well, Primus Pilus, it has been awhile, hasn't it?"

"Yes, ma'am."

"Still the formidable warrior, I see. The question is, can we count on your bravery and skill in the coming great battle?"

I felt my jaw clench, for the words were spoken in a mocking tone, as if she doubted me. I felt a shiver of fear run through me, the thought hitting me that somehow she knew my innermost thoughts and what I was planning.

"Queen Cleopatra, I will do as I have always done, and that is my duty."

I was angry, but I had enough self-possession not to say what I normally did in these situations, leaving "to Rome" out of my statement, knowing that someone as clever as Cleopatra would pounce on it. However, she was clearly not impressed.

"So you say," she sneered. "But words are easy. It is deeds that are more difficult."

"You're absolutely right, ma'am. Deeds on the battlefield are more difficult. Perhaps you could tell me of those that you've performed in combat?"

As soon as I said it, I knew that I should have bitten my tongue off rather than let it run loose like that. One would have thought I had slapped her from the look on her face, the rest of her body going rigid with shock.

"You . . . insolent, low-born brute!"

She was practically spitting with rage, but I was no less angry.

"Insolent I may be, low-born I certainly am, but you better hope that I'm just as much of a brute as you claim me to be, my lady, if you have any hope of winning a victory over Caesar."

To my memory, this was the first time I had ever referred to Octavian as Caesar in public, which enraged her as much as I knew it would.

"Don't you *dare* refer to that little vermin as Caesar! He is not Caesar's son, no matter how much he claims to be! My son is Caesar's only true son, and when he sits in judgment of all those who denied his birthright on your precious Capital, you would do well to remember that, Pullus!"

The instant she said it, she knew she had made a mistake. It was as if the air was sucked out of the room. I felt all eyes turn on her, and none of them were friendly.

"Be careful, my lady." I said this only loud enough for her to hear. "That sounds dangerously close to saying that he'll be sitting as a king. Perhaps you don't know that it was on the Capitoline Hill where our kings did just as you say Caesarion will, but I'm sure you know what happened to those kings. I wonder how Marcus Antonius would feel to hear you make such pronouncements."

Oh, any warm feelings she ever had for me were gone, her hatred for me and all that I represented suddenly seeming to ooze from the very pores of her skin. Nonetheless, she also knew that she had gone too far, in front of too many witnesses, and she did not want Antonius involved in this dispute, although she had to know that he would hear her words.

"You are right, Primus Pilus Pullus." I know she was trying to sound gracious, but it is hard to do so through tightly clenched teeth. "I misspoke. All I meant to say is that when my son Caesarion, Caesar's *legitimate* and naturally born son," she was clear to emphasize the status that Antonius had conferred on Caesarion, though I do not see how he had the right to do so, "inherits what is his due from Caesar's estate, he will remember who served him well in the restoration of his status."

I knew that it was the smart thing to do to accept this offering, no matter how weak it was, but I was too angry, all the frustration and pent-up rage threatening to spill over. I had come to see that standing before me in this tiny woman was the cause of all this grief and turmoil, all to further her dream of making her son truly worthy of the title King of Kings. I raised an eyebrow, this time not lowering my voice.

"I must admit I'm confused, my lady. I thought that this fight was to put Marcus Antonius back as First Man, not to make sure your son gets what may be due him from whatever is left of Caesar's."

"Of course it is to restore to Marcus Antonius his proper status," she said, tight-lipped, now clearly aware that all eyes and ears were turned in our direction and trying to limit the damage of her words. "But that doesn't mean that the claims and status due to Caesarion can't be recognized as part of what must be done to help Marcus Antonius."

"That's completely understandable. I would just hate to think that it was part of your plans to put your son on a throne as King of Rome, for I seriously doubt that Marcus Antonius would agree. And he is, and has been my general."

"Must I remind you that Antonius and I are co-commanders in this venture? And what my plans are, such as they may be, are only your business as far as it goes to execute those plans, not to question them. However," she said as she turned, facing the rest of the men in the room so that they could hear her more clearly. "I'm well aware of the customs and traditions of Rome. I was instructed in them and what they mean to you Romans by no less a personage than Gaius Julius Caesar, who your people rightly revere as a god. I can assure you that Caesarion has no wish to be King over Rome any more than you wish him to be."

She turned to look back at me, her hatred blazing from her eyes, but there was no less in my gaze as I moved my stare from the spot on the wall to look directly into her eyes. I was satisfied when I saw her take an involuntary step backward, flinching as if I had lifted my hand, despite the fact I had not moved a muscle.

As if realizing she had done something that showed weakness, she tilted her chin upward, then said in what I was sure she thought of as a commanding tone, "That will be all, Primus Pilus. I'm glad to know that I can count on you."

"Every man in the 10th Legion will do their duty, my lady. I can assure you of that."

Such is the duplicitous language of royalty, I suppose, and as I turned away to make my retreat I wondered if I were any better than Cleopatra, knowing as I did that we were both lying.

Naturally, I had to discuss what happened with Scribonius immediately, walking on wobbly legs back to my quarters as quickly as I could without running. My hope was that Cleopatra was as shaken by our confrontation as I was, while the others who heard it would waste no time in going to Antonius. The thought crossed my mind that Cleopatra might now try to remove me, but I dismissed the thought for a number of reasons, not least among them that I did not want to lie awake at night listening for every creak in the floor, wondering if someone was coming to kill me. Also, I believed that my sudden death, especially after what just transpired, would cause enough of an uproar that it would prove more difficult for Cleopatra to advance her plans. Not lost on me was her declaration that her son had no desire to be king, recognizing it as the kind of mealy-mouthed words that might throw off the more slow-witted among the lower classes. As far as it went, I thought and still think she was telling the truth; nothing I had seen in the few times I was around Caesarion, and nothing I heard about him leads me to believe that he held any desire to be anything other than Pharaoh. His mother, on the other hand, was a different story and it was she who worried me and the rest of the army. She was the serpent that had to be watched, and she had not said a word about her desires.

Immediately on my arrival back at my quarters, I sent Eumenis to fetch Scribonius, while I regret to say that I took my frustrations out on Diocles for unknowingly walking me into an ambush. Thankfully for both of us, Scribonius arrived to cut my diatribe short, since I was still angry and working myself up to a higher pitch of fury. As it was, Diocles was shaking all over, although I can see him smile about it now as he is writing. Scribonius did not say a word, just looked at each one of us, then pulled up a stool to sit as if he were watching a gladiatorial contest, his demeanor perfectly mimicking that of a man avidly waiting for blood to be spilled in the sand. My anger immediately evaporated as I began laughing, and it did not take long before it was out of control. I had seen men act in a similar fashion after a battle, despite it never happening to me, though I suppose that what I had just endured with Cleopatra was similar to a fight. After I finally calmed down, I sat down heavily, my legs just giving way, and I grabbed the pitcher of wine on the table, pouring a full cup and not adding any water. I drank a cup straight down, something I rarely did, causing Scribonius' eyebrows to crawl almost up to his hairline, such as it was.

"I take it something interesting happened."

"You could say that," I agreed, then proceeded to tell him everything that had transpired shortly before.

When I was finished, he sat for several moments, then let out a low whistle.

"Well, I'll say this for you. When you decide to put your foot in a pile of *cac*, you stick it in all the way up to the ankle."

His tone was one of mild rebuke, but I expected no less.

Turning to more practical matters, he continued, "But I think you did the right thing in forcing her to at least imply that she wants to set Caesarion up as king. There's no way that this isn't going to reach Antonius. The question is, what's he going to do about it? If your, and my, suspicions are correct, and he's under her control in some way, the answer will come with this."

"It doesn't really change anything though, does it?"

"Only if he sends her packing, but I doubt that will happen."

"Not likely," I agreed, and later that day, we were proven right.

I was not entirely surprised when a runner came from the *Praetorium* to inform me that Antonius demanded my presence immediately. Since I had only removed my helmet and harness, it took but a moment before I followed the man sent to fetch me. When I entered the *Praetorium* for the second time that day, I suppose I noticed that most of the clerks who were there earlier seemed to be missing, but I did not think much of it at the time, my mind occupied with other matters. I caught the sympathetic glances thrown my way from some of the Tribunes who were there, so I expected to see Cleopatra with Antonius in his office, or at least Canidius to be there if only to gloat, but the Triumvir was alone, sitting at his desk. He looked exceptionally weary, with dark circles under his eyes. However, he did not have the appearance that he exhibited in the past when he had been drinking heavily. I supposed that was at least one good thing that Cleopatra had done for him, despite it being for her own purposes. Marching to his desk, I came to *intente* and saluted, but he did not acknowledge the salute for a long moment, until my arm began to ache. He was scribbling in a tablet, then finally looked up, returning my salute before he sat back, chin in his hand with one finger tapping rhythmically against the side of his face as he regarded me.

When he spoke, his tone was as weary as I had ever heard him, even in those dark days during our first campaign against Parthia.

"I understand you had a conversation with the queen."

"Yes, sir."

I saw no point in making things easy, and a look of irritation crossed his face.

"And?"

I recounted the conversation word for word, as I remembered it. When I was finished, he grunted before heaving a long sigh.

"That's exactly what I heard as well, just not from the queen."

He gave me a look that could have either been a grimace or a smile, it was hard to tell which.

"You understand this puts me in an extremely awkward position."

"I would imagine so, sir," I agreed, still playing the role of the dim Legionary.

"Cleopatra shouldn't have spoken as she did," he continued. "But you shouldn't have baited her."

"Sir?"

I tried my very best to look surprised, but he was not buying what I was selling.

"You know exactly what I'm talking about, Pullus," he snapped. "Don't play the stupid Legionary with me. I've seen it too many times, and I know you too well. You knew exactly what you were doing. It's just a pity she fell for it."

"Truly sir, I didn't plan anything," I replied, which was at least partially true.

I had let my temper get the better of my tongue and had no plan originally to try to make Cleopatra say something intemperate, but when the opportunity arose, I admit I took it.

"Your queen angered me with her slur against my honor, and I admit that I let my tongue get the better of me, but I was as surprised as anyone that she went as far as she did."

Now, that last part was an outright lie, but I saw nothing to be gained by total honesty.

"Here in the East, men's tongues have been cut out for much less of an offense than you gave to the queen," he said coldly.

"Then it's good that I'm a Roman citizen, and not one of her Eastern minions," I immediately replied, inwardly wincing the moment the words left my mouth.

Titus, will you never learn? I wondered, but Antonius reacted in a completely different manner than I expected.

He threw back his head, roaring with laughter, slapping the table in obvious delight.

"No, you're not, Pullus, I'll give you that. You are Roman through and through."

I was absurdly pleased by the compliment, except as quickly as he had been full of mirth he turned serious again, reminding me how ever changeable this man really was.

"Still, you've put me in a really tight spot, or rather you and Cleopatra have. You know, she thought very highly of you, Pullus. She told me that during Caesar's time in Alexandria you distinguished yourself under very difficult circumstances."

I was not sure how to respond, so I said nothing. He leaned forward, putting his head in his hands, giving another one of his bone-weary sighs.

"I would ask you to forget all that she said, but I know that's both impossible and unrealistic. Who have you told of this?"

"No one, sir."

"Liar," he said, but it was in a genial tone as he shook his head. "I'm not going to order you, I'm asking you, Pullus, that whoever you told, you tell no others. I have my hands full at the moment, and I don't need an army ready to mutiny because my queen can't keep her mouth shut."

"I won't tell anyone else, General. I give you my word."

"Good. Unfortunately, I'm afraid some damage is done already, because the *Praetorium* seemed to be stuffed with clerks at the time. Fortunately, all but two of them were slaves or freedmen, but now I'm afraid I'll have to raid the Legions for qualified clerks, and it will take time for them to become versed in how things run here in the *Praetorium*, but that can't be helped, I suppose. The Tribunes are another story, but I can deal with them. They're all ambitious young men, and the queen's purse runs very, very deep."

The shudder was involuntary, but it was very real as my mind struggled to fully understand the import of what Antonius had just said.

"You put the clerks to death?" I gasped.

He looked up, clearly surprised. I was relieved when he shook his head, but it was short-lived.

"Oh, I didn't. Cleopatra did, moments after you left, before any of them could get out to make mischief by tattling on her. You know how slaves talk; they're almost as bad as Legionaries. She used her Nubians for the job."

I took a staggering step back, too shocked to speak. He mistook my clear distress, holding up a hand in a dismissive wave.

"Oh, don't worry. You're quite safe. I made sure that the queen understood the consequences of a Primus Pilus being murdered by her. In fact, I suppose I should thank you. I think the prospect of being torn to pieces by the army is more than enough to keep her tongue in check. The gods know I haven't been able to. And Pullus," he finished grimly, "like it or not, the queen is here for the entire campaign. I won't send her away again as I did the last time. And she *is* co-commander, though I'll try to make sure that you deal only with me. It will be better for everyone that way."

For the second time that day, I left the *Praetorium* on shaking legs.

"She did what???"

I imagine Scribonius' expression matched mine when Antonius had told me. Returning to my quarters, I immediately told Diocles, knowing that he had friends among the clerks. He was still speechless from the news I had brought, sitting on a stool in the corner, facing the wall. I suspected he did not want me to see him crying, but it would not have mattered, for I felt much the same way. True, they were slaves, and I had seen much worse things done to slaves in front of my very eyes, yet to have their lives taken simply because they were in place doing their jobs, at the whim of Cleopatra, was a tragedy and an injustice.

Facing Scribonius, I waited for the shock to wear off; when he finally spoke, his tone was grim.

"This is worse than I thought. And you say Antonius will do nothing about it?"

I shook my head.

"He was very clear that she's not going anywhere. But he did promise me that I was safe from her, that the prospect of the men tearing her apart made me secure. He didn't say it outright, but I got the very strong hint that he let her know that he'd tell the men if something happened to me."

"I hope the threat is enough," Scribonius mused. "Because if he's as lovesick and in her control as we think, I doubt seriously he'd make good on his threat." That did not make me feel better, so he added hastily, "But as long as she believes that he will, then I think he's right."

"That's an awfully thin shield to protect me." I was made gloomy by Scribonius' words, knowing that he was right.

"Not necessarily." Scribonius put his hand on my arm, causing me to look up to see him staring at me earnestly. "Think about it this way. Cleopatra is one of those people who can only look at the world through her eyes. So she's going to think, 'What would I do in this situation?' Do you have any doubt that she'd throw Antonius to the dogs if it suited her purpose?"

I thought about it for a moment, then shook my head.

"No," I admitted. "She would do it quick as Pan."

"Exactly. And she's going to accept it as fact that Antonius would do the same, because that's what she'd do in his place."

That made me feel a bit better, but not by much.

"What now?"

Scribonius considered, then shrugged.

"Nothing much to do at this point. Stay on our course. And watch your back."

"I'll need help with that." I hated to hear the words come out of my mouth, because it ran against every fiber of my body to ask for someone else's aid in the matter of defending myself, but I had to sleep sometime.

"Balbus and I will take care of that. I'm sure we won't have any trouble getting Vellusius and a few of the other old-timers to help."

"That's only part of it."

Both Scribonius and I turned in surprise, for it was Diocles who had spoken from his spot in the corner. His mouth was set in a thin line, his chin up, the anger in his eyes something I had not seen often before.

"She's Eastern. I doubt that she'll send a section of Nubians after you, or even a hired knife. She'll be more subtle than that. I'll check your bed every night for snakes." He paused to think as I suppressed a shiver at the thought of finding a serpent in my bed. "We'll also make sure that we watch your meals being prepared and bring them to you ourselves and then we'll taste everything before you eat it."

While I appreciated the gesture, I did not see the point.

"If you're watching my meals being cooked, and then bringing it to me, why taste it as well? That seems a little excessive."

"Because that's the only way to be sure that the ingredients of the meal aren't poisoned," he said quietly.

"Wait. Are you suggesting that she could poison a whole sack of grain that might be eaten by others just on the chance that it would poison me?"

"What do you think?" Scribonius asked quietly. "Do you think she would care if a few other men died to get to you?"

I had to admit that when he put it that way, it was hard to argue.

"And those are just the ways I can think of where you're vulnerable off the top of my head," Diocles continued. "But these Easterners are incredibly imaginative when it comes to doing away with someone. When we were in Alexandria, the palace slaves filled my head with stories of the ways that the Ptolemies did each other in, and she not only grew up in that world, she's the only one to have survived. The rest are all dead, and a good number of them were at her direction."

Scribonius paused to consider what Diocles was saying, thinking of a question. "Did you happen to hear how much she was willing to pay someone to dispatch a rival or threat?"

Diocles thought a moment. "I heard that she paid 10,000 sesterces to have one of her guard commanders killed by one of his own men."

My stomach twisted in a knot as I let out a whistle. "If she's willing to pay that much, one of my own men is likely to do me in." I said it as a joke, but I was half-serious.

"You sell yourself too cheaply." Scribonius patted my arm. "It would take 15,000 at least."

I had to laugh, except it sounded hollow in my own ears, as Scribonius turned serious. "I think you have nothing to worry about from the men, if only because they hate Cleopatra as much as you do. And for every man who'd be willing to take the money, that's not enough for him to drop off the face of the Earth, because there'd be ten who would hunt him down and gut him like a fish."

It was nice to hear the words, but I fervently hoped that Scribonius was right. My thoughts turned to Miriam, whatever comfort I had been feeling evaporating in a wave of icy fear.

As if reading my thoughts, Scribonius said, "We'll put Vellusius in charge of guarding Miriam, and of course what Diocles will do with your food will protect her."

"Send for him now," I commanded Diocles, who jumped up and ran out of the office.

No matter how disturbing the thought about my own safety was, it was nothing compared to the fear I felt for Miriam. It was a completely helpless feeling knowing that the richest, most powerful woman in the world would likely stop at nothing to do me harm, and would view Miriam as a way to strike at me. I could easily imagine Cleopatra's minions worming about to find out how attached to Miriam I was, then how the queen would view that as a perfect way to hurt me, and I felt the tremors return to my legs.

How do I get myself into these messes? I thought to myself as we waited for Diocles to return with Vellusius. Too many times in my career I had let the combination of my temper and my tongue get me into situations where I aroused the hatred and anger of people more politically powerful than I was, or would ever be. I thought of Lepidus, which in turn reminded me of Octavian's dark gift, one with a powerful cord attached to it that he could yank at any time, feeling in my bones that the time was coming when I would feel the tug. It certainly helped that all this turmoil was taking place with Antonius and Cleopatra, making the decision easier, yet I knew that I was fooling myself with the thought that I had any choice in the matter. Diocles returned, interrupting my musing, with Vellusius, whose wrinkled, leathery face was pinched in obvious worry. When my eyes fell on my old comrade, I was struck by how old he looked, making me wonder if I looked the same, careworn and creased by wind and weather. He was a few years older than I was, but not by that much, and I consoled myself with the thought that at least I still had all of my teeth, despite the fact that they were giving me more trouble by the day.

"I told Vellusius that you needed him for a special assignment, but I thought I'd let you tell him why," Diocles said as soon as Vellusius rendered his salute.

I quickly explained to him the situation, leaving nothing out, not feeling that it was right to send him to guard Miriam without knowing why. If it had been one of the newer men, I would have been less forthcoming, but I knew and trusted Vellusius as I did few others in the Legion. His face turned grim, and I recognized the look of determination on his face as the same he had before going into battle. I was thankful that it was this man who would watch over the woman I loved. Reaching for a tablet to scratch a quick note to Miriam, I suddenly remembered she could not read our words. Instead, I wrote out the symbols that she said made up my name in her language so that she would know it came from me, then sent Vellusius on his way.

Before he left, he paused at the door. "Primus Pilus, I'd like to take a couple of men with me. Is that all right?"

I thought about it, then nodded. "Only men that you trust with your life," I added, which he answered with a grin.

"I wouldn't bring anyone other than them, Primus Pilus. This old dog has lived too long to throw it away now."

Then he left, and that act made me feel a bit better.

Scribonius and Balbus walked with me out of camp to my apartment, where Vellusius was standing guard, along with one other old veteran named Kaeso. Their presence drew curious glances from passersby, but Legionaries were crawling all over Ephesus, so it was only passing on the part of the civilians.

I frowned at the sight of just two men. "I thought you wanted two other men."

Vellusius saluted, giving me a toothless grin. "Oh, Primus Pilus. You don't think that I'd let some nosy bastard see exactly how many men are guarding the lady, do you? In fact, I've got Herennius and Cornelius tucked away out of sight. One of them's watching the back of the building, and the other one.....well, I'd prefer to keep that secret. If you don't mind, sir."

"If either Herennius or Cornelius doesn't mind me running my sword through their guts because they surprise me, then no, I don't mind at all," I said pleasantly.

Vellusius' face fell as he realized the flaw in his plan; deep thinking had never been one of his strong points. "Oh. Yes, sir. Completely see your point. Well, I have Cornelius out back, and Herennius is up on the roof. We were poking around, you know, scouting the lay of the land and he found a hatch on the roof that leads into a crawl space. A sneaky bastard could use that to get into the building easy like, and we don't want that. So he's camped out up top."

I commended Vellusius for his thoroughness, asking what seemed to me to be an obvious question, only to see that this was another point Vellusius had forgotten to consider.

"Who's going to relieve you? I can't expect you boys to stay out here through every watch. You need to eat and rest sometime."

"Oh."

His voice was very small, and he looked down at the ground, clearly ashamed.

I put my hand on his shoulder. "That's all right, Vellusius. I'll take care of the relief." I turned to Scribonius, saying quietly, "When you go back to camp, fetch Gaius. Have him pick the same number of men that he trusts with his life."

Scribonius looked at me with some surprise. "You really want Gaius for this? That's a lot of responsibility for a young man."

I shrugged. "You clearly believed him capable of being a Sergeant. I trust your judgment. And I know that Gaius loves Miriam well. He'd rather die than let anything happen to her."

"It won't come to that," he assured me.

"I hope not."

Even as I was deciding that Gaius would be involved in this, I cursed Cleopatra for putting me in a position of putting one person I loved at risk to protect another, but I had watched Gaius since his promotion, and I saw that he was more than just a good Legionary, that he had the potential to be a real leader. It was time I stopped protecting him and started to trust in his abilities and training, and this was as good a time as any to start that, even while it did not make me feel very good in doing so. I also realized that there would never be the perfect time, that there would always be a nagging doubt in the back of my mind as I wondered if the situation was the right one in which to expose him to greater danger. Balbus had said nothing this whole time, and I wondered what was going through his mind as he stood, slightly apart from us, watching the street. Sensing that he had something to say, I decided to try and find out what it was.

"You haven't said a word about any of this," I began. He turned to look at me, his face as flat and expressionless as it usually was, but I could see that he was troubled by the look in his eyes.

"Go on," I said. "You have every right to speak your mind. If you don't want to be involved in this, I won't hold it against you in any way."

A look of alarm flashed across his scarred visage. "It's not that. I have no desire to be anywhere else but where I am. I was just thinking."

"Of what?"

He did not answer for a moment, then finally he asked, "Does it bother you that we're on the defensive?"

"Of course it does," I replied. "It's not in my nature, and I know it's not in yours."

"Then why are we?"

I did not take his meaning, but I saw Scribonius step forward, the corners of his mouth turned down almost to his chin. "You're not suggesting that we try and kill Cleopatra, are you?"

My heart started hammering, and I took a look around to make sure that nobody was close enough to hear our conversation.

Balbus shrugged, but his tone was defensive, replying, "Why not?"

"Because we'd bring the wrath of Marcus Antonius down on our heads, that's why," Scribonius retorted.

"And who else?" Balbus asked quietly. "Who in this army would Antonius use to seek retribution?"

For once, and perhaps the only time, I saw Scribonius was completely flummoxed, for Balbus was right. As hated as Cleopatra was, it was highly unlikely that we would be considered anything other than heroes by the army and Antonius' own generals. Most importantly, it would put us in the good graces of Octavian, not to mention erase whatever debt I owed him, although I know that was not part of Balbus' thinking.

"In that you're certainly right." Scribonius sounded grudgingly admiring of Balbus' turn of thinking. "But that doesn't answer the question of how we'd get to someone as closely guarded as Cleopatra is. How many in her Nubian bodyguard?"

He turned to me for the answer. "About a thousand. They lost a few when one of their ships went down on the voyage here, but only about 50, I think."

Scribonius turned back to Balbus, regarding him with a raised eyebrow. "So how would you propose we penetrate that screen to get to her?"

Balbus shrugged again, but I could see the beginning of doubt in his eyes. "I haven't thought that through yet. But what I do know is that we won't have to go through a thousand, because they won't all be guarding her at the same time. They work just like we do, in shifts. We could go in fast, with maybe three Centuries, and cut through them before they knew what hit them."

Balbus' plan, such as it was, certainly had an appeal to it, as I am sure he knew it would. I looked at Scribonius, who did not seem nearly as tempted as I was, and I sighed, knowing he was about to tear Balbus' idea to shreds.

"That might work," Scribonius began, much to my surprise, but he was not through, "getting us in. And it might be enough of a surprise that we could actually get to Cleopatra. But what exactly were you planning on doing to Antonius, who will undoubtedly be sleeping at her side? I mean, that's when you were planning on going in, sometime during the night, correct?" Without waiting for an answer, Scribonius continued. "So let's say we get in, and we get to where Cleopatra and Antonius are sleeping. And let's say that we decide to restrain Antonius in some way, though I can't imagine that he'll take it well, no matter what we do or how we do it. If Antonius raised the alarm, do we go ahead and kill him too? Or knock him over the head? How long do you think it takes for the Nubians who aren't on guard to get roused and get in position to stop us from getting out?"

Balbus was seeing where things were going, and he was turning sullen. I cannot say that I blamed him all that much, his heart clearly being in the right place.

Scribonius turned to me and asked, seemingly in all seriousness, "Titus, how well do these Nubians fight? You worked with them in Alexandria."

"Well, enough that three Centuries wouldn't be enough if the whole guard were roused," I admitted, not particularly wanting to help Scribonius destroy Balbus' plan.

Scribonius turned back to Balbus, eyebrow raised, which Balbus did not take well. "Fine," he fumed. "Then we'll just let Titus fend for himself."

"That's not what I'm saying and you know it," Scribonius snapped, clearly as irritated now as Balbus. "What I'm saying is that while I would love to strike Cleopatra down as much as you would, it has a very small chance of success, if you want to bring men out alive. I don't know that Titus would be willing to sacrifice three Centuries of men on such a risky proposition."

"No," I said instantly, despite this being more of an emotional reaction than anything logical.

If killing Cleopatra ended the chances of a larger fight that would see many, many more men killed in what we all felt was a doomed cause, then it was probably a small price to pay. But when it is your men, men that you have trained, led, and seen suffer through so much already because of the mistakes made by your generals, then it is not quite so easy.

With that question settled, I thanked Scribonius and Balbus, reminding the former to alert Gaius that he would be needed, then I entered the apartment to find a petrified Miriam waiting for me.

"Titus, what is going on? Your man Vellusius brought me the tablet with your name on it, which you misspelled again, by the way." She was babbling the way she did when she was nervous or scared.

The other sign of how frightened she was showed in her use of only my first name, and I tried to comfort her by taking her in my arms, making the same soothing sounds one makes for a skittish horse, but she continued as if I had done nothing.

"He would not tell me what was happening; just that he and three other men, who are very fierce looking,! He said they would be guarding the apartment and that nothing would happen to me. What is going on?"

She was repeating herself, and I finally could only get her to stop by kissing her. Then, taking her by the shoulders as she caught her breath, I looked at her with what I hoped was a soothing and calming demeanor.

"It's just a precaution. I had a disagreement with Cleopatra . . ."

"Her! I *knew* this had something to do with her! She is evil! She cannot be trusted! Have I not told you that those Macedonian Egyptians are serpents? They came as conquerors, and they will not leave! And that one! She will do anything to make her son king of the whole world, and her the queen! From what I've heard, she has relations with her own son!"

In an instant her demeanor had gone from frightened to spitting angry, and I wondered how much this had to do with her belief that I had some sort of unrequited love for the queen of Egypt. That may have been true in the past, but I would gladly have wrapped my hands around the queen's scrawny neck to squeeze the life out of her and enjoyed doing it. I must admit that I had been seduced by Balbus' idea, enjoying the thought of standing over Cleopatra with a sword in my hand, seeing the fear in her eyes as she knew that her life was over, and the bitterness in her mouth that it would be at the hands of an insolent, low-born brute like me. I suppressed a smile at Miriam's show of defiance and anger, oddly proud that my normally shy and retiring woman should display a surprisingly fierce side. I let her go on for a few moments as she lapsed into her native tongue, something she often did when she was upset, and despite finding it a difficult language to master, I knew enough to understand that Cleopatra's mother was not well thought of by my woman.

Finally spent, she looked up at me, her brown eyes wide and searching as she gave a shy smile. "I am sorry, Titus Pullus, for my show of temper. I beg your forgiveness."

I laughed, hugging her tightly. "You have nothing to be sorry for. I'm happy to see that you have some fire in you."

"Anyone who tries to hurt the man I love will find out just how much fire I have," she said with such a fierce scowl that I stepped back in mock fear, throwing my hands up.

"*Pax*, Miriam, my love. You've nothing to worry about, either for me or for yourself."

Turning serious, I decided to be as honest and forthcoming with her as I thought it prudent to be. She had already guessed that Cleopatra was behind this new development so I saw no point in denying it, knowing myself well enough that she saw in my face that it was true when she said it.

I described our confrontation, enjoying the look of anger when I detailed her slur against my honor, appreciating her obvious delight in my witty retort, wagging a finger at me to scold. "You outsmart yourself sometimes, Titus Pullus. I know that you have to defend yourself against the lies she is speaking against you. The nerve of her to insinuate that you are a coward! But you pushed her when perhaps it was better that you just let it lie."

"I know," I admitted, for she was right.

None of this would have been happening if I had just kept my mouth shut, said what was expected of me, and gotten out of there. But I am a warrior; fighting is what I do better than anything, except I was not nearly as skilled in the war of the court as I was the battlefield. I also decided not to tell her what happened to the slaves in the *Praetorium*, knowing it would upset her needlessly. Her business of putting me in my place finished, she turned back to the kitchen, where a pot was simmering, and before I could stop her, she picked up the ladle to taste what she was preparing. I was about to shout a warning before I shook my head at my alarm.

Get hold of yourself Titus, I chided, but just to make sure, I asked her, "Did you go to the market today?"

She gave me an apologetic look, shaking her head. "No, I am sorry. I am using some vegetables and pork I had left from yesterday. I will go in the morning."

Despite knowing the extremely small chance that Cleopatra had been able to work so quickly, I felt my body go limp with relief.

"No," I said quickly, causing her to turn back around with a questioning look.

"From now on, you're going to have help with that. You won't go to the market, and we're going to let Diocles, Eumenis, and Agis help with the cooking. And tasting the food," I finished weakly, looking away.

"Oh."

Her voice was very small as the import of why this was necessary hit her.

She stood completely motionless for a moment before she seemed to gather herself. "That is probably a wise choice, but I do not know how I feel about those three putting their lives at risk for us."

"It was their idea," I protested, suddenly not liking the sound of it any more than she did, which was not exactly true anyway.

It was Diocles' idea, and he had been with me the longest and was the one of the three I was closest to. I wondered how enthusiastic Eumenis and Agis would be at the prospect, although as slaves they had no choice in the matter. This suddenly moved my thoughts in a new direction, since in the past when poison was used the most likely suspects were the slaves of the victim's household, making me think of all the unkind things I had done to Eumenis and Agis, wondering if these slights were enough to entice either of them to be willing to listen to the blandishments of one of Cleopatra's agents. I had never flogged either of them; in fact, I had never done that to any slave I owned, the image of Phocas and Gaia always springing up in my mind. That did not mean I did not cuff them about the head every once in a while, especially Eumenis, who was exceedingly clumsy, but I thought that I also showed them small kindnesses that I hoped would be enough to keep them loyal. Nonetheless, I resolved to talk to Diocles about it at the first opportunity to get his thoughts on the matter, then I sat down to eat the last meal that others would not taste first for some time to come.

The days passed, slowly becoming weeks, the members of my household and those closest to me establishing a new routine during that time. After the first few days of being guarded through every watch by four men, I made the decision to reduce the guard shift to three men, adding one more man to the detail so that the men would not have to spend half a day on watch, instead splitting the day into thirds. Gaius was as angry as Miriam at what had happened, and insisted that he be part of the escort whenever I left camp to go to the apartment the first several days. It was hardest on Miriam though, since Scribonius and I deemed it best that she not leave the apartment for any length of time, and when she did go for a short walk that she do it at random intervals that made her movements impossible to predict. Those times when she did leave, one of the men would go with her, and I believe this upset her more than anything, because a woman seen in the company of different Legionaries is usually thought to be working in a professional capacity. For the neighbors who knew that she was my woman, it had to be extremely puzzling, and it was unfortunate because she had become friends with another woman about her age who was the woman of a Centurion in the 19th, and suddenly Miriam was refusing her invitations, with no explanation.

Talking with Diocles, he assured me that neither Eumenis nor Agis were worthy of suspicion, insisting that compared to the other slaves in a similar position, they were the envy of their lot. I did give them an exceptional amount of freedom, and I was aware of some of the friction this caused among other slaves, knowing that there were other Centurions who did not appreciate my policy either. Still, it appeared that all involved had become settled into this new reality, and Antonius was good to his word in keeping Cleopatra and me from being together in settings where there were not many others around, although there was no way he could completely avoid having us in the same room. The only time this occurred was with meetings of all Primi Pili and senior officers, so there would be more than 40 men and Cleopatra. It did not keep the queen from glaring daggers at me, which did not go unnoticed among the other Primi Pili, though as far as I could tell Antonius was successful in squashing word leaking out of what happened. It made me wonder how much it had cost him to buy the more than half-dozen Tribunes that were present.

Even Ahenobarbus seemed to be in the dark, pulling me aside after one meeting to try to find out what was going on. "It seems that your romance with the queen has gone sour," he said with a sly smile.

I felt my face redden, but I kept my tone as neutral as I could make it. "Seeing that we never had one, it's hardly surprising, General."

"Still, the last time I saw you two together, she was waving at you like you two were old friends. Now, she gives you Medusa's frown. You're just lucky she's not Medusa or you'd be stone."

I shrugged, saying casually, "Who knows what makes her run hot and cold? I'm not going to lose any sleep about it."

"Interesting you say that." His voice dropped as he glanced around. "Because from what I hear, you should be sleeping with one eye open."

I had been walking out of the *Praetorium,* but that made me freeze in my tracks and I took my own quick look about.

Still, nobody appeared to be listening, but I knew that could be deceiving. "What exactly do you mean, General?"

"I think you know exactly what I mean," he said quietly. "Gods know that in some ways Cleopatra having you murdered would be a good thing, since it would expose her to the wrath of the army, though I have no idea why she hates you so. But I can't say that it would sit well with me to know that that Macedonian bitch can have a Primus Pilus murdered."

"Thank you for that, I suppose." Looking around again, I asked him, "Have you heard anything specific? I mean, about how she'll attempt something?"

He shook his head. "Nothing more substantial than a whiff of smoke," he admitted. "But those Eastern types favor more subtle means like poison, and I hear that one of the members of her court has been seen in the market shopping among the herb sellers."

Thanking him again, I returned to the Legion office, immediately calling Scribonius to pass along what I had just been told.

"It appears that our hopes that Cleopatra would let this lie are in vain," was his only comment, both of us sitting glumly sipping wine, wine that had already been tasted by Agis.

Despite it only confirming our suspicions that if she would attack, this would be her most likely method, it was good to have this information, though I could not say with any certainty that Ahenobarbus' information was accurate. Where it helped was in giving us an area in which to be extra vigilant, since it was left to Diocles, Eumenis, and Agis to go to the market every day, but make their purchases from different merchants. This would keep a would-be assassin from being able to bribe a merchant to slip one of my men a bag of tainted vegetables or poisoned pork. This was the world in which I walked in those days in Ephesus, waiting for the fleet to be finished to ship for Greece.

There are always delays when undertaking a task as massive as the building of a fleet that would protect and carry 19 Legions, along with the attendant cavalry and auxiliaries, and that is not even taking into account the creation of the artillery that would be fitted on the decks of the warships, or the sea trials each craft must undergo. Entire forests in Judaea and the Levant were denuded of trees, which had to be hauled to the shipyards along the coast where the craft were being built. The huge logs had to be hauled down slippery mountain slopes, made more difficult by the snows that were especially heavy in the mountains that year, which of course thawed, turning the tracks traveled by the carts into ribbons of mud. Journeys that were supposed to take a single week were taking three, causing delays as inevitable as the change of seasons. So when Cleopatra had announced that the transports would be ready by the end of the summer, none of the Primi Pili paid much attention, knowing that just because the queen wished it to be so did not make it that way. The problem, at least for me, was that it gave her more opportunities to remove me as a possible threat, although as time passed and no word of her indiscreet remarks leaked out, I began to wonder why I was so worried. I reasoned that it must have become clear to her that I was not going to say anything, or I would have already done so by that point, meaning that I did not see why she would risk Antonius' and the army's wrath by trying to kill me.

One evening after my walk home with Scribonius, I decided I would get a feminine view on the matter before I mentioned to Scribonius my latest thoughts. After we sat down for our meal, for which Agis was responsible that evening, and seeing that he survived, we began eating. In between bites, I asked Miriam for her opinion. She chewed her food as she listened while I explained why I believed that I could relax my guard against Cleopatra at this point. When I was finished, she said nothing, continuing to look at me as she munched her bread. Finally, she gave a sad shake of her head, regarding me in a way that reminded me of how Scribonius looked when he was about to lecture me on some point that I had missed.

"You really do not understand women, do you, Titus Pullus?"

In fact, by that point in time I thought I did have a fair understanding, but apparently once again I was wrong, since she proceeded to explain why.

"You are thinking as a man would think. You don't like Cleopatra, but as long as you do not pose a threat, you see no reason why she should be threatened by you. It is, how do you call it, logical?"

She tilted her head when she tried the foreign word, something that I found absolutely charming, and I nodded.

"But a woman is not logical; she is ruled by her passions. You know this, do you not?"

I nodded again, for that was true, making this fact part of why I believed that I had finally begun to understand women.

"But you also think that she is Cleopatra, she is the ruler of all Egypt, and that she was taught Roman ways by Caesar. So you think in your head that, unlike other women, a queen like her cannot be ruled by her emotions, that she has to think like a man. Is this not so?"

I have to say that I was impressed, because that is exactly what I was thinking.

I got another shake of her head before she leaned forward to tap me on the forehead with her first finger. "That is where you are wrong, Titus Pullus. She is a woman; first, last, and always. She hates you, and a woman does not need a reason to hate because it is part of her passions. She has no control over it. You think if you do not give her a reason, she will have no desire to end your life, but that is exactly when she will strike, because her hatred for you will only die when she dies, may the god Baal make it happen soon. She probably does not know herself why she hates you, though she will tell herself she has reason for it. All she knows is that she hates, and she is Cleopatra, and when Cleopatra wills it, you will die."

I had rarely heard Miriam speak so many words, with such conviction as she did then. Sitting back, I digested her words along with my food. I cannot say that I completely agreed or even understood her explanation, but something inside me told me that it would be wise to heed her words, and I had resolved earlier that I would stop ignoring that voice of caution.

I patted her hand, saying, "I'll heed your words, my love. The guards will stay, and we'll continue with testing the food."

Her relief was obvious, and we resumed our meal, each lost in our own thoughts the rest of the evening. As it turned out, Miriam's advice was some of the best I ever received, despite it coming at a high price. It was perhaps two weeks later as I was walking to the apartment for the evening, this night with Balbus, and we were just a dozen buildings away when I saw a sudden movement, squinting to see Herennius sprinting toward us. My heart leapt into my throat and I grabbed Balbus by the arm, running to meet the Legionary.

He skidded to a stop, trying to render a salute, but I snapped at him, "Stop wasting time! What is it?"

He was gasping for breath, so it was hard to understand him, but finally I made out the name he was blurting out.

Once I made it out, I went limp with relief, although I do not suppose I should have felt that way. "Your slave, Eumenis. He was tasting the food and something happened. I'm sure he's been poisoned."

We ran the rest of the way back to the apartment, where Vellusius was standing in the doorway, his arm protectively around Miriam's shoulder, who was weeping uncontrollably. A small knot of people were gathered, the type of onlookers always attracted to excitement, the grimmer the better, and I was none too gentle when I shoved them aside.

Reaching the pair, I asked Vellusius, "Where is he?"

Vellusius jerked his head back into the apartment, his weathered face a shade paler than normal. Before I entered, I asked if he was still alive.

Vellusius shook his head, saying grimly, "He died a few moments ago, and it wasn't a pretty sight. I think he choked to death." He shrugged. "We tried to help him, but there was nothing we could do."

I nodded my understanding before pushing past into the apartment. Eumenis was sprawled on the floor, his face almost unrecognizably contorted in a rictus of agony. The skin of his face was a purplish hue, his tongue protruding between swollen lips, his mouth still ringed with foam. I have seen men die in innumerable ways; I had seen my first Optio Vinicius burned to death with boiling pitch. In the intervening time, I had seen men disemboweled or rendered limb from limb, but this was the most horrible death I had ever seen, and I felt my stomach lurch at the sight. It was clear that he had died in horrific pain, his nails torn and bleeding where he was clawing at the stone floor, and I could see the bloody scratch marks he left. An upturned bowl was lying next to him, its contents spread over the floor, Miriam cooking a porridge for the night's meal, by the look of it. I had made her promise that she would never taste her food, but I knew that sometimes she forgot, and I thanked the gods that she obviously had remembered this day. I doubted Eumenis felt the same way. A pool of what I assumed to be saliva was around his head, while his belly was grossly distended, as if whatever it was that had been used created some noxious gas inside of him that threatened to burst out. I knelt beside the body, saying a silent prayer, realizing that I did not know much about Eumenis, though I was sure that Diocles would. He was Thracian, or so I believed, and I wanted to at least send him to the afterlife in the manner of his people, thinking it was the least I could do. Slave he may have been, but he gave his life for Miriam and me, so for that I owed him a debt that I could never repay.

Returning to where Vellusius and Miriam were still standing, I took Miriam gently, nodding my thanks to Vellusius, whispering to him to remove the body. Herennius had rounded up a cart from somewhere, and he and Vellusius wrapped Eumenis in a piece of linen before they carried him out. Miriam's sobbing had subsided, but it began afresh at the sight of Eumenis' corpse, which was rigid, his limbs splayed out in the position in which he had finally died, something I attributed to the poison since the stiffness that comes with death should not have occurred yet. Kaeso, the third man on guard, had come into the apartment to clean up; he informed me when he was done, and I took Miriam back inside.

"Disperse this crowd," I ordered Kaeso. "And I don't care how you do it."

Vellusius and Herennius carted Eumenis' body back to camp. In a move of cunning, Vellusius "accidentally" let the makeshift shroud slip from the dead slave's body, ensuring that all in the vicinity could view the handiwork of Cleopatra's poisoner, much in the same way that Caesar's body was displayed when he was assassinated. From all accounts, it created quite a stir, men calling to each other to come look, it quickly becoming a parody of a triumphal parade with men lining the Legion streets to watch the grim procession. When men called out to Vellusius to ask him who did this horrible deed, he did not answer, instead giving a grim jerk of the head in the direction of the compound that served as the queen's palace. From what I learned later, word shot through the crowd, and as Vellusius described, he was followed by an angry rumble as men informed each other of the identity of the suspect. Before long, Vellusius and Herennius had drawn a tail of men who followed the progress of the cart back to the 10th's area of the camp. By his dress and the disc around his neck, it was clear that Eumenis was a slave, yet that did not stop these hard-bitten men from being outraged at his fate, and in a strange way, they honored Eumenis in a way that I think he would have appreciated. There is no doubt that their impromptu demonstration was an expression of their outrage against Cleopatra more than it was any grief over the death of a slave, no matter how horrible it may have been. Nonetheless, I know that most of them would not have wished this on a helpless and powerless victim. Meanwhile, as Vellusius and Herennius were finishing their task, I was with Miriam, who had calmed down enough that she could answer my questions.

"Do you remember anything about Eumenis saying where he purchased the food today?"

She shook her head, her brow furrowed as she tried to think. "No, he did not. You know his Latin was not very good, and we did not speak each other's tongues, so we did not talk all that much." She gave a sad laugh, her eyes refilling with tears. "Though that did not stop him from chattering away about only the gods know what. I do know that he seemed to have been in a much better mood the last few days. I do not know why that was."

I had taken the sack that Miriam identified as being what Eumenis had brought from the market, still half full of grain. There were a few apples, most of which he had sliced for Miriam to put in the pot, along with the stalks of vegetables that were the remnants of what had gone into the meal. While Miriam talked, I examined these items. None of them looked suspicious, yet I also knew I had no idea what I was looking for. Picking up an unsliced apple, I was careful to hold it by the stem, inspecting it for any signs that the skin was punctured by a needle through which poison could have been dripped, but not finding anything. Next I took a cautious sniff, wondering if the concoction was potent enough to create vapors that would kill me if I inhaled, relieved that there was only the tangy scent of apple. Turning my attention to the sack, I continued my inspection while Miriam watched apprehensively. I think we both had the same feeling in our gut that the likely cause of Eumenis' death was contained in that sack, but like the apples and vegetables, I could see nothing untoward in the appearance of the kernels of grain nestled in the bottom of the snack. Then, I took a sniff. At first I smelled only the familiar must of the combination of grain and sacking. I started to put the sack down, about to turn away, then on an impulse I took another pass at the sack, drawing in another breath. It was the second time that I caught a whiff of something that seemed out of place with the other smells, my mind struggling to place it. Was it . . . almonds? There was a tug at the back of my mind, recalling some conversation about a certain poison that smelled like almonds, although I could not remember when it took place or who said it. Whatever the case, I immediately tied a knot in the sack before setting it aside, telling Miriam I would have to leave to attend to Eumenis. I called Kaeso to tell him to stay with Miriam inside the apartment, which was unusual, but I knew him well enough to know that he could be trusted with her alone.

Pointing to the loaf of bread made from the grain left over from the day before, I said jokingly, "I guess you're going to have to eat like a Legionary tonight."

My attempt at humor did not go over well with her, so I gave her a clumsy pat before I left. In my defense, my thoughts were elsewhere. Taking the sack of grain, I went back to camp to begin the search for Eumenis' killer. I knew where the trail would point, and accepted that there was nothing I could do to strike back at the ultimate perpetrator, but I could make the people who carried it out pay with their lives.

When I arrived back at my quarters in camp, it was a somber place. There was a small group of men gathered outside the door to the Legion office, talking quietly, Vellusius standing among them, clearly telling them the gruesome details of Eumenis' death. Upon my approach, the men came to *intente,* but I was in no mood for formalities, or to listen to their questions and cries that they wanted to avenge this insult to their Primus Pilus, knowing that on the part of many it was more of an attempt at ingratiating themselves with me than any real sincere outrage. Even after all these years, here near the end of their enlistment, it never ceased to amaze and irritate me that there were men who insisted on trying to flatter me in some vain hope that it would be useful to them in the future. I had been a Centurion and Primus Pilus for almost 20 years by this point, meaning that I knew every trick the men did, and was immune to them all. Nonetheless, it did not stop men from continuing to try to find a new tactic that would keep the *vitus* from their back or a shovel out of their hands digging a *cac* hole. Now they were using the death of a slave that they cared nothing about in a new attempt to get into my good graces, and the thought angered me.

"Get back to your duties," I suddenly roared, taking a measure of enjoyment out of seeing the sudden rush of alarm and fear in their faces as they went scrambling, not before a couple of the slower ones got a helping prod from the *vitus*. Vellusius turned to run as well, but I stopped him with a barked command. He turned to stand at *intente*, his expression a mixture of apprehension and confusion.

"Where's Herennius?"

"He went to get our rations for the night, Primus Pilus."

That was certainly a plausible reason, and one I was not prepared to hear, expecting some Legionary's excuse.

"Very well," I grunted. "As soon as he returns, get back to Kaeso and resume your post. I don't think it'll take long for her to find out she wasn't successful, so she might send some men to try and finish the job."

"I hope so," he said fervently. "We owe that bitch a few more bodies."

I did not know what to say, nodding instead before turning to enter the office.

"Primus Pilus," Vellusius called out. I looked back to see him fidgeting. "I know he was just a slave, and I didn't know him all that well, but that was no way for anyone to die. I mean it. That bitch owes the gods a blood debt for putting someone who hadn't done a thing to her through something like that."

I was touched at Vellusius' obvious sincerity, and I thanked him, assuring him that if we got the chance we would make amends in Eumenis' name, then entered the office. Scribonius and Balbus were there, sitting while Diocles stood beside the table on which Eumenis' body had been placed, the Centurions watching as Diocles washed the corpse. Agis was assisting, both of them crying as they worked. Despite the absence of tears in the Centurions' eyes, their expressions were suitably grim.

Scribonius turned to me, shaking his head. "I had begun to think that she'd forgotten about the whole thing."

"I'm glad I listened to Miriam this time," I replied, recounting the conversation where she had warned me to continue to be on guard.

He was clearly impressed, admitting that he had not thought of it in that way, and despite the gravity of the situation, I grinned. "See, women are good for more than just scratching an itch."

Balbus gave a grunt that we had learned signaled his disagreement, but I was in no mood to argue the point. Turning my attention to Diocles, I stood behind him, placing a hand on his shoulder. I could feel him trembling, though I did not know if it was through grief or anger; I suspect that it was equal parts of both.

"Diocles," I said gently. "I need to talk to you about this."

He did not turn to look at me, but nodded his head. I asked him what he knew of Eumenis and his trips to the market. "Did he use different merchants like he was supposed to?"

Diocles shrugged as he said, "I reminded him every day it was his turn, but I didn't follow him to make sure he was doing as he was told."

I thought I detected a hesitant note in his voice, so I waited to see if there was anything else. He said nothing more, continuing to stroke Eumenis' skin gently, which had turned a purplish hue, with a wet cloth. Out of the corner of my eye, I noticed Agis staring at Diocles, his lips moving and I turned suddenly, clearly catching him by surprise. The young slave's face reddened as he turned his eyes immediately downward, but I was not going to be deterred.

"Agis," I said sternly. "What do you know?"

While Eumenis was physically the clumsiest, and when compared to Diocles was slow-witted, Agis made Eumenis look like a combination of Homer and Achilles in comparison. He also had a severe stutter, which was exacerbated whenever he was under stress, and he certainly was at this moment. In truth, I would have sold him long before this, but he had an endearing sincerity and earnestness that softened my heart, while the tasks he had to perform were sufficiently low-level that he took up enough of the drudge work by which he earned his daily bread and place to sleep. I knew that he was saving to purchase his freedom, since he had not been captured in war, but had been sold by an impoverished family, the youngest of many children, a not uncommon fate for poor people not lucky enough to be born Roman citizens.

"M-m-master, I-I-I d-d-d-don't k-k-know . . ." he began before I cut him off.

I turned to Diocles to ask him, "Do you really want to put Agis through this?"

Diocles sighed, shaking his head as he laid the cloth down. He turned around to face me, his eyes red and swollen, and I could see the guilt in them.

Before he spoke, I told him quietly, "Diocles, it's not your fault. The fault lies on my shoulders because I allowed this to happen."

"But it was my idea," he replied.

I shook my head, not wanting him to feel the burden of a man's death, as I had so many times in the past. "No, I would have thought of it in time. You just came up with the idea first, but I assure you, it would have occurred to me as well. And," I did not want to speak ill of Eumenis, but I felt it had to be said, "if Eumenis didn't obey his instructions, he has to bear some of the burden of this as well."

"I think he's bearing all of the burden," Diocles burst out bitterly, and this I could not argue.

Turning back to the question, I asked him again.

He bowed his head, closing his eyes before saying quietly, "I didn't know for sure, but I had my suspicions and this confirmed them. He had been talking about a girl he met at the market, a slave girl that worked for one of the merchants that he swore he didn't shop at every time it was his turn, but that he would stop and talk with."

Something about this did not sound right; I found it very unusual that a master would let one of his slaves have enough leisure time to hang about a market stall to talk to other slaves. Immediately after that thought hit me, I was forced to admit that the number of ways that slaves can wriggle out of work to steal some moments where they can act as if they are not slaves are too numerous to count, so I supposed it was not as unusual as it sounded.

"Do you know which merchant it was? Or the girl's name?"

"I-i-iras," Agis spoke up, saying the name with some difficulty, but the name was clearly recognizable enough that Scribonius and I exchanged a look.

That was an Egyptian name, which could mean nothing; somehow, I think we both sensed that it was not a coincidence. Diocles thought about it for a moment before coming up with the name of the merchant, Deukalos as I recall, and where his stall was located. I patted him on the shoulder, then went to sit with Scribonius and Balbus.

"It looks like we have a merchant to visit," Scribonius said grimly.

Turning to Balbus I told him, "This is the time."

He gave me a quizzical glance, not taking my meaning.

I had to fight back a grin as I told him what I meant. "This is the time when you get to make someone's ball sac into a purse."

The thought seemed to cheer him greatly while we made plans to go visit the merchant Deukalos.

After talking it over, we decided it was best that we not descend on Deukalos at his stall, since there would be too many witnesses and more importantly would likely tip anyone watching for Cleopatra that we were onto her. The first job was to follow the merchant to his home, go in at night, then snatch him, taking him someplace where we could question him. This had to be done without any chance of word leaking back to Antonius, meaning that the group involved was very, very small. We chose Gaius to be the man to tail Deukalos, since he was still sufficiently fresh-faced and unassuming, enabling him to wander about the market area in tunic and Legionary's belt, appearing to just be a man on off duty time. Immediately upon locating the merchant's home, he would come back, where we would be waiting for darkness to fall, for the team of men that were to snatch Deukalos. We would then be guided by Gaius to the house, whereupon we would slip in and take him. I split the men into two teams, one to get Deukalos, the other to search the slave quarters for the woman Iras, despite none of us expecting to find her, since after discussing it, we were sure that she was no more a slave than any of us were. Still, on the slight chance that she was, we would take her as well, if we found her.

I sent Balbus in search of an appropriate spot for us to conduct our questioning, and he returned shortly before dusk with the location of an abandoned building outside the city walls that had apparently been a farm and was relatively isolated. Shortly after Balbus' return, Gaius arrived with his part of the mission complete, describing the house, which sounded as if it would pose no problems. As Centurions, we had the freedom to come and go out of the camp at any time of the day or night without requiring any pass from a superior officer, but the rankers in our party, consisting of Vellusius, Herennius and, over my initial objections, Gaius, would require a written pass. I occupied myself with writing these out while we waited for it to be time to set out. Ideally, we would have left during the third watch, since we would not be striking the house until we were sure the occupants were asleep for the night. However, the sight of men leaving the camp so late, even with signed passes or being of Centurion rank, would arouse suspicion.

Therefore, we left in two parties, starting with Gaius and his companions talking excitedly about the night on the town they were about to enjoy, joking with the guards on duty, who looked on enviously at their counterparts as they swaggered off. Scribonius, Balbus, and I were following not far behind, while I was carrying a sack in which were our swords, rope, and material for gags. Along with these were some implements that Balbus had in his possession that I had decided I did not want to know much about. All the weapons were wrapped in the sacks we would use for our kidnapped subjects so that the blades would not bump together and make that distinctive clinking sound that any military man would recognize. Naturally, the bag was heavy, which was why I was carrying it. Following the men, we all went to the apartment, where Miriam was still awake, her eyes reddened and puffy. Kaeso did a good job cleaning and there was no sign of Eumenis' demise left, but her gaze seemed as if it were pinned to that spot as she sat at the table. She did not ask any questions, just watching as we took pieces of charcoal from the edge of the hearth with which to blacken our faces and exposed skin. I was sure she knew what we were about to do, but if she had any objections, she did not raise them then, or later. I think a part of her thirsted for vengeance, the need overcoming her fear and concern for me or the rest of the men.

We sat sipping watered wine while we waited, one of us popping our head out to judge the passing of time by the moon, which fortunately was only a quarter full that night. Taking Miriam into the bedchamber to bid her good night, she clung tightly to me, forcing me to pull gently away.

"Try to get some sleep," I told her.

She sat on the edge of the bed, looking up at me, but shook her head. "I will not be able to sleep until you come home."

"I might be gone all night," I warned her.

"Then I will be up waiting for you."

That did not make me feel better, but I also knew there was no point in arguing. Instead, I kissed her, then left the room. The men were ready and waiting; I took a moment to go over our plan one more time before we left the apartment, heading for Deukalos' house.

Ephesus is a port city, the largest in the area as it is the provincial capital. Because of its location near the Hellespont and straits leading into the Euxine Sea, it is a city where people are up and about at all watches. As usual, this is a blade that cuts both ways. It allowed us to move freely without arousing too much suspicion, since we were not the only people out on the streets, yet it meant the chances of being seen carrying one, and possibly two bodies was that much greater. Gaius led the way, and as we got closer to the merchant's house, the streets became almost deserted, there being no wineshops or whorehouses in this area, the usual nighttime attractions that brought people out. He stopped across from a well-built house, surrounded by a low wall that I could see over, although Scribonius was the only other man who could. Taking a good look about, I saw no movement in the yard, which was a substantial size. There was a low outbuilding with shuttered windows that I assumed were the slave quarters, with another directly across that, judging by the smell, was a stable. A wagon was hard against the stable, while barrels of various sizes lined the rest of the wall of the stable. All in all, it was a tidy yard, without any objects over which we might trip, though in the dim light it was impossible to say that with any certainty.

We took a moment to cover ourselves with the charcoal, then I quietly opened the sack to distribute the weapons. Inevitably, there was sound, which on a dark and quiet night sounded loud enough to wake the dead, despite knowing from experience that this was mostly in our minds. Scribonius was leading the team that would search the slave quarters for the woman named Iras, while I would lead Balbus and Gaius to find Deukalos. It was the one demand I made, that Gaius would be with me since this was his first such type of operation, working in the dark and outside the rules of the army, since what we were doing was highly illegal. I had not made any inquiry into whether Deukalos was a Roman citizen, partially because I did not want possibly to alert the *Praetor* of the province, where those records are kept. The other, and probably the more powerful reason was because I knew that if he were a citizen, this would make what we were doing an even higher crime and I did not want to knowingly endanger the men involved any more than I had to. Thin porridge for an excuse, I know, but it was all I had. One at a time, starting with me, we vaulted over the wall, each man landing with a soft thud, pausing for a moment to listen. The air was still, the only sound that of the harsh breathing around me. After waiting a moment, I gave the signal to begin, both teams moving quietly towards their target.

Fortunately, the house was a Roman style villa. In fact, it was almost identical to the one belonging to Uncle Tiberius in Damascus, so I was fairly certain I knew where to go. There were no lamps lit, as of course some people do so that if they have to go to the privy at night, they do not trip and bash their head, and I had to bite my lip to keep from cursing. I was hoping that the occupants would be people like that, but evidently their fear of fire was greater than the fear of the dark, making me stop for a moment while closing my eyes, both to let my eyes adjust to the deeper gloom of the villa and to let my ears do the work. I heard a shuffling sound behind me, then I was bumped from behind. Putting my hand out, grabbing quickly to stop whoever it was that was advancing blindly, I gripped an arm, telling from the musculature that it was Gaius. Knowing what was coming, I moved my hand up to clamp it over his mouth before he could utter the whispered apology. I felt his mouth open under my hand, which I squeezed shut, reminding myself to talk to Gaius about this moment, then opened my eyes wide to peer into the darkness. I could just make out vague shapes that I assumed were couches and chairs arranged around the outer edge of the atrium, the opening in the center above the only real source of light. Taking a deep breath, I stepped from the atrium, carefully moving my foot ahead of me, wishing that I had remembered to wrap my boots in rags so the hobnails would not make any noise. Moving slowly, I felt Gaius' hand grabbing onto the back of my belt while I made my way out of the atrium, moving down the short hallway that I hoped led into the sleeping chamber of the merchant. At the end of the hallway, I reached out, expecting a door, but my hand only waved open air. Confused, I took another step forward, squinting in the gloom to try and understand where I was. I could barely make out the arrangement of couches and low tables, then I realized we were in the *triclinium*, and I sucked in my breath. I had been wrong; while the house was laid out in the same manner as Uncle Tiberius' villa, it was reversed, so that the bedroom was on the other side. Turning around slowly, I exhaled before leaning forward to whisper to Gaius that we needed to reverse our course. This was a bad business, since the likelihood of one of us tripping or bumping into one another and knocking us all off balance was extremely high.

Somehow, we managed to negotiate the change of direction and I squeezed past Gaius and Balbus, their breath rank with the high nerves of the moment. Moving back out into the atrium, I headed in the opposite direction. Since we had already passed through once I was able to move a bit more quickly, although Gaius still clutched at my belt. I knew time was growing short; I expected at any moment some sort of alarm or commotion to come from the slaves' quarters, simply because there were more slaves and hence more people to control. I had considered sending Balbus with Scribonius to handle the larger numbers, but I was also somewhat expecting that Deukalos would have a guard somewhere in the house. Usually, these men are hired from the ranks of former gladiators, while sometimes they are former Legionaries, and this was the reason I kept Balbus with us. Making it through the atrium again, I began moving up the hallway that I could now see was to the bedroom, where the blackness was absolute, signaling that there was indeed a door blocking the light that would come from the windows in the bedroom. Holding onto one wall, I was moving my foot forward when two things happened, although I am not sure which occurred first, or if it was simultaneous. There was a shout from the direction of the slaves' quarters, shattering the stillness, just as my foot struck something soft and yielding that immediately reacted to the touch with a jerk of movement and a muffled exclamation. I barely had a moment in which to react to the sudden disturbance of air, the movement that caused it more sensed than seen. However, the sudden slamming of a wildly aimed fist that landed squarely on my shoulder, numbing my entire left arm and sending stabs of pain shooting through my body was very real. I reeled backwards into Gaius, knocking him off balance and I heard him careen into Balbus, one of them letting out an explosive grunt that coincided with the same sound from my attacker as he followed up his punch by slamming his body into me. I could tell that he was smaller than I was, my size keeping me from keeling over backwards, though he was very strong. One hand groped for a purchase on what he thought would be a tunic but was instead my armor, while the other reached out, trying to claw me in the eyes. Not surprisingly, he misjudged my height, yet that was actually worse as his hand found my throat, vulnerable because I had not tucked my chin down quickly enough. While he was trying this, I reached down for my dagger, thinking to end this quickly with a thrust to his body. Somehow, he sensed my purpose because he released his grip on my armor, whipping his hand down to grab my forearm in a crushing grip, clearly intent on stopping me from pulling my weapon. All this took the span of a dozen heartbeats, while I could hear Gaius and Balbus struggling to their feet, telling me I was still on my own. We continued to wrestle, both of us endowed with the desperate courage that comes from the knowledge that the next few panting breaths could be our last.

Behind my opponent, down the hallway and emanating from the bedchamber, I heard cries of alarm, so I knew that time was slipping away. If this Deukalos had his wits about him, he could very likely escape through the window. It was this idea that decided my next move, as I whipped my head forward, striking blindly at where I thought the other man's head would be. I guessed correctly, stars exploding in my head with the impact, but I was rewarded with the crunching sound of gristle as the man's nose was squashed flat against his face. His grip loosened as he let out a howl of pain, giving me all the opening I needed, jerking my arm from his grasp to draw the dagger and bringing it up in one motion, feeling it punch deep into his side. His breath left his body, washing me in the odor of garlic, wine, and garum as he fell to his knees. Surprisingly he did not let out a scream, emitting more of a low, despairing moan when I wrenched the blade free, feeling the warmth I knew was his blood spurt onto my hand. Without waiting, I moved past the inert body of the guard, reaching out to feel the door. The instant my hand touched the wood, I lowered my shoulder, smashing it open, the door swinging to slam into the wall, making the loudest sound to this moment, even causing me to jump in surprise. It took a heartbeat to make out the scene before me, but I quickly saw that the window shutters were open and I could make out a dark bulk trying to climb out of the window. Moving as swiftly as I could, I crossed the room in two or three strides, reaching out to grab hold of the fabric clothing the body of the person trying to escape. There was a surprised yelp when I yanked backwards to pull the person down out of the window frame, but there was only a ripping sound as the gown came away in my hand. Now that the person was naked, I could see that it was a man, an enormously fat man, whose legs were scrabbling for purchase on the wall as he continued trying desperately to get away. There was no way to get a good purchase on bare skin, so I pulled out my sword, pressing the point of it directly into the fat man's rear end. Immediately the legs stopped working, his body sagging back into the room. I became aware that someone was standing next to me, their breathing harsh from the excitement and exertion.

"Deukalos the merchant?"

I now saw no point in keeping quiet, my voice rasping from the effects of a hand being on my windpipe just moments before. There was no immediate answer. Pressing the sword a little harder, I was rewarded by a whimper of pain.

Finally, a surprisingly high voice answered in Greek, "No, you have the wrong man!"

"Really?"

I sounded surprised, but said over my shoulder to Balbus and Gaius, "Kill everyone in the house."

"No!"

As I expected, the threat to his family and slaves was more than enough, while I was just happy that I did not have to carry it out.

In a defeated voice, he said, "Yes, I am Deukalos. What do you want with me?"

"I think you know," was my only answer.

I directed Balbus and Gaius to tie the fat merchant up before putting him in the sack, which was yet another problem. After he was trussed and a gag stuck in his mouth, Balbus and Gaius tried to stuff him in the sack, except that it became clear very quickly that it was not big enough. Cursing bitterly, I directed one of the others to light a lamp so that we could look around to find something suitable to use as a substitute.

A moment later, the lamp came guttering to life, its flickering light seeming bright as the sun after the total darkness in which we had just been immersed. That is when I became aware that there was another person present, and I looked over to the bed to see a smallish figure with the sheets pulled up to the chin, while Gaius stood gaping open-mouthed, sword in hand. I walked over, seeing the long, tousled black hair and a set of enormous eyes, the only part of her face visible, peering up as they darted from Gaius to me. Gently reaching down, I pulled the sheet away from her face, and there was a collective gasp from all of us in the room. The girl was a rare beauty, with the kind of face that made men stop and stare, and I was sorely tempted to pull the sheet down further to see if her figure matched the promises of the full lips. They were slightly parted and moist as she was shallowly panting in obvious fear. Fortunately, or unfortunately, I am not sure which, the thought of Miriam suddenly chose that moment to force its way to the front of my brain, so I refrained.

As if reading my thoughts, Gaius said helpfully, "We need that sheet to wrap him up. Should I take it?"

I glared at him. Even in the dim light from a single lamp, I could see his face redden, and he became defensive. "We need something to wrap his fat ass in," he protested.

"Fine," I snapped.

His hand was a blur of motion as he whipped the sheet away from the girl, who gave a frightened shriek, trying to cover herself with her hands. I will not deny that given the opportunity, I got an eyeful, and her figure matched the face in perfect harmony. It was immediately clear why the fat merchant had this girl as a bedmate. I searched about for a gown to give to the girl, except that I did not move particularly quickly. Finding what looked like a woman's garment in a cupboard, I pulled it out, throwing it to her and telling her to put it on. She had not spoken a word, but she clearly understood what I wanted, since she put the gown on. It swallowed her up, clearly much larger than her frame required. The meaning of that hit us all immediately, and we began laughing.

"It seems that our merchant here is having someone keep the bed warm while the wife is away somewhere." Balbus poked the fat man with the tip of his sword, whose eyes were rolling about in obvious fear, sweat pouring down his body despite the coolness of the evening.

Deukalos tried to speak, but his words were muffled by the gag, though none of us were interested in hearing whatever excuse he had for this young bedmate. There was a commotion down the hallway, so to be safe I signaled Gaius to stand off to the side while I turned to face the door.

"All clear?"

I recognized Scribonius' voice, and I replied that it was safe for him to come in. He entered the room, a long livid scratch down one side of his face.

"Run into a cat?" I teased, but he was not amused.

"Something like that," he replied grimly before telling me that the slaves' quarters were secure.

"And?"

He shook his head. "No Iras."

I had not really been expecting to find her, but it was still disappointing nonetheless and I cursed bitterly.

"Uncle?"

I turned, about to bite Gaius' head off for calling out a name, even if it was not my given name, but he gave me a warning look as he approached.

Leaning close, he whispered into my ear, "I think that Iras is right here."

It turned out that Gaius was right. Not surprisingly, he only had eyes for the girl, meaning that he was watching her when her name was mentioned. He said that her eyes widened as she shot a glance at the fat merchant, a look that Gaius naturally followed, to see the merchant staring at her, shaking his head in a clear warning. This was confirmed a moment later by the merchant himself, albeit with the gentle persuasion of again having the tip of a sword placed in a very sensitive area of the male body. That mystery solved, we wrapped the merchant in the sheet, tying the ends into a knot to make a makeshift sack, then between Scribonius, Balbus, and Gaius, they managed to half-drag, half-carry the bulky object, after being rendered unconscious, of course, down the hallway and out into the yard. I had the girl by the arm, trying to concentrate on the job and not the sweet scent of her young body, which was a challenge. I also became aware that she seemed to walk more slowly than need be, so that I naturally bumped against her. It might have been my imagination, but I was fairly sure that she was trying to press her body against me, and it seemed to take a long time to navigate our way out of the house. We returned to the yard, Deukalos' inert form now lying in a lump on the dirt, the others panting for breath from the exertion of carrying him just the short distance out of the house.

"There's no way we're going to be able to carry this piece of *cac* all the way to that farm," Balbus said.

I looked about, seeing nothing useful, knowing the wagon was too large and bulky, and would take too long to hitch it up, not to mention the noise created in doing so. Turning to Gaius, I told him to go to the stable to look for a cart that was able to carry the fat man. Returning my attention to Iras, she seemed eerily calm as she looked up at me. To my astonishment, I could see her smiling up at me in the gloom, then felt the press of her body, which was not my imagination. The others noticed this as well, and I heard Balbus chuckle.

"It looks like Miriam has some competition." Scribonius seemed as amused as Balbus, but the mention of Miriam's name was like a dash of cold water, and I pushed her away from me with a shake of my head.

Immediately, her demeanor changed and I felt her arm go rigid in my hand, the hatred in her glare clear even in the darkness of the night as she spat on the ground, making her contempt plain, still without speaking a word.

"Seems we've just seen the true Iras," Scribonius commented wryly.

I do not know why, but it made me feel better seeing her act this way. Perhaps it was because I knew that I was going to kill her in the near future.

Gaius returned with a pushcart just big enough to fit the merchant, who was still unconscious, and he was hauled into the bed, the wood of the cart creaking in protest at the weight. Iras was bound and gagged, still spitting defiance and hatred. At first, she refused to accept the gag, until I pressed a dagger to her throat. She was thrown into a sack, with room to spare, Gaius charged with carrying her. Scribonius gave a low whistle, whereupon Vellusius and Herennius came trotting from the slaves' quarters where they had been guarding the occupants. I grabbed Vellusius by the arm, giving him an inquiring glance, which he understood immediately.

To my relief, he shook his head. "They're all alive," he said. "A couple were a little roughed up, but the bruises will heal." He grinned. "Now, how they manage to untie themselves is another matter, but I don't think they'll starve to death."

With that off my mind, we opened the gate and, pushing the cart, our party left the villa, headed for the city gate and the farmhouse. The next obstacle was getting past the city guard, but I had enough gold denarii in my purse to make that no problem at all, and we passed easily out of the city. While we walked along, I felt a tug on my arm, turning to see Balbus, his expression grim, made more so by the pale light.

"Titus, there's something you should know," he said before pressing something into my hand.

I felt the cool metal of a round disc in my palm, and while it was too dark to examine closely, I knew what it was immediately. What Balbus had pressed into my hand was the metal token that a retiring Legionary is given, inscribed with his name and the identity of the Legion from which he retired, usually worn by men on a leather thong around the neck. There is one dangling from my own neck as I dictate this, and that night, I felt a creeping dread when I asked Balbus where he had gotten it, despite already knowing the answer.

"From around the neck of the guard that you killed," he confirmed, my heart sinking.

"What Legion?" I asked.

"3rd Gallica," he said flatly.

He was a man who had retired just a few months before. I swallowed hard, debating whether to ask the next logical question.

Finally, I could not stop myself. "Did we know him?"

I saw his head nod, giving the name of a man from the ranks, well known as a good fighter but heavy drinker, one of those men who had spent most of his bonus money on debauching, meaning he had to work because of his fondness for Bacchus. I closed my eyes, saying a brief prayer for the man, mentally chalking another debt up to Cleopatra, whom I blamed for all that we were doing this night. We passed the rest of the way in silence, reaching the farmhouse a short while later. It was obviously derelict, weeds growing up in the yard and all around the buildings. One of the others pushed the door open, the leather hinges cracking with the movement, whereupon the door fell away with a loud thump that startled all of us, causing some nervous laughter. Balbus and Vellusius produced a couple of lamps that they had taken from the merchant's house, and in a moment the inside of the house was illuminated, revealing a dusty, dirty single room that was not dissimilar from the home where I had grown up, even if quite a bit smaller.

Vellusius, Herennius and Gaius came in grunting and groaning, dragging the sheet containing Deukalos. I directed them to open the sheet, then place the fat merchant on a chair that was next to a table. Like the cart, the *numen* of the chair did not appreciate the sudden burden, squeaking in protest at the weight. For a moment, I thought it would collapse, but somehow it held up. While Deukalos was being strapped to the chair, Balbus rounded up some charcoal and wood to feed into the discarded brazier, which was soon heating up nicely.

Balbus retrieved his tools, placing them on the grill of the brazier to heat up. With this happening, we took another chair, placing Iras on it, a short distance away from Deukalos, but where she could see what was about to happen to him. She came out of the bag the same way she had gone in, spitting hatred and bile, but when she saw what was about to take place, the fear in her eyes was plain to see, causing her to subside in her struggles. Once all was ready, Balbus, apparently determined to be the man who did the dirty work, walked over, slapping Deukalos, starting with gentle smacks across his fat cheeks, making his jowls quiver. When these had no effect, he increased the force, until the merchant's head began to bob and he moaned his way back to consciousness. Finally lifting his head, he opened his eyes, blinking blearily as he looked around. It took a moment for his situation to become apparent to him, his breathing immediately increasing rapidly, and it was as if an invisible wellspring suddenly started from the top of his head, sweat quickly pouring down his fat, naked body, making it glisten like a roasting bird in the dancing light, which, I suppose, was appropriate, since his goose was plucked and cooked. I nodded to Balbus to begin the questioning.

It did not take much persuasion to get Deukalos to talk. Something I have noticed over the years is that very fat men do not seem to have much tolerance for pain or even discomfort, and I have often wondered why that is. Just the sight of the glowing red blade of one of Balbus' implements got him babbling, but as he spoke Greek, which only Scribonius and I understood, making it so that we were also the ones who asked the questions, translating the answers for the others.

"I was approached by one of Cleopatra's people," he told us. "He offered me a small fortune if I would allow Iras to work in my stall."

He looked over at the girl, who was glaring at him over her gag, her head tossing as she still tried to spit curses through the cloth.

I gave Vellusius a nod, who gave her a gentle cuff on the head, telling her, "Quiet, girl. You'll get your chance to talk soon enough."

I turned back to Deukalos, whose eyes were rolling in his head, his gaze constantly shifting from me to Balbus, who was continually stoking the brazier to keep his tools hot should they be needed. Blood trickled down the fat merchant's lip and nose from where Balbus had slapped him a few times to loosen his tongue.

However, he was apparently unwilling to divulge everything, saying, "But I did not know what she was doing there, I swear it on all the gods! I thought Cleopatra had put her there to keep an eye on another merchant for some reason."

I laughed at this, but it was not a pleasant one, shaking my head at this nonsense. "What would Cleopatra care about what some merchant in the market at Ephesus is doing? No, you did not become so obviously successful by being a fool, Deukalos. And I see that you're not blind ... yet," I added menacingly, gratified to see the ripples passing through his blubbery flesh at the threat. "No, all you had to do was watch her and know that she had made my man her target."

He shook his head wildly, still not ready to give in all the way. "I swear I did not know!"

I motioned to Balbus, who looked at the merchant impassively for a moment, as if considering something, then he turned to pick up another tool, this one a straight thin rod with a wooden handle, with a wicked looking hook at the end that came to an obviously sharp point. It was glowing red, and it was easy to see the air around it shimmering with the heat when Balbus stepped toward the fat man in the chair. Deukalos lost control of his bladder at the sight, the smell of urine filling the air. The men surrounding him mocked his fear, cursing him in disgust at his weakness, while he began babbling incomprehensible words, a mixture of Greek, Latin, and a number of other dialects. Seeing that he was out of his mind with fear, I waved Balbus back, squatting next to Deukalos, waiting for him to regain his senses.

After a moment, I asked, "Are you ready to be completely honest now?"

"Yes! I will tell you whatever you want to hear! Please do not let him hurt me!"

"I don't want to hear anything other than the truth," I told him, patting his sweaty shoulder, causing him to give me a pathetically grateful look.

He swallowed several times, then began speaking again. "I knew that she was up to no good, and I suspected what she had been instructed to do, but I swear that I did not know it was you she was trying to poison!"

He had just given himself away, as I said in apparent puzzlement, "Who said that it was me she was trying to strike?"

I looked at Scribonius, who was regarding Deukalos with a raised eyebrow, instantly picking up the same thing I had and playing along.

"Do you remember hearing me say anything about me being her target?"

Scribonius shook his head. I turned back to look at the quivering mass of flesh before me, who closed his eyes and dropped his head.

Without looking up, he said dully, "I asked your slave who he belonged to the second time he showed up and he told me it was you."

"And knowing that, and knowing what Iras here was up to, you chose not to warn me."

All he could give was a helpless shrug. "And draw the wrath of Cleopatra by betraying her plans for you?" He looked up, giving a sad smile. "With all due respect, Primus Pilus, I think that Cleopatra makes a worse enemy than you."

"And yet, here you are under my control," I pointed out. "Does it seem that she has more power right now?"

"No," he admitted, and despite myself, I felt a flash of sympathy for the man.

He had truly enmeshed himself in a scheme where he was almost guaranteed to draw the enmity of either or both parties. I shook the thought off, reminding myself that he could have simply turned down the offer, and thereby gone on to see another sunrise.

There was something that puzzled me though, so I asked Deukalos, "Why is Iras still with you? Was she part of the deal?"

A strange look passed over the man's face that I could not immediately identify. However, his words clarified why he had the expression. It was guilt, both for what he did and did not do.

"I was supposed to get rid of her after she did what she had been sent to do."

There was no mistaking what was meant; he was not to sell her, he was to kill her. I turned to see Iras' reaction. It was not what I expected, assuming that she would have at least some gratitude to Deukalos for not following through, but her eyes blazed with hatred.

"I could not do it. Look at her! She is the most beautiful creature I have ever laid eyes on."

Iras was now trying to shout something through her gag, ignoring her earlier instruction to remain silent, but I did not bother stopping her, since it was almost time to remove the gag.

"She doesn't seem particularly happy that you showed her such compassion. Maybe you're too heavy to be on top of her," Scribonius commented wryly, evoking laughs from everyone in the room, except Deukalos, of course.

"That was probably not a wise decision," I admonished Deukalos. "You might have gotten away with it, but I suppose your greed for money and other things got the best of you."

I indicated that I was finished with Deukalos. The gag was stuffed back in his mouth then he was dragged, chair and all, into a corner, with considerable effort, of course. Iras' chair was brought to the spot where Deukalos' had been, and I reached down to remove the gag.

Before I did, I asked Iras, "Are you going to try and do something silly like spitting on me?"

She refused to answer, just glaring at me, and I sighed, but took the gag out anyway, jumping aside just in time to miss the stream of spittle that flew from her mouth. I turned to Balbus, who was stepping forward to teach her some manners, stopping him. Instead, I was the one whose hand swung backwards and with a fair amount of force, slapping her once, twice, three times across the face. I took care not to use my fist since that would have knocked her unconscious at the very least, if not worse. Nonetheless, blood spurted from her nose and began to trickle from her lip. After a moment, she began whimpering, her defiance gone at least temporarily, so I stopped my assault.

Now I saw a healthy dose of fear in her eyes as she looked up at me, but there was still defiance when I asked her, "Why are you willing to undergo such pain for someone who had given orders to throw you away like so much trash?"

She did not answer immediately, shaking her head before she began speaking rapidly. I swallowed my irritation, since she had chosen to speak in the Egyptian tongue, of which I knew a little from my time in Alexandria, and I saw that she was trying to convince me that she did not speak either Greek or Latin.

"That's not going to work," I said gently, in Greek. "We questioned Deukalos in Greek and you followed every word perfectly, so don't play with me, girl."

Iras tried to maintain the pretense for a moment, then slumped. She seemed to gather herself; when she looked up, the defiance and hatred had returned.

"Roman, you ask me why I am willing to undergo torture, knowing that I was to give my life? Because it is my duty and my honor to die for Pharaoh! She is Isis! She is a god! You and all Romans are worms under her feet!"

To emphasize the point, she spat again, except this time I was not quite so quick, some of her spittle landing on my feet. I lashed out, this time with a fist, but I was careful to strike her on her arms and legs. She screamed as I pummeled her for the space of several heartbeats before pausing for breath. Now she was sobbing in pain, and normally seeing a young and pretty girl in such distress would have troubled me, but my heart was hardened by her deeds and words. I had expected to hear that she was forced to do this, because of her status as a slave or because Cleopatra and her minions held something like her child and its fate over her head. To hear that she had apparently done this willingly, knowing that she was to die after her part was played, shook me. I was absorbed in these thoughts when she turned her head to look at Deukalos in open contempt.

"But this fat piece of excrement did not do as he was told! He wanted me for himself, he did not care about saving me for anything other than to grunt and sweat all over me. He is disgusting and I piss on him and his ancestors!"

She turned back to face me. "Do with me what you will, Roman. It does not matter because I have been blessed by our priests and I will be waiting in the afterlife to serve Pharaoh whenever she chooses to come to join her subjects."

I had been toying with the idea of keeping Iras alive, bringing her back to camp to put her on display, despite knowing that she could do nothing more than serve as an embarrassment, the word of a slave counting for nothing against a queen. But that would have only been useful, however slightly, if she had been cooperative, which she clearly was not, and in fact, her proud admission of her deed was problematic. Under our law, the only way the confession of a slave is valid is after torture, and what I had done to her would not qualify. Oh, I could have turned Balbus loose and after he was through there would have been no question that she had been properly tortured, but suddenly it did not seem to have any value. As Iras sat there, I waved Scribonius over to a corner to get his thoughts.

"I don't see that bringing her back is going to serve any purpose, and in fact, might make an antagonist out of Antonius," he pointed out. "Truly," he continued, "it would be highly embarrassing for the queen to be confronted with proof that she tried to have a Primus Pilus murdered. But I also think that there's a significant chance that Antonius will be just as angry with you as

Cleopatra will be. And not even Titus Pullus is strong enough to fight both Cleopatra and Antonius."

I looked over at the girl, rubbing my chin. Maybe you are getting soft, I thought, because even as clearly evil as this girl was, there is something about killing a beautiful woman that somehow seems wrong. I sighed, knowing Scribonius was right, so I clapped him on the shoulder, then returned to face Iras. Balbus was looking extremely disappointed, since neither of the subjects had required extensive use of his tools. Seeing this, I decided that I would at least let Balbus tell Deukalos what plans he had for his ball sac, even if I saw no point in carrying it out. If Deukalos had been a harder man, I had every intention of allowing Balbus to fulfill his dream, but alas, the merchant was as soft as mushy porridge in every way. He was sitting over in the corner quietly sobbing, and while Iras had tears streaming from her eyes, it was from the pain I had inflicted on her, and she still looked up at me defiantly, giving no sign that she would ask for mercy. It was probably because she realized that she would not receive it, and I imagine that her faith that she had a spot reserved in the curious version of the afterlife that these Egyptians have gave her the courage she needed. I could respect that, and in that moment I decided that I would kill her quickly, despite what she had done to Eumenis, who had suffered greatly. Her blood would avenge the murder of Eumenis; causing her suffering would not enhance the quality of the vengeance as I saw it.

I leaned down, still careful to stay out of her spitting range, asking her, "You said that your priests have blessed you?"

She swallowed hard, but nodded.

"Do you have any words that you would like to say?"

Iras looked surprised, and there was a flash that I thought might be gratitude in her eyes. She nodded.

"Then say them now, girl," I said grimly.

While she was thusly occupied, I walked over to Balbus, pointing to Deukalos and telling him that he could amuse himself, to a point. He gave me a grin, and turned to walk over to the fat merchant, who began wailing in fear. Returning to the girl, drawing my dagger as I did so, I was interrupted by the sound of a clearing throat. I looked over to see Vellusius, Herennius, and Gaius standing together a short distance from the girl, all of them with a peculiar expression on their faces as they glanced at each other. There was a whispered argument, and I was beginning to get irritated, when Herennius and Gaius, apparently working in concert, shoved Vellusius forward.

"Primus Pilus, me and the boys here were wondering, sir, seeing that we came along and are taking a risk ourselves," he saw my face, prompting him to hasten to add, "not that we aren't happy to do whatever you need us to do. It's just that, it just strikes us as a shame that you're about to do in that tasty bit there, and we were wondering . . ."

His voice trailed off, but I now understood what they were asking, and I was assaulted by a wave of different emotions. A combination of amusement, revulsion, and the gods only know what else washed through me as I considered the request. Rape has never been to my tastes, but I was not blind or deaf to the fact that there were a fair number of men who found it appealing, remembering old Didius, one of the original tentmates of Vellusius, Scribonius and me. While I was not surprised at either Vellusius or Herennius, I was shocked to see Gaius clearly part of the plot, his face a mixture of guilt and interest in my answer.

"Fine," I snapped. "But make it quick."

They played odd man out to see who would go first, and Iras, realizing what was about to happen, began thrashing wildly, moaning with fear as the winner, Gaius as it turned out, approached.

"Please, master," she called to me, every trace of defiance and anger gone, "don't let them defile me in this manner. Just kill me now, I beg you. Please!"

Gaius stopped short, suddenly looking as if he wanted to be somewhere else, but Vellusius and Herennius, both of them old hands at this and accustomed to the begging hysteria of a woman about to be ravaged, just grinned, pushing him forward.

"Go on, boy! She looks ready to give you a ride you won't forget," Herennius called out.

I took a step forward to halt Gaius, both for Iras and for him, somehow knowing that it would relieve both of them, when Iras called out again, saying something that stopped me in my tracks.

"The queen has another plan to strike at you! It's probably happening as we speak!"

Everyone froze in place, while I felt as if an invisible hand gripped my heart and squeezed it. I held up a hand to stop Gaius, but it was not needed.

"What are you talking about?"

My tone was low, but she could not mistake the menace in it, and she visibly flinched.

"I heard her telling Apollodorus that if you discovered that Deukalos was involved, you would do as you have, and that it would be a good time to strike at your woman. She still wants to kill you, but she has learned that you love your woman and wants to hurt you any way you can!"

I stood, mind reeling, trying to make sense of what the girl was saying, but it in fact did not make sense.

"You're saying that Cleopatra said this in your presence?" I asked, to which she nodded, and I was about to turn away to let Gaius resume what he and the others planned, sure that she was lying.

"She wouldn't tell Apollodorus something like that in front of the person who's going to carry out her poisoning attempt, for the very reason that you're sitting here now. She wouldn't take that risk," I said over my shoulder.

"She would if she thought I was going to be dead," she said quietly.

I looked quickly to Scribonius, who gave me a grim nod.

"That's true," Balbus spoke up from where he had stopped before doing whatever he had planned to do to Deukalos, who had momentarily stopped his constant moaning, as arrested by the words of the girl as the rest of us, it seemed. Gaius looked stricken, and for the space of several heartbeats, none of us moved before Scribonius' voice broke the spell.

"Who's on guard at the apartment right now?" he asked Vellusius.

"Kaeso, Cornelius, and Secundus," Vellusius answered, which made me feel a bit better, since they were all hard-bitten veterans. The question answered, I called to the others.

"We need to go, now."

I pointed to Iras, directing that she be rebound, gagged, and thrown back in the sack. "If you're lying," I warned her, "I'm going to let my whole Cohort have you. We won't have to cut your throat by the time we're through."

She looked extremely frightened, but before the gag was stuffed in her mouth, she assured me that she was telling the truth, and suddenly I believed her. Turning to Balbus, I told him to finish Deukalos, not needing to tell him that it had to be done quickly. In a couple of strides, Balbus crossed to the fat merchant, who had resumed his moaning, and with a quick, practiced motion, cut the man's throat. Blood sprayed from the gaping wound, but Balbus had done this often and jumped aside to avoid the splatter. In just a few moments after Iras had uttered the words, we left the farmhouse, and with the girl slung over Gaius' shoulder, we were running back towards the city.

We heard the fighting before we came within sight of the apartment, about two or three blocks away. All of us were panting for breath, while my legs were on fire, but I was powered by the fear that we would arrive too late, making me merciless with the others as well, though they needed no urging. Despite the late time of night, now just a couple thirds of a watch before dawn, people had been awakened by the noise, coming out of their homes to try and see what was happening in the gloom. Nearing the apartment, the crowds grew thicker, and we had to shove people aside, which I did without breaking stride. Ignoring the cries of alarm and pain as people of all ages and sizes were sent flying, we turned the corner onto the street where the apartment was located to a scene illuminated by torches that had apparently been brought by the assault force. There was a group of men, dressed in a motley assortment of castoff armor, most of it leather while some had mail shirts similar to ours, carrying a similar collection of weapons. A number of the attacking party were already on the ground, but there were still more than fifteen men left, and they were pressing the three Legionaries, who were standing shoulder to shoulder with their back to the doorway into the building to prevent any attempt to circle behind them. Taking this in and seeing that the men at the apartment were not in immediate danger of being overwhelmed, I snapped an order to Balbus, who took Herennius and Vellusius back to make a wide circle down the street, across an alley, then back up the street on the far side so that they could hit the attackers on the left flank. While we waited for Balbus to get into position, I ignored the people who understandably gave us a wide space, directing Gaius to wait, which he did not like one bit.

"I need you to keep hold of what's in that sack," I said patiently, despite not feeling that way.

I gave a jerk of the head to indicate the people gathered a short distance away, most of them still dressed in their nightclothes, jaws agape at the battle taking place in front of them.

"I don't want any of these bastards making off with it while we're taking care of that bunch."

He nodded, but said nothing, then I heard Balbus' whistle. I turned to Scribonius as I drew my Gallic blade, taking comfort in the feel of the handle that had been worn to fit exactly the shape of my hand.

"Let's give 'em a surprise," I said, catching Scribonius' grin before we turned to rush into the melee.

Our attack from both sides achieved just that, since these men were not of a high quality as soldiers. They had not posted men as a rearguard, apparently completely confident that any hope of rescue for the men guarding the apartment was so minimal that it did not warrant one. Intent on trying to force their way into the apartment, every man was facing the three Legionaries who, despite not having shields, were keeping the attackers at swords' length simply by being better with their blades than their opponents. The shouts of the attacking force turned to cries of alarm as the men on either flanks found themselves under assault. I picked a swarthy, squat man in a leather cuirass armed with a sword that would have been useful from the back of a horse, but was worse than useless in a close-quarters fight. He whirled when I was just a couple of steps away, trying to bring his blade up and around. He was too slow and too late, the point of my finer Gallic sword punching through the leather cuirass as if were not there. I struck with such force that I made the *tiro's* mistake of burying the blade too deeply, it lodging in the backbone of its victim, who was now hanging dead on the end of my sword. I tried to wrench the blade free, it finally coming out on the third attempt, giving the man next to him just enough time to take a swing at me with a club studded with spikes. He could have bashed my brains in, since none of us were wearing our helmets, but his aim was terrible, striking a glancing blow off my shoulder instead, just under the edge of my tunic, one of the spikes digging a bloody chunk of flesh out of my left arm. I roared with the pain, bashing the wielder of the club in the face with the pommel of my sword, the few teeth he had left splintering in his mouth while I was sprayed with blood. The man fell as if all the bones in his body had disintegrated instead of just his teeth, while I turned my attention to the next attacker in my line of vision.

Scribonius was fighting a man who was surprisingly skilled, but I could see my friend was not hard pressed. Pushing forward, I noted that Balbus was making similar progress, his blade making short, economical thrusts that inevitably scored. My feet slipped a bit, and I realized that it was because the blood was flowing freely, the rich, coppery smell filling my nostrils, some of it my own. The attack had disintegrated; now men were just concerned with escaping with their lives, but there was no mercy to be had at our hands this night, all of us chopping the men down before they could escape. Almost as quickly as our counterattack had started it was over, with 25 men lying dead in the street, after we finished off the wounded of course, surrounded by gaping citizens of Ephesus who seemed rooted in their spot, clearly shocked by the sudden violence and brutal efficiency of what Roman Legionaries can do. Standing there, catching our breath and taking stock, I thought that the reaction was understandable, it being highly unlikely that any of these city dwellers had ever seen a Roman Legion in action.

"Is that the best that bitch could send for us?"

Kaeso spat on one of the corpses, evidently the leader and as a result the first to fall, a former gladiator from the look of his broken, battered face and scarred body, now marred by the gaping wound in his side from which blood still leaked, adding to the pool collecting on the paving stones about him. Kaeso was slightly wounded with a cut up his left arm, which normally would have been protected by his shield. Cornelius was unmarked, his sword bloodied to the hilt, while Secundus had a serious stab wound to his thigh. Fortunately, while bleeding freely, it was not spurting bright red, which would be a sign that the major vessel in the thigh was severed. Cornelius helped him bind up the wound and I asked Kaeso what happened.

"The bastards came roaring up the street," he reported, pointing down the avenue that led past one side of the apartment building. "Oh, it was a bit hot for a few moments, until Secundus came from the back. Cornelius was here right away." He pointed to the overhanging wooden balcony that overhung the front of the doorway. "He dropped down on them from his spot on the roof, and they never knew what hit them."

I surveyed the bloody mess before me, then heard the cries of the city watch, which apparently had finally been roused out of their barracks, as they drew closer. Now that the fighting had stopped, they could not easily follow the sound, so I was sure they were now wandering about trying to find the site of this disturbance, undoubtedly cursing whoever dared to rouse them from their comfort. Without waiting for me to tell him, Scribonius directed Herennius and Vellusius to help him disperse the crowd, which not surprisingly, did not need any urging to flee back into their homes. I debated what to do; there would undoubtedly be some questions from the commander of the city guard, while it was possible that the *Praetor* would be roused to be told that a small battle had taken place in his city. I cocked an ear for the city guard, relieved to hear that their cries seemed to be receding as they wandered around the streets of the city. That gave us more time, but I could not take the chance of being found with the gory evidence at my feet. I called Balbus over, telling him what needed to be done. His face, spattered with blood that was not his, reflected his doubt, yet he moved quickly and in moments we were all very busy, our work for the night not quite done.

The dead men were dragged into the nearby alley, along with the various bits and pieces that had been separated from their bodies, but there was still a huge dark mass of blood and gore spattered on the paving stones. Directing Gaius, Vellusius, and Herennius to scrounge some buckets and go to the nearby public fountain, we tried to wash the blood away, while I kept my ears and eyes open for the sounds of the city watch.

They had drawn nearer, the sound growing louder as they continued their search for the disturbance. After a few bucketfuls of water, it was clear that it would not be enough to disguise the signs of a fight completely, even with the darkness, the spot still clearly showing up black in the night. However, the gods were with us, because after more searching the city watch clearly gave up, their clomping feet and shouts receding back in the direction from which they had come. Once it was clear that the immediate danger was over, my thoughts turned back to what had brought us to that point, and what we should do about it. I had Iras, who was still alive, but would not be much longer, and I had the bodies of the men who were hired, probably by Apollodorus since I did not see Cleopatra dirtying her hands, to try and kill Miriam. I wondered how I could use these to send a message to Cleopatra. Turning to Scribonius, I gave him my idea, and I cannot say that he took it well.

"Are you out of your mind?" is how I believe he put it, though I do not remember his exact words.

"Why?"

I know I sounded defensive, yet I had thought it was a good idea.

My friend sighed, looking at me with what looked dangerously close to pity. "Why do you insist on continuing to try and antagonize this woman? Isn't it enough that you and Miriam are alive? Why can't that be enough?"

"But how else do I convince her that she needs to stop?"

For once, I had brought up something Scribonius had obviously not considered, and he rubbed his chin as he thought.

"I don't know," he finally admitted, frowning at my whoop of triumph that I had come up with something he had not. Still, he was not convinced. "I don't think that dumping a pile of bodies in front of her door is the way to do it, though."

"I need to do something," I argued.

"That's true." He nodded. "I can see that. I was thinking of something a bit more…subtle than what you had in mind."

I gave a snort, not wanting to hear about anything subtle. It was one thing to try and kill me, but when she sent the scum lying there in the alley after Miriam, that had enraged me more than any attempt on my life could. Now, I wanted to show my contempt for the queen of Egypt. Although I must say that there was a tiny, small voice of caution that knew that in all likelihood Scribonius was right, that I would only goad the queen into increasing her efforts. The reality was that I could not hope to compete with her if she really wanted to eliminate not only me, but every member of my family and those that I loved. I gave a bitter curse as I gave in.

"Fine, you win."

I poked him in the chest with enough force to make him to take a step back as he blinked in surprise at my vehemence. "But you better think of that subtle thing you think would be better."

With that settled for the moment, and with the threat from the city watch gone, I turned my thoughts back to other matters. Realizing that it would not be smart just to leave the bodies in the alley, I called Balbus back over from where he was standing with the rest of the men. Gaius was still there with Iras in the sack over his shoulder, which kept twitching as she struggled inside.

"We need to get these bodies out of here," I told him, ignoring the irritation that flashed across his features, knowing that he was thinking that they had just worked to drag them into the alley and now I wanted to move them again.

"Find a wagon or cart that we can load them up in, and then drag them out of here."

"Where are we supposed to take them?" he asked incredulously.

"I don't care," I shot back. "I just don't want them here by the apartment stinking the place up, and I don't want them drawing attention to this area. Someone will bring the city watch here as soon as it's light, and they'll be poking around."

I looked up, dismayed to see that the sky above was already turning gray, and while I could not see the eastern horizon, I had seen enough sunrises to know that it was already pink. We would not have time if we wanted to get back to camp, and have the men in place for morning formation. Despite the fact that I was Primus Pilus, and these were my men, it would still arouse some attention and suspicion to have not just rankers missing, but the Secundus Pilus Prior and my Pilus Posterior missing as well. Realizing that the lesser of the evils would be to have the rankers missing, which I could cover, especially since their Centurions were here with me, I called the men over to tell them what needed to be done. They clearly did not like it any more than Balbus had, but they knew better than to complain, at least until after I was gone. I had Gaius hand Balbus the sack containing Iras, still not having decided when to kill her, then I had an inspiration.

"Bring her with me," I told Balbus, then entered the apartment.

I am ashamed to say that until Scribonius mentioned her name, I had not thought about Miriam, making me feel guilty that she had been sitting quaking in fear inside, listening to the sound of fighting beyond her front door. I went to push the door open, found it barred, and I called to Miriam.

"Titus Pullus, is it really you?"

Even muffled by the door, the fear in her voice was clear to hear, and I replied soothingly that it was indeed me. I heard the bar being lifted, the door opened a crack, a large brown eye peering up at me before the door was thrown open and she flew into my arms, clutching my neck so tightly that I was afraid I would choke.

"I have never been so frightened in all my life. I did not know what was happening."

I quickly explained to her what had taken place, assuring her that she was now safe, and motioning to Balbus to follow me into the apartment. I directed him to dump the sack on the floor, and Iras let out a grunt as her body hit the stone floor, muffled by her gag, causing Miriam to start at the unexpected sounds coming from the sack. Untying the end, I whipped it off her, leaving a glaring Iras blinking at the sudden light of the lamps that Miriam had burning. She immediately began cursing us through the gag; at least that is what I assumed she was doing. Miriam gave me a sharp glance as she moved instinctively to loosen the girl's bonds and remove the cloth from her mouth.

"I wouldn't do that if I were you, Miriam," Balbus said mildly, but he sounded a little too casual for my tastes, and I suspect that he was looking forward to whatever came out of the girl's mouth and Miriam's subsequent reaction.

I was not about to let that happen, so I reached out to restrain Miriam, but she shook my arm off, clearly angry with me for my treatment of Iras. I could understand her reaction; looking at Iras, one would not think of her as the viper that she was, but she was dangerous and I was not about to put Miriam at risk.

"This is the person who poisoned Eumenis," I told her, gratified to see Miriam's hand immediately freeze, looking up at me with shock and horror.

Directing her gaze back down at the bound girl, I saw the two exchange a look that told Miriam it was true, her face changing from disbelief to a cold anger that I had never seen before.

Straightening up, Miriam turned to look at me, asking me in an eerily calm voice, "What do you bring her here for? So that I may kill her?"

I confess I was not prepared for that question, at least not coming from Miriam, and I stood rooted for a moment while I tried to come up with an appropriate answer.

"Why not?" Balbus asked me. "She deserves to have her vengeance just as much as you do."

I looked over at Miriam, and her face was as if it was carved from stone as she stared down at Iras, who was looking up at my woman, quaking in more fear than she had shown to that point. I did not clearly understand, nor do I now, why she was obviously so much more frightened of Miriam than she was of any of us, but I suppose it has something to do with gender. I have seen women fighting more times than I can count, and they have a viciousness that men seem to lack, so I suppose that Iras had good cause for fear.

"Is this what you want?"

I watched Miriam closely, who did not take her gaze from Iras.

Finally, she shook her head. "No," she said dully. "It will not bring Eumenis back."

"I understand," I said, putting my hand on her shoulder, feeling the trembling clearly through the cloth covering her body, and I wondered if it was from the residual fear, or her anger and hatred for Iras was more powerful than I imagined. "But I do need you to watch her for a while," I said, relieved when she nodded. "I'll be back to fetch her after we get back to camp and have morning formation."

"You're going to kill her, aren't you?"

She did not look at me as she asked, but I sensed that my answer was very important to her, despite not knowing what she wanted to hear.

I took a deep breath, hesitating before I finally answered, "What do you think?"

That is when she turned to look at me, her eyes locking with mine as she seemed to try and peer into my soul for the answer.

Evidently she found the answer, giving a brief nod, but not saying anything more than, "I will watch her. If she tries anything, you will not have to kill her."

With that, we left the apartment, where Scribonius was supervising the men who were now stacking the bodies of the slain while they waited for Gaius to return with a wagon. Seeing nothing left to do, the three of us turned towards the camp. We had to hurry to make it before the *bucina* sounded the signal for morning formation, so there was not much talking, which I think all of us welcomed. It had been a busy, harrowing night, and we knew from experience that while none of us were tired at the moment, whatever *numen* that inhabits the body in moments of danger that keeps us from experiencing fatigue would be fleeing soon. We reached camp, it actually working out perfectly, since men were streaming in from where they stayed out in the city overnight, most of them Centurions of course, and we mingled with them and had no trouble getting in. The last hurdle overcome, I could feel the tension draining from my body, immediately flooding in behind it the fatigue, my legs suddenly feeling as if they were filled with lead. I could see that Scribonius and Balbus felt much the same, and when we caught ourselves eying one another, obviously looking for signs of what we each were feeling, we had to laugh, rueful as it may have been.

"We aren't getting any younger," Scribonius acknowledged what we were thinking.

"No, but we can still kill anyone that tries to stand before us."

I could count on Balbus to boil things down to its simplest essence, and as usual, he was right. We were slowing down, but we were not done, not by a long stretch, and it was this thought that was in my mind as we made our way to the forum, where the Legions were already forming up. There are always two formations in the morning; one for the whole army, where the orders of the day for everyone are relayed, such as they are, and a second for each Legion, where the specific tasks for that particular Legion are passed along.

As we walked to our spots, thankful that our respective Optios had done their jobs of rousing our Centuries without having to rely on us, Balbus commented, "Don't be surprised if when you get back, Iras is already dead."

I was caught off guard, stopping still as I thought about it, wondering if he had seen something in Miriam that I had missed. While I had been shocked that she would even consider avenging Eumenis' death herself, she seemed to discard the idea immediately. My mind was occupied with these thoughts while the daily ritual of an army in camp began. As it would turn out, I would be surprised, but not in the way that Balbus predicted.

The day dragged by with me counting the moments until I could safely slip away from camp and return to the apartment. Neither Antonius nor Cleopatra had appeared at the morning formation, which was not unusual. In fact, if either of them had shown up, I would have been instantly suspicious, such was my frame of mind. The men returned from their chore of disposing of the bodies, allowed back into camp with the passes that I had signed for them, and Gaius immediately came to find me to report that they had managed, albeit with some difficulty to remove the dead men.

"We took them to the docks and found an isolated spot. We threw them into the water, but we weighted them down first," he told me, clearly proud of himself because of the responsibility I had given him.

I thanked him, even though I did not need to, but he shook the thanks off.

"They tried to kill Miriam," he said, his mouth a thin line, which I had learned was a sign of his anger. "I love her, Uncle, and I'd rather die than see anything happen to her. Not in the same way you love her, of course," he added hastily, his face turning red, but I took no offense, knowing what he meant, or at least thinking that I did.

After catching up on some reports that the *Praetorium* had been clamoring for, and updating Diocles on all that had transpired the previous evening, I was at last ready to return to the apartment to finish the business with Iras. Before I left, I found Scribonius, overseeing his Century working the stakes, and pulled him aside.

"Well? Have you come up with something more subtle than what I wanted to do?"

He shook his head and said, "Just kill her and be done with it. It'll be enough that Cleopatra sees that you're alive."

I did not like it, and I said as much before I left to return to the apartment. Miriam was sitting at the table, with Iras still bound but with the gag out of her mouth. They both looked up guiltily when I entered, as if I were interrupting a private conversation. Iras looked away from me, making me wonder what she was hiding, as Miriam rose to greet me. Before I could say a word, she pulled me into the next room, closing the door.

"I don't think that's wise, to leave her alone like that," I told her, but Miriam was dismissive.

"She will be fine. She knows what I am going to talk to you about."

I did not like the sound of that at all, and it only got worse.

"Titus Pullus, I think you should spare Iras' life."

I felt my jaw drop open as I stared down at her, trying to understand what she had just said.

"Spare her life?" I was incredulous, my tone causing her own jaw to clench, her chin tilting up in a sign I knew far too well.

"Do you know anything about her? Do you know what she has been forced to endure because of Cleopatra?"

"I know that she poisoned Eumenis, but only because she was trying to kill us," I retorted.

"That was because she was forced to do so by that . . . woman." Miriam would rarely utter a foul word, but her feelings for Cleopatra were such that I could see she was sorely tempted to say something else.

As I listened to her, I realized what was going on; Iras had been working on her, changing herself into the exact opposite of what I believed to be her true nature, which we had seen in Deukalos' villa. It was easy to understand how Miriam could be fooled, I thought. After all, I had been lulled into a false belief that such a young, beautiful girl could not have the heart and nature of a viper coiled to strike. With that in mind, I tried to explain patiently that Miriam had been fooled, but while she listened quietly to my description of how Iras acted when we had captured her, she was unmoved.

"She told me all that," she said quietly. "She just wanted not to appear to be frightened by you and thought if she showed loyalty to Cleopatra you would be impressed by her bravery and spare her life. She says she hates Cleopatra, and I believe her."

I was completely dumbfounded and did not know what to say to convince Miriam that she was being fooled by this girl. Seeing my hesitation and mistaking it for wavering, Miriam grabbed my arm, squeezing it hard with the urgency she was feeling.

"Titus, I am asking you to trust me. I know that she is telling the truth, I know it in my bones. My people are blessed with the gift of being able to see a person's true nature at times, and this is one of those times."

I shook my head, readying the argument in my head that would convince her that this was not one of those times, even as I knew that it would be close to hopeless.

Then Miriam said something that changed everything, as quickly as a bolt of lightning chars a tree. "Think how angry Cleopatra would be if we spared her life, and took her into our household."

Her words cut through my brain, and I felt a shock of excitement. Miriam was looking up at me earnestly, her hand still on my arm as my mind began churning on the idea.

"It would make her angry enough to chew through nails," I said slowly, surprising myself that the words were coming out of my mouth.

Miriam nodded emphatically. "Yes! And it would let her know that we are not afraid of her, and she will always wonder what secrets her slave is telling us about her and Antonius."

That clinched it for me, and I looked down at my woman, admiring the cunning turn her mind had taken, but as quickly as that came, I was struck by another thought, more unwelcome.

"Is this Iras talking? Did she plant this idea in your head?"

Miriam's face flashed with a rare show of anger. "Why do you think that I can't think of this on my own? Iras was telling me how much she hated Cleopatra, but she never said anything about sparing her life, or staying in our household. I just listened to what she said, and the idea came to me."

And that is how Iras came to live in our household, although it was a long, slow process before she was trusted enough to be given the same amount of freedom that the rest of the slaves and Diocles had. At first, I locked her up every night, less out of fear that she would run away than what she might try to do to us in our sleep, and she was never allowed anywhere near our food for the first several months. As time passed, I began to suspect that Miriam's intervention was due more to her desire for a companion than any genuine compassion for the girl, but that is getting ahead of this tale of mine. That day, I do not know who was more surprised when I walked out with Miriam to face the girl, who stared up at me with a mixture of fear and hopefulness. I squatted down next to her so that we were at eye level, and I bored my eyes into hers as I spoke, searching her face for signs of guile.

"You need to thank your gods that my woman has such a kind heart, girl."

Before I could say another word, Iras burst into tears, throwing her body at Miriam's feet. I got the distinct impression that if her hands had been free she would have wrapped them around my woman's legs as she sobbed her gratitude.

"Mistress, thank you, thank you, thank you! I will make offerings to Isis and Ptah and to your god Baal every day! There is no way I can repay this kindness, and I shall be devoted to you for the rest of my days!"

Miriam looked equal parts pleased and embarrassed at Iras' display, and I was not very gentle when I grabbed the girl by the arm to pull her back upright so that we could continue our conversation, one-sided as it may have been.

"Understand this." I made my tone as grim as I could to impart how serious I was. "You're going to be treated fairly, but I don't trust you, and I don't know that I ever will. That means that you're not going to have the same kind of freedom my other slaves have. You're going to be locked up every night, and you're never going anywhere alone, but that's for your safety as much as it is to keep an eye on you. You told me how you were willing to die for Cleopatra, but now you're singing a different song to the lady."

She dropped her eyes, breaking her gaze from mine. I grabbed her by the chin so we reestablished eye contact, and I was pleased to see there was real fear there, with none of the defiance and as far as I could tell, no cunning or artifice.

"I'm going to listen to my lady, for now. But know this, Iras," I used her name to let her know how serious I was, "if you betray us, or try to harm us in any way, even if you succeed, you've seen my friends. You know that they'll fulfill my wishes. I'll have you thrown to the men of not just my Cohort, but to my entire Legion, and I'll set aside part of my considerable fortune to hire physicians who will keep you alive long enough for every man in the 10th Legion to have their way with you. And some of them have, shall we say, peculiar tastes when it comes to how they treat women. After they're done, what's left of your body will be fed to the dogs that skulk around camp. Do you understand me?"

I waited for her answer. Finally, she nodded her head, but I was not quite through.

"And do you believe me?"

I could see her swallow hard, but she nodded again. I stood and pulled Miriam, beaming with happiness at getting her way, back to the other room.

"I hope you know what you're doing," I told her. "But there are conditions to keeping her."

I outlined what I expected, and she agreed readily enough, which did not make me feel particularly good, but I confess I was seduced by the thought of seeing Cleopatra's face when she saw Iras for the first time as a member of my household, and I began to think of ways in which I could make that happen.

Scribonius, after his initial shock over what had transpired, rubbed his chin, then gave an approving nod. "I think Miriam would make a good Roman patrician," was how he put it. "That's exactly the kind of devious behavior that the upper classes would approve of, and I have to say that I agree. More than seeing a pile of bodies on her doorstep, seeing Iras as part of your household will drive her apoplectic with rage."

That sounded good to me; now I just had to figure out how to let Cleopatra see Iras in a way that let her know that she belonged to me. First, I had to let Cleopatra know that her attempt on my life had failed, since I imagined that she still did not know for sure, though she had to have her suspicions. After all, Deukalos had not come to tell her, through Apollodorus, that Iras was successful, and that he had disposed of her as he was paid to do. I suspected that she would send Apollodorus to the merchant's house, where he would find the place in turmoil, despite the fact I had not done as Balbus suggested and put everyone in the house, slave and free, to the sword. I did not see the point in such slaughter, especially since I did not really hate Deukalos, and I certainly held no malice towards his slaves or family. I decided that I had pressing business at the *Praetorium*, hoping that I would find Cleopatra, or at the least Antonius present, thinking that he might find reason to comment to her that he had seen me. Looking back, I know that I was being extremely foolhardy in provoking the queen, and if I had better sense I would have not gone out of my way to antagonize her, instead just letting her find out in her own good time that I still lived. But a man cannot change his nature, and it had never been in my nature to hide from a fight, no matter who it was with. I imagine that this attitude can be attributed to the fact that I had always been the biggest, and usually the strongest in almost every contest of any sort in which I had been involved, making walking away from one an idea foreign to my thinking.

I arrived at the *Praetorium* to find Ahenobarbus berating one of the Tribunes for something, and the door to Antonius' office closed, which usually indicated that he was present. I saw Spurius talking to another Tribune, and seeing that he was positioned directly across from the door, I made my way over to him. Waiting for the conversation to end, I asked Spurius a question about something completely inconsequential, and he gave me a quizzical look, but answered readily enough. Still, the door remained closed while I fished about for something else to talk about, with Spurius looking more and more confused, since he was not a man with whom I normally engaged in the kind of small talk that was taking place at that moment. I had almost exhausted my supply of queries about the best way to keep the men from getting seasick or things we could do to keep the men occupied while on board their transport, neither of which I actually had any interest in, when at long last the door opened and Canidius emerged. The door was not open long, but I had enough time to see Cleopatra seated on her couch reading a scroll, dressed in her ridiculous armor, which did not allow her to recline. She was clearly absorbed in what she was reading, but as people tend to do, she glanced up when Canidius exited. At first, I did not believe she saw me, or it did not register, then I saw her head freeze in mid-motion as she was returning to her examination of the scroll. Very slowly, she looked up, our eyes met, and I smiled and nodded, gratified to see the blood drain from her face just as the door swung shut.

"I don't know what's wrong with her, but that bitch is on rampage," I heard one of Diocles' friends, a clerk from one of the other Legions that had recently been sent to the *Praetorium* to take the place of the men she had removed, told him.

This conversation was taking place a day or two after the queen had seen me at the *Praetorium*, with Diocles and his friend in the outer office while I sat at my desk in my private quarters.

"Really? No idea why? I mean, other than she's a queen and can do that sort of thing without a reason?"

To one who did not know him, Diocles' tone was casual, just one slave gossiping with another, but I could tell that he was avidly interested and was probing for my benefit, his voice getting slightly louder.

"None," his friend replied, and obviously Diocles made some sort of face that showed his disappointment in not hearing some juicy bit of talk that would liven his day, with the other slave adding in a seeming afterthought, "although I know that whatever it was that set her off just happened in the last day or so. And she has been clawing the general to shreds about the least little thing. He's at a loss, and you can tell that he just wants to get drunk, but she won't let him touch a drop of the stuff. He looks absolutely miserable."

Diocles gave a noncommittal grunt, while I smiled as I worked. It was perhaps two days after this that we were told that at long last, the fleet was finished, and we would begin the transfer to Greece within the next few days. To commemorate the event, Antonius announced that he would host a dinner for all the senior officers of the army. Primi Pili and Pili Priores would represent the rankers, while the Tribunes and Legates would be attending as well. Finally, this was the event that gave me the opportunity I was looking for.

"I'm going to bring a guest," I told Scribonius that evening, after passing the word to the Pili Priores. He saw immediately where I was headed, and he grimaced at the thought of the turmoil that was likely to erupt because of it.

"Well, that will certainly let Cleopatra know that you're not intimidated, which I suppose is what you're after," he conceded. He glanced at my face, giving a sigh. "I don't suppose there's any way I can talk you out of this, is there?"

"Not really," was my reply, then I went home to let Miriam know that she would have the opportunity to get dressed up.

Not surprisingly, Miriam was torn about the idea. On the one hand, like every woman, the thought of an excuse to buy a new dress and have her hair done in the Roman style, which I had insisted on, excited her. The prospect of coming face to face with Cleopatra, no matter what the physical distance, was not so appealing, her indecision easy to read on her face.

"Are you really sure this is a good idea, Titus Pullus?" she asked anxiously.

Whereas I had been confident in front of Scribonius, facing my woman and her doubts, suddenly I was not so sure.

"No," I admitted. "But we're going anyway." I grinned at her. "Besides, you haven't had an opportunity to show off your new slave while you shop for a dress."

As I expected, this was just too powerful to resist, but she gave me a mock scowl, putting her hands on her hips. "Shop for a dress? Titus Pullus, I cannot just buy a dress for something like this. I will have to have one made."

"But the dinner is day after tomorrow," I protested. "There's no way that a dress can be made in time."

"Of course it can." She smiled sweetly at me, which told me that I, or more accurately, my purse, was in real trouble. "It just costs more," she finished, confirming my fear.

I opened my mouth to try putting an end to this idea, then shut it as I realized that I had been the instigator. Titus, old boot, you are just getting what you deserve, I thought, fishing in my purse to take out some denarii. The coins clinked heavily into her palm as I counted out what I thought should be enough, but when I stopped I was rewarded with a raised eyebrow that spoke more eloquently than any words could that I was being a silly man. A few more coins later, she closed her palm, her fingers barely wrapping around the stack, then turned to call to Iras that she was going shopping.

I had brought Agis with me, and I went to tell him that he needed to accompany the women wherever they went, something he was clearly not happy about, but I did not chastise him. My decision to spare Iras, after they learned that she was the instrument of Cleopatra, had not been well received by either Diocles or Agis, although after explaining it to him, Diocles understood. I did not feel disposed to explain anything to Agis, expecting him to accept whatever I decided without complaint, yet I was not so insensitive not to understand why he was unhappy, hence my somewhat lax attitude towards his displeasure. Leaving Miriam to her own preparations, I returned to camp to attend to the real business of making sure the men were ready to embark. We would be loading onto the transports the day after the dinner, beginning at first light, making our area a swarm of activity as men ran about, dodging between the piles of sacks containing our grain supply, barrels of pitch, and amphorae of olive oil and wine, each man with a specific task given by his Centurion. Even as many years as I had done this, it never ceased to amaze me how such a seemingly disorganized mass of confusion could suddenly result in the delivery of men to their ships, at exactly the moment they were supposed to be there, with exactly the gear they were supposed to have. Once on the sea, of course, it was in the hands of Neptune whether or not he delivered us to where we were supposed to be, but we would make sure that we did our jobs once we got there. To an untrained eye, I am sure that the sight of a Legion preparing to move looks remarkably unorganized, with every appearance that men are running in circles, but it is deceiving to believe so. The Centurions were striding about, bawling out orders and smacking laggards with the *vitus*. All in all, it was a normal day in the life of an army preparing to move.

The day of the dinner arrived, and I will admit that I had a case of nerves not dissimilar to those that I felt before going into battle. Shortly before the dinner, which was being held in the open space of the forum in order to accommodate the large numbers, I went and picked up Miriam. I had decided on one more surprise for Cleopatra, something I had kept to myself until this moment when I informed Miriam.

"Iras is going to be your attendant at the dinner."

Miriam, looking even more beautiful than she had the night of the dinner with Uncle Tiberius, was standing framed in the doorway of our bedroom, and I had to admit that the dress, made of some filmy material that seemed to cling and drape her body at the same time, had been worth every sesterce. As I stood examining her, I saw that there was something subtly different that at first I could not identify, finally seeing that her face was made up, with special attention paid to her eyes. They were underlined with kohl, while somehow her lashes seemed to be even thicker than normal, and I recognized the style as being distinctly Egyptian, which I thought was a nice touch. She was oblivious to my admiration, focusing instead on the words that had just come out of my mouth, her own dropping open in shock.

"You cannot be serious," she gasped. "Titus, I am nervous enough as it is. To have Iras come where Cleopatra can see her, that is too much! She will kill us, right there on the spot!"

"She can try," I retorted, instantly regretting the words, knowing that they were not helping. I stepped forward, speaking soothingly while putting my hands on Miriam's bare shoulders and feeling the tremors. "But she won't, my love. She can't, not in a public setting like that. Not even Cleopatra would dare. Besides, remember that we're going to be with Scribonius and the rest of the

Pili Priores. You don't think that they'd let anything happen, do you?"

That seemed to settle her down, but she was still clearly nervous. To take her mind off the prospect of Cleopatra leaping across her couch to attack us, I asked her about her makeup.

She touched her face, replying absently, "It was Iras' idea. She thought it would make me look more like a highborn lady."

"It makes you look even lovelier, which I didn't think was possible." I was trying to be kind, having learned that flattery will do more to soothe a woman than any other thing one can do.

I was pleased to see her blush, and it did seem to take her mind away from her fears of Cleopatra. I called Iras, who had been in the main room, telling her gruffly to make herself presentable because she was going with us to the dinner to attend to Miriam. If Miriam had been nervous, Iras was clearly petrified, without a trace of the fighting spirit I had seen just days earlier.

"Master, I beg you do not make me go," she told me in Greek. "I cannot face the queen! If she sees me, she will kill me!"

"Didn't you just hear what I said?" I asked coldly. "She wouldn't dare to try and attack us, let alone a slave like you, in such a public setting."

"But she'll know that I'm alive," she begged. "She won't tolerate that insult to her pride! Please, reconsider!"

I knew that she was speaking sense, and in truth she was not saying anything I had not already heard from Scribonius when I had told him, but pride is not confined to the highly born, and I had perhaps more than my share of it, so I was unmoved by her pleas.

"Well, think of it this way," I made a grim jest. "You were supposed to be dead already, so what does it matter?"

We left the apartment, with Iras following behind on clearly shaking knees and Agis tagging along just in case she decided to make a break for it. Making our way through the city, I enjoyed the admiring glances from the men as they stopped to watch us pass, and I was not blind to the women who did the same, which seemed to please Miriam immensely.

"We make a handsome couple, don't you think?" I teased, causing Miriam to blush and give me a happy smile, but it was fleeting.

Arriving at the forum, we stopped to wait for the Pili Priores, and a few moments later, they came marching up in double file with Scribonius, as the ranking Centurion, leading the group. They crashed to a halt, saluted, then stood at *intente* while I inspected them, making sure that their tunics were freshly laundered and clean of stains, since this was not an affair where full uniforms were required. As I expected, there was nothing to find fault with, although they would have been more surprised if I did not wipe away a nonexistent speck of dust or straighten a perfectly aligned buckle.

I turned to Scribonius, who was eying the two women, and he murmured, "It's not too late to send the girl home."

"What, and miss the look on that bitch's face?"

For perhaps the thousandth time since I had known Scribonius, he heaved another sigh that communicated more of his true feelings than any words could.

With a wave of his arm, he said, "Then by all means, Primus Pilus Pullus, lead the way. I must admit that I'm looking forward to seeing the show."

I turned, beckoning to Miriam and Iras, who had been standing off to the side, and they approached nervously, Iras holding the hem of Miriam's gown out of the dirt. As beautiful as Miriam was, Iras alone would have turned men's heads as she passed, despite the fact I had wisely made her wear something drab, knowing that Miriam would not appreciate Iras being dressed up. It was my one concession to making as much of an entrance as possible; my original intention had been to dress her almost as richly as Miriam, having her wear the gown that Miriam wore at Uncle Tiberius' dinner, but I was quickly disabused of that notion by a visibly angry woman when I mentioned it. Instead, I had to content myself with having her dressed plainly and walking behind the two of us, with the Pili Priores following behind us, as we were ushered to a series of tables and benches. I was disappointed to see that we would not be dining in the style of the Roman upper classes on couches, but I supposed that finding so many couches and tables in the proper configuration must have been difficult, even in a city the size of Ephesus. Not to mention that more than a few of the Centurions had probably never been exposed to such finery and would not know what to do. Thinking about it, I had to admit that it was wise of Antonius to make such arrangements, since his relationship with the army was so tenuous that it could easily have been viewed as an attempt to embarrass the men who were guests at this dinner by putting them in an unfamiliar position, so to speak. It just meant that Miriam would not be as easy to spot seated among the men, but I was relieved to see that I had not been the only Centurion to bring a female companion. Taking our places, the air soon filled with the buzzing of conversation while we waited for Antonius and Cleopatra to appear.

My stomach was in knots, and I could see that Miriam was in much the same state, despite Scribonius trying to occupy her with conversation about the table settings and decorations, something I barely noticed. The other Pili Priores could sense my tension, and while none of them knew the details of all that had gone on, they undoubtedly knew enough to understand that something momentous might be occurring. Then, the *bucina* sounded the call that told us that the commanding general was present, all the Legionaries coming to *intente* at the first note. The open forum was quiet and still as we waited, then out of the corner of my eye, I saw the figures of Antonius and Cleopatra mount the raised platform where their table was placed. We were some distance away, which I suspected was by design on the part of Antonius, not wanting my big body in the line of sight of his queenly wife. Gauging the distance, I began to wonder if this was a futile exercise, thinking that we were too far away to be seen from their spot. The couple was dressed richly, in embroidered matching tunic and gown, obviously deciding that armor was not appropriate garb for such an event. Immediately after we were seated, Antonius made some remarks, completely forgettable, which I believe was due as much to my nerves as the quality of his speech. I am sure that it was up to his usual high standard; of all the orators I have heard, Antonius was second only to Caesar in his ability to communicate to the rankers in a way that did not make them feel stupid. He spoke for a few moments, not long enough for the diners to start fidgeting, then signaled to the slaves waiting in the back to bring forward the platters of crackling pork fresh from the spit, followed by others carrying boards piled with heaps of bread still steaming from the oven. Not far behind that were slaves carrying pots of chickpeas, lentils and a variety of vegetables. It was simple soldier's fare, but there was plenty of wine, making the atmosphere convivial as men regaled each other with tales of past battles or wild nights spent on the town. Naturally, the talk was toned down in deference to the female guests present, at least at first. The more wine that flowed, however, men's tongues loosened, soon enough making it sound like a normal night around the fire. I was barely paying attention, and I believe that it was due to Scribonius more than my presence that kept the Pili Priores at the table under control out of respect to Miriam.

My focus was pinned to the rostra where Antonius and Cleopatra were seated, since it became apparent that we were too far away to be seen, at least at a casual glance. I was beginning to think that this had been a waste of time and effort, and I was really regretting the whole idea, thinking about the amount of gold that had gone into the gown draping Miriam, when Antonius and Cleopatra rose from their table.

They stepped down from their perch to begin circulating among the guests, Antonius waving the men to stay seated when they came to *intente* at his approach. They started on the far side of the forum, spending a few moments at each table, long enough for Antonius to tell a joke, or ask a man about his Cohort and how their preparations were going, the normal kind of small talk that generals like to engage in to show the men that they are interested in their well-being, even if in reality they could give a rotten fig about anything we had to say. Ever so slowly, the pair made their way up and down the rows of tables. I felt Miriam grip my arm and I turned to see her looking at me with wide eyes.

"What are we going to do?"

Her voice was quivering with the tension she was obviously feeling, so I patted her arm, trying to keep her calm while fighting the growing knot in my own stomach. Cleopatra was now walking down the next row of tables, next to Antonius, but their backs were turned to us as they continued their small procession. Standing just behind and to the side were two men, one from the Brundisium Cohort, and one Nubian, the latter carrying the large curved axe that they favored. The sight of the huge plum-colored man was not helping Miriam's state of mind, but Iras, who was kneeling behind us, was having the most violent reaction, shaking in such obvious fear that she was drawing the attention of other guests. Her eyes were glued to the queen, as I suppose mine were as well, though to that point Cleopatra was oblivious, her back still turned.

Cleopatra remained facing away from us while she followed Antonius down the row, and I took the opportunity to examine her closely, noticing the lines that had not been there the last time I was this close. Her hair was plaited in its normal fashion; even so I could see a few strands of silver, not as thick as the gray in Antonius' own curly locks perhaps, but visible nonetheless. Her great beak of a nose seemed even more prominent, and I surmised that it was due to her losing what little spare weight she carried, seeming to be all sharp angles and edges. What little physical allure she held was long gone, although it did not seem to deter Antonius from slavering over her as if she were Venus herself. They reached the end of the row, making the turn up ours, and for a moment both Antonius and Cleopatra stood with an unobstructed view of the entire length of the dozen or so tables, each of them with several guests seated. There were a few other slaves kneeling in the space between tables, those nearest to the royal couple jumping up to move out of the way. Iras started to rise, but I reached out, putting a hand on her shoulder.

"Stay where you are until I tell you to move," I said, using the tone I reserved for commands to Legionaries.

Her eyes were wide with fear, and she shook her head in mute appeal, but remained kneeling. At that moment, Antonius took a step closer to the first table in our row as he leaned down to say something to one of the Centurions seated there, making it so that Cleopatra was not blocked in her view. Our eyes met; immediately her lip curled back from her teeth in an involuntary snarl, her eyes blazing with a hatred that I could almost feel as a blast of radiant heat. I returned her stare with equal hatred, while Antonius continued talking, completely oblivious to this small drama being played out behind him. Then, he took a step to the side towards us, forcing Cleopatra to break her gaze so that she moved with him, making it natural for her eyes to move downward, and that is when she saw Iras. The gods blessed me by keeping my attention on the queen, enabling me to see the full bloom of reaction as she took a halting step, her eyes taking in the sight of the shaking girl kneeling at my feet, just before her mind comprehended that it was Iras. Her face looked suddenly drained of blood as she took a staggering step to the side, reaching out in reflex to grab Antonius' arm. As he turned, an annoyed look on his face, Cleopatra's eyes moved back to me, then to Miriam, and I could see the bitterness of defeat written as plainly on her face as I have ever seen in the expression of a man I have slain. Antonius was looking at her, his irritation changing to puzzlement at her expression, then he followed her gaze to see me sitting there, with Miriam at my side. I nodded gravely to Antonius, which he returned, but I could see him struggling to understand exactly what was taking place in front of him. Cleopatra suddenly reached up, pulling him down to her level, whispered something in his ear that caused him to react sharply, followed by a whispered exchange. Then just as quickly, the queen turned to walk away on clearly unsteady legs, beckoning her Nubian to follow. Without a further word to anyone, she left the dinner, leaving Antonius looking bewildered, and me feeling better than I had in some time.

Turning to Iras, I said quietly, "You can stand up now. The general's coming and you don't want to be in the way."

She was able to rise, but only on the third try, her legs clearly wobbling. I suddenly became aware of Miriam's breathing, harsh and rasping as if she had just run a great distance, and I looked over to see her staring straight ahead, clearly trying to regain her composure.

I put a hand on her arm, thinking it would calm her, but she went rigid to my touch, her voice shaking as she said, "I would like to leave as soon as it is possible, Titus Pullus. I understand if you need to stay here, but I want to go home."

"We can't leave now," I tried to assure her. "But we'll be leaving shortly, I promise."

Antonius continued to speak to the seated guests, though I saw him continually glance over at me, his gaze then shifting to Miriam. On his second or third glance, he looked over at Iras, a frown creasing his face as he tried to place her face, or so I assumed.

Scribonius was silently watching this playing out, then he whispered to me, "I think Antonius recognizes the girl as belonging to Cleopatra. This could get awkward."

"Really? You think so?" I snapped at him, irritated at his grasp of the obvious, despite realizing now that he was just needling me.

The other Pili Priores were paying avid attention, sensing that there was something very interesting occurring, something that might fill a boring evening around the fire with conversation. Antonius' exchanges were getting shorter, since he was clearly intent on getting to me, making it only a matter of another moment or two before he was standing before me, looking down at me with cold eyes.

"Well, Primus Pilus Pullus, it seems that you have a talent for upsetting the queen."

"I can imagine, general." I was proud that my voice sounded in control and cool, because I was feeling anything other than that, my heart beating against my chest with enough force that out of the corner of my eye I could see my tunic pulsing from the impact.

I heard a sharp intake of breath at my reply, while Antonius' eyes narrowed, the Triumvir clearly not liking either my words or tone.

"I can't," he snapped. "I can't imagine why your very presence seems to provoke her to such anger. I thought we had settled your . . . disagreement."

"I can't speculate about why my existence so displeases the queen, general. Perhaps you should ask her about it." I should have stopped there, I suppose, but I could not resist adding, "Mayhap it's the fact that I'm still *in* existence that's the cause of her anger."

There was not a whisper of sound from anyone sitting at the table, Miriam suddenly gripping my arm with surprisingly strong fingers, while Antonius' jaw clenched, the blood rushing into his face. Our eyes were locked together, but I sensed that more than just our table was paying attention to this exchange, and I believe it was that fact that kept Antonius from exploding. He suddenly exhaled so violently that it was almost a snort, before the corners of his mouth turned upward in what I clearly recognized as a smile meant for everyone watching except me.

His laugh was forced, but his tone was even as he said, "I have no doubt that has something to do with it, Pullus."

He turned his head to regard Iras, who was standing with downcast eyes while the Triumvir examined her in the same manner a man appraising a horse will.

"Girl, what is your name?" he demanded.

"I-Iras, master."

He cocked an eyebrow, looked over at me while saying a bit more loudly than before, "Isn't that a coincidence! Cleopatra once had a slave by that very name, if I remember correctly. And she looked remarkably like you. I haven't seen her about for a few days, though. Do you have a twin, girl?"

I do not know what possessed her, but as I had already seen glimpses, Iras was a smart girl. "Yes, master. In fact, I do have a twin."

The look on Antonius' face told me that he was as surprised as I was, yet I did not miss the flash of relief that passed over it as he saw a way out of his dilemma.

"Ah. That explains it. I'm relieved that I can assure the queen that her property hasn't somehow been stolen from her by one of my Primi Pili."

That stung me, and it was my turn to feel the flush of heat rising to my face as the men around me laughed at Antonius' wit, even if they did not fully understand what was happening.

"I can assure you that I came by Iras honestly, general." I tried to keep my anger from showing. I do not think I was altogether successful, because I felt a kick under the table from Scribonius. "I didn't steal Iras from your wife, I can assure you."

Now, I still do not know to this day what the exact truth of that statement was, and is. Is it possible to steal property when that property has essentially been discarded, and was supposed to be destroyed? And does the fact that the property in question tried to kill you affect the balance of the scales in any way?

"I never thought you did, Pullus," Antonius said lightly. "And I'll be sure that the queen understands that this is a case of mistaken identity."

Antonius made as if to leave our table, then he stopped and slapped his forehead. "This business has made me forget my manners. Who is this lovely creature with you, Pullus?"

Marcus Antonius was famous, and rightly so, for his amorous conquests throughout the Republic, and his charm was on full display at that moment. It was as if Miriam's fear evaporated with the speed of a raindrop falling in the desert, blushing with pleasure at the attention of the Triumvir. I stood, pulling Miriam to her feet to present her to Antonius, who kissed her hand and complimented her extravagantly on her beauty and dress.

"Pullus is a lucky man, lady. I can't imagine how a big ugly brute like him managed to secure such a flower. He obviously has talents outside of the army that I am unaware of. Isn't that right, Pullus?"

He turned to look directly into my eyes, and we both knew that he was not referring to matters of love. Releasing her hand, Antonius turned to go to the next table.

As he passed me, he whispered in my ear, "This is a dangerous game you're playing, Pullus. You have no idea what Cleopatra is capable of, or the lengths she'll go to protect herself. And me."

"Tell that to them," I jerked my head at the seated Pili Priores, all of whom were trying very hard to appear not to be listening. "The queen needs them, and I think we both know that there are no secrets in the army. Whatever happens to me, I respectfully request that you impress that fact on her."

"Don't you think I've been doing everything I can to make sure she understands that?"

His voice tightened, and as close as we were, I could clearly see how worn down he was. "You're still alive, aren't you?"

"And I'd like to stay that way," I assured him, then decided to take yet another risk. "And as long as I don't have to sleep with one eye open, or lose another slave to someone's poison, the queen doesn't need to worry about Iras' twin showing up."

I do not believe that his look of surprise was feigned at the news that I had lost Eumenis, and he seemed at a loss for words for a moment. However, I could see that he understood the implications of what I had said, and he turned to look at Iras again. His shoulders slumped as he put the pieces together, or at least enough of them to know that she had been a tool of Cleopatra, and the true cause of Cleopatra's turmoil at the sight of her. Finally, he nodded his understanding, stepping away with a whispered promise to do what he could. This did not make me feel very secure at all, but I supposed it was the best I could hope for. Marcus Antonius had been unable to rein Cleopatra in for some time; only time would tell if he managed now.

"He didn't know, did he?"

Miriam's question intruded into my thoughts on our walk back to the apartment.

I considered it, then shook my head. "No, I don't think he did. It makes me wonder what else she's up to that he doesn't know about."

"He was right about one thing," Scribonius, who was walking with us, interjected. "You're playing a dangerous game."

"Don't you think I know that?"

I had been aware for some time that I was swimming in very deep, very rough waters, but I did not see that doing nothing was an option. If I had just absorbed the loss of Eumenis and not retaliated, would that have stopped her from trying again? I did not believe then, nor do I believe now that being passive with a woman like Cleopatra was the smart or right thing to do.

"Do you think she will stop?" Miriam asked.

"I think so." This came from Scribonius, surprising me considerably.

I turned to look at him, trying to determine if he was just saying this to make Miriam feel better, but he seemed to be serious.

"Why do you think that?"

"Because she's about to have a lot bigger things to worry about than you," he said frankly. "We're about to embark for Greece, where Octavian is either waiting, or will be arriving shortly. I think that you've proven that coming after you won't be easy. And now that Antonius is aware of, or at least has an idea of what's happened so far, it's in his best interest to keep her under control."

I looked at him, and could not resist gloating a bit. "Why Sextus Scribonius, that sounds like you think what I did was a good idea."

He gave me a frown. "I never said it was a bad idea. But I agree with Antonius that it's a dangerous game. I just think that you tend to take things farther than they need to go."

"What do you mean?"

As an answer, Scribonius simply pointed back at Iras, who was following along behind us.

"Oh, that." It was all I could think to say.

"Yes, that. There were other ways to let the queen know that Iras existed, other than throwing the girl in her face in a public setting. Otherwise, I think you did the right thing."

I was content with that, and we finished the walk back to the apartment in silence, each of us clearly lost in our own thoughts.

Before we left, I decided to take further precautions, hiring a man from the recently retired 4th Macedonica, just one of the number of men still about who decided they had enough of the army, but did not save enough money to retire without an income. The man's name was Decimus Flavius, and he came highly recommended by Corbulo, who was now one of the Evocati attached to Antonius' *Praetorium*. I interviewed the man, a grizzled veteran missing an eye, a result of the first Parthian campaign. The empty socket was covered with a patch, the scarring from the wound clear to see tracing out from the edges. He was about the same age as Vellusius, which meant he was missing about the same amount of teeth, yet he had a competent air about him, and I was confident that he could handle almost anything that might come up in my absence. I still did not trust Iras, so I went to great lengths to instruct Flavius to keep a close watch over her, but just to be safe I was leaving Agis behind as well, who had surprised me in the last few days. The death of Eumenis had thrust upon him more responsibilities, and I was not hopeful that he would be able to step into the role, but aside from his stuttering problem, he had done so quite capably. He was also devoted to Miriam, and hated Iras for killing Eumenis, no matter what the circumstances might have been, although I must admit I was beginning to think that perhaps Miriam was right, that Iras had been forced to do what she did, and her display at Deukalos' villa had indeed been false bravado. I was not willing to put Miriam at further risk to test that idea, however, and I was in a better frame of mind knowing that Flavius would be there.

The process of loading the Legion took an entire day, which of course meant that the men who embarked first had to sit in the cramped holds of their ships, bobbing about in the harbor. Even in the calm waters of the protected harbor of Ephesus, there is enough motion in the water to make men with more sensitive stomachs seasick. This misery is shared by all those sitting next to the unfortunate, meaning that it is not unusual to see one man start to retch from the movement of the ship, causing those around him to do likewise. Soon the bottom of the hold would be filled with the contents of men's stomachs, and the ordeal is just beginning. One could stand on the deck of their own ship and hear the sounds of vomiting emanating from the holds of every vessel, accompanied by cursing and prayers to the gods to relieve the suffering. This was a time that I was thankful that as a Centurion I was above it all, so to speak, on the main deck, vividly remembering the trips to Britannia crammed in the hold. The loading process took all day and the better part of the night, then we had to wait for the following tide to sail out of the harbor late the next morning. Fortunately, the trip was uneventful, if a little rough. We traveled northwest, sailing around the Peloponnesus and up the coast, landing at a dreary, marshy spot called Actium.

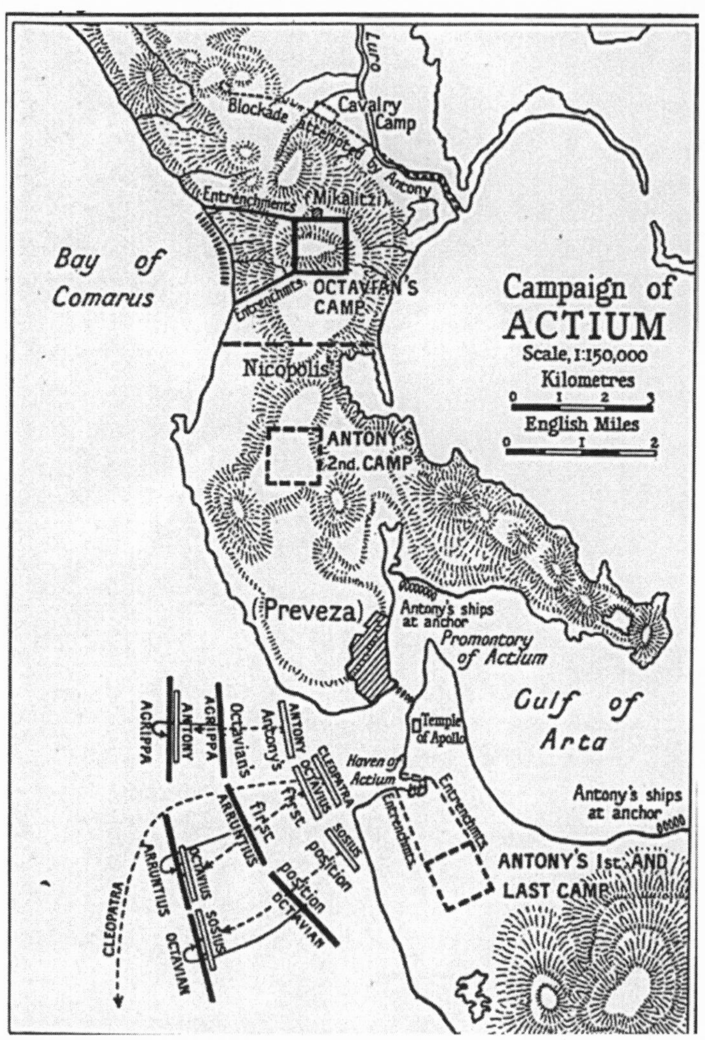
Campaign of
ACTIUM
Scale, 1:150,000
Kilometres
English Miles
Bay of
Comarus
Luro
Blockade
Cavalry
Camp
Attempted by Antony
Entrenchments
(Mikalitzi)
OCTAVIAN'S
CAMP
Nicopolis
ANTONY'S
2nd. CAMP
(Preveza)
Antony's ships
at anchor
Promontory
of Actium
Gulf of
Arta
Temple
of Apollo
Haven of
Actium
Entrenchments
Antony's ships
at anchor
ANTONY'S 1st. AND
LAST CAMP
AGRIPPA
ANTONY
Octavian's
Antony's
first
position
CLEOPATRA
OCTAVIUS
SOSIUS
ARRUNTIUS
OCTAVIAN

Chapter 4- Actium

Although I understood why Antonius and his engineering officers chose the spot and that they did so from a tactical standpoint, its isolation and the boggy ground made Actium a miserable place on which to build a camp. The only civilization nearby was a tiny village, home to pearl divers and housing a few temples that had clearly seen better days. The nearest trees of sufficient size were located on a promontory to the south about two miles away, so that as soon as we disembarked, I put half the men to work, sending them to fell the trees we would need for the towers. Meanwhile, the rest of the men worked to unload the gear, supplies, and livestock. The other Primi Pili were doing much the same, although some chose to have their men unload before putting them to work. The engineers had already staked out the outlines of the camp, which was huge, and was another reason that Antonius had selected this spot, it being large and barren enough for the entire army. The marshy ground also guaranteed the presence of bugs, with millions of marsh flies and mosquitoes swarming about the men, obviously celebrating this sudden feast of flesh and blood that presented itself. Bugs flew up our noses, into our mouths and our ears, causing men to gag and spit out the tiny vermin as they worked. By necessity, the camp was huge, and there was no way that just the eight Legions that came over in the first wave would be able to complete it, so in a hasty meeting of the Primi Pili with Ahenobarbus, who was in command of the leading contingent, it was decided that our first task should be to drain the swampy ground as much as possible. The hope was that draining the ground would rob the bugs of a home, making them go elsewhere, along with reducing the clinging, sticky muck that would soon coat everything. We had a few *alea* of cavalry to act as scouts and as soon as they landed they began ranging out about the countryside, looking for signs of the enemy.

Actium was on the southern tip of a narrow inlet that led into a large protected bay, called Arta as I recall, with enough space for the entire fleet to harbor, another reason that Antonius had selected this spot. The northern point of the inlet jutted down so that the entrance into the bay was very narrow, and the way that the northern and southern points overlapped, it was much like a man with a bit of overbite, requiring the masters of the ships coming into the bay to steer slightly north before bearing sharply south to navigate past the upthrust point of land that formed the southern tip.

The men were grumbling about being placed here in the middle of nowhere, far from the distractions and enjoyment of wineshops and whorehouses. They had gotten soft from all their time in cities, first in Damascus, then Ephesus; it was now than two years since we had marched into Armenia, while our transfer across the water to Greece took place late in the season, meaning we would be spending the winter in this spot. I believe that the knowledge that we would be spending the winter in what the men considered to be little better than the privy where they squatted further contributed to the overall low morale that the Centurions faced. Things were not made easier by the fact that in our hearts even the Centurions wished we were elsewhere. I found it hard to stop worrying about Miriam, wondering if Iras had fooled her, and to a certain extent me, as I had begun to believe that she was not the evil bitch that I had first thought, despite still having strong reservations.

However, nothing could be done about it here in this marsh so I forced myself to concentrate on the job at hand. In a manner similar to what we did at Philippi, we dug a series of shallow ditches, making them progressively deeper as they emptied out into the outer ditch so the water would drain. The advantage of marshy ground is that it is easy to drive the spade into the earth; the disadvantage is that each spadeful is soaked with water, making it that much heavier and the straightforward task of digging even more exhausting. The cavalry scouts returned to report that there was no sign of Octavian's forces, which eased the pressure of building a marching camp in the face of the enemy. The first day saw the men who worked on the camp covered in muck and filth, while the men cutting wood were relatively clean, and I made sure that the men who escaped the bugs and muck this day would not be so lucky the next.

At the end of a week, we were reinforced by the second wave, which landed to find a much drier and less bug-infested camp than when the first wave landed, though you would not know it to hear the complaining of the new arrivals. Not surprisingly, this did not sit well with men who did all the work, and before the first night passed, men had to be separated and punishments given because of the bad blood. With the additional labor force, the camp was almost completed, with the exception of the stakes to finish the palisade that were still with the third and final wave. Fortunately, there were still no signs of Octavian and as we were to learn, he was in no hurry to cross the water from Italia to face us, more concerned with consolidating his power first. His first step was to "encourage" every male citizen in Italia to swear an oath of loyalty to him, including the men of the

Legions who had recently been discharged and elected to return to Italia despite Octavian refusing to give them any land. He also continued his assault on Cleopatra's image, emphasizing her role as the seducer of Antonius, who he was careful to avoid speaking ill of in public. Little by little, day by day, in the patient manner that he was becoming famous for, Octavian chipped away at Antonius' power base in Italia, winning over the other Triumvir's remaining supporters in the Senate. When possible, he used soft words and flattery, but there were whispered tales of harsher measures, of midnight visits to Senator's homes, and mysterious disappearances. As was usual with Octavian, there was nothing more substantial than those whispers, so I cannot say whether they were true or false. My suspicion is that these acts were not nearly as numerous as his enemies implied, but I am not so naïve as to think that it never happened. Both Octavian and Antonius were playing for the highest stakes imaginable; control of the strongest, greatest civilization in the known world, making it hard to fault either of them for doing whatever they thought was necessary to come out on top. Regardless of the truth, Octavian's campaign was paying off, while Antonius was not doing himself any favors.

Antonius seemed to alternate between ignoring Octavian, then doing something that would not only antagonize his colleague, but the lower classes as well. Yet of all the things he did, his order to Octavia to quit his house, supposedly giving her one day in which to pack her belongings, along with those of all of the children she was caring for, I believe severed the last tether of sympathy and support he had with Romans of all classes. He had divorced Octavia some time before, but seemed to be content to let matters lie between them and, as I was to learn later, his divorce of Octavia was common knowledge only on our side of Our Sea. Octavia's humiliation so enraged and inflamed the people that it gave Octavian the opportunity to pass a Senatus Consultus Ultimatum against Cleopatra, declaring war on the queen while specifically not naming Antonius. Whereas prior to this there had still been enough support for Antonius to block this motion, now it passed handily, his former clients seeing that to refuse to back Octavian would be injurious not only to their public fortunes, but their lives.

All of this took place as the rest of the army and navy moved to Actium to settle into winter camp, although we would be spending the winter under leather and not building huts as was normal. Instead, we worked on improving our tactical position by digging a double line of entrenchments from the northern edge of the camp further north to the shore to enclose a small natural harbor known locally as the Haven of Actium. It was in this harbor where the transports carrying our supplies would land and be unloaded, hence the double entrenchments protecting it. The bulk of the fleet, the warships and transports, were anchored in the Bay of Arta, with a line of picket boats always on station across the narrow neck entering the bay. To guard our supply line that ultimately led all the way back to Alexandria, we built a series of small forts and naval stations, ranging down the coast, with a guard of at least one Cohort's strength at each one. Each Legion had to detach one Cohort for these duties and I selected Metellus and the Third, who were sent to the base on the island of Leucas, which was separated by a narrow strip of water between the island and mainland. This base was constructed on the northwestern tip of the island, giving us a position where artillery could be brought to bear on any ships of Octavian that ventured near to our fortifications. From where our main camp was located to Metellus and the Third's redoubt was perhaps a matter of eight or nine miles, and the heights on the island were clearly visible. The forward supply base was established at Patrae, and there was a steady stream of ships ferrying supplies to the Haven, where a wharf had been built. Working parties were required on a daily basis, rotating among the Legions, to unload the ships, which helped keep the men busy. Slowly and steadily, we established a solid operating base, with a steady and protected line of supply, prompting the feeling among the Centurions that at least Antonius had learned his lessons from the Parthian campaigns. I wish I could say that the rankers felt the same way.

As the army labored and settled in for the winter, Antonius and Cleopatra were in Athens, feasting and holding lavish parties that lasted for days. Quite naturally, the news of their debauchery did not go over well with the men, not least because they were unable to indulge themselves in similar activities, even if it was on a more modest scale. Then, there were the omens and signs that occupy the minds while exciting the fears of men in the ranks, and not a few Centurions as well. I have never been particularly religious, or superstitious, but I believe that we are all at the whim of the gods, so even I had to give pause to some of the things that were happening all about us. The difference between me and the men who put so much faith in these omens is that I do not automatically believe that they actually occurred, and am willing to accept the possibility that reports of these happenings could be the result of overactive imaginations.

First, there was news of an earthquake at Pisaurum, a veteran's colony established by Antonius on the Ionian

Sea, supposedly swallowing the colony up, leaving no trace. In Alba Longa, a statue of Marcus Antonius erected in the forum began to sweat and would not stop, even after it was wiped clean every day. There was a statue of Bacchus in Athens at one of the theaters and a violent wind blew it flat. This was connected to Antonius because of his claims to be the new Dionysus, which as I am sure you know, gentle reader, is the Greek name for our god. Despite the fact that the reports of these happenings excited the men greatly, what I noticed was that nobody seemed to be able to name someone who had seen any of these events firsthand. However, the one report that did concern me, because it was witnessed by a number of men that I knew personally, was the bolt of lightning that struck the statue of Hercules in Patrae. Since Antonius claimed direct descent from Hercules, that seemed to me to be a clear sign of the gods' disfavor and it did give me pause. The men spent many thirds of a watch about their fires muttering about these signs, and there was nothing that the Centurions could say that seemed to help. I suspected that for most of the Centurions, the problem was that they did not believe their own words coming out of their mouths, because they read the signs the same way as the men did.

Either oblivious to or ignoring these omens, Antonius continued his preparations, sending for his client kings, either demanding their presence in person or requiring more troops. From far-off Libya came Bocchus with a few thousand cavalry, armed and trained in the same manner as the Numidians; Tarcondemus of Upper Cilicia brought a levy of spearmen and some cavalry of indifferent quality; Philadelphus of Paphlagonia, the mountainous country on the Euxine Sea between Bithynia and Pontus, brought a few thousand horsemen.

Mithridates of Commagene, the son of Antiochus and his successor, brought about 5,000 men of foot, armed with wicker shields and long spears, while Sadalus of Thrace supplied another 5,000 men, evenly split between infantry and light cavalry. Perhaps most telling were the client kings who did not show up, since in the past they had been the men whose lips were most firmly attached to Antonius' backside. Polemon of Pontus sent a contingent of cavalry, although I personally thought that he could be excused, given his experience of being held hostage the last time he marched with Antonius. Herod the fat toad made his excuses as well, sending a force of 5,000 Jews, well-armed and trained, and if half of what I heard about what happened whenever Herod and Cleopatra were in the same room was true, I suppose he also had a good reason to absent himself. Finally, Artavasdes the Median, who was by agreement Antonius' future son-in-law, sent a force of cataphracts and archers, but not his royal personage. Their absence did not go unnoticed by the men of all ranks and, coupled with the omens and portents I have described earlier, created a sense of futility that I had never seen or experienced before.

The men seemed resigned to the idea that our defeat was a foregone conclusion and in the Legions where the ranks had been filled with men from the East, desertion became a problem, men slipping over the rampart to make their way back to wherever they came from. Some of them were caught and were executed the next day in front of the army, but it did not stop men from trying to escape. For the most part, most of the veterans stayed put; in the 10th we only had a half-dozen men who decided they wanted no part in what was about to happen, and none of them were much loss. It might sound strange, since all of them escaped, meaning that their close comrades had to be flogged, but there was still a sense of pride in their accomplishment, such as it was. All of the deserters from the other Legion had about as much chance of being caught as escaping, half of them either being grabbed trying to slip past the sentries, or in the first day after the alarm was raised. Only the men of the 10th all got away clean, none of them ever being seen again, something that the men quietly gloated about. I found it surprising that after seeing how easily the deserters made their escape that more men did not follow them, particularly given their mood, but for reasons I could not completely fathom they chose instead to stay put, despite their conviction that the cause they were fighting for was doomed. This was the mood of the army of Marcus Antonius in those last months of winter, while we waited for Octavian.

"Agrippa has crossed the Ionian Sea and landed at Methoni," Ahenobarbus announced at our morning briefing early in the year. "He attacked our base there, and it's been captured, along with the garrison."

It was the year of the third Consulship of both Octavian and Marcus Antonius, although Octavian had his former colleague stripped of his Consulship, putting a nothing named Marcus Valerius Corvinus in his place. Despite this being expected news, it still caused a stir, as the reality that the battle that had been looming on the horizon for so many years was drawing close enough to be recognized. Upon hearing it, men glanced at each other, exchanging quiet remarks, while I was assailed by the thought that the moment when Octavian would most likely reach out to me was perhaps just days away. It all depended on how quickly Octavian followed with the rest of his fleet.

Agrippa established a forward operating base at Methoni and in his always efficient manner, sent a number of seaborne patrols out in an effort to find the naval stations protecting our supply line. In doing so, he chanced across a convoy of transports making their way from Alexandria to Patrae, loaded down with grain and ingots of iron and lead that we needed to make repairs to weapons and armor, as well as making the sling bullets that had proven so effective against the Parthians. Although the grain was important, the loss of the iron and lead was even more crushing since this was our only source of supply, Octavian now controlling all of the mines in Greece and Hispania. Our grain supply was ample, at least for the time being, but that also depended on how long we would be in Greece and on campaign; according to the tallies for which I bribed a clerk in the *Praetorium*, we had enough for three more months at our current consumption, without resupply. These were not our only problems. Spending the winter in the unhealthy air of Actium, even with the marshes drained, caused an outbreak of fever that took a heavy toll on the men. It got to the point where one in ten men were afflicted and on the sick list; of those, about a quarter of that number ended up dying. Without knowing exactly when Octavian would be moving, there was not much we could do other than to wait, despite stepping up our training regimen with more forced marches. Even with Agrippa many miles away on the southwest tip of the Peloponnesus, all of the Primi Pili began making the men train and march ready for battle, which of course the men hated since it meant marching wearing their armor. That was a mark of the respect we had for Agrippa; all of us worried about when and where he might show up, knowing that if he did, it would be to fight.

In early March, we heard that Octavian had moved to Brundisium to begin embarkation, taking 700 Senators with him, most of them the creatures of Antonius. In his coldly logical way, Octavian apparently decided that the best way to keep an eye on potential troublemakers was to keep them nearby, though how he managed all 700, I have no idea. It was early in the year to move an army across the sea, it not being practical to hug the coast all the way up the peninsula and then down the coast of Illyricum and Greece, so Octavian was taking a huge risk. However, the winds were blowing from the west instead of their normal easterly direction and he managed to cross the water without losing a ship, something the men took as yet another sign that he had the favor of all the gods. Landing at Panormus, not the city in Sicily, but the colony by the same name on the Epirot coast, Octavian quickly invested the town before moving south to Toryne. It was here that one of the Liburnians that Antonius used for scouting first spied Octavian's fleet and, being much faster than anything Octavian had, was able to outrun the pursuit to report to Antonius, who had moved from Athens to Patrae when Agrippa made his crossing. Whatever the scout had to report, it got Antonius and Cleopatra moving, both of them leaving for Actium within the day of receiving the report.

"Have you seen her yet?"

I was munching on a piece of bread, bemoaning to Diocles the sad fact that I had lost my first tooth, so I was not in a very good mood to begin with when Scribonius entered and asked the question. There was no need to ask to whom he was referring and I was sure that he was just trying to put me in a worse mood.

"Not yet," I grunted. "But we're having a briefing in the morning and I'm sure that she'll be there, all dressed up in her armor."

"Hopefully you won't do anything to make her want to pick up where she left off," my friend commented, ducking out of the way of the cup I flung at him. Turning serious, he asked, "Have you heard anything from Octavian?"

I shook my head. It was something that occupied my every waking thought, wondering when Octavian would reach out to me, along with whomever else among the Primi Pili he had in his purse, and how he would do it.

"You haven't spoken to the other Centurions about this yet, have you?"

"No. I plan on waiting until the last moment, like you suggested."

"Good. Let me know when Octavian contacts you."

I assured him that I would. The next morning, I arrived at the *Praetorium* fully dressed, with freshly varnished leathers and whitened crest, cursing for the hundredth time Antonius' insistence that all crests and plumes be white instead of black, which is much harder to achieve and maintain. The tent was already crowded with the other Primi Pili and Tribunes, gathered in small knots, usually arranged by rank. The conversations were whispered, but the urgency and tension was palpable as we waited for Antonius and Cleopatra to make their appearance. After what seemed like a full watch, the royal couple finally arrived. From their rigid postures and set expressions, it was fairly clear that they had been arguing. Antonius had a harried, haggard look that indicated to me that Cleopatra was after him about something, and I felt a pang of sympathy for the man. Even knowing that he had willingly done this to himself, I still felt badly that he was in this position. With that harpy constantly gnawing at his bones, I could not imagine that the man had a moment's peace as she dripped poison into his ear every waking moment. Cleopatra was dressed in her armor, but this time she was even wearing a sword, and had an Attic-style helmet perched on her head, although it was made of gold and studded with precious jewels.

"That's not going to do her much good," was Balbinus' comment. "One good crack with even a mediocre blade would split that golden helmet like a pear."

"Do you really think she'd get anywhere near a battle?" I asked, my tone as sour as my mood.

"Probably not," Balbinus conceded as we settled down in our seats while Antonius and Cleopatra made their way to the front of the room.

It took a moment for so many men to quiet down, but soon enough we were all paying attention as Antonius scanned our faces, clearly trying to communicate that a momentous event was awaiting us.

"You all know that little prick Octavian has finally gotten off his pampered ass and crossed the water," Antonius began.

He had our complete attention as we waited to hear what he had planned for us, but we were to be disappointed, since he seemed intent only on insulting Octavian while Cleopatra looked on with a smile. For the next several moments, he ranted about Octavian's perfidy and not surprisingly, the reading of Antonius' will drew his most bitter comment. Not content with stopping there, he went on to make a number of slurs against Octavian's sexual tastes, yet despite his wit drawing appreciative laughter from most of the men, there was more than one sidelong glance about to see if anyone else was disturbed by his seeming lack of concern about actually doing something other than calling Octavian names. Finally, he finished with a vague remark about waiting for Octavian to commit himself to a strategy before responding, which did not make any of us feel any better. Of course, we could not relay that feeling back to the rankers when we returned to our Legions; instead, we had to project an attitude of confidence in our general while pretending that we actually had a plan.

"It was never like this with Caesar," I complained to Scribonius that evening, who I had called on to commiserate with me about the state of affairs.

"Why are you acting surprised?" Scribonius was anything but sympathetic. "He's never been Caesar's bootlace as a general. I heard from one of the Tribunes that he's commanded that the fleet be gathered here in the bay."

I felt a tightening in my chest as the import of what Scribonius was saying hit me.

"The whole fleet?"

He nodded grimly.

"That's what he told me, and he's the one who had the scribes copy out the orders so I'm guessing that it's true."

"So much for the initiative," I said glumly, for that was the crux of the matter as far as Antonius' order.

While it was protecting his fleet, it also meant that we were essentially blinded, unable to make any serious effort at protecting our supply line. Conversely, Octavian would be able to land his troops anywhere he wanted, then force us to come to him, since he would have an uninterrupted line of supply back to Italia because Antonius was keeping his fleet penned up. I was completely mystified by this decision, and I told Scribonius as much.

"That's because I don't think Antonius is planning on fighting on land," Scribonius said.

I looked at him incredulously. That had never occurred to me.

"Why would he want to do that? What did he ship us over here for if he plans on doing his fighting by sea?"

"That I don't know." Scribonius shrugged. "But I suspect that it has something to do with his queen. And, it does make a certain amount of sense if you think about it. I'm not saying I agree with it," he added hastily, reacting to the look on my face. "But if the numbers are right, we outnumber Octavian's fleet by two to one and we have all of those Egyptian quinqueremes. If Antonius can crush Octavian's fleet, he can't prevent Antonius from moving wherever he wants and doing whatever he wants."

As Scribonius spoke, it became clear to me his reasoning was sound, and I also understood, or believed that I did, what the larger game was.

"He's saving the army for an invasion of Italia," I said slowly.

Scribonius nodded. "I think so."

"That smells of Cleopatra through and through," and he nodded again, but said nothing.

"Well, think of the bright side," Scribonius said, with a twisted grin that was more ironic than humorous. "It won't matter to us because Octavian is sure to call in his debt any day now."

Somehow, that thought did not cheer me greatly.

One thing about Octavian; he does not move often, but when he does, it is with blinding speed. Now that he made up his mind to move, he wasted no time. Establishing his forward base on the island of Corcyra, we were now essentially pinned between Octavian to the north and Agrippa to the south. Still, Antonius refused to unleash his fleet. Keeping it penned safely behind a row of ships linked together by a huge chain, much as was done at Brundisium in the first civil war, our fleet was safe but impotent. Ahenobarbus at least had the foresight to establish a pair of forts on both sides of the inlet, emplacing a disproportionately large number of artillery pieces in each one. A fire was kept perpetually burning in each, with a large stockpile of combustible ammunition, ready to rain fire down on the heads of any of Octavian's ships that were foolish enough to try to run the gauntlet. Duty in the two forts was rotated, with a Cohort in each fort standing duty for a day at a time, while Octavian and Agrippa's ships cruised back and forth out in the open water in plain view from the watchtowers placed at each fort. Occasionally, they would venture just within artillery range of our larger ballistae, but after the first time or two, the men learned not to waste their ammunition, recognizing that the enemy was testing our defenses.

Then, Octavian made his next move, after a probing attack on the inlet, which was easily repulsed, landing his army at a spot about five miles north of our position, near a town called Toryne. There was a shallow bay there, suitable for beaching the bulk of his fleet, despite the fact that it was not nearly as protected from the spring storms as our bay. Overlooking the bay was a high flat-topped hill a few hundred feet high and it was on this height that Octavian constructed his camp. Immediately, our cavalry scouts returned with a report and for the first time we learned the size and composition of Octavian's forces. After the briefing, I returned to call a meeting of the Legion's Centurions, minus Metellus' Cohort, which was still on detached duty.

"Octavian has eight Legions, plus five Praetorian Cohorts," I reported.

The Centurions treated this as good news, at least until some of the more observant took notice of my grim expression.

"Primus Pilus, we outnumber them by a huge amount. Why are you looking as if you just ate a lemon?"

"Because they're all Italians, they're all veterans, and I suspect that there are a fair number of them that were with us not that long ago."

This quieted them immediately. One recurring topic of conversation among the few veteran Legions remaining in Antonius' army concerned the quality of the men filling the ranks of the new Legions that were raised in the East. After the first Parthian campaign, when we combed the region to fill our ranks, we had essentially picked the cream of the Roman citizens that populated the regions on the far side of Our Sea. When it came time to re-enlist Legions like the 3rd, 4th, and all the others, Antonius had been forced to waive the requirement of Roman citizenship in order to fill the ranks. This was the first time that non-citizens were enlisted into the Legions on such a large scale, causing quite a bit of grumbling among the men. Antonius was offering every man citizenship at the end of their enlistment, which was a powerful enticement as far as we were concerned, but we Romans also believe strongly in the sanctity of our traditions and customs. Despite these men being Roman-trained, the fact that they were not Romans was never far from any man's mind. Adding in their unblooded status, it was an open question as to how these Legions would perform. My Centurions were all veterans of long-standing, most of them having been at least in the ranks at Pharsalus when our veterans, whittled down to slightly less than half our numbers, had routed a far more numerous army. In our minds, one truly Roman veteran Legionary, blooded and tested in battle, was worth five or ten men from the East, no matter what their training. The thought that Octavian's army, or at least the portion which he had shipped over with, was composed almost entirely of such veterans was sobering to all of us.

"So what do we do?"

I did not see who asked the question although I recognized the voice as belonging to Plautius, the Princeps Posterior of the Fifth Cohort. I had been dreading this question, knowing that I had to provide more of an answer than I was given.

"We wait for the general to finalize his plans, which he's working on as we speak."

"Which means we sit here with our thumbs up our asses and let Octavian fortify his position and do nothing about it," someone whispered.

I do not know if I was meant to overhear or not, but it was something I could not let pass.

"*Tacete,*" I roared suddenly, gratified to see men jump, blinking in surprise. "I don't know who said that, but you're lucky, because I'd break your bones, both for talking out of turn and for being blatantly disrespectful to your commanding general." I lowered my voice to a menacing growl as I finished. "And if I hear one more word like that, I'll hurt somebody."

With my duty done, in the event that one of my men was working for Antonius, I dismissed them to their duties for the day. I had just lied to my Centurions, the first time I had ever done so, at least to this degree. In the past I had lied more by omission than directly, choosing not to tell them all of the information that I had, but I did not and do not believe that this is wrong. Sometimes it is in the best interests of the men you are leading that they not know all of the details of their situation, but this time

I had just fabricated something out of the air, since there was no planning of any sort going on in the *Praetorium* of Antonius and Cleopatra.

Octavian took advantage of our period of inactivity, or paralysis would perhaps be a better description, to fortify and improve his position outside Toryne. To protect his ships in the unprotected bay, he constructed a breakwater extending from the shore out several hundred paces. In addition, he created a double set of entrenchments similar to ours, leading from the camp on the hilltop down to the water. During this time, the Senators and others of similar rank were allowed to pass back and forth between the two camps, something which both Antonius and Octavian allowed, mystifying me completely.

"It's for us," was the way Scribonius explained it. "Octavian knows that we'll hear about all that they're doing and how well prepared they are for a fight."

"I can see why Octavian would want that," I agreed. "But why would Antonius allow it? Our morale's for *cac*; half of the Legions here barely know which end of the sword to hold, and the Centurions are unhappy."

"How many Senators do you think can look at us and see those things? Out of this current crop, there aren't many left of Caesar's men. Oh, most of them have at least been under the leather for a campaign season, I'll grant you that, but how long ago was that?"

I mulled over what Scribonius said. I did not like it, but I knew that what he was saying was most likely true. Scribonius was not finished, however.

"And as ignorant as they might be, do you think Antonius is any better? He's either ignoring the true state of this army, or Cleopatra has indeed slipped him some potion or performed some magic that makes him blind to what's really going on."

When Scribonius was like this, there was no sense in trying to stop him. I could tell that this agitation had been building up inside him for some time and now he was letting it out before he burst. I was just thankful that we were in the privacy of my tent, though I was somewhat worried that our voices would carry.

"No," he finished. "Those men come and go because both of them think it's in their best interests to let them and neither of them are blind to the fact that there are friends and relatives on both sides of this fight. No matter who wins, Rome has to keep going and those are the men that run Rome. As powerful as Octavian and Antonius might be, they can't afford to alienate them."

As it turned out, the Senators turned out to be as effective as any of our scouts in relaying not just information on enemy dispositions and numbers, but in the exchange of messages between the two generals. It was not long before word leaked out that Octavian had sent Antonius a letter, offering to meet in battle five days later, at a spot mutually agreed upon. Antonius ignored the letter, leading to a huge argument between him and Ahenobarbus, who emphatically urged him to accept the challenge and end the struggle once and for all. Feelings had been growing tense between our most competent general and the royal couple for some time, the strain clear to see at every briefing. With the camp and defenses constructed and the presence of a nearby enemy curtailing training outside the walls, there was little for the men to do as they waited for Antonius to announce his plans. Days passed with men listlessly playing at dice or tables, not even having the interest or energy to fight over disputed throws. The desertion problem spread to the crews of the ships, with rowers slipping away at seemingly every opportunity, so that Antonius was forced to start pressing local fishermen into service on the benches. For my part, I waited for the message from Octavian, and worried about Miriam and Iras.

Days dragged into weeks, the seasons changing from spring to summer, the heat rising every day, increasing the lethargy of the army. Then, the defections of the higher-ranking men who were still with Antonius began in earnest. The numbers of the Senators who once came flocking to Alexandria with Ahenobarbus and Sosius the year before now reversed direction, heading back to Octavian, all of them with the same complaint: Cleopatra. And it was not just Senators; Legates began leaving as well and none of them were stopped by Antonius, despite Cleopatra's furious demands that these men be punished. The defections were clear to see at every morning briefing, with more empty stools almost every day. Antonius had long ceased bothering to show up, letting Ahenobarbus conduct the briefings as the ranking officer. Then, Ahenobarbus took ill, coming down with the fever that was sweeping the camp. The 10th had an average of one man per tent on the sick list, most of them from fever, although there were a fair number of men ill from other reasons. As bad as it was with the 10th, we were still better off than most of the other Legions, particularly those filled with the Eastern *tiros*, who seemed to be more susceptible to illness for some reason. It was something I had noticed throughout my career in the army; Legions filled with new men usually had a higher rate of sickness early in their enlistments than veterans did, though I do not know why. Canidius was now the ranking general conducting the briefings and for some reason he had managed to stay, if not in her good graces, at least sufficiently out of range of Cleopatra's wrath.

Cleopatra had taken to trying to conduct surprise inspections of the men, but she was met with such open hostility from the Centurions that she quickly abandoned this course. Fortunately for both of us, she gave me a wide berth, while I did the same, turning to head the other way whenever I was around the *Praetorium* and it looked as if our paths might cross. Ahenobarbus' condition steadily worsened, but he rose off his sickbed to make one last plea to Antonius to come to grips with Octavian and end the war, pressing forcefully for the use of the army instead of Antonius' fleet. Diocles' spy in the *Praetorium* reported that Cleopatra became enraged, mercilessly ridiculing Ahenobarbus for daring to second-guess her and Antonius. According to the scribe, Antonius sat mute during the exchange, as if he were helpless to stop her from berating and alienating a man who had cleaved to Antonius through the worst of times. This proved too much for Ahenobarbus to bear, so despite his feeble condition, he somehow summoned the strength to mount a horse to ride out of the camp, then hired a boat to take him across the bay to Octavian's camp. While Antonius could not stop Cleopatra from running off most of his highborn supporters, he did brave her anger by sending all of Ahenobarbus' baggage off to him after he had departed.

I do not know if Ahenobarbus' words were the spur to Antonius that prompted him to take action on land, but from somewhere a plan was concocted to try and cut off Octavian's water supply. Fortunately, we were not involved, since this seemed to be a plan doomed to failure from its inception. Using a mixed force of cavalry, he shipped a contingent across the bay to land essentially behind Octavian's camp, between the camp and a river that was Octavian's supply of fresh water. The bulk of the cavalry, Galatians mostly, although the overall command was led by the Paphlagonian king Philadelphus who led the blocking force, were sent the long way around the entire bay, which measures some 20 miles deep and 11 miles across, to reinforce the men holding their tenuous position blocking the river. The reason I state that the plan was destined to fail was not that the idea was bad. The problem lay in the fact that to effectively cut off Octavian's water supply, the river had to be guarded the entire length from where it turned up into the mountains and down to where it emptied into the bay. It could have been held, but not by cavalry, except that is all that Antonius sent to accomplish his goal. Even if the main body of the cavalry had reached the holding force, I doubt they could have accomplished the task set for them, but they were intercepted by a mounted force led by none other than our old quartermaster Titius, who was one of the first to defect to Octavian over Cleopatra. The main body was commanded by Amyntas the Galatian, while Philadelphus commanded the holding force and when Titius routed Amyntas' men, both men promptly surrendered, defecting to Octavian. This was a disheartening setback, but it was nothing compared to the disaster that was about to befall us, as Agrippa struck again, and it would cost the 10th Legion dearly.

There is an island, a craggy upthrust of rock named Leucas Island that acts as a guard to the mouth of the bay. Anyone holding that island could fall on the rear of any enemy trying to force its way into the bay, making it strategically important. That is why Metellus' Cohort was placed there, along with a squadron of triremes, both to protect the island and to serve as a deterrent to an attack on the fleet in the bay. One feature of the marshy ground at Actium was that during the night as the land cooled off, a heavy, misty fog would form that usually lasted until mid-morning. Some days it was barely visible, but other days it hung over our shoulders like a sodden cloak, effectively blocking our view more than a few hundred paces out into the water. It was on just such a morning that Agrippa chose to descend on the island, landing a force of several Cohorts on the island, while his own fleet attacked the triremes anchored in the small bay.

Because of the fog, no alarm was raised that might have sent aid to the garrison and squadron, at least until it was too late. I only became aware that something had happened when the *bucinator* for the guard Cohort manning the western side of the camp facing out to sea sounded the call that signaled an enemy was sighted. Not knowing if it was a probe or an all-out attack, I took no chances, having Valerius sound the call to arms and assembly in the forum, while I hurried to the *Praetorium* to find out what was happening. Arriving to total confusion, I saw there were Tribunes scurrying about, shouting what I soon recognized to be groundless speculation about what was transpiring, while Canidius and a few of the other generals stood in a knot, looking anxious. Spotting Corbulo, dressed in his uniform as Evocatus, and standing with Spurius and Caecina, I walked over to them. Their faces were grim and when they turned to see me coming. I saw Corbulo and Spurius exchange a glance that put me on my guard, though I could not say why.

"What's happening? Do you know any more than this bunch?" I jerked a thumb over my shoulder at the

Tribunes, who seemed intent on acting like a bunch of panicked women.

Corbulo shot Spurius that same look, as if they were trying to decide who should speak and I found I did not have patience for such behavior at that moment.

"What is it?" I snapped. "Both of you look like I caught you trying to fuck a Vestal."

Finally, Corbulo spoke, his voice low. "It looks like Agrippa has taken Leucas."

I heard a sharp hiss of someone sucking in a breath, only dimly aware that it was me, as my stomach lurched.

"How do you know this?" I demanded, despite somehow already knowing that it was true.

Caecina spoke. "Because it's my Cohort on guard duty. Curtius, my Decimus Pilus Prior is in command. He's a good man and not likely to make a mistake. Once the fog cleared, his men on the southwest tower saw what was happening."

"That's a long way off," I said doubtfully, knowing that I was desperately looking for any chance that the lookout was wrong. "I don't see how your man could tell exactly what was going on."

"He couldn't see the fighting on land," Caecina conceded. "But he saw at least two of the triremes go down and the others scatter. How about your Pilus Prior out there? Is he a good man? Do you think he can hold out long enough to send relief?"

"He's one of my best," I said emphatically, thinking of all the times Metellus had performed with skill and bravery while under my command. "I would put him just behind Balbus and Scribonius as my best Centurion."

"Then maybe there's hope yet." Corbulo tried to sound reassuring, but it rang hollow in my ears.

Apparently, he felt the same way, since he reached out to give me an awkward pat. Looking over to

Canidius, who was still standing there talking, I felt a surge of anger that we were not moving to save not only my men, but the island from being invested. Resolving to press the man to take some action, I began walking over to him, girding myself for what I was sure would be an unpleasant encounter, the bad blood between us from the first Parthian campaign obviously still lingering. Before I could reach him, however, there was a commotion at the entrance and a man came bursting in, panting for breath. I recognized the man as a squadron *navarch* belonging to the Egyptian segment of our fleet, despite the fact he was spattered with blood and his uniform was torn. Spotting Canidius, he headed directly for the general, just as Antonius finally emerged from his private quarters, followed immediately by Cleopatra. That stopped me in my tracks since I was not willing to get any closer to the queen, instead watching as she and Antonius joined Canidius. Instead, I moved off to the side out of her line of vision, but I did not need to worry, her attention being pinned on her fellow Egyptian. Approaching the three people, the *navarch* faltered for a moment before turning to kneel in front of Cleopatra, his head bowed. There was a shocked gasp from most of the onlookers at this effrontery to Antonius' authority, but he did not seem to notice.

"Well?" he snapped. "What's the situation?"

Looking confused, the *navarch* turned his attention to Antonius, speaking in Greek with an accent that told me he was one of the Macedonian Egyptians, which partially explained why he deferred to Cleopatra first.

"General, I regret to inform you that the island of Leucas has been taken by the forces of Marcus Agrippa."

Even though I knew what he was probably going to say, I felt a shock jolt me and I could see by the faces of the others standing there that they felt much the same way. Antonius' face drained of all color, his jaw hanging open, and he took a staggering step backward. Only Cleopatra seemed to have any self-possession, asking the *navarch* to describe what had happened.

"They used the fog that hangs around the coast," the man explained, continuing in Greek.

Knowing that I spoke the language, Corbulo, Spurius, and Caecina came to stand next to me, and I whispered the translation as he continued.

"They attacked just as the sun was coming up, so that between the fog and the sun hanging low in the sky, they were shielded from view. At least," he added, "until it was too late." His head dropped as he described the attack, clearly not wanting to look his audience in the eye. "While part of their squadron engaged our ships, another portion landed an assault force that launched an immediate attack on the camp. They came prepared with ladders and hooks to pull the palisade down."

My chest tightened as he talked, knowing that under such a well-prepared assault even a man as good as Metellus was fighting against overwhelming odds.

"Most of our own ships were unable to pull anchor and maneuver, so it quickly degenerated into a boarding action," the *navarch* said, explaining the blood on his body and garments.

"And how did you escape?" Cleopatra's tone was cold as she looked down at the still-kneeling man.

"By the sacrifice of most of my squadron," he said quietly. "We were able to repulse the first attempt to board our vessel, then Lysander was able to get underway and he rammed the ship we were engaged with, allowing me to break free."

"How . . . *fortunate* for you." Her voice dripped with contempt and sarcasm, eliciting another gasp at the insult.

The *navarch* stiffened, but his tone was even as he replied, "If you call seeing many of your friends sacrifice their lives for you, then yes, Highness, I am fortunate."

Before Cleopatra could respond, Antonius interrupted. "What of the garrison? Are they holding out?"

The man looked genuinely sad as he shook his head. "I regret to say, general, that there is no chance that they are still fighting by this point. The last I saw of them, they had formed into an *orbis* in the middle of the camp and they were beset on all sides."

As I translated this to the others, my jaw felt tight as the words seemed to stick on my tongue. I said a silent prayer for Metellus, the rest of the Centurions, and men of the Third Cohort. This was the second full Cohort that I had lost while marching for Antonius and it was a bitter, bitter potion to swallow.

"General, I can tell you that your men fought valiantly. I saw many enemy bodies around them as they fought, but I am afraid the numbers were too great for there to be any hope that they could hold them off for the length of time it took for us to get here."

"What does it matter how they fought if they were not victorious?" Cleopatra interjected bitterly.

Antonius spun to face her, his face twisted with what I perceived to be rage and grief.

"What does it matter?" he echoed. "It matters everything, you silly woman! Even when we don't win, it matters to a Roman how we fight!"

Now it was Cleopatra's turn to go bloodless, stiffening not only from the rebuke, but I imagine from the tone and the fact that it had taken place in front of witnesses.

She managed to maintain her composure, but it was plain to see that it was a struggle.

"I can see that your grief has affected you, husband," she replied coolly. "Otherwise, I could not imagine you speaking in such a manner to your co-commander, let alone your wife."

Antonius instantly deflated, his shoulders sagging, and the only reason I did not shake my head in disgust is because it might have drawn Cleopatra's attention to me.

"You're right, my queen. I shouldn't take my anger out on you." Antonius turned back to the *navarch.* "I thank you for your report, even if you don't bring me welcome news. You're dismissed to see to your crew."

The man stood, saluted Antonius, bowed to Cleopatra, then hurried out, leaving Antonius, Cleopatra, and Canidius standing huddled together, talking in low tones. After conferring a few moments, Antonius turned to address us as we gathered closer. I lingered toward the back of the group, taking care to remain on the edges of the small crowd and out of Cleopatra's line of vision, though she was looking grimly pleased while Canidius was visibly fuming.

"So there's no point in mounting an attempt to dislodge the enemy," Antonius announced in a tired voice. "They overwhelmed the men holding the camp there, and no doubt, by this time, have invested the position with more men. Sending the fleet out would expose it to attack from the north and south by Octavian and Agrippa's remaining fleet. I have no intention of risking the fleet to hold an island that would be under constant attack."

Now I understood why Canidius was so agitated, especially since I shared his feeling. Again, it seemed to me that Antonius was picking his navy over his army and I knew that the men would feel the same slight when the inevitable word leaked out of what had taken place. It also explained why Cleopatra was standing there looking triumphant, since she had been pushing Antonius to rely on her navy instead of his army. No one dared to protest, not with Cleopatra standing there. Instead, we filed out to return to our respective Legions. Before I could make my escape, however, Antonius called to me. Bracing myself, I turned and marched back to face the general, keeping my eyes on him, not allowing myself to look over at Cleopatra. I could tell her gaze was on me, almost feeling the blasting force of her hatred washing over me, but I managed to maintain my focus on Antonius.

"Yes, general?" I asked as I saluted, which he returned.

"It was your Cohort on the island, wasn't it?"

"Yes, sir, it was. Tertius Pilus Prior Metellus, sir."

He blinked at the name, clearly struggling to recall the face to put with the name. Then he nodded. "Ah, yes. Short, squatty man, but a good man with a sword, if I remember?"

I was thankful that he did seem to remember Metellus, and I nodded in return.

"Well, I'm sorry that he was lost, but you should be proud that he died fighting so bravely for Rome."

Before I could answer, Cleopatra's voice cut through the air as she sniffed, "Brave he might be. I just wish he had fought better. Then perhaps we wouldn't have lost the island."

I knew that she was baiting me, but it did not make it any easier to endure and I kept my eyes locked on Antonius, it feeling as if my jaw would grind my teeth into powder. His gaze turned sympathetic and he gave an almost imperceptible shrug, but he ignored Cleopatra and I took my cue from him.

"I am proud of him, general. I just wish there was something we could do for all of the men lost today."

That was as far as I dared to go, but Antonius did not seem to take any offense, reaching out to give me a pat on the shoulder.

"So do I, Pullus. So do I."

I wanted to scream at him, to grab him and slap some sense into the man, anything to rid him of the *numen* that Cleopatra had conjured up to take over the man that had been Marcus Antonius, but my courage failed me. I know that it would not have done anything other than get me executed, but it did not make me feel any better. I do not remember the rest of the conversation, such as it was, only taking away the small victory that Cleopatra was unable to provoke me. Returning to the Legion, I prepared myself to tell the men that some of their friends, and in some cases relatives, had in all likelihood been killed or captured, and what was worse, we were going to do nothing to avenge them.

Looking back, I believe that the hands of the gods were busy pulling the strings that control events and thereby indirectly our actions, since I believe that the loss of Metellus and the Third Cohort set the stage for what was to come later, making my task easier when the time came. Ordering the Legion assembled, I told them of the fight on the island. By this point, most of them had heard rumors to this effect, but this was the first confirmation, and I watched the shock and anguish ripple through the ranks, the faces of the men matching what I was feeling. Scribonius looked particularly sad, because he and Metellus had been almost as close friends as Scribonius and I. There was not much else that I could think to say, so after telling the men, I dismissed them back to their areas, and they shuffled off, talking morosely among themselves. Calling the Centurions to me, I ordered a double wine ration for the evening meal, knowing that it would be needed to dull the pain of what happened. After that, I retired to my quarters, telling Diocles that I did not want to be disturbed, sitting down heavily in the chair behind my desk and putting my head in my hands. It was only then that I began to weep.

The bad news did not stop there and as much of a tragedy as the loss of the Third was to the 10th, what happened next was a catastrophe for the entire army and navy. Agrippa, clearly not wanting to waste the momentum gained from his capture of Leucas, continued sweeping southward and on to Patrae, seizing our supply base. In a stroke, Agrippa cut our lifeline, not only by taking our existing supplies still waiting to be shipped to us from Patrae, but by taking control of the sea route along with it. We now had to rely on everything coming by mule train over a torturous mountain track originating in faraway Thrace. The path where it cut through the mountains of Macedonia was too narrow for wagons, cutting the flow of supplies to a mere trickle. Suddenly our situation was close to desperate, having barely a month's supply of grain on hand, with perhaps five weeks' worth of chickpeas and other staples. There was no way that our stocks could be replenished or even maintained at their current levels with a plodding train of mules coming in once a day, so Antonius immediately ordered our rations cut to three-quarters. It was a small blessing that we were as inactive as we were, or the reduction would have caused more trouble than it did, yet the men were so lethargic as it was that there was not even much grumbling about it.

Word also reached us from one of the Senators still traveling back and forth between the camps that Ahenobarbus had died, just a day after he left our camp to go to Octavian. It made me wonder if he had spent the last of his strength trying to convince Antonius to abandon his current course of action, whatever it was. Spending my time walking through the Legion area talking to the men, I tried every trick I could think of to keep morale from sinking lower by the day. I had long given up thinking that each day it could not get any worse, instead trying to focus on finding ways to keep the men somewhat interested in their duties. While I dug deeply into my own purse, I am afraid that I also put some pressure on the other Centurions to come up with funds of their own, putting the money up as prizes in a series of games and contests. We did not have the room or energy for mock battles, meaning I had to keep the contests short and of a sufficiently small scale that the men were not exhausted or did not want to participate.

Although other Primi Pili were cracking down on the discipline, marching men out almost daily to witness punishments ranging from flogging to executions, I, along with the Primi Pili of the more veteran Legions, took the opposite approach. I had never seen the value of trying to beat men into being in a better frame of mind, and I did not think that watching other men being punished would help either. That is not to say that I stopped punishing my own men, but I did it without making a spectacle of it, or whenever possible I substituted onerous duties instead of a flogging.

Unfortunately, Antonius chose to start taking the hard road as well, as his frustration with the continuing defections of high-ranking men mounted. Any man wishing to visit the opposing camp first had to seek permission from Antonius, stating his reason for visiting and how long he intended on being there. Evidently he was lied to so many times, with men telling him that they were visiting a friend or cousin for an afternoon never to return, that he ordered the practice to cease altogether. This did not stop men from seeking to escape, but when they were caught, Antonius once again showed a viciousness that almost defies description. When Iamblichus, one of the client kings of Arabia tried to escape and was caught trying to sneak out with a cavalry patrol, he was dragged to the forum before Antonius. Calling for all the client kings to be assembled, Antonius ordered his summary execution, and he was beheaded in front of the other kings as an example. One would think that would be enough to discourage others from attempting to leave and resigning themselves to waiting to see what the Fates had in store for them, but one foolish man, Quintus Postumius was his name, tried his own chances at getting away. The unfortunate fool was caught, his ruse trying to mingle with the muleteers leaving for the return journey back to Thrace, but he was easily discovered. Highly born people have an arrogance and posture that proclaims itself no matter how they're clothed, even if it is in the meanest rags, so it did not take exceptional alertness on the part of the guard Cohort to spot him. He was taken to Antonius, who flew into a rage at this latest desertion, then ordered all the Centurions of the army to the forum.

"Do you have any idea what this is about?" Scribonius asked as we strode to the forum, but at that moment, I did not.

"No, but I don't imagine it's anything good."

I was more right than I knew. When we arrived, we saw that there was a large cleared area and we were directed to a side of a square enclosing the area by one of the provosts. The square was made of not only Centurions but all of the Tribunes, with the remaining Legates and Senators on one side, all facing inward. In the middle of the square lay a naked man, over which stood two of Antonius' Brundisium Cohorts, looking down to make sure he did not try to escape, or so I presumed. He was bound, but not in the normal fashion; instead of his hands being tied together each wrist was secured by a length of thick rope, the other end of which snaked away several feet where it was attached to the rigging of a horse. His legs were similarly bound, so there were four horses, each facing in a different direction. It became immediately apparent what the punishment for this man was to be, even if I did not know why.

"I've heard of this but I've never seen it before," I heard a man whisper, several heads bobbing in acknowledgment.

Once we were assembled, Antonius stepped forward, his face twisted and cruel as he looked down at the naked man, who was understandably shaking uncontrollably.

"This miserable excuse for a man you see before you is Quintus Postumius. He *was* a Senator of Rome. Now he is a traitor, a traitor who was caught trying to skulk out despite taking a solemn oath before Jupiter Optimus Maximus and his household gods to remain true to me. But the gods are watching us, always. And they saw what this bag of excrement was attempting to do and called attention to him by putting a rock in his path, causing him to trip and fall. When that happened, his disguise as a mule driver fell away and he was revealed to the guards, who did their duty and apprehended him."

Although I had no idea whether this was true, I was skeptical. While I believe that the gods are watching us, I was doubtful that they intervened to the extent that Antonius claimed. Regardless, I also knew he was saying this so that his words would be relayed back to the men, since the men in the ranks are much more likely to believe such things. Postumius was on the young side, but he had evidently been living well, his white, flabby skin rippling with each tremor of fear that seized his body. Antonius, seemingly impervious to the man's sheer terror at the prospect of a gruesome death, continued talking.

"I called you all here to witness what happens to those who break their oaths to me. I am still Triumvir of the East, no matter what that worm Octavian says! I am still Marcus Antonius! And I will be obeyed!"

His voice rang out, hard and cruel, without a drop of mercy in his tone. He turned to signal to the men holding the bridles of the horses. They did not slap the horses and get them to a full gallop, as I expected. Instead, they merely gave a tug on the lead rope of their respective beasts, each of them plodding forward. Postumius' head was whipping around as he watched the slack being taken out of the rope, very slowly, his eyes rolling back in his head so that only the whites showed.

"Surely he's not going to go through with this," whispered Scribonius.

"I think he is," Balbus muttered, and I agreed with Balbus.

The horses moved until the slack was taken out of the rope, Postumius' limbs spreading out as he vainly tried to ease the strain by extending them. In a few moments, Postumius' moans became screams as the horses were urged forward, their ears twitching at the sounds coming from the tortured man. When Postumius was suspended in the air, his head twisting back and forth in agony, Antonius raised his hand to halt the horses. I heard Scribonius exhale in clear relief.

"I told you," he whispered. "He's not going to go through with it."

But Scribonius was wrong. All Antonius was doing was prolonging the man's agony. While he stopped the horses from continuing, he did not have their handlers back up, so Postumius hung suspended, his muscles slowly being pulled apart. He screamed, the sound piercing our ears like needles, a high-pitched wail that was unsettling to both man and the beasts involved in the punishment, their ears twitching as their heads tossed nervously. After a moment like this, Antonius waved his hand again, the horses resuming their pulling. I will not go into any more detail about the death of Quintus Postumius, other than to say that next to Eumenis, it was the most gruesome death that I have ever witnessed. He did not die easily, nor did he die well, but I do not imagine many men would under those circumstances. During the whole ordeal, which caused some of the most hardened Centurions in the army to turn away, Antonius watched impassively, his face betraying not the slightest emotion. I thought it strange that Cleopatra was absent, though I supposed that it made sense in that this was a purely Roman matter. Once it was over, with the gore that had been Quintus Postumius lying spread across the dirt of the forum, Antonius closed with the command to tell the men what we had witnessed here, then dismissed us back to our Legions. It was a quiet but sullen group of Centurions that walked with me back to our area.

While Antonius shut down all traffic out of the camp, for some reason he continued to allow high-ranking men to enter ours, to visit what were now essentially captives. I cannot imagine that the Senators and clients being held forcibly inside our camp had anything good to say about Antonius, although it is probable that they were too scared to say anything of that nature lest some Antonian spy be listening. The series of reverses that we had suffered caused Antonius finally to make some decisions. About two months before, just after Octavian had made camp at Toryne, Antonius enlarged the fort on the north side of the inlet, sending a third part of the army across to occupy the new camp. His intent was to create a blocking position strong enough to withstand an assault by a large force that would allow time to bring the bulk of the army across the inlet to reinforce or counterattack. Now, he pulled this force back to the original camp, leaving two Cohorts along with some extra artillery at the fort, guarding the mouth of the inlet.

After this action, he called a council of war that for the first time in months included the Primi Pili, Evocati, Tribunes, and Legates of the entire army, along with each *navarch* of the navy, with the client kings acting in their role as commanders of their respective contingents. It was held in the forum and guards were posted around the edges to keep the rankers from lingering and overhearing what their fate was to be. Of course, Cleopatra was present, seated on a throne that I recognized as the one from her palace in Alexandria, and I wondered how much trouble it had been to drag that thing all this way to this bog in Greece. Antonius sat in a curule chair, but it was raised up on boards so that it was on the same level as Cleopatra's, while both were dressed in their best armor. Cleopatra had a diadem draped around her golden helmet, although I noticed that she also had the crooked staff that represented her relationship with one of her Egyptian gods propped up next to her. She was not wearing the hideous makeup that usually marked her royal appearances; I suspected that this was intentionally done to reduce her foreignness. Antonius' face was puffy, but his eyes were clear and his speech was not slurred as he began to speak.

"We are at a decision point," he announced. "Our supply situation has become tenuous, and I don't want to go to half-rations, but I may be forced to. We've suffered a series of setbacks, it's true, for which I take full responsibility. The fault doesn't lie with any of you."

So far, Antonius was hitting all the right notes, I thought.

"The purpose of this meeting is to discuss the best next step for us to take. I know that it has been some time since we last held a council of war that included all of the senior officers of both army and navy, but I thought this would be the right time."

Now, I did not remember ever having a meeting that included both arms of the might of the East, but I supposed it was better late than never. Because of the many different tongues spoken among the men of this force, Antonius was forced to pause to allow interpreters to translate. He was speaking in our tongue, and while I imagine that if he had spoken in Greek it would have been easier, since I was sure that every client king and Egyptian, almost exclusively Macedonian, spoke fluent Greek, it was not lost on me at least that he had chosen to speak in his native tongue. Was it a mark of respect for his army, a sign that he recognized on whom he truly relied? Or was it to lull us into a false comfort, before he sprung some surprise on us? Even as this thought occurred to me, I wryly chided myself that I had been in the East too long and had begun thinking like one of them.

"I would hear from the commanders of each contingent of the army now." Antonius turned, nodding to Canidius, who stood to face us, striking the classic pose of an orator about to address the Senate.

"Thank you, Triumvir Antonius and Your Highness, for hearing my words." He bowed to Cleopatra, while I suppressed a smirk at his choice of the word "hearing" as opposed to "listening," sure that they would not do much of either. "The Triumvir is of course correct," he began, using the title Antonius had now held for more than ten years. Despite the fact that he technically no longer held the office, according to Octavian and his Senate at least, that was still the most common method by which he was addressed, at least by fellow Romans. "We are in a situation that I won't call desperate, but it is serious. It's become clear to me that we have nothing to be gained by staying put, trying to force Octavian into a confrontation. A confrontation, I might add, that he has consistently refused our invitation to participate in, that we might settle this matter once and for all. But he is behaving in a cowardly manner, and as he refuses to engage with us, I see no point in remaining here."

This, of course, was a bald-faced lie and I could tell by the faces of the men around me that they knew it. In fact, it had been Octavian who issued an invitation to meet in battle, which Antonius had refused. There was nothing to be gained, other than a quick trip to a slow death in pointing this out, so none of us said a word, listening stone-faced as Canidius continued.

"I propose that we make a strategic withdrawal of the entire army, into the interior of Macedonia towards Thrace, where we can not only find terrain that's more suitable for battle, but puts us closer to what has now become our main source of supply. In doing so, we can draw Octavian farther away from his own base of supply and can reverse our position, putting him on the defensive."

Heads, mostly Roman, I noted, bobbed up and down at Canidius' proposal, and mine was one of them.

Antonius sat for a moment, seeming to consider, then asked, "And what about the fleet?"

"The fleet can break out of the bay, it's clearly strong enough, and once it does, we can regain control of the sea. It should operate independently of the army but in a supporting role, reestablishing our supply line back to Alexandria to augment our line of supply from Thrace."

Cleopatra's face looked as if it was made of stone, her lips a thin line as she sat silently, listening to Canidius. Canidius waited for more questions or objections, but there were none, so he sat down. As far as I was concerned and I could see I was not alone, Canidius' argument would be hard, if not impossible to beat. It made sense, both from a strategic and tactical standpoint, yet I was disquieted by the look on the general's face, which looked anything but triumphant. Although I tried to interpret his expression, I could not think of a solid reason why I felt unsettled. Antonius was impassive as he looked over to Cleopatra, who plainly intended to speak for the naval arm of this endeavor. She stood, her demeanor as haughty as ever and I wondered where the softer, feminine side of the woman had gone, the side that I had seen in Alexandria and on the Nile. I was forced to admit that it was possible that it had never truly been there in the first place. Perhaps it was an illusion, one of her conjurer's tricks, pulled from the same bag as the one she used to bewitch Marcus Antonius, the most powerful Roman of his time, after Caesar. And Octavian, came the unbidden thought popping into my head. Do not forget Octavian. He may prove to be more powerful than even his adopted father, a thought I would have immediately dismissed just a few years before, but now I was not so sure.

"There is much merit in what you say, Canidius," Cleopatra began and I could see the surprise register on some faces, which made me want to shout a warning to them not to be fooled, since I had no doubt whatsoever that she was about to tear Canidius' argument into tatters, at least in her own mind.

"However, I would propose that we accomplish the same thing, but in a different manner."

I saw Canidius' eyes narrow in obvious suspicion, he at least knowing that there was an attack on his flank coming.

"I would argue that it is the fleet that is the most precious asset that we have, followed closely by the army, but not all of the army. I do not think it is any secret that there are Legions that are of a higher quality than others."

Suddenly, a low growl began issuing from the throats of the Centurions. Two spots of color appeared on her cheeks, while her voice raised just a bit in volume.

"I do not intend in any way to cast aspersions on the abilities of the Primi Pili. I know that you have done a magnificent job in training the men to the highest standards available to you. But let us be frank; training is not the same as battle, and a large portion of this army is unblooded."

"As if she would know the difference," someone whispered, causing a few snickers, but if she heard, she chose to ignore it.

For the most part, her words had somewhat soothed the feelings of the men listening, because the brutal truth is that she was right, and we knew it. I still did not know exactly where she was going, but she was not finished, not by a long shot.

"That is why my proposal is that we save the most veteran part of the army, and the entire fleet, as in my view the fleet is the most important. The fleet can control a much larger area of territory than an army can. It is more mobile and it is vital to keeping our supply lines open."

"And where do you propose that we go, my wife?"

I think it was the way that Antonius posed the question that convinced me that this was all a sham, that everything had already been decided, making me realize that the look on Canidius' face was one of resignation, because he knew he was wasting his breath.

"Well, it would seem that since our most pressing problem is keeping a supply line open and that a large part of the reason is the length of that line, it would make sense to shorten it. The best way to shorten it is to sail back to Alexandria."

Now it was the turn of the Eastern heads to start nodding up and down in approval, although I noticed that it was not unanimous.

"So you're proposing that we just abandon most of our army to save your precious fleet?"

I turned in some surprise, since it was Spurius who asked this question, making no attempt to hide in the crowd, in fact stepping forward to be recognized. Perhaps he was counting on his status as being a favorite of Antonius, but it was a courageous thing to do no matter what his reasoning.

"No, Spurius, I am not proposing that," Cleopatra replied coolly. "I would not just leave those Legions to their own devices. I would emplace them at strategic points along the coast and in the interior, forcing Octavian to devote some of his own troops to counter this threat. He cannot leave a substantial force in what would become his rear as he turns his attention to Egypt, where the army would be able to refit and prepare defenses that no army could penetrate."

Spurius looked to Antonius, who said nothing, choosing instead to examine the large signet ring on his finger. The Primus Pilus of the 3rd stood helplessly and I could see his fists clenching and unclenching as he struggled to guard himself from voicing his anger and frustration. Careful Spurius, I thought, or you could end up choking on your own tongue like Eumenis. However, Spurius had not achieved and maintained his position by being stupid, so he said no more. For several moments, nothing was said by anyone. Finally, I heard the sound of a throat clearing and I looked away from Spurius to see Canidius standing again.

"Your Highness, as you have complimented my plan, allow me to compliment yours for having some merit. However, it is a military axiom that you never, ever divide your army. Despite understanding your attachment to the fleet, I respectfully disagree that it is the most important. Navies can help control territory, but only armies can take and hold cities, towns, and countries. Weakening the army by dividing it makes each part more likely to be defeated, and every defeat makes holding territory impossible. But I understand your attachment to your fleet, which is why I am making an alteration to your proposal."

He paused, the silence as we waited for what he was going to say next hanging like a blanket over the entire forum.

"I believe that the best course of action, given our respective opinions, is that the fleet does exactly as you say. It should fight its way out and return to Egypt. And of course, they will fight all that much harder if you command the fleet. Then, we will remain here, under the command of the Triumvir, and continue the fight."

Cleopatra looked as if she had been slapped, while Antonius sat upright, only slightly less shocked. This obviously was not part of the plan and I suspected that there had been a discussion before this meeting among the three about how it would go. Evidently, this new proposal had not been part of that discussion. Cleopatra's mouth opened but nothing came out, then she looked to Antonius for help. Antonius frowned at Canidius, clearly irritated that he had not followed the plan.

"General," he said coldly. "It's out of the realm of possibility to do as you suggest. We can't hope to achieve victory without the fleet in support of the army. I'm surprised that you would suggest otherwise."

Canidius affected a look of surprise.

"Triumvir, I'm not suggesting that we send the whole fleet back to Egypt. I'm sure that the Egyptian *navarchae* would fight to the death to protect the queen. We should allow them to escort the queen back, while our Roman and other allied commanders would stay in support of the army."

So there it was, out in the open. One last-gasp effort on the part of a Roman to become a Roman army again, commanded and supported by a Roman general and Roman navy respectively. The silence that followed stretched for several heartbeats, with both Antonius and Cleopatra glaring at Canidius, who stood, unyielding. Any bad feelings I had continued to hold for Canidius had evaporated in that moment, since I knew perhaps better than anyone else in that crowd what he risked in crossing Cleopatra. Finally, Antonius spoke again, his tone as hard and unyielding as it had been on the day that Quintus Postumius was torn apart.

"Your proposal is not accepted, General. I will not weaken the fleet by dividing it. That would make it easier for Octavian and Agrippa to capture each part. As it is, now that Agrippa and Octavian have combined, the fleet is outnumbered, though not by much. Dividing the fleet would make that disparity in numbers much larger."

"Then burn it," Canidius said. "Burn the fleet so that it can be of no use to Octavian."

Cleopatra leaped to her feet, livid with rage.

"Burn it? Burn the fleet?" She was shrieking now, clearly beside herself. "Do you realize how much money it cost, the amount of work that went into building it, you stupid man? And you're suggesting that we burn all that money? All of *my* money?"

I had never seen Cleopatra so angry, but Canidius refused to back down, as now Gaius Sosius, who had been made one of the commanders of the Roman contingent of the fleet stood from his spot arrayed behind the royal couple, coming to stand next to Canidius.

"I agree with Canidius, Triumvir. We can't win unless we do as he suggests."

He turned to squarely face Cleopatra, then said in a louder voice so that there was no chance he would not be heard, "In fact Triumvir, I'll go farther than the General. I say that we can't win as long as the queen is present."

There is no way adequately to describe the shock that accompanied Sosius' statement, on the part of everyone present. Cleopatra took a staggering step backward, then in the next instant she sprang forward, clumsily trying to pull her sword, clearly intent on running Sosius through, but Antonius was too quick for her. Reaching out he grabbed her wrist, restraining her with ease, while she spit and clawed, screaming at Sosius in what I recognized was not Macedonian Greek, but the native Egyptian tongue. Men began shouting, shaking their fists in approval at Sosius' words, as all the pent-up frustration and rage at the queen came pouring out. It quickly became impossible to distinguish one man's voice from another, complete pandemonium reigning for several moments. Antonius was now holding Cleopatra around the waist, and she was flailing her arms in an attempt to get at Sosius, still standing next to Canidius, both men shaking their fists at Cleopatra. I saw Antonius' mouth open as he took a giant breath.

"TACETE!"

At first, nobody obeyed, but then he bellowed the order again and again, so that finally things calmed down. Antonius, to my surprise, did not look angry. In fact, he looked more tired than I had ever seen him and the moment order was restored and Cleopatra was seated, still glaring daggers at Sosius, who glared back, he slumped into his own chair.

"We're not burning the fleet," he said tiredly. "We can't burn it because it would strand us here, and there would be nothing to stop Octavian. He could go straight to Egypt and there would be nothing to stop him. So, we're not burning the fleet. We're going to do as the queen proposes. We'll take the veteran Legions with us to Egypt. The other Legions will be deployed at strategic points along the coast to tie down Octavian's own army. Canidius," he turned to face the general, "you'll command that effort. The queen and I will be commanding the fleet and the accompanying Legions."

He stood, signaling that the meeting, if that is what it could be called, was at an end.

"You'll be informed where each of your Legions will be heading in the next day. I expect each of you to do your duty to Rome, and to me in this matter. That is all."

We were then dismissed to go back to our Legions to make them ready. I had little doubt that as the most experienced Legion left in the army, the 10th would be expected to board ships to go with Antonius and Cleopatra, something that I had no intention of doing.

I immediately called for Scribonius to tell him what was happening, along with some others. We sat in my private quarters, with Gaius, Diocles, and Balbus present as well, and I had taken a chance by asking Macrianus to attend. Because I had not spent as much time with the man as I had hoped, it was something of a question in my mind how much he could be trusted. They sat on stools in front of my desk while I told them what had transpired, then outlined what I was sure would be the plan for the 10th Legion. As I talked, I watched Macrianus carefully, trying to judge his reaction to what I was saying; I was pleased to see his face cloud at the idea of getting on a ship and sailing to Egypt. Once I was finished, I looked at the others, giving Scribonius a silent signal that I did not want him to speak, knowing that neither Balbus nor Gaius would be comfortable speaking first, for different reasons. Macrianus sat looking back at me, gradually becoming aware that I was waiting for him to say something. He opened his mouth, then shut it.

"Speak your mind, Macrianus," I told him. "I give you my word that nothing you say will leave this tent."

"I don't want to take my men to Egypt," he replied instantly, seeming to be relieved to be able to get it out. "I don't see the point in prolonging this any more than we already have."

I took notice that his first concern was not for himself, but for his men. With some of the other Centurions, if they had said as much it would have sounded false, but I had come to know Macrianus well enough to know that he was being genuine in his concern. However, I decided that it was time to push Macrianus further.

"That's understandable," I acknowledged. "But what exactly does that mean? If I were to tell you that we would refuse the order to go, what would you do? It's easy to talk here in the tent. It's another thing entirely when the moment is at hand."

The younger man said nothing for a moment, giving me a level stare that did not betray his thoughts in any way.

Finally, he said, "If you give the order, Primus Pilus, I'll follow it."

"And if I give the order to get on the boats?"

He paused again before nodding his head. "I would obey that as well. But I wouldn't like it."

"I wouldn't expect you to," I agreed. "But I would expect you to obey."

I looked over at Scribonius, asking him, "Do you still think I should wait?"

He nodded. "Do you want to end up like Postumius? Antonius and Cleopatra are clearly at the end of their tether, and if they get wind of anything they think is a plot, your guts are going to be scattered all over the forum."

There was no need for any more convincing than that. I do not know exactly when it happened, but somewhere between the council and that moment in the tent, I had decided that I would not wait to hear from Octavian to lead a mutiny of the 10th Legion.

After this flurry of events occurred, there was a period of inactivity for us that stretched for several days. An air of gloom and despair hung over the entire army, the men waiting for whatever was going to happen next. While the men in the army waited, Antonius' naval contingent was hard at work, inspecting and refitting the best of the ships in the bay, most of them riding at anchor idle or beached for the last several months. It was now the end of Sextilis; we had been at Actium more than nine months and had been on short rations for the last several weeks. Despite the fact that the ground had dried out somewhat, there were still hordes of mosquitoes that came out in the evenings, drawn to the host of fleshy targets sitting about their fires. Men were still sick with fevers of varying origins and severity, while their condition was not helped by the reduced rations. The leather of our tents was wearing thin and I was worried that the first bad storm would rip them apart, and the only thing keeping us from starving was the daily arrival of at least one and sometimes two trains of mules carrying grain and other supplies. Still, men from Octavian's camp were allowed to visit friends in ours, creating an air of unreality about the impending battle.

I was still waiting for a message from Octavian, but the atmosphere was so oppressive, with the men entering the camp so closely watched that I did not see how he could send word to any of the men working for him in Antonius' army. However, I should have known him better than that; Octavian is not a man easily thwarted, and is as clever a man at deception and guile as I have ever met. The day that I had been dreading happened on the same one that Quintus Delius again changed sides, somehow managing to slip out of camp to run to Octavian, carrying in his head all of Antonius and Cleopatra's plans. Taking advantage of the uproar at the *Praetorium*, with Antonius ordering a search for the missing man, one of those visiting the camp slipped away from his host and asked his way to our area. He ran into Ovidius, my Quintus Princeps Prior, who directed the man to my tent, where Diocles was sitting in the front office, going through the motions of compiling the daily report. I was lying down in my quarters, when Diocles came to tell me that I had a visitor.

"He's a Senator, but I've never seen him before," he whispered. "I think he might be from Octavian."

That got my attention, my heart beginning to thud against my ribs as I sat up. Telling Diocles that I would be out momentarily, I straightened myself up, then entered the outer office. The man who was standing just inside the front flap had iron-gray hair, cut almost as short as mine. He was perhaps ten to fifteen years older than I was, but still fit for his age. He was wearing a tunic of expensive linen, edged with the senatorial stripe, but even if he was not wearing it, his badge of rank was plain to see in his face and in the way he carried himself. Proud nose, head slightly tilted upward, skin gleaming from the oil that some slave applied every morning and evening, mouth turned slightly downward to show his distaste at being in such surroundings. I instantly hated the man.

"Primus Pilus Titus Pullus?"

His voice was surprisingly raspy, as if he had spent a fair amount of his time bellowing at the top of his lungs.

"I am," I replied.

"I am Gaius Amulius Marcellinus and I bring greetings from Caesar Octavianus Divi Filius. We do not have much time, so I will be brief. I am instructed to give you a message from him."

Swallowing the lump in my throat, a thought suddenly struck me. Before he could continue, I held up my hand.

"My apologies, Gaius Amulius Marcellinus, but how do I know you are who you say you are, and that you truly bear a message from the man you name?"

He stiffened at the question, but his tone was even as he replied, "Caesar says that there is still an open dinner invitation that neither of you have had the time to fulfill. In case you asked that very question."

I relaxed, but only a little, remembering that long-ago evening when I dined with Caesar and Octavian, when he gave his invitation to dine with just him and me. Satisfied, I nodded for him to continue.

"Caesar sent me to remind you of a debt, I believe? And he suggests that this would be the appropriate time to repay that debt. Of course, he leaves it up to you as to the best way to do so."

I took a deep breath, trying to control the shaking of my body, but I said nothing.

"Primus Pilus, I require an acknowledgment that you have received and understood my message before I can depart," Marcellinus said, making his voice as gentle as I suppose was possible.

Gulping, I nodded, then realizing he expected more, I replied, "I understand the message you have given me."

I was surprised at the sound of my voice, it sounding hoarse, as if I had been yelling all day.

Marcellinus gave a slight bow, then turned to leave.

"If you will excuse me, Primus Pilus, I have more messages to deliver while your general is still occupied elsewhere."

With that, he left the tent, leaving me suddenly bathed in sweat as if I had just been working at the stakes for a third of a watch. When I looked over at Diocles, he was staring back at me wide-eyed, but was already up and moving.

"I'll go get Scribonius," he said as he left the tent.

The moment was now at hand. Later the same day that Marcellinus showed up in my tent, Antonius gave the order to burn a large number of the ships in the bay. Because of the desertions and sickness, there were not enough crews left to man all of the vessels of the fleet, so the best had been selected, with the remainder put to the torch. The sky filled with an inky, greasy smoke, carrying huge particles that deposited themselves on anything in the way. Additionally, the order was also given for the Legions designated to leave with the fleet to pack their personal belongings. Our tents and stakes that were part of the rampart of the camp were to be left behind, along with our artillery and other items of heavy gear, both to save room and to supposedly fool the enemy about our departure. We were told that we would begin loading the next morning, although there were to be no transports used; most of the ships were the huge quinqueremes and quadriremes, with perhaps a quarter of the fleet triremes, along with a smattering of smaller scout ships. Despite the fact that I had no intention of going through with putting my men on ships, I had to participate in the fiction to a certain degree, so I gave the order for the men to pack.

Walking about the Legion area, I saw that the men were sullenly obeying, moving slowly, just quickly enough to avoid being smacked with the *vitus* of their Centurions. Sensing the eyes of the Centurions on my back as I passed by, I felt their probing gazes seemingly searching my soul for a clue about what lay in store for them, but I kept my face a mask. After seeing to the men, I returned to my tent to make my own preparations for what was about to happen. Shortly before dark, Scribonius arrived from seeing to his Cohort, his face taut with the tension that we were feeling.

"Are you ready for this?"

I shook my head, not able to find the words. How does one get ready to lead men into mutiny, no matter what the reason?

"Well, that's not very reassuring," Scribonius tried to joke, but it was hollow and we both knew it; I was just too tense to engage in any banter. Changing the subject, he asked, "Have you picked a spot to hold the meeting?"

"Not yet," I replied, which caused his frown to deepen even more.

"You better think of one," he snapped. "It has to be someplace away from prying eyes and ears."

"I know that," I shot right back. "I just can't think of a spot that fits our needs. Not in camp anyway."

He was silent for a moment then made a suggestion.

"How about the stables?"

I thought about it, then replied, "That might work. They're practically empty now, and they're not taking many animals with them. Yes, I think that will do."

Between the capture and defection of most of the cavalry, the stables were only used to hold the personal animals of the senior officers, meaning they were now holding a fraction of the animals they had originally. All of the pack and draft animals were held in a large pen outside the southern edge of the camp; they were going to be left behind as well, to be used by Canidius' portion of the army when they made their move. With that determined, the next step was to decide the best time to hold the meeting. Since this was to be the last night in camp, I decided to wait until after dark before I sent Diocles to summon the Centurions and Optios to the stables. Normally, men moving about the camp after dark would be subject to arrest by the provosts, but on a night like this, nobody would be sleeping. Besides, there would be men scurrying about attending to last-minute tasks, so the danger was lessened considerably. Everything had been prepared as much as possible to that point, so I lay down on my cot to get some rest, marshaling my thoughts for what was to come.

The fleet was ready. Out of the more than 400 ships that were part of the original force, there would be roughly 250 actually sailing, divided into four squadrons, with 60 of the best ships designated to protect Cleopatra. For the rest of the night, the sky was illuminated by the lurid light of the ships that were still burning down to ashes. Sometime in the late evening, the wind shifted, pushing the smoke through the camp, the sounds of men coughing and choking almost drowning out all other noise. Fortunately, the presence of the smoke actually helped mask movement, enabling me to walk through the combination of gloom and smoke without drawing attention to myself. I had waited in my tent for a bit to give the Centurions time to gather in the stable and I specifically instructed Diocles not to divulge any reason for my summons. In short, I was doing everything I could think of to keep Antonius and Cleopatra from learning that something was afoot. Nevertheless, I was still more nervous than I had ever been before battle as I made my way towards the stable. One difficulty was that our area was on the opposite side of the camp from the stables, with the *Praetorium* in between, meaning that I had to pass by the bustle of activity and confusion that is a headquarters on the eve of a move. Luckily, I was able to pass by without being spotted by a senior officer, or at least nobody called my name.

Coming to the stables in the darkness, I could see the men gathered, barely illuminated by the light of the torches around the *Praetorium* and on the ramparts. Despite the choice of the stables being good to avoid attention, it also meant that it was not well lit, so the men would not be able to see my face as well as I would have hoped. That was important on this night; I was about to make a speech that would determine not only my fate, but the fate of the men of the 10th. If I did not have the support of the Centurions then I would be faced with a choice of meekly obeying Antonius, loading my men on the boat, in the hope that he defeated Octavian, or falling on my sword. It was as simple as that; if I was forced to follow the rest of the Centurions that meant that I was spurning Octavian, with my only hope then being that Antonius came out on top, which I believed in my heart could not and would not happen. Refusing to join the Legion would see the same end result; the only difference being that my demise would happen more quickly, since Antonius would promptly have me executed for treason. For the first time, walking towards the stables, I finally understood how Caesar must have felt when he stood on the banks of that muddy creek. Everything; my career, my fortune, and my life came down to one throw of the dice and I knew that I had to give the speech that would salvage it all. Looking back, it is easy now to say that what happened was a foregone conclusion, given how the men felt about Antonius and more importantly, Cleopatra. But that was certainly not how I felt that night, fighting a strong urge to vomit. Fortunately, I was able to avoid the shame of showing such weakness in front of the men, but it took quite an effort. They were a solid mass of darker black, although when I drew within a few paces I could dimly make out some men's faces enough to recognize them.

Calling for both Centurions and Optios of the remaining Cohorts as I did meant there were 108 men packed in the stables, which still smelled strongly of horse manure and piss. The remaining animals were stabled in the far corner from where the men gathered, putting them closer to the *Praetorium*, where they were nickering nervously at the scent of so many men packed together. Hearing the low buzz of the men talking, I knew they were asking each other why they were standing in a dark stable the night before a movement. However, only Scribonius, Balbus, and now Macrianus knew for sure what was happening, and I trusted them not to say anything beforehand. Someone spied me approaching, calling to the men to come to *intente*, the smacking of heels striking together and hands slapping thighs making me wince at the noise, sure that it would attract attention. Thankfully, the gods were protecting us as I stopped to listen for any sound of alarm, hearing nothing except the shouted commands and curses of men still working to make preparations to leave. Saying a silent prayer asking for the gods' blessing on what I was about to do, I quietly told the men to stand easy as I took a deep breath. Then, I began to speak.

"First, I want to apologize for the setting. I would have liked to have used Pompey's Theater."

"So would we. That means we wouldn't be here in this *cac*hole." The men laughed heartily at Balbus' remark, which we had rehearsed beforehand.

I wanted the men relaxed and receptive to what I had to say, and a good leader should never underestimate the value of making men laugh during tense moments.

"This is a *cac*hole," I agreed. "And I, like you, would rather be back in Ephesus, or Damascus even. But we're here, and that's what I wanted to talk to you about tonight." Now that I had their full, undivided attention, I plunged on. "You know that we've been ordered to board the ships bound for Egypt in just a few thirds of a watch. So I suppose that might be considered by some to be cause for celebration, because that means we're leaving Actium and Greece. But I don't feel that way, and I don't think any of you do either."

Waiting a moment, I saw heads nodding slowly up and down, although most of the men still stood silently, arms crossed looking at me, their faces giving nothing away.

"In fact," I continued, "I've reached a decision, but it's one that I can't make alone. You all know me. For most of you, I've been the only Primus Pilus you've ever known. For some of you, you've known me long enough to remember when I was Secundus Pilus Prior. And for a very, very few, you and I were *tiros* during the first *dilectus* of the 10th, when Divi Julius was just a *Praetor* and known simply as Caesar."

As I said this, I looked over at Scribonius, remembering the tall, gawky young man who was the next tallest man in our tent section and stood next to me, when my original Primus Pilus, Favonius, punched me in the stomach moments after we met.

"You've seen my scars, and you've seen me bleed and fight and kill for Rome. I've done this, as each of you have, mostly without complaint, going where we were told and obeying orders without question. Like all of you, I have lost friends, seen them die in front of me, sometimes in ways so horrible that it can never be spoken of again."

The image of Vinicius, covered in boiling pitch, but still climbing the ladder of that town in Hispania leapt into my mind's eye, a lump forming in my throat that I forced down as I kept speaking. The men were looking at me, fully engaged, with grave expressions, but I still had no sense of where their hearts were at, so I continued on.

"Now, we're asked to do something yet again, to take ourselves far away, to continue a fight that we all know is lost, and has been for some time." Pausing to let this sink in, I could see the beginnings of some new emotion forming in the faces of the men, as some of them looked sidelong at the man standing next to them. "That's right, I'm saying what we've all been thinking, what the men have been saying at the fires every night for the last few months. We have no hope for victory, not as long as we're led by a woman, and a non-Roman woman at that."

Now, more heads began to nod as men started muttering to each other, because I had just prodded the boil of the problem with the needle as far as most of the men were concerned; a woman has no business commanding an army, queen or not. It goes against everything that makes us Roman, while the fact that Cleopatra was a foreigner was like rubbing salt into an open wound.

"It is Cleopatra who's led us to this spot. It is Cleopatra who wants to sacrifice part of the army to save her precious ships. She cares nothing for the men we lead. And don't think that just because we're one of the Legions that have been selected to protect her precious fleet and thereby escape to Egypt that she won't throw us away the first chance she gets." The muttering was growing louder now, striking me with the fear that we would be overheard before I could finish, so I held my hands up for quiet. "You don't need to speak. I know you agree; I can see it in your faces. So please remain quiet as I finish what I'm saying." Although I did not want it to sound like a rebuke, I nevertheless needed to impress on the men the need to be quiet, and I could not tell how that was received. They immediately quieted down, however, so I continued, "Brothers, I'm tired of seeing our blood shed in order to further this woman's ambitions. And I know what those ambitions are, better than almost any man, because I've heard her speak the words myself."

If they had been paying partial attention, I now had them listening avidly, and I could see men leaning forward, eager to catch every word out of my mouth. They all sensed that I was about to reveal what had been a source of much speculation and rumor.

"And it's because I heard her speak those words that she tried to kill me. Not only me, but my woman Miriam as well. You all have heard the talk about the strange happenings several months ago in Ephesus. Well, I'll tell you now that what happened was at her command. You all know that I lost a slave; Eumenis was his name. Slave he might have been, but he died to protect Miriam and me. He was poisoned and it was done by the slave girl, Iras, the girl you heard about attending the banquet that caused such a stir."

Despite my plea for silence, I understood that this would be too much for them to bear and I watched as they turned to talk to each other excitedly, although they did try to keep their voices low. Observing and listening for a few moments, I finally raised my hand and I was rewarded with a sudden silence. Clearly, the men wanted to hear me, which I suspected that they would.

"Yes, I spared the girl's life, for reasons that I prefer to keep to myself, other than to say this. One reason I kept her alive is because I knew that it would anger and worry Cleopatra, and to show Cleopatra that a Centurion of Rome fears no woman, even if she is a queen." The men liked this, and I could see the gleam of teeth as they smiled at my defiant words, making me decide that it was time to make the kill, so to speak. "That's why I've decided that I will take the outrage and insults no longer. Cleopatra will command me no more, and make no mistake about it. All of this," I swept my hand in the direction of the bay, where some boats were still flickering as they burned, "is her doing. The Marcus Antonius we followed to Parthia no longer exists. In that I believe Caesar is correct."

There were a few looks of surprise, this being the first time I had referred to Octavian as Caesar in front of these men, but that was also by design. Taking a deep breath, I knew that we were at the moment of truth. In the next few moments, I would know where I stood with the Centurions and Optios of the 10th Legion.

"But I need your help. Without you, my gesture would be futile, and for me it would be suicidal, but I still have many years left to live, if the gods will it. I've given my life and all that I have to give to the 10th, and I can't let it be destroyed because of the mad ambition of the queen of Egypt. The only way that we can save the Legion is if we work together. I can't do it alone. I've never been able to do it alone." I took a moment to look into as many man's eyes as I could, trying to send to them a message of how I felt about the Legion and all that it represented. When I continued, I spoke in a lower tone of voice. "In the morning, when I'm given the order to march the 10th Legion to their designated ships, I intend to refuse that order. But I can only do that if I know that each and every one of you is with me. I know that what I'm asking you to do Antonius will consider mutiny, but I'll tell you that Antonius is not Rome. He may have once been the lawfully appointed Triumvir, and Consul, but that's no longer the case. He's been stripped of his titles. But those are just words. Brothers, you all know that Antonius is no longer Roman. He's Eastern. So while we may be defying our general, or more accurately, his wife," this elicited some harsh chuckles, "we're not defying Rome. We're being faithful to Rome." Stopping again, I surveyed the faces hopefully, but I still could not tell how men were feeling. "I'm asking much of each of you. If Antonius is victorious against Octavian, even if he was willing to forgive us, I can assure you that Cleopatra wouldn't, mainly because of me. But truly, is there a man among you who thinks that Antonius will win? Please, speak freely. I give you my word that I won't hold it against you if you think so." I waited, but no man spoke, their eyes for the most part studying the dirt in front of them. "That's what I suspected. And it's because of that belief that I'm not willing to throw the lives of the men we lead away. I'm taking this step for them just as much as it is for me, and for each of you. They have less than three years before they can retire, with honor and all that they have coming to them."

This was the part of the speech I worried about the most, even more than actually asking them to follow me, and my worry was immediately justified. A subtle change came over the men before me, a low-pitched muttering beginning among many of them, some shaking their heads as they talked. Deciding to wait for someone to speak, what happened instead is common with large groups of men; they were waiting for someone else to voice the concern that many, if not all of them were feeling. Finally, it was Gellius, the Pilus Prior of the Sixth who spoke up.

"Primus Pilus, how do we know that Octavian will honor the promises made by Antonius to all of us? Or that he'll even allow the men to end their enlistments? Half of the army facing us right now is past their enlistments. Why would Octavian worry about us when he has his own men to provide for?"

This was the very question I had been worrying about for some time, and it was a valid concern on the part of Gellius and the others. I suppose I could have lied and said that I had received assurances from Octavian. If I were younger, I probably would have done just that, then hoped that I could somehow make good on whatever came out of my mouth. But I was at least older and more experienced, if not wiser, so I told the truth.

"You're right, Gellius, to ask that question. And the honest answer is that I don't know for sure. What I do know is what's likely to happen to us if we follow

Antonius. Even if we make good our escape or if by some miracle of the gods Antonius is victorious in this battle, he can't win this war, and we all know it. So it becomes a question of whether or not we choose to take a risk today and trust in the gods and Octavian, or trust in Antonius and Cleopatra. I've already told you my choice, but as I said, I can't do it alone."

Gellius nodded thoughtfully, and I saw others doing the same. But I saw just as many men, if not more, who gave no sign that would indicate their thinking, and I felt the knot tightening in my stomach. I was also beginning to feel the desperation threatening to claw its way up and out of me, making me want to shout at them, knowing that to do so would just make things worse. Taking a deep breath, I forced myself to remain calm while I waited for the men to digest all that I said. Finally, I knew I could wait no longer to ask the question that would ultimately determine my fate.

"Are you with me? Will you *all,*" I emphasized the last word, "and I mean all, stand beside me when I tell Antonius that the 10th Legion has marched its last mile and fought its last battle to help the queen of Egypt bring down Rome? Because it must be unanimous. We must act as one, for our sake and for the men's sake. And for mine," I added this last, acknowledging what I knew some men would be thinking anyway.

The plan at this point was for Scribonius and Balbus to step forward, but they did not move quickly enough.

First, Macrianus took a step forward, saying just loudly enough to be heard by everyone assembled, "I'll stand with you, Primus Pilus. I'm tired. My men are tired, and we've had enough."

Scribonius and Balbus joined Macrianus, followed by Gellius, then one by one the other Pili Priores; Nigidius, then Frontinus, Scaevola, Glaxus and Marcius. Laetus,

Celadus, and Vistilia, the remaining Centurions of the First Cohort came next, then finally Trebellius, the last of the Pili Priores. Lutatius, my Optio was next, which seemed to send a signal to other Optios, adding their numbers to the men standing with me. Then, when things seemed to be going well, with perhaps two-thirds of the men standing at my side, the remainder stopped moving. For several very tense moments, we were staring at each other across a few feet. There was nothing more that I could think to say that had not already been said, and suddenly I was assailed by the strangest feeling I had ever experienced. Tremors started in my legs, moving rapidly through my body, my heart suddenly accelerating as if I had broken into a full-out sprint. I could feel cold sweat trickling down my spine and beading my forehead as I recognized that for the first time in my life I was experiencing panic. In all the battles I ever fought, big and small, I had felt excitement along with a certain amount of fear, but never before had I been stricken by the type of all-consuming, mindless dread that I had seen overcome so many of the enemies I had faced. For the first time I understood how it felt to be almost paralyzed by fear, and it was not something I liked at all. Clenching my fists, I forced myself to remain calm and think, which was extremely difficult. Looking over to Scribonius, he seemed as confused and helpless as I felt. Moments dragged by in total silence, the tension growing with each breath before someone in the group of men still to make their decision cleared his throat, causing all of us to jump, eliciting a nervous laugh. Stepping forward a few paces so he could be seen, Numerius Sacrovir, the Optio of the Ninth who had tried to engineer the mutiny in Parthia spoke up.

"Primus Pilus, we appreciate what you say, but we have concerns about what you propose. We're all loyal

Romans, as are you. We just don't know if what you're suggesting will work. What if the Triumvir and the queen order the rest of the army to strike us down? We would lose everything, including our lives, and have nothing to show for it. It seems that there should be some extra profit for us if we're going to take this huge risk."

He licked his lips, eyes shifting nervously about as I stood staring at him. I should have known that there would be someone like Sacrovir who would try to squeeze something out of this. What troubled me is that it looked like were at least 40 men who either thought the same way, or had some other objection that I had yet to hear. Keenly aware as I was that time was running short, if I had to convince the rest of these men individually, the plan was doomed to fail.

Not wanting to waste any more time on Sacrovir than I had to, I asked him coldly, "What do you want, Sacrovir? Name your price."

He blinked in surprise, clearly taken aback that I had put matters so bluntly. I saw men on both sides eying Sacrovir with outright hostility and it relieved me to see that most of the men remaining to commit seemed displeased at Sacrovir's blatant attempt to squeeze me.

"Primus Pilus, you misunderstand me," he began, but I cut him off before he could say more.

"It seems that this is the second time I've misunderstood you, Sacrovir. The last time I misunderstood you was when you were part of a mutiny of the Ninth. I'm surprised that now you seem reluctant to do something you've already attempted to do once before."

Even in the dim light, I could see his face flush as he opened his mouth to protest. Again, before he could speak, he was interrupted, but this time it was by Vibius

Pacuvius, the Hastatus Posterior of the Eighth and one of the remaining holdouts.

"Primus Pilus, I don't want you to think that Sacrovir speaks for me, because he doesn't. My hesitation is not to try and get a few coins or a promotion." His mouth twisted into a sneer, his voice dripping with contempt as he looked over at Sacrovir. "It's just that some of us don't trust Octavian any more than we trust Antonius. We haven't been around him much and when we were at Philippi, we didn't much like what we saw. He may be Caesar in name, but he's not Caesar, at least from what we've seen of him. That's the reason I'm concerned, and I think I speak for most of the men still standing here."

Pacuvius looked over his shoulder at the others, but they were already nodding or speaking their agreement. Suddenly, I did not feel quite so bad, since I was on firmer ground knowing where things stood.

"That's fair, Pacuvius. Here's what I can tell you. I do know Octavian, not that well, but I believe well enough that I can put some of your fears to rest. No, he's not Caesar, at least when it comes to the battlefield, but in other ways, he's very much like Divus Julius. He's as brilliant at organization as Caesar, and I believe that this is an important trait to have in what's to come. He's also much like Caesar in his political views, and more importantly in recognizing that things need to be changed for the lower classes."

While I talked, the slightly better feeling that had been developing evaporated as I saw men shifting about, their eyes wandering, their fingers tapping against forearms, all the signs that they were losing interest. Immediately, I realized that I had been talking about ideals, high-flown and not concerned with the things that Centurions of Rome particularly cared about. My mind raced, trying to think of one thing I could communicate to these men about Octavian that would strike home.

"He saved me from being executed by Lepidus," I blurted out. "I know you all remember when we were on the Campus Martius, and we lost Tetarfenus because he avenged the death of his men." The men were paying attention again, indicating that they indeed remembered that drama by nodding their heads or muttering their assent. "Well, it was Octavian who directly interceded with Lepidus and stopped him from having me tried and probably executed for dereliction of duty. He told me at the time that he couldn't afford to lose a Centurion, let alone a Primus Pilus."

Octavian had said no such thing, but I reasoned that it was worth telling a small lie at a moment like this. Tale it may have been, it nevertheless made the impression I had hoped; men looked at each other, talking quietly among themselves.

I was not out of danger yet, because Servius Varro, the Princeps Prior of the Tenth said bitterly, "But that didn't save Tetarfenus, did it?"

Recalling that Varro and Tetarfenus had been close friends, I cursed my oversight in bringing up the name of a man still mourned by his comrades.

"Tetarfenus was a dead man no matter what," I replied firmly, and in this, I was telling the truth. "He disobeyed regulations and killed other Legionaries without benefit of trial. His fate was sealed when he did that."

Varro did not like my words, though at this point I was not worrying about him as much as the others and I was relieved to see that they clearly accepted this as truth. Pacuvius, the man who had asked the question, was the first man of the remaining holdouts to step forward, stopping in front of me, looking up into my eyes.

"Very well, Primus Pilus. You can count on me and the men of my Century to follow you, wherever you order us to go. I trust you and know you wouldn't be doing this unless you thought it the right and only thing to do."

Pacuvius saluted, the first and only man to do so, which I returned, the weakness in my knees threatening to make them buckle. The rest of the men quickly followed, leaving Sacrovir standing for a moment by himself before he quickly joined the rest of the men. As he tried to lose himself in the crowd, I saw him shoot me a poisonous look, his lips curled back in a grimace of hatred and anger at being thwarted. That was a matter I would have to attend to sooner rather than later, I thought to myself, but I was not quite through with this ordeal. Stepping to the side so that I could face the men again, my throat was tight with emotion and relief, making my next words sound as if I had been yelling.

"There are no words I can summon that would convey the gratitude for the loyalty you're showing me, but I swear to you on Jupiter's Stone that I won't let you, and the men you lead, down, or I'll die in the attempt. Now, I must ask for an oath from each of you. I trust you men with my life, but I'd also remind you that you now are trusting each other with your own lives as well. For if any of you make a careless remark in the next few thirds of a watch, and the wrong ears hear it, there will be a bloodletting the likes of which we have never seen before. So I'm asking you to swear that none of you will whisper a word of what has transpired to any of the men, or to any of your friends in other Legions. Nobody must know of what we are going to do and that includes your slaves. Is that understood?" I saw heads nodding, but I was not satisfied. "As each of you leave, I'm going to offer my hand to you, in a gesture of both brotherhood and as a symbol of the oath I'm asking you to take. With this oath, you're pledging on your honor that you'll say nothing, to anyone. Is that agreed?"

Naturally, Scribonius was first and I felt a little foolish clasping his arm, but he uttered his oath to me just the same, winking at me before stepping to the side. One by one, each man stepped forward, clasping my arm, some of the hands firm and dry, others cold and clammy, yet every man looked me in the eye, and I did not get the sense that any of them were lying to me. This took several moments, most of the men milling about when they were finished so that a crowd formed around me, making it somewhat confusing. I imagine that is what encouraged Sacrovir to slip by without taking the oath, something I missed entirely. However, Macrianus did not.

Quietly ordering the men to disperse, I advised them to take different paths back to the Legion area, while I stayed behind with Scribonius, Balbus, and Macrianus. It took a few moments for the others to disappear, during which I felt my heart start to slow and the shaking gradually stop. My tunic was drenched under my armor, the dampness and cooler temperature of the pre-dawn chilling me, but I shook it off. There were other things to worry about.

"Now we'll see if they all live up to their oaths," I said this more to myself than to the others.

"They will."

Scribonius sounded confident. I wondered if he was being sincere or just trying to make me feel better.

"I know one who won't."

I looked sharply at Macrianus, he being the one who had uttered the words. That is when he relayed what he had seen Sacrovir do, slipping out without taking the oath. Hissing a curse, despite not really being surprised, I spat onto the ground as I considered what to do.

"We're going to have to stop him," Balbus said grimly. "We can't wait."

"Balbus is right." Scribonius rubbed his chin. "I seriously doubt he'll go straight to the *Praetorium*. Too many men heard him try to extort you and they'll be watching him. He'll go back to his area, then try and slip away."

"I'll take care of it," Macrianus said, surprising all of us. I looked at him closely, but he only shrugged. "I'm in this up to my eyeballs already. My neck is on the block just like yours."

While I appreciated the sentiment, I could not allow this.

"No, none of you are going to do anything. I'll deal with this myself."

"What are you going to do? Just walk up and gut him? He'll see you coming long before you can reach him." Balbus asked the question, and it was a valid one.

Still, I was not willing to delegate this task.

"Don't worry about that," I told him. "I'll deal with it."

He just shrugged then, and repeating my own gesture, spat on the ground to show his disapproval.

"Suit yourself," he said flatly.

Beginning my walk back towards the Legion area, the others followed a few paces behind. Sticking to the shadows, we slipped around the *Praetorium*, avoiding detection. Immediately after getting back to our area, the others departed, with the agreement that we would meet back up in the third of a watch before dawn. That gave me barely two parts of a watch so I hurriedly stripped off my armor and sodden tunic, fighting the shivering from the cold as I rubbed myself dry. There was no need for my armor for what I was about to do; I needed to be able to move quickly and quietly, without any hindrance. Calling Diocles, I told him to bring me some charcoal. He eyed me curiously but said nothing, returning shortly with a lump. Rubbing the charcoal all over the exposed parts of my body, I did not stop until I was sure that the only thing that would be visible in the night would be the whites of my eyes and teeth. Keeping my belt on, I hung only my dagger, after testing its edge to make sure it was still sharp. Preparations done, I had Diocles extinguish all the lamps in the tent, waited for my eyes to adjust to the darkness, then slipped out, moving quickly but silently around the corner, then across the Legion street behind my tent. Breathing through my mouth so that it hung open slightly, which helps one hear better at night, I lifted my feet carefully in order to avoid the stakes and guy ropes that litter the ground in the space between tents. I could have made my way to Sacrovir's tent blindfolded, since it was in the exact same place in every camp, just as mine was, along with every section of the Legion for that matter. I was going to come up behind his tent, which he shared with the Century *cornicen, tesseraurius* and *signifer*, one of the few options given to men of this rank being whether they shared a larger tent, or had one to themselves that was smaller. My experience and observation over the years had been that it seemed that most of those men who were sharp operators chose to have companionship. Why this is, I have no idea, although I suspect that it comes from a desire to build a confederation of like-minded men who will do your bidding. Perhaps my perception is colored by the memory of Sacrovir on this night.

Reaching his tent, I squatted down, cocking my ear to listen for sounds that might tell me what was happening inside, somewhat expecting to hear talking since I did not believe that Sacrovir would be able to keep his mouth shut and would be telling his tentmates of all that had transpired. Instead, I heard the sounds of gentle snoring coming from at least two men. After straining my ears, I thought I detected the breathing of a third man that suggested that he was sleeping as well. Those were the only three that I heard; my heart pounded even faster, assailed by the fear that Sacrovir had already left the tent, or worse, not ever returned. Raising myself to a half-crouch, I tried to decide what to do. Certainly I did not want to head towards the *Praetorium* for a number of reasons, not least of which was that the threat of discovery was dramatically increased. The fact that I was covered head to foot in charcoal and armed with a dagger would be impossible to explain away, should I be caught. Still, if Sacrovir was not in his tent, it would seem I had no other choice, so I began to move slowly away from the back of the tent. Just then, I heard a stirring from inside and I froze in place, waiting for an eternity. At last, there was the rustle of the tent flap being pushed aside, as a dark figure emerged from the tent. Instantly I could see by the shape of the shadow that it was Sacrovir; somehow I had not detected his presence inside earlier. Giving a silent prayer of thanks that he had appeared and that he was alone, I waited a moment for him to pick a direction in which to head towards the *Praetorium*. It relieved me to see that he was not taking the most direct route, giving me more time to stalk him, waiting until he was almost out of sight before setting off after him. Taking care to stick to the darkest parts of the path, I stopped when he stopped, which he did often, peering about in the darkness to see if he was detected. Once we were a short distance away from his tent, I rushed forward a few steps, closing the gap between us. Evidently, he heard something, freezing in place and I could dimly make out the lighter blur of his face turning in my direction. Pressing hard against the side of a tent, I tried to control my breathing to make as little noise as possible, although it still sounded incredibly loud to my own ears. However, Sacrovir seemed to be satisfied, turning about to continue on his way and I moved with him, using my longer legs to reduce the distance even more, closing now to just a matter of a few quick long strides away from him. He turned in the direction of the *Praetorium*, meaning it was time to strike, so I waited as he paused one more time, and I thought I detected the sound of his muttering something under his breath while he looked carefully about. Sacrovir did not move for several moments, then turned to stare right at me, or at least where I was crouched, my side brushing the wall of a tent, where I heard men snoring soundly. I was sure that he had seen me, his neck craning as his eyes bored into the spot I was occupying and I was close enough that I could see him shake his head, muttering again before turning to resume his journey. Fighting the urge to let out an explosive sigh of relief, I stood back up while shaking the feeling back into my legs.

Sacrovir had gone a few paces before I moved again, but this time I did not go slowly. Using my longer stride, I covered the ground between us quickly, picking up my feet to avoid making a sound or tripping. When I was just a pace away, Sacrovir sensed something and began to turn, his hand going down to his own dagger, but it was too late and I was too strong. Using my left hand, I clapped it over his mouth to grasp his jaws with all my strength, forcing his head to face directly away from me. In the same motion, I brought my dagger up to shoulder level, pulling my arm all the way back as I did, then drove the point straight into the base of his skull. The sound of the metal grating on the bone of his neck seemed loud enough to wake the dead as the point punched through and into his brain, though I knew that it was only in my imagination. His body stiffened, every muscle seeming to go rigid for just an instant before his body then reacted as if all the bones had magically disintegrated and he collapsed, forcing me downward while I shifted my balance to compensate for the weight. Twisting the blade free, I felt the warm blood and gore pulse onto my hand, his heart continuing to pump for a few moments. Letting him fall gently to the ground, I was careful not to make any noise, then wiped my blade on his tunic before sheathing it. Even in the darkness, I could see his eyes staring up at me, wide in the surprise he felt, the last emotion he experienced before I ended his life. His mouth hung open, his tongue hanging out to the side, and I smelled the blood pooling in it from where the point of my blade had punched through.

"That was a better death than you deserved," I whispered to him, then picked him up, slinging him over my shoulder.

I had only solved part of the problem; now I had to decide what to do with his body. Moving quietly, his weight threw me off a bit, making things more awkward, but I managed to avoid tripping over anything in my path while I made my way back to the Legion area. Throwing him over the wall would be tricky; I judged the risk of being discovered to be too great. I could deposit him in a corner of the stables then cover him over with hay, but that would mean that I would have to sneak by the *Praetorium* one more time, so I discarded that as well.

Then I was struck by an idea that was as absurd as any that I had ever had before, and I had to fight the urge to keep from laughing. However, the more I thought about it, I realized that it was not such a bad idea after all, so I headed back to my tent.

Arriving at my tent without being seen, I pushed through the front flap, startling Diocles, who was dozing in his chair behind his desk. He took a look at what I was carrying, his eyes growing as wide as denarii as he sat upright.

"Master, may I ask what you're doing?"

"I'm hiding a body," I replied in what I assumed was a reasonable tone.

"In here???" Diocles jumped to his feet, obviously alarmed.

"Where else?" Despite my grim cargo, I was trying suppress a laugh at the sight of Diocles so upset. "Nobody would think to search my quarters and who knows, if things don't go well in a couple of thirds of a watch, I might be joining Sacrovir."

It was a grim joke, but it was not far off from being the truth. Deciding to put Sacrovir in my private quarters, my reasoning was that since we were supposed to be leaving the tents behind, it would give me at least a few thirds of a watch before scavengers came poking about to see if anything valuable was left behind. By that time, our collective fates would be decided one way or the other, making it of little matter if we failed and he was discovered. If we were successful in our endeavor, I would be returning to the tent and I could decide what to do about the body then. I placed the body under my cot, after thinking about putting him in it before discarding the idea. Sacrovir was a small man, so when I stuffed him against the far wall, he was almost completely out of sight. Draping a blanket over the edge of the cot, I knew that it would look odd, but I did not want anyone happening to come into my private quarters immediately spotting the body. Calling again for Diocles, I told him to bring some water to wash the blood off my hands while I checked myself carefully for Sacrovir's blood. There was a small stain on my tunic, but it would be hidden by my armor, so I did not change again. Diocles returned and I washed quickly, knowing that time was running short. Once I dressed myself, I took care to don my decorations, despite there being no real reason for it. However, I wanted to let my record of all that I had done for Rome be visible, not only to Antonius and Cleopatra, but the men. Once I was satisfied, I stepped into the outer office to find Balbus, Scribonius, and Macrianus standing there.

"Is it done?" Scribonius asked the question and I gave Diocles a surprised look, since I had expected that he would tell the others.

Instead, he just shook his head. I told Scribonius that I had indeed taken care of Sacrovir.

"Where's the body?"

In answer, I just jerked a thumb over my shoulder towards my private quarters, but it took them a moment to comprehend.

Scribonius and Balbus exchanged a puzzled look, then Balbus asked, "Are you saying that you dumped him in your tent?"

I nodded. For several heartbeats, nothing was said, all three men staring at me as if I had lost my mind, then Balbus roared with laughter, slapping his thigh at the idea. The others joined in, and it was contagious, all of us standing laughing for several moments until tears were streaming from our eyes and we were gasping for breath.

"I will say this for you, Titus," Scribonius managed to gasp. "You're not boring."

Emerging from the tent after a quick conference, it was decided that I would postpone the actual act to the last possible moment. This was to avoid giving Antonius time to react by sending other Legions after us, which was the one possibility that worried me the most. I knew the men would defend themselves and in truth, especially if Antonius sent the Eastern Legions after us, they would not have any problem in cutting them down, both physically and mentally. However, I did not believe that Antonius would be that stupid, no matter how angry he might be. He would most likely send Balbinus' 12th, which was almost as veteran as the 10th, and perhaps the 19th as well. Not forgetting that I was certain Balbinus was an agent of Octavian, I still could not afford to risk everything on that belief. Therefore, I had to be prepared for the possibility that the 12th would come after us. If we refused to march out of the camp and down to the ships designated for our use, it would give Antonius too much time in which to react, not to mention that if we were forced to fight, doing so in camp would be the worst possible spot.

The *bucina* of the *Praetorium* sounded the call to start the day, prompting the Centurions and Optios to leap into motion, yelling and cursing at the men to rouse them. From all outward appearances, it was just a normal day of an army on the move, the men moving quickly and smoothly, albeit not very happily. As I walked the Legion streets, I watched carefully, but I saw no signs that the men were aware that momentous events were about to occur, other than a possible sea battle, of course. They were grumbling quite a bit about the idea of having to fight on the pitching deck of a ship, another sign that none of the Centurions or Optios had said a word. Only Gaius appeared even more tense than normal so I took him aside to calm him down and assure him that all was proceeding as planned to this point, reminding him to keep his mouth shut about what he knew. He was slightly offended that I should admonish him about it, but at that moment, I did not particularly care about his feelings. All around the camp the sounds of men rousing to start their day broke the pre-dawn stillness, where just moments before it had been completely silent. For reasons I did not understand the feeling of nerves and near-panic that I experienced the whole night had disappeared, and I was as calm as I had ever been before a battle, despite my hope that this would be a bloodless one. Perhaps it was because I was committed now; I had thrown the dice, and now it was just a matter of seeing if they came up Venus or Dogs. There was no reason to be nervous at this point and I made sure that I bantered with the men, chided a few of them, while with a couple of them who were moving particularly slowly, gave them a smack with my *vitus*. Some of the more sharp-eyed among them seemed to notice that I was wearing my decorations, yet no comment was made. A few moments later, the *bucina* sounded the call for all Primi Pili to report to the *Praetorium*. Taking a deep breath, I turned to head for the meeting with Antonius and Cleopatra, where we would be told which ships we were loading onto. Or not, as the case may have been.

Entering the *Praetorium*, I saw that perhaps half the Primi Pili had arrived to that point. The Tribunes were mostly present, along with the Legates. Antonius was there, dressed not in his ceremonial armor, but in a relatively plain cuirass, although it was still inlaid with gold while the curled edges were leafed in the same material. His greaves matched his cuirass and his *paludamentum* was about his shoulders, freshly laundered and bright. Cleopatra stood beside him, also wearing her armor, minus the helmet, which she carried under her arm. She stood stiffly and I knew that she wanted to strike a martial pose, but anyone with a set of eyes could see how nervous she was, the sweat beading on her upper lip. Turning to survey me coldly, her eyes narrowed at the sight of my full uniform.

"We're not marching in a triumph, Pullus," she snapped. "I don't think the enemy will be able to see your decorations from the deck of their ships."

"It's not for the enemy, Your Highness. It's for my men. They like seeing all that their Primus Pilus has done in the service of Rome."

She opened her mouth, no doubt to shoot back a sharp reply, but Antonius was in no mood for our bickering.

"Pullus, is the 10th ready to load?"

"Yes, sir. They're fully packed."

I spoke carefully, but neither he nor the queen seemed to notice that I had actually dodged the question.

"Very well," he grunted. "You'll load on the following ships."

He reached out to offer a wax tablet, which I took. Written on it were the names of fifteen ships, most of them quinqueremes.

"You'll be in my squadron, in the center of the line, so expect some heavy action. I hope your men are ready."

"They're ready for whatever comes their way, General."

I do not know whether it was the words or my tone, but he looked up sharply from what he was doing, signing something held by a scribe, to give me a searching stare that I was sure looked into my heart and saw all that was there. For the space of several heartbeats, our eyes were locked together, before he gave a minute shrug, as if it was not worth pursuing. Heaving a silent sigh of relief when he nodded to me, indicating that I was dismissed, I turned to head for the door of the *Praetorium*.

As I was leaving I passed Balbinus, who gave me a nod as he passed, although he seemed distracted. I was tempted to pull him aside to see if he had anything planned, but decided I could not take the risk. Instead, I made my way back to the Legion to find that the men were in the last stages of making themselves ready. Calling for Valerius, I had him give the signal for all Centurions to gather at my tent, then waited. Diocles was responsible for supervising the loading of the mules that would take our baggage to the ships to be loaded, so I handed him the wax tablet, which contained the location in the bay of the ships along with their respective names. As I did, I arranged to meet with Diocles and the rest of the slaves, with all the baggage, on the eastern side of the upthrusting promontory about a half-mile from the first of our ships. Wanting to continue the fiction as long as possible, I knew that the absence of the baggage would alert Antonius, so it was imperative that we be seen together. The Centurions began arriving at my tent, their faces taut with the tension of the moment. Watching the men carefully, I looked for any signs of deceit; furtive glances, whispered conversations, anything that might indicate that treachery was in the works. It relieved me to see that while the men were sober, and some even grim, they all appeared to be committed to our course of action. Once they were together, I announced loudly enough for any of the men nearby to hear that we had been told which ships we would be boarding.

Then, in a softer tone, I asked the Centurions, "Are you ready?"

They either nodded or murmured that they were prepared for what was to come. Satisfied, I explained what was going to happen and what I expected. With that done, I resumed my normal tone, telling the Centurions to assemble the men.

Marching out of the camp, we did so along with the three other Legions assigned to ship out with us. Those Legions staying behind lined the streets but not much was said, since most of those men were from the East and we did not have anything in common with them other than the uniform we wore. Our men were silent; their eyes straight ahead, shoulders back, the tramping of their feet made it sound as if a giant walked the Earth. As is always the case, the men marched better because the eyes of the new Legions were on them. Seeing Canidius standing by the *Praetorium* with his Legates about him, he could only watch as the best of the army marched away. Not knowing what was going to happen after the next third of a watch, it made me wonder if I would see Canidius again or serve under him, although I doubted it. As we exited the camp, the sun had crested the horizon, shining over the bay, illuminating the ships waiting for us. Smoke hung in the air from fires that still smoldered, but there were no longer raging flames burning. In the growing light, I saw another Legion marching in front of us, recognizing it as the 12th. Directing the Legion, we cut across the inlet, the hills where we had initially cut our wood now standing denuded to our right. As we marched, I noticed that now that the trees were down, we had an unobstructed view of the sea, the stumps dotting the slopes serving as an obstacle to anyone choosing to attack us. Spotting Diocles waving to me, walking in front of the mules, I gave the commands to angle the Legion over to where he was. Stopping next to the baggage train, I gave an order that was met with quizzical glances by the men, although the

Centurions seemed to understand my intent immediately. We were still about a half-mile away from where our ships were pulled up to the shore, their gangplanks lowered from their sides down to the beach. Breaking formation, the men went to find the mules on which their gear was loaded, taking it off the beast's back. That was not unusual, even if it was still a good distance away from the ships. What puzzled the men was my order to dump their baggage on the ground next to the mules to perform an inventory at that moment. They began going through their gear, mumbling to each other about the oddity of their Primus Pilus. Standing there, seemingly watching them, my eye was really on the knot of people that I recognized as those surrounding Antonius and Cleopatra, who were directing the loading of their respective squadrons. Knowing that it would take several moments before someone noticed that the 10th was not moving, I was also wagering that what we were doing would cause puzzlement, enough that it would draw Antonius himself.

It was one of Antonius' Legates who first noticed what we were doing, and I saw his black-plumed helmet turn to examine us. After a moment, he walked slowly over to Antonius, got his attention, then pointed in our direction. Antonius turned, shielding his eyes from the sun with one hand, which was now halfway over the line of hills to the east of the bay. He stood still for several moments as I watched closely, knowing that Antonius was obviously trying to determine what we were doing. Finally, he turned to call the slave who held his horse, which was about to be loaded onto his flagship, and the beast was led to him. Without waiting for a saddle, Antonius leapt aboard the horse, using the lead rope as a makeshift rein to head in our direction. Turning about I snapped an order to the Centurions, who had remained standing in their spots, whereupon they immediately began bellowing orders to assemble, telling the men to leave their baggage at once and return to their spots in formation. Despite their obvious confusion, the habit of obedience had been drilled into them and they were veterans, so they moved quickly. At the sight of the men returning to their formation, Antonius pulled up short, seemingly undecided whether to keep heading to us or to turn back and go get help. At least, that is what I assumed, and the delay gave me the chance to give the next order, which the Centurions immediately relayed to the men. If they had been confused before, they were positively befuddled now, yet they still obeyed, dropping their packs at their feet before taking their shields out of their leather cases. Seeing the men hefting their shields, with their two javelins in their free hand, Antonius furiously kicked his horse in the ribs with his heels, making the animal leap forward. If Antonius had not been a superb horseman he would have been thrown, but he managed to stay aboard, the horse galloping the remaining distance as I turned to face the oncoming Triumvir. His face was a mixture of rage and confusion as he approached, and for a moment, I thought he intended to run me down, so that I tensed my legs, ready to leap out of the way. At the last moment, he yanked hard on the halter, the horse skidding to a stop while showering me with clods of dirt.

Looking down at me, he pointed a finger as if it were a javelin, jabbing at my face and snarling, "Pullus, by Pluto's cock, you better have a good reason for whatever this is."

"I think I have a very good reason, General," I said loudly enough for the men immediately behind me to hear, knowing that it would be relayed back down the column quickly. I gestured back towards the men of the 10th. "These men are the reason that I'm refusing to board your ships. We're not going to Egypt. We're not fighting for you any longer. We're through."

For a moment, I thought he would fall from his horse as he reeled backward, his face white with shock. I heard the excited whispers of the men behind me when they finally realized what was happening, that they were involved in a mutiny. This was the moment of truth, when I would know how strong a hold I had on this Legion, but I did not turn to look to see how the men were reacting, relying on the Centurions and Optios to alert me in the event there was trouble.

"You faithless, gutless, cocksucking son of a whore!" Antonius' face was contorted with rage. "I'll have you flayed alive for this, Pullus! I swear it by all the gods I will!"

He twisted around to see that one of his Brundisium Cohorts, probably alerted by the Legate, was now marching in our direction. Cleopatra had stopped what she was doing as well and was now looking in our direction; hand over eyes, along with most of the other people gathered on shore. Only one Legion, I could not tell which one from this distance, was actually loading onto the ships. Another Legion had stopped and they were facing in our direction. I suspected it was the 12th and Balbinus, and that he was watching to see what would happen before he made his decision. So be it, I thought grimly, it will be up to us. Risking a look back over my shoulder, I saw that at least the men of the First and Second Cohorts, having heard and understanding what was happening, looked grimly determined to follow my lead.

Catching Balbus' eye, I nodded to him before turning back to face Antonius, whose hand was resting on the hilt of his sword. My heart began hammering on the realization that he seemed to be seriously considering drawing his weapon and charging. Behind me, Balbus ordered the *cornicen* to sound the call to move from column to double line, the notes ringing out through the air. Immediately the Centurions and Optios took up the call, yelling at the men to move quickly and I was gratified to hear the crashing of sound that signaled men running, with no hesitation whatsoever.

Over the noise, I called to Antonius while pointing to his sword, "General, I have no wish to fight you, but if you pull that out, I'll kill you, and we both know it. I may be all the things you say I am, but I'm also Titus Pullus of the 10th Legion, and you know that I'm one of the best men in the army with a sword. And even if you did strike me down, you can see the men are determined to stay here. I have no doubt that they'd kill you to do so."

My words had frozen his hand and he stared down at me from his horse, his face still a mask of impotent anger. The white had been replaced by the rush of blood and I had seen that look before, when he seemed to lose his head, giving in to the overwhelming fury that he was feeling, even his eyes seeming to glow red. However, he made no move, instead looking back over his shoulder to see the Brundisium Cohort suddenly come to a crashing halt at the sight of a full Legion deploying in line, ready for battle. All pretense of work had stopped, the men of the Legion that was in the process of loading now openly watching the drama unfold. The standing Legion still had not moved, but I saw that they had also unslung their shields, making me worry that they might actually want to engage with us. The 10th finished moving into line, whereupon the Cohorts in the second line faced about so they were looking roughly in the direction from where we had marched. This was pre-arranged, to avoid the possibility of a Legion marching out from camp to fall on our rear. The Brundisium Cohort was now faced with the prospect of tackling a full Legion, something that they clearly had no intention of doing, since they had stopped and were not moving.

"Why, Pullus? Is the idea of having Octavian's cock up your ass too alluring?"

I ignored the insult, looking at him with a mixture of incredulity and scorn.

"Are you seriously asking me why, Antonius? Your wife tried to kill me simply because she couldn't guard her tongue and made it clear that she intends to have her son sit as king of Rome. And she tried to kill my woman, just because she was in the way. I won't let the 10th contribute to that kind of insanity."

He slumped over at the reminder of what Cleopatra had done, giving a tired wave of his hand, as if to dismiss all that I had said.

"That was just talk, Pullus. She's a woman. Women talk, it's what they do. You don't think I'd let her do such a thing, do you? As far as that other business, that was regrettable, and I've ordered her to stop in her ridiculous attempt to exact retribution on you."

He turned eyes drained of rage on me, his gaze tired and sad. I thought I detected a plea for sympathy and help, but too much had happened.

"I don't think you have any more control over Cleopatra than you do over the tides, Antonius. And you can't win, of that I'm sure. Sosius was right, and so was Canidius."

"So you're going to be one of Octavian's lackeys now, is that it?"

"Octavian has nothing to do with this," I lied. "This has everything to do with the last ten years of following you, with no prospect of it ever ending if we go to Egypt.

We're tired, Antonius. And I don't plan on the 10th being thrown away to advance Cleopatra's plans."

"You're a traitor to Rome," he said coldly. "And I assure you that you'll be punished for this, Pullus."

"Only if you win," I shot back, happy to see him flinch. "And I'm so sure that you won't win that I'm willing to take that risk, for the sake of my men."

"This has nothing to do with your men," he sneered. "It has everything to do with being in Octavian's purse."

"Believe as you wish, General. It doesn't change the fact that we're not boarding ships and going to Egypt."

He hissed a curse at me before looking again over his shoulder, but no help was forthcoming. An idea struck me, and I called out.

"As I said, General, you have no control over Cleopatra, and neither do you control the tides. They wait for no man, and if you want to be ready to try and break through Agrippa and Octavian, you need not be wasting time trying to change my mind. The 10th isn't going."

My hope was that the mention of the tides would break this moment between Antonius and me and I could see his eyes shift seemingly involuntarily towards the bay. Clenching his teeth, he wrenched the horse around, calling over his shoulder that we were not done, then galloped back towards the ships.

I wasted no time, sure that he was going back to try and rally the remaining Legions. While Antonius and I were arguing, Diocles had supervised the Legion slaves who were almost finished packing the baggage back on the mules. It was a haphazard job and would have to be done over, but it was sufficient for our purposes and I gave the order to form a Legion square, with the baggage in the middle. As the men moved into position, I watched

Antonius reach Cleopatra, where a wild argument seemed to be raging, both gesticulating furiously, in my direction and at each other. Tribunes were now running back and forth, one going to the Legion that was loading, another to the Legion that I suspected was the 12th. With the men now formed in square, the mules were becoming restive at the tension in the air so I gave the command to march, leading the men towards the bare hilltop. Once we got going, I trotted over to the Centurions of the trailing Cohorts, telling them to keep an eye on what was going on behind us in the event that one or both Legions obeyed orders to chase us down and engage us. We began marching over the broken ground as I called again to Balbus, who trotted over and pointed to the top of the far hill.

"That's where we're going, to the high ground there."

Balbus grinned. "That'll give them something to think about if they want to come get us. But I don't think they will. They don't have time."

"Neither do I," I agreed. "But we're going to be prepared nonetheless."

Telling Balbus to take the lead, I dropped back to the rear of the square, closer to the fleet so that I could watch what was happening. Antonius was conferring with what looked like the Primus Pilus of one of the Legions and I could tell by the size of the man in comparison to Antonius that it had to be Galba of the 19th, one of the other three Legions scheduled to take ship. The fourth Legion, the 22nd, was just marching to the bay, crashing to a halt when one of the Tribunes galloped up to undoubtedly tell the Primus Pilus of the latest developments. That made the Legion standing in place the 12th and I could make out the figure of Balbinus having a spirited conversation with one of the Legates, who continued to point in our direction.

"Primus Pilus, are we really not going to Egypt?"

I was expecting the question, so I turned to address the man who asked, seeing that it was a man from the Fifth Cohort.

"I get seasick on long voyages, Terentius. Didn't you know that? No, we're not going to Egypt."

The man Terentius flushed with pleasure at being recognized, reminding me how it was the little things like the Primus Pilus calling you by name that make men feel a bond to their leaders. My attempt at humor seemed to be appreciated, drawing a hearty round of laughs, followed by a cheer, which I assumed to be for the announcement that we would not be going to Egypt.

I held up a cautioning hand.

"Don't be so happy, boys. It looks like Antonius isn't going to let us stay without making a fuss about it."

I pointed to where Galba and the rest of the 19th was falling into formation, while the 12th had already begun to move.

"Let 'em try, Primus Pilus," I heard someone shout. "If you tell us we're going to Hades, we'll storm the gates and kill anyone who tries to stop us!"

The men around whoever had called out roared their approval and then, despite still marching, some of the men began to tap their javelins against the rims of their shields. Very quickly, this was picked up by other men, until in a matter of a few paces the entire Legion was rapping their javelins in time to the beat of their feet as they marched. Looking back over my shoulder, I saw that the 22nd, which had been diverted to come after us, had stopped dead in their tracks, presumably by the sound. Many an enemy has heard that sound and it always spelled doom for them, so doubtless this was in the minds of the men and Centurions of the 22nd. Antonius was running back and forth between groups of men, waving his arms, then I saw him gallop his horse to the 22nd. We had put a bit of distance between us by this point so I could no longer see gestures, but I imagined that there was a fair bit of pointing and shouting going on. Moving across the rear of the formation while the men continued to march, the slope of the hill was now less than a half-mile away. My purpose in moving was more to have similar exchanges like I had just had with Terentius than for any tactical purpose, and men obliged by calling out their questions, all of them essentially same.

"Are we really not going to Egypt?"

Every time I was asked, I used the same line I had given Terentius, mainly because it was well received, and I wanted the men as relaxed as possible under the circumstances. This was a moment where they needed to see their Primus Pilus in a similar frame of mind, the father figure who was looking out for their best interests and had everything under control. Every trick, everything I had learned during my time in the Legions and as a Centurion I was using now, all in an attempt to assure these men that they were not making a horrible mistake in following me. Things had happened quickly and they had happened that way for a reason, since I was gambling on the force of habit being too strong to overcome when the men were given an order that was contrary to what they were expecting. Also, I did not want to give men time to think; it is when men begin thinking that problems can start. There would be time to explain and for the idea to settle in among them, yet this was not the time, particularly if we were going to be fighting. And it looked like we would have to, as the 12th

Legion continued marching behind us, seemingly in pursuit.

Reaching the base of the hill, the front rank of the square began to climb the slope. Naturally, the speed slowed down, meaning that the 12th started to gain on us, making me worry that they might pull within javelin range before we could get into position. Diocles pulled the baggage train ahead of the front rank, the men moving aside as the mules trotted by. They would be placed on the opposite slope, out of the range of the fighting, because I did not think that Balbinus could afford the time to envelop the whole hill. There was still a larger battle to be fought out on the water and I was sure that Antonius had ordered Balbinus to launch an all-out assault, but I did wonder if he had tried to send the other two and they had refused, or if he believed that just one Legion would be enough. Whatever the case, I was surprised that it was Balbinus, now that I knew for sure that it was he and the 12th, the front ranks closing the distance enough to recognize his face. Obviously, I had been wrong about Balbinus working for Octavian, I thought, as my men reached the top of the hill.

I sent Decimus Silva, the Legion *aquilifer,* to plant the standard just below the crest on the easternmost point facing downhill, and as he did this, I called the Pili Priores over. Using Silva as the reference point, I indicated the spots where I wanted the other Cohorts to line up. This was the first moment I had with Scribonius and he lingered for a moment, both of us looking down the hill where the 12th had come to a halt.

"I didn't really think he would come after us." Scribonius was looking down at the 12th, while I looked past them towards the ships, which were visible, while individuals were barely distinguishable. Yet another

Legion had left the camp and I worried that Antonius had sent for them. If they were an Eastern Legion, I suspected that they would not hesitate to do as he ordered.

"Neither did I, but here we are," I admitted.

We turned to face each other, then he smiled as he offered his hand.

"May the gods protect you, Titus."

"And you, Sextus."

With that, we both turned to head to our respective spots in the formation to wait what was to happen. It puzzled me that the 12th had made no move to begin the assault, and I was beginning to feel that the reason had to be to wait for the other Legion leaving the camp. However, as I watched, the Legion on the march out of the camp turned to head for the bay, convincing me that they were going to replace the 10th on the ships. The two Legions that had stayed behind, the 19th and 22nd, were in various stages of loading on their assigned ships. By this time, the sun was now well clear of the eastern hills, the tide was running out, and Antonius could wait no longer. Some ships were already moving, weighing anchor, their oars beginning to sweep them ponderously towards the entrance to the bay. The squadron of ships that had been guarding the mouth was moved out a short distance, apparently waiting for the rest of the fleet to join them, while the fleet of Octavian and Agrippa was moving from their anchorage farther north. Occupied as I was with these sights, it was not until Lutatius called to me that I turned my attention back down the hill. The 12th had still not moved, but a man wearing the transverse crest was walking up the hill towards us, his hands empty and out to his sides. It was Balbinus and once he was out of his men's javelin range, I walked down to meet him. I assumed that this was one last attempt to try to change my mind, and I thought that it must have been on Balbinus' own initiative because I could not see Antonius doing such a thing, or delegating it to another Primus Pilus. But it was a day of surprises, and this was just the latest one.

"If you're here to try to make one last attempt to change my mind before you try and take us, you're wasting your breath."

I was not speaking in a rude tone of voice, but I did not want to waste time in useless talk. Balbinus was standing a few feet away; he stared at me for moment, before he burst out laughing. I tried to cover up my confusion, this not at all what I was expecting.

"Don't worry, Pullus, I won't try and change your mind. You can be sure of that. I actually am here to join you."

Now it was my turn to stare, sure that this was some sort of ruse. Taking a careful look over his shoulder, I saw that his men had grounded their gear and were standing there, not looking the least bit interested in charging up the hill.

"What do you mean?" I asked cautiously.

"What do you think? You're not the only one who works for Octavian. I must confess when I was told that there would be at least one other Primus Pilus involved, I didn't suspect that it was you."

I bristled at the suggestion that I was working for Octavian, despite the reality that is exactly what I was doing.

"I owe Octavian a debt, that's true. But I'm not his agent, and I would have refused to let my men board even if I didn't owe him."

Balbinus just shrugged.

"If you say so," he replied, his tone clearly implying he did not believe me.

I opened my mouth to argue the point before thinking better of it.

Instead, I asked, "What did you tell Antonius?"

He looked away, refusing to meet my eyes, although I could see a smile tugging at the corner of his mouth.

"Nothing actually. He sent me after you, that's true enough. I just didn't tell him that I wasn't going to do what he wanted me to do when we caught up to you."

My mouth dropped open, then I looked again over his shoulder, first at the bay, then at the camp, half-expecting to see a line of Legions marching in our direction. However, the loading process was still taking place, with the newly arrived Legion clearly about to do the same. No Legions were leaving the camp either, which was a good thing.

"He must be figuring it out now," I said.

Balbinus turned to look back at the bay as well, then shook his head. "Even if he does, he won't have the time or the men to do anything about it."

"How can you be so sure he won't send for Canidius and have him send the rest of the army after us?"

He turned to give me a long look, then said, "I don't think Canidius is going to find the men very willing to come after a couple of veteran Legions."

Balbinus said this with an assurance that convinced me that he knew something that I did not, but I decided not to press the matter. I was certain that he was telling the truth and I felt better that my suspicions about Balbinus had turned out to be justified. I also suspected that he was right, yet I resolved to keep the men ready until I was sure.

Pointing to the spot where the 10th was standing, I said, "You can take our spot and we'll move to the west side of the hill."

"That means you'll have a better view of the fighting," he protested, but I just grinned at him.

"We were here first."

"Fine," he grumbled, and for the men, we clasped arms, then embraced.

Cheers erupted from both Legions when they realized that there would be no fight, at least between us.

Our viewpoint on the hill was perfect for watching the coming battle and after we rearranged ourselves, I allowed the men to sit in place. Deciding that it was time to address the Legion, I walked to the crest of the hill, using a pile of baggage as a makeshift rostrum that I stood on so that I was visible to all. The men turned about, and it was one of the few times I did not have to call for silence. Looking down into their upturned faces, the questions and apprehension were written plainly for me to see. The Centurions with the Cohorts in the middle of the Legion stood so that they could relay my words back to the rest of the men. Once they signaled they were ready, I began.

"Most of you by now have figured out that we're not going to Egypt. Some of your slower-witted comrades may not have at this point, so I'll give you a moment to turn to explain to them that we're indeed sitting on a hill and not on a ship."

This brought the roar of laughter I had hoped for, the men making a great show of turning to one of their friends to explain that fact, prompting more than one punch or shove from the offended party. Letting this continue for a few moments, finally I raised my hand, the men falling immediately silent. Turning serious, I continued.

"I suppose I should say that this wasn't an easy decision to make, but the truth is, comrades, that it was exceedingly easy. We've marched for Antonius for many years now, and we've all seen that the Marcus Antonius we knew is gone, replaced by a minion that's a slave to the bidding of Cleopatra."

The men responded positively, nodding their heads or clapping their hands to show their agreement.

"And make no mistake about it. Cleopatra wants nothing less than the destruction of Rome, and she'll stop at nothing to achieve her goal. She'd use the 10th, she'd use each and every one of us," I swept my arm across the ranks to emphasize the point, "to help her bring Rome to her knees. Our beloved city, our beloved republic! And when she was through with us, she'd send us off without a single sesterce or acre of land to show for all that we've done. That's exactly what she'd do, because that's the Egyptian way. Brothers, I've served in Egypt. I know how the soldiers of Egypt are treated. They're not given any land; they're not given any bonuses in recognition for all that they've sacrificed when their service is done, because their service is never done! They march under their standards until they can no longer hoist a shield or wield a sword, then they're cast aside to beg in the streets for crusts of bread. If Cleopatra did that to her own people, how do you think she'll treat you?"

A low growl rolled up the hill, issuing from the throats of the men of the 10th Legion at the thought of suffering the type of outrage that I had just described. I had no idea if what I was saying were true, at least as far as how the Egyptian soldiers were treated, although I knew that the Nubian royal guards retired as rich men.

This was not the time to worry about such niceties, and I built on the men's growing outrage.

"Look at those men over there." I pointed to the tiny figures still loading on the ships. It looked as if a fourth Legion was almost to the bay, and I assumed that Antonius had by now realized that Balbinus and the 12th was not coming back, so he had sent for yet another Legion to load on the ships. The 19th and 22nd had clearly finished the process, the ships they had boarded now moving out into the bay, headed for the entrance.

"Those men are being carried away to do the bidding of the queen of Egypt, not the people of Rome. That's why I couldn't obey the orders of Marcus Antonius, because I knew that they weren't truly his orders, but *hers*! And I don't recognize the authority of Cleopatra to order me or the men of my Legion to go anywhere and do anything! That's why we're here and not there, like those poor bastards who will never, ever see their homes again!"

The men leapt to their feet, roaring their approval while shaking their fists in the direction of where they thought Cleopatra was, although I was sure she was onboard a ship by this point. I allowed the men to carry on for a bit before holding my arms up again for them to quiet down.

"Brothers, we're not out of danger yet." I paused to let that sink in before continuing. "So far, Canidius has made no move to confront us, but that doesn't mean he won't. I need you all to stay vigilant while we watch what happens between Antonius and Octavian, and be ready for whatever happens. To this point, things have gone easily. I can't guarantee that it will continue like this, but I remind you that nothing worthwhile is ever easy to attain, and this is no exception. Once we see what happens between those two, then we'll have a better idea of what our future holds."

"What if Antonius wins?"

Someone from the ranks shouted this question and it was immediately picked up by other men.

"Who here, knowing what they know and having heard of all the portents and omens, truly believes that will happen?"

The silence was thunderous, men glancing at each other, but none of them willing to voice the opinion that Antonius might come out on top.

"But I'll acknowledge that this is a possibility, since none of us truly know what the gods have in store for us. Whether Antonius wins or not, he's going to Egypt with Cleopatra. That's why he wanted the most veteran Legions with him, not to try and win a battle, but to escape with the best part of his army intact. I'll tell you this now; even if Antonius were to win this battle, he's not going to win this war. We'll never see the face of Marcus Antonius again."

The men were silent, digesting what I had said.

"What about them?"

I did not have to look to see where the man who asked was pointing, knowing that he referred to the 12th, who were sitting on their packs as well.

"Their Primus Pilus felt as strongly about protecting his men as I did," I lied. "He couldn't allow Cleopatra to throw the lives of his men away any more than I could."

"So they'll fight with us?"

"They'll stand next to us to keep anyone from trying to force us to serve Cleopatra," I responded, knowing that it was not exactly the answer they were looking for.

The truth was that I did not know what Balbinus was going to do should Canidius rouse enough men to come up the hill after us, but the men seemed satisfied, giving another rousing cheer for the men of the 12th, who looked somewhat bemused by the whole thing. With the men solidly behind me, I finally started to relax, feeling the tension drain from my body while I was almost overwhelmed by a desire to lie down and sleep, despite it being barely mid-morning. Instead, I gave the order for the men to break out their rations while we awaited further developments. Calling to Scribonius and Balbus, I moved farther up the crest out of earshot of most of the men. They joined me, looking as tired as I felt, but both of them were smiling.

"At least we'll have a good view." Scribonius looked over his shoulder down at the bay and sea beyond.

"And we'll know if we're going to end up with our heads separated from our shoulders if Antonius manages to win." Balbus' sense of humor always tended to be heavy and grim.

I had to laugh, even if it was a gruesome jest.

"That's certainly one way to look at it."

"Balbus always does look at the bright side of matters," Scribonius said dryly.

We stood then for a few moments, none of us speaking; I imagine that we were still struggling to cope with the enormity of what had just taken place, at least I was.

As if reading my thoughts, Scribonius turned and asked me lightly, "How does it feel to be the leader of a mutiny?"

I knew he was jesting, but the words fell heavily on my shoulders nonetheless. Scribonius was not telling anything but the truth. However, when one hears it put as plainly as he had, it carries a huge amount of weight, a burden that felt like it was going to push me down into the ground. Thinking back to the moment when the 10th mutinied the first time at Pharsalus, one in which I had refused to participate, that had led to the rift between my best friend Vibius Domitius and me. That had been under different circumstances, I told myself, but the instant the thought crossed my mind a small voice in the back of my head chided me. Do not make excuses, Titus Pullus, it said. No matter what the cause, leading a mutiny is a crime, the most serious crime in the army. Now I would have to wait to see if Octavian actually meant something else when he sent his message to me through Marcellinus, but I could not imagine what other action I could have taken. Maybe he wanted me to use the Legion to attack Antonius, I thought, immediately dismissing that as foolishness. Only when I faced him would I know if I had fulfilled my debt to him, at least in his own mind. Until then, we could only watch and wait, so the three of us turned our attention to the waters below.

The battle of Actium was fought entirely on the water and it was the largest naval engagement I, or everyone else for that matter, had ever witnessed. With the Legions loaded aboard the ships, the Antonian forces exited the bay, although it was impossible to make their disposition out on the decks from our vantage point. Seas were calm, allowing Antonius' fleet to arrange itself into three wings, with Cleopatra's fourth squadron of 60 of the best ships right behind a man named Marcus Octavius, who had been serving Antonius as a fleet commander for some time, and was placed in the middle. Their plan called for Sosius to command one wing, the southernmost, while Antonius would take the right wing. Antonius' red pennant flew from the very top mast of his flagship, attracting the attention of Scribonius, who noticed something odd.

"They all have their masts and sails in place."

The truth was that I had not noticed, but when I squinted, I saw that he was right. This confirmed, to me at least, that Antonius' first intention was to flee and not fight, since it is highly unusual for ships going into a fight to leave their masts and sails upright. Usually they are hauled down and lashed to the deck, while all the maneuvering is done by oar power. The presence of the masts and sails made it clear that Antonius was counting on speed to outrun Octavian's fleet. That fleet had positioned itself, also in three wings but without a reserve squadron, some distance out to sea, making them just visible as individual ships from our vantage point. They made no attempt to stop Antonius' ships from forming up, seemingly content to wait for Antonius to start the action. The wind had dropped to almost nothing as the sun rose higher in the sky. The men ate their bread and salted pork, talking among themselves and of course wagering on every imaginable thing. The betting was brisk; when the attack would begin, who would begin it, which side would sink the first enemy ship. All of these questions became fair game, the men seeking to relieve the boredom of sitting there out of the action. Underlying the boredom was an air of tension as well, since this was not just any battle we were watching, but would have an enormous impact on our future. Diocles had come with some food, also bringing a stool for me to sit on, a move that both Scribonius and Balbus copied, sending their own slaves to fetch them. Once settled, we munched on our bread talking idly while we waited for something to happen. Balbinus joined us, and it was turning into a bit of a party. Neither Scribonius nor Balbus openly questioned Balbinus about why he took the action that he had, while I was content to let the matter lie, at least until later. The day grew warmer, until I could feel the sweat trickling down my back, the lack of breeze not helping matters.

At some point, Scribonius made the comment, "It looks like Antonius made a mistake not lashing his masts. There's no wind and those masts make the ships harder to maneuver when they're erect."

I did not know that, and I was curious. "How so?"

"It makes the ships top-heavy," Scribonius explained. "It makes it easier to capsize a ship with its mast extended. Watch and see if that doesn't happen to a lot of those ships."

"That's if they actually do any fighting," Balbus observed sourly. "They've just been sitting there and it doesn't look like they're going to be moving anytime soon."

He pointed to a small boat that was being rowed from its spot in the right squadron, heading towards the squadron in the center. If I squinted, I could just make out a swirl of red at the rear of the boat, telling me that it in all likelihood it was Antonius in the small boat, wearing his *paludamentum*.

"I think that's Antonius," I said. "He's probably trying to whip the men up, making one of his speeches like he does before we fight on land."

"It'll take more words than he knows to get those men ready to fight."

There was a certainty in Balbinus' tone similar to when he had assured me that Canidius would not rouse himself to come after us, making me further wonder what Balbinus knew that I did not. I must say that I did not like the idea of someone like Balbinus knowing more about what was happening than I did, and I was about to ask him to explain his statement, but Scribonius beat me to it.

He was looking at Balbinus steadily, his eyes not blinking at all as he asked, "Why do you say that?"

Balbinus seemed about to say something, hesitated, then just gave a shrug instead.

Seeing that we would not be content with that, he mumbled, "It's just what I think. No reason, really."

"Good. I'd hate to think that you know something that we don't. Seeing how we're now essentially in this together now."

True to his habit, Scribonius had cut right to the heart of the matter and also as was usual, his words had not caused any offense, or at least Balbinus did not seem upset.

Instead, he gave a wry smile, then replied, "Fair enough.

He took a look around to make sure there was nobody listening, but still pitched his voice low so that only we could hear.

"There are other Primi Pili and Pili Priores that are secretly for Octavian. I'm sure some of them are onboard those ships, and they were going to surrender after putting up a bit of a fight first, you know, to avoid making it look obvious."

"How do you know this?" I demanded.

He did not reply, instead just putting a finger to the side of his nose and winking, as I bit my tongue to keep from trying to pry the answer out of him. Thinking about it, it really did not matter that much how he knew, at least for the time being. Glancing at Scribonius, I saw that he had his frown in place as he thought about what Balbinus had said.

"So you don't know for sure that any of these agents are on board?"

"No," Balbinus admitted. "But it stands to reason that he has men in the Legions that are on the ships."

"How many are there?"

"I don't know." Balbinus was beginning to sound irritated. "Maybe a dozen, I suppose."

"That's not very many." Scribonius was doubtful. "I think it's just as likely that they're still in camp as they are on ships."

"Well, we'll see, won't we?"

Now Balbinus was clearly upset, while I found myself in the unusual position of trying to keep the peace between Scribonius and Balbinus. Fortunately, there was a distraction, and I pointed to it.

"It looks like we'll be putting that idea to the test, Balbinus."

He turned to look where I indicated while I let out a string of curses. Out of the camp gates came marching the entire remainder of the army, appearing very much as if they were headed our way.

"On your feet!"

Roaring the command while I came to my own, I watched the stream of men leaving the camp. Our men, many of them with mouths stuffed full of food, looked startled as they climbed to their feet. A number of them were looking at me, then following my gaze, saw what looked like every man in camp in their formations, either marching or preparing to march when their turn came. An excited chatter arose, men pointing and calling to each other, which not even the Centurions could quell. I looked down at Balbinus, who was still seated, seemingly more concerned with gnawing on a piece of pork than the sight of an army marching.

"It looks as if you were wrong about Canidius not getting off his ass, Balbinus."

"I doubt it," he replied placidly, his jaws working on a stubborn piece of gristle.

"Don't you think you should get your men ready?" Scribonius asked him, clearly as worried as I was about this latest development.

"There's no rush."

Balbinus still refused to be concerned, which made me wonder yet again what he knew.

"How can you be so sure that they aren't headed this way?"

Balbinus sighed, then shook his head.

"Just watch," is all he would say, so I did.

Our men of the 10th had hefted their shields, while their Centurions made sure their alignment was what it should be, walking among the men and talking about what was likely to come.

"They're going to be slaughtered, boys. They're walking up this hill to their death."

"We'll cut them down with the javelins before they can get close. We won't even draw our swords, mark my words!"

Keeping my eyes on the lead Legion, I saw they were led by a small group that I was sure was Canidius and his staff. While I watched, they suddenly wheeled, turning away from the hill and towards the coast, just a half-mile from the western edge of the camp. Men began talking again, trying to determine what was happening, but I was as mystified as anyone. Looking back at Balbinus, he just gave me a smile, looking very much like a cat who has just stolen the cream.

"I told you," he said smugly. "They're not headed here; they're headed to the beach to watch the show."

"Why didn't you tell me that in the first place?" I snapped, but he just laughed at my irritation.

"Would you have believed me?"

"Probably not," I said grudgingly.

Continuing to watch, I was unconvinced that there was not some ruse in the works. However, the rest of the army followed Canidius, so that after a few more moments, I ordered the men to stand down and resume their meal. While this was taking place, the respective fleets still had not moved, drifting more or less in place, though every so often their rowers would have to make adjustments with a few strokes in order to keep their spot.

"How did you know that Canidius wasn't headed for us?" I could no longer resist the urge to ask, expecting to hear about some highly placed agent of Octavian, or that even Canidius himself was secretly working for the young Caesar.

I was to be disappointed, since it was nothing that mysterious.

"I overheard Antonius send one of the Tribunes to tell Canidius he wanted the army to make a demonstration on the beach and watch the fight."

I stared at him a moment, trying to determine if he was being deceitful, but I saw no guile in his gaze. Giving a snorting laugh, my amusement was more at myself for my suspicious mind than for anything else. It was well past midday now, the heat was oppressive, but finally there was the first stirring of wind, coming from the west. A few moments after I felt the breeze on my cheek, the ships began to move.

Sosius, on the left, moved first, his squadron suddenly beginning to advance, the water around each ship churned white from the men on the benches bending to their oars. Slowly, the huge ships began to head towards the squadron facing them, which at first did not react. Only after Sosius began his advance did the other two wings of Antonius' fleet start to move, while the commander of the northernmost squadron of Octavian, deployed into a double line of ships, sent his second line rowing suddenly to the north in a clear attempt to get around Antonius' right flank. At the time, I did not know the identity of the commander of the left wing, but when I learned later that it was Agrippa, I was not surprised. Antonius, seeing the threat, changed his course, turning his squadron more to the north as well while the other two wings of the Octavian forces finally reacted. Instead of moving forward to close with the oncoming attack, both wings began rowing backward, moving away from the Antonians, who had begun to pick up sufficient speed to ram. The problem was that Octavian was not giving either Sosius or Marcus Octavius the chance to use the overwhelming power of their ships, all of which were equipped with massive brass beaks just under the waterline.

"They can't maintain that speed for very long," Balbus commented while we watched the Antonian fleet vainly trying to come to grips with the smaller ships facing them.

There was no doubt that the ships belonging to Antonius were more powerful, many of them equipped with high turrets at both ends of the ship on which several ballistae and scorpions were mounted. Each vessel carried a contingent of archers as well, along with the Legionaries, but unless they could actually close with, then grapple an enemy ship, they were essentially useless. Consequently, all that power came at a price; these ships were huge and took an extreme amount of effort to get them moving. Once in motion, they slowed quickly if the oarsmen did not keep up a steady momentum, which was draining their energy with every stroke. In order to get a ship of this size to ramming speed, it took a supreme effort that could only be sustained for moments at a time before the rowers had to be given a rest, which of course then killed the momentum of the ship. To observers like us it looked as if ships were moving in fits and starts, suddenly lurching towards an enemy ship that it had selected as a target, gaining speed as it closed, leaving a churning white wake that looked like the letter "V" behind it. Then the opposing ship would begin retreating and because they were much smaller, their movement would begin almost immediately after the oars first dipped into the water. Since they were not moving to engage, they were instead pulling farther away from the pursuing ship, drawing it farther from the coast with every stroke. This scene was being repeated across the water; it was clear that Octavian or Agrippa had given orders to try and wear the Antonian fleet down. In doing so, they were also drawing them farther away from the protection of the bay. In the event that Antonius should decide to retire, it was no longer a foregone conclusion that he could just have his men back-oar to retreat into the bay, for the simple reason that his huge ships could not go fast enough to make it to safety before being fallen upon by the Octavian fleet.

In terms of numbers, Scribonius had counted more than 400 ships for Octavian, while less than a hundred were anywhere near the size of most of the Antonians. However, what they lacked in power they clearly made up for with speed, so that after perhaps a third of a watch of this maneuvering back and forth, Antonius gave the order to rest, the ships sliding to a halt once again. The only difference was that Antonius' wing was now separated slightly from the other two in order to counter Agrippa's flanking attempt, and the entire fleet was now almost a mile farther from the shore. After the initial excitement from the men in seeing movement they had settled back down, breaking out the dice and tables to play while they waited to see what happened next, which looked very much like nothing.

"There's a gap now between Antonius and Marcus Octavius," Scribonius mused. "I wonder if Cleopatra will order her squadron up to plug the gap. If she does, then Antonius might be able to carry the day."

I shook my head, sure that she would do no such thing.

"All she cares about is getting away back to Egypt. I think she's going to wait for the rest of the fleet to engage, then I think she's going to make a break for it."

As we continued to watch, the lull was seemingly over, Antonius ordering his ships forward again. This attack, however, Octavian and Agrippa did not try and avoid. In fact, they began closing the gap as well, their ships seeming to leap forward when compared to the ponderously slow charge from Antonius. With astonishing quickness, the sea was suddenly churning with movement as ships began to engage each other. It quickly became clear that even when their opponent did not flee and chose instead to face the attack, the Antonian ships were usually just too slow and clumsy to be able to ram the Octavian vessel they had targeted. Just a few strokes of the oars on one side or the other would see the smaller ship neatly slip to the side, letting the attacker churn by. We could just make out bright lines arching from one ship to the next, signs that they were firing flaming missiles at each other. With the battle progressing, the cohesion and spacing of the ships began breaking down, with gaps growing between the Antonian ships that gave the Octavian craft the opportunity to surround individual ships with multiple opponents.

Balbus summed it up when he said, "It looks like a bunch of bears being baited by a pack of dogs."

In essence that was what was happening; the smaller but quicker Octavian ships were nipping at the lumbering Antonian vessels, darting in when they saw an opening, firing darts and missiles in an attempt to sweep the decks of Legionaries before they closed to grapple. Fairly quickly after this second phase of the battle started, smoke began to roil up from a number of the Antonian ships, with perhaps a dozen quickly surrounded and grappled by three and more Octavian ships. Despite being unable to see the fighting, we knew from experience that men were now trying to throw planks across the gap between ships or just leaping across to land on the deck of the other craft. Others would be hurling javelins to try and clear a space that would allow them to board without immediately being cut down. In short, it was the same as a fight on land, just in a much smaller space. And of course, if you fell in between the two ships you would either be crushed as they bumped together, or drown because your armor took you to the bottom. Otherwise, the same tactics applied and it was frustrating because we were far enough away that we could not tell how things were going once the fighting on the decks started. Men were now talking excitedly, pointing and alternately cheering or groaning as they watched individual battles, while the betting was spirited. Since they could not see how the hand-to-hand fighting was going any better than we could, they bet on individual ships and whether they caught fire, sank or capsized. I began watching the gathered army on the shore, which Canidius had arrayed on the beach, giving all the men a view of the action, and it was actually from their reactions that I gathered what was happening on the decks. One moment they would raise their fists, shaking them in jubilation, the next cover their faces or drop their head at the sight of another Antonian ship defeated. After another third of a watch, the sky was filling with columns of smoke, while true to Scribonius' prediction several of Antonius' ships toppled over after being struck by an Octavian vessel. Men appeared as tiny black dots bobbing in the water, along with the scattered wreckage of masts, spars, and oars, the black dots disappearing after a few moments when they were pulled under after becoming too tired to struggle any longer. The wind, which was gradually strengthening to a healthy breeze, shifted, now coming from the north. This was not unusual, although it did not happen every day and I doubt that Antonius and Cleopatra could have planned on it. However, at least one of them was quick to take advantage of the shift.

"I'm guessing that must be Cleopatra's ship." Scribonius pointed to a quinquereme that had hoisted a purple sail, the other ships in her squadron following her lead. "And it looks like she's decided the battle is lost."

I had heard about the giant sail of Cleopatra's, that it had cost the staggering sum of 5,000 sesterces just to dye, using the best Tyrian purple, but seeing it fill with the wind above the deck of her ship was in fact quite a sight. Her squadron, gaining speed more quickly than the craft in the other squadrons, thanks to the stronger wind and use of oars at the same time, pointed themselves for the gap that had opened up earlier between Antonius and Octavius' wing. The men of both Legions on the hill were watching Cleopatra's ship and guessing the identity of its commander were openly jeering the departing queen, more than one man turning to bare his backside.

"Why do they do that?" Scribonius turned to me as he asked this, and I was not sure if he wanted an answer, so I said nothing. "It's not like she can see their bare asses from the deck of her ship," he persisted. "I just don't see the point in making a futile gesture like that."

I could tell that he was genuinely upset about it, and curious, I asked, "Haven't you ever wanted to do something like that?"

He stared at me in astonishment. "By the gods no! Why would I want to expose my ass when there's no point in it?"

"I seem to remember a young *tiro* who wasn't shy about showing his ass to Gauls," I pointed out, happy to see him blush a deep red.

"That was different," he protested, albeit weakly. "They were just a hundred paces away and they could see it."

Both Balbus and I roared with laughter at this, even Scribonius unable to pretend that he was offended as he joined in. Turning our attention back to the fighting, I pointed and I must admit that I was gloating a bit.

"See? I told you, she's making a run for it."

The leading ships of Cleopatra's squadron had pulled roughly even with the first of the combatants scattered on either side of them. Making no attempt to change course to head in either direction where the fighting was taking place, Cleopatra was now clearly intent on escape, drawing even more jeers from the men.

"It's a good thing I didn't bet on it," Scribonius said ruefully.

"For you, maybe," I shot back.

The fighting was continuing, seemingly unabated, and it was not all one-sided. Some of the Antonian ships managed to either ram an Octavian vessel or had grappled it, subduing the men on the deck, then setting fire to the vanquished vessel before moving on. Other Octavian ships fell victim to the heavy artillery on the

Antonian ships, sinking within moments of having a huge rock crash through their hull. It had become a confused mess of a battle, with the sun sinking lower in the sky, which would make matters even more difficult. Cleopatra's ship was now sailing clear, despite several of the Octavian ships turning to head her off. From our vantage point, it was clear that they had moved too late. This was what I was watching unfold when Scribonius nudged me, pointing to the north.

"What's going on over there?"

Following his finger, I saw the ship that we knew to be Antonius' flagship sitting in the midst of the remnants of his squadron, those ships that were still operable heavily engaged. While Antonius' ship had managed to avoid being grappled, the others in his squadron around him all had multiple craft surrounding them. What had drawn Scribonius' attention was a lone trireme, one of the smaller galleys in the fleet, drawing alongside the Antonian flagship. At first, I thought that one of Agrippa's vessels had managed to slip past the cordon of Antonians, but neither ship fired at each other. I could barely make out what was happening and I shaded my eyes, cursing for the thousandth time the blurred vision that comes with age.

"Is that a small boat going between the flagship and the trireme?"

As much as I hated asking that question, I was thankful Scribonius did not give me any grief about it, seeing how I had always had the keenest vision among us for many years. He squinted, making me feel better that he was obviously having problems as well.

Finally, he said doubtfully, "I think so. What do you think it means?"

"Antonius is getting on a faster ship so he can catch up to that bitch," Balbinus interjected, again with a certainty that caught my attention.

"And how do you know that? Something else you overheard and forgot to mention?"

I knew that my tone was less than friendly, but I could not contain my irritation.

Balbinus refused to meet my gaze, and for a moment, I thought he was not going to answer.

"They had it planned beforehand. If the battle wasn't going well, Cleopatra and Antonius had arranged for one of her Egyptians to lag behind the fighting, then when Antonius gave the signal, come alongside and take him aboard."

"You mean he's just leaving the rest of them behind?" I asked incredulously, hardly able to believe it, yet somehow knowing it was true.

Balbinus just nodded and I forgot to press him about how he knew.

I exchanged looks with Scribonius, who said quietly, "If that doesn't convince you that you made the right decision, nothing will."

Balbinus was right. Antonius boarded the trireme, heading immediately for the open gap, the rowers pulling so furiously that their oars foamed the water with every stroke. The ship leaped across the bay, making us suspect that it had also been stripped and it was not carrying anything in the way of troops or supplies that would slow it down, its only purpose being what it was doing now, carrying Antonius to safety. Cleopatra's squadron was still just visible on the horizon, sailing south towards the Peloponnesus, with the scattered wreckage and remnants of Antonius' fleet spread all over the sea. There were still isolated fights going on, with a few Antonian ships trying to flee back to the bay, hounded every stroke by several of Octavian's craft. Some of the surviving ships whose *navarchae* were a bit more quick-witted or who somehow knew in advance what Antonius was about had broken off to follow him. The sun was now hanging just above the western horizon, reflecting off the sea and making it very difficult to see, but one thing was clear from our vantage point; Antonius' fleet had lost, and lost decisively. A group of Octavian's ships set off in pursuit of what was effectively all that was left of Antonius' fleet. The battle was obviously winding down and men were becoming bored and tired as the novelty of betting on the outcome had long worn off.

Balbus asked, "What do we do now?"

The truth was that I had not thought that far ahead; all that I had focused my thoughts and energy on was making sure that my Legion did not board the ships then dealing with the immediate aftermath of that decision. We had left our tents behind in the camp, along with our heavy baggage, and I had no intention of going down and getting all that, nor could I imagine Canidius just letting us in to retrieve it. As I thought about Balbus' question, it became clear that we would have to spend the night on the hill and that it would be prudent to post a strong watch. We carried enough rations for two more days; after that we would have to procure more, along with our grinders and ovens. I was fairly confident that when Canidius vacated the camp he would burn all the tents, along with everything else flammable to keep the gear from falling into the hands of Octavian. The one good thing if Canidius did put everything he was not taking to the torch is that it would take care of the body of Sacrovir lying under my cot, but losing our gear would create more problems than it solved. Immediately after his men marched back into camp, they began striking their tents and packing, indicating that they planned on not waiting until the next morning to begin the march. That gave me some hope that perhaps he would not spare the time to burn everything, but there was nothing to be done except wait and see. Then, I was struck by a thought, so I walked over to Balbinus, who had rejoined his own Legion, pulling him to the side.

"Is Canidius going to leave us our tents and other gear when he pulls out?"

He looked startled at the question, but it was still light enough to see a look flash through his eyes that told me he knew the answer. Staring at him hard, he finally nodded.

"Yes, he's going to leave everything behind that doesn't belong to the Legions marching with him."

"That's another thing you forgot to tell me?" I was angry now, and he took an involuntary step backward as he held his hands up.

"I was going to tell you," he protested.

"When?"

"Later," he said vaguely.

Biting back my reply, I stalked away. Balbinus was proving to be an untrustworthy ally and I resolved that I would not relax my guard around him at any time. Calling the Pili Priores, I gave the orders to get the men settled down as comfortably as possible, having them pull their cloaks out of their packs to wrap up in since it got cool at night. The breeze had been blowing steadily now for some time, not feeling like it would slacken, making me hesitant to have fires built. Without the protection of the walls of the camp, on this exposed hilltop, I was worried that sparks would fly if a strong gust of wind came, causing a fire. Deciding that the men would be grumbling anyway at the prospect of being deprived of the shelter of their tents, I took the risk. Diocles brought the animals and baggage back to the top of the hill, where he supervised the unloading, the men retrieving personal items that would make their night more comfortable.

Despite being fairly confident that there would be no trouble that night, I still ordered a half-strength watch, but cut the length of the shifts down so that men could get more rest. The ships of Octavian's fleet had begun to retire back to their anchorage, leaving a few dozen still in various stages of destruction. Some were still burning fiercely, illuminating the sea around them as the light grew dim, but most had already burned down or capsized. A few of Octavian's vessels had captured Antonian ships in tow, while other Antonians that were still able to move under their own power but had surrendered were being escorted back to Octavian's camp. Watching them, I wondered what would happen to the men on board, particularly the Legionaries. I did not believe that Octavian would act harshly with them, but only time would tell. There were a handful of Antonian ships that did not escape with the remnants of the fleet in pursuit of Cleopatra, yet had managed to evade capture by escaping back into the bay and in the last light we could see the crews and Legionaries trudging back to Canidius' camp, leaving the ships on the beach. The battle of Actium was over, the only thing left seeing what happened in the morning. Sitting and talking quietly with the Pili Priores, I prepared them for the next day before we retired. Rolling up in my cloak, the ground was hard beneath my body and I knew that I would have aches in the morning that had never been a problem when I was younger. My last thoughts before drifting off were not of what the next day would bring, but of Miriam, wondering what she was doing, and when I would see her again.

I was roused shortly before dawn by a call from the duty Centurion. Dragging myself to my feet, my back and hips aching from the cold and the hard ground, I stumbled a bit while I tried to shake the sleep from my head, wondering what had happened to cause the alarm. Moving carefully among the men, most of who were just sitting up themselves, I went to the spot lower on the hill where the sentries on the north side were placed. The duty Centurion happened to be Glaxus and I greeted my former Optio with a growl that he better have a good reason for rousing me. In answer, he pointed down towards the camp, where I could see that more torches were lit and in the pools of light thrown by them, we watched men moving about.

"I think that Canidius and the army are about to move out."

I just grunted, not particularly surprised, but Glaxus was not through.

Pointing farther north, on the other side of the inlet, beyond the remnants of our old camp, he added, "I saw torches over there, heading this way."

Peering into the darkness, I could not see anything at all. Then, just when I was about to tell him he was seeing things, I caught a glimmer of reflected light, just a brief flash. A moment later, the light grew in strength, several other pinpoints finally appearing behind the first. It took a few heartbeats for it to register before I recognized that I was seeing a column of men, marching by torchlight and they were indeed headed south. There was little doubt that it was Octavian, explaining why Canidius was on the move as well. As I watched, the leading light disappeared, and I remembered from my previous study of the ground that there were undulations in the terrain, meaning they had obviously dipped down in between small hills. They had yet to reach the point where the ground leading up to the shoreline flattened out, allowing them to march along the beach, and I estimated that they were still a good third of a watch away from reaching the mouth of the inlet. Looking back to the camp, Canidius' men were formed up and it appeared that they were just moments away from starting out the gate of the camp to make their escape. They would be exiting the Porta Decumana, meaning that they would actually head in our direction before turning to the east to follow the southern shore of the bay, then turning into the interior, but I was positive that Canidius would not spare the time to try and do anything about us. Seeing that nothing was likely to happen that would involve us for some time, I decided not to rouse the men yet, letting them get an extra bit of sleep. Telling Glaxus that he had done the right thing in sounding the alarm, I turned to walk back to my spot, telling the men, some of whom had climbed to their feet in anticipation of being roused, to go back to sleep. Daylight would be coming soon enough and we would see then what happened next. The big question in my mind was whether the men in the fort on the other side of the inlet, all two Cohorts, would put up a fight, despite it being a futile gesture, at best only buying Canidius a full watch or less should Octavian choose to pursue. Lying back down to try to rest before the dawning, I knew that this day was likely to be as difficult as the previous one, even if in different ways.

The sun rose to the sight of Octavian's army just reaching the beach on the east side of the inlet, barely a mile north of the fort. Canidius' army, or the tail end of it anyway, was still visible off to the east, marching along the southern stretch of the bay where a surprisingly large number of ships were gathered, growing from the night before. These turned out to be more Antonian stragglers that managed to escape the fighting under the cover of darkness. Evidently not knowing what else to do, they came back to the bay. Their crews were gathered in small knots about their respective craft and I imagined that there were discussions, likely very heated, about whether to surrender or run after and join up with Canidius and the army. As Balbinus had informed me, the camp below was not a smoking ruin, though a large number of the stakes of the palisade and tents were missing, making the rampart look like an old Legionary missing half of his teeth. The light, growing as the sun climbed over the eastern hills, allowed me to see that the fort on the north side of the inlet was deserted. Evidently, also under cover of darkness, Canidius had withdrawn those men, so there would be no resistance to Octavian's army as it crossed over to the camp. My men, and those of the 12th, were already into their morning routine, the Centurions and Optios hurrying them along, preparing them for our orders. Deciding that I needed to consult with Balbinus again, by this point I was convinced that he had specific instructions about what to do next from Octavian, and I found him bawling orders to his Century, once again pulling him aside.

"What are we supposed to do next?"

"What do you mean?"

Finally, I had enough and I reached out to grab his arm, squeezing it with as much force as I could muster. He flinched, almost crying out in pain, but stopped by biting his lip, not wanting to shame himself in front of his men. Normally I would never have treated another Primus Pilus in such a manner, but I was beyond caring.

"You know exactly what I mean," I hissed through clenched teeth. "I know Octavian well enough to know that he wouldn't leave a detail like the two Legions who mutinied against Antonius unattended to, and I know that you know a lot more than you're telling me. So what is it? What did he tell you to do next?"

He rubbed his arm, seeming more rueful than angry.

"You don't have to get angry, Pullus. I was going to tell you."

"Apparently I do, because I keep finding myself coming over here begging for information, which you should be giving me freely."

"The Legions are to stay up here, and you and I are supposed to go down to meet him in the camp."

That alarmed me a great deal.

"Alone?" I asked, and he nodded.

Looking down towards the group of men on horseback leading the way in front of the standards of the first Legion, I knew that Octavian would be one of them. They were almost to the fort and it would take a bit of time for them to get loaded aboard the boats that would ferry them across the inlet. I did not think that Octavian would lead the way; he was much too cautious and wily for that, preferring to send at least a Cohort ahead to smell out a trap. Also, I imagined that he would want some men sent across to go and deal with the crews of the ships, who had apparently made their decision and were now all clustered together, seemingly waiting for Octavian to present himself so they could surrender. That gave us a bit of time, but I did not like the idea of going down to face the younger Triumvir with just Balbinus at my side, and I shook my head.

"I won't go down there alone. Not with just you."

Balbinus looked unhappy, strengthening my suspicions. He shook his head. "Octavian won't like that. He was very specific that it should just be you and I."

"I don't care," I had made up my mind, and it had been Balbinus who had done it for me. "I'm going down there with the whole Legion."

Now he looked positively petrified. "You can't do that, Pullus," he gasped. "Octavian will think you mean to fight if you disobey his instructions and come with the whole damn Legion."

As much as I did not want to admit it, I could see Balbinus had a point.

"All right," I relented, but very grudgingly. "I won't bring the Legion. I'll bring just my Cohort. He can't possibly think that I plan on fighting his whole army with just them. And I'll leave them just outside the camp when we go to see him."

He was clearly unhappy, but he could see that I was not going to budge, so he sighed and said, "I hope you know what you're doing."

"Well, if you had been more forthcoming in the beginning, I would have been more likely to trust you."

Without waiting for a reply, I spun on my heel to go get the First ready to meet Octavian.

I did not explain to the Centurions why the First was to accompany me down to the camp, and they did not ask. The men, probably sensing my unease, were on edge, looking very wary as we marched down the hill. Ordering them to march in column and not in closed formation, the way we would if we were expecting contact, I understood that I was taking a risk as it was and did not want to exacerbate matters with Octavian. However, I was so tired of all the intrigue and treachery that I was not taking any more risk than I had to, so I was especially alert as the camp drew closer. Balbinus was not talking; he looked very uneasy himself and I wondered why, since he had been so assured about almost everything that had taken place to this point. Reaching the bottom of the slope, just outside the Porta Decumana I ordered the Cohort to halt. Octavian had posted men on the ramparts and they stood watching as I called Balbus over.

"I'm putting you in command. If you see me come running, wait for me and we'll get back up the hill. If you think I'm in trouble, I'll leave it up to you to decide what to do."

He regarded me steadily, then looked up at the men on the rampart. Finally, he just gave a shrug.

"I think you're making a big mistake, but we'll be here whatever happens."

"I don't see where I have a lot of choice," I said. "I have to meet with Octavian at some point, and Balbinus seems to have arranged it already."

"You're a fool if you trust him." Balbus was adamant, though I was not sure whether he meant Octavian or Balbinus.

"I'm no fool," I assured him. "If something goes wrong, I'll gut Balbinus before I go down."

"Hopefully it won't come to that," were his last words, then we clasped arms before I joined Balbinus, who was standing off to the side.

"You ready?"

Looking over at him, I saw that he looked extremely nervous, which did not make me feel ready at all, but I nodded anyway. We walked towards the Porta Decumana, then when we were perhaps 50 paces away, a Centurion stepped forward from the small group of men who were standing waiting. Squinting at the figure, I knew that he looked familiar but was unable immediately to place the face. We were almost to him before it came to me; the man's name was Aulus Lappius, and he was the Primus Pilus of Octavian's 3rd Legion, not to be confused with the 3rd Gallica of Spurius. The two of us were slightly acquainted from our time on the Campus Martius and what I knew of him was that he was competent, but was also firmly attached to Octavian. His face was neither friendly nor hostile; his manner that of the professional as he greeted the both of us.

"Caesar is waiting for you. You're to come with me," he told us after our initial greeting.

Without waiting for an answer, he turned to walk back through the gate, Balbinus and I on his heels. The men who were with him, all rankers, but looking like hand-picked men, very tough and experienced, fell in immediately behind us, which did not make me feel any easier.

As we marched by what just two days before had been the 10th's area, I could tell from a cursory look that it appeared that nothing was disturbed, the tents still standing and everything else looking intact. Naturally, I was most interested in examining my tent and was happy to see that it also looked untouched. Approaching the center of the camp, I saw men gathered on the large empty spot where the *Praetorium* had been. Two of them were mounted and, as we drew closer, I saw that with Octavian was Marcus Agrippa, the latter leaning down, presumably giving orders to the Tribune standing next to his horse. Octavian was addressing a small cluster of men, stopping when we came into his view. Sitting upright, he watched us approach, his demeanor cold and anything but welcoming. Gone was the prettiness that had dogged his youth, leading to all those whispered rumors about his sexual tastes. In its place was a coldly handsome man, clearly in the prime of his life although he still looked young for his age. He was now 32 years old and I felt a jolt as I realized that it had been 13 years since that night when I had joined Caesar and his young nephew for dinner.

Lappius approached to salute Octavian, saying something in a low voice to his general that got Octavian's attention. Nodding a dismissal to Lappius, he fixed his gaze on me as I saluted, which he did not return, staring down at me for several moments, his face betraying nothing. When he spoke, his voice was cold and despite the fact he did not speak in an excessively loud tone of voice, it was clear that he meant for the others around us to hear his words.

"Well, Pullus, it seems that you're still doing things in your own way."

I was unsure what he was referring to, so I decided that the best course was to play the stupid Legionary.

Finishing my salute to Octavian, I remembered to address him in his preferred manner.

"I'm reporting that the 10th Legion is at your service, Caesar."

I had hoped that this would soothe whatever hard feelings he was having, but it clearly did not work. Ignoring what I had said, he turned to Balbinus.

"Balbinus, did you relay the instructions to Pullus exactly as they were relayed to you?"

Balbinus was not about to stick his neck out for me, snapping to *intente* and wasting no time in answering that he had indeed very specifically told me to come without an escort. Once Balbinus finished, Octavian turned back to me, his pale blue eyes boring into mine.

"So Balbinus here claims that he told you my instructions, which you apparently chose to ignore. Would you care to explain why?"

It had been a trying two days, with my patience sorely tested by Balbinus as it was, and I felt the anger that had been churning in me come boiling out, even as I knew that nothing good could come from displaying my temper.

"Because you're not my commanding general, Caesar. It's true I'm repaying a debt to you, but I'm loyal to Rome, first and foremost. I would ask why it was so important that you demand that we come alone?"

Agrippa's jaw dropped, while Octavian looked as if he had been slapped. The men standing about were looking at me like I was possessed by some *numen*, but I did not care.

It took Octavian a moment to find his tongue, though his voice was strangled, I assume with anger, as he gasped, "Are you insinuating that I planned some sort of violence against you?"

"Are you insinuating the same thing, Caesar? What would it matter if I brought my men? They've been up on that hill for two days and they need to come down to the camp to retrieve their gear and to pack up to join up with your army. I assume that you're going to waste no time in going after Canidius, and you'll need one of the most veteran Legions in the army. The more time they spend sitting on that hill, the longer it will take them to be ready."

Finished, I stood, feet apart, half-expecting him to snap an order to have men seize me, or try at any rate, while for a long moment he looked as if he were about to do that very thing. Then, he exhaled sharply, giving a harsh chuckle.

"Fair enough, Pullus. I can see now how ordering you to come alone could seem to be suspicious, though it was only to save time. And now that you mention it, I can see that having your men and Balbinus' men to stay up on the hill and not down here, packing up, is wasting it."

Octavian urged his horse forward, walking it to where I was standing so that he could look down on me.

"I'm happy that you have chosen to continue to serve Rome, Pullus, and I welcome the 10th Legion into my army." Leaning down, he stared into my eyes as he finished quietly. "But now that I am your commanding general, you will never question my orders again. Is that clear, Primus Pilus?"

I knew better than to push my luck any farther, so I nodded, giving him another salute as a sign that I had received his message very clearly indeed.

Satisfied, he said, "Send for your Legion to come pack up. Then I want to speak to you and Balbinus privately. I want to know everything about the army we're chasing."

"How did it go?"

"I'm alive, but just barely, I imagine," I said grimly to Balbus, when I returned to the First.

Recounting the conversation, Balbus gave a toneless whistle after I finished.

"Sometimes I think that you truly want to die, Titus."

"I just don't like being pushed," I retorted. "And he had no business pushing me that way."

Balbus gave me a hard stare.

"No business?" he repeated. "What kind of nonsense is that? He's the most powerful man in the Republic, he can do anything he likes and you and I and everyone like us must do as he commands. That's what business he has."

"But we're citizens, just like he is." I knew I was being stubborn, but I was still simmering over the confrontation. "Just because he's higher born and is a Triumvir doesn't mean that we don't have rights."

Balbus just snorted at this, making it clear what he thought of my high-flown notions. Deciding that there was no profit in continuing the conversation, I let it drop, ordering Balbus' Optio to go up the hill and retrieve the rest of the Legion.

"You might as well go into camp and start breaking things down," I told Balbus. "I have to go have a private talk with Octavian."

Balbus' eyebrow lifted in a clear question, but I waved his concerns away.

"No, it's not like that. He wants to talk to me about the state of Canidius' army, and I imagine he's going to ask about Antonius."

"And Cleopatra," Balbus added.

"Her too," I said grimly. "And I have quite a bit to tell him about her."

Balbus laughed as he walked away to rouse the First.

Since the *Praetorium* was missing, Octavian had to find a smaller tent near the forum, choosing a Legate's tent that had somehow been left behind. Two guards were standing outside and I noticed that they were dressed differently, wearing red plumes instead of black, while their armor was highly polished. They were both almost as large as I was. When I appeared, I was clearly expected and waved in without a challenge. The inside of the tent was essentially bare, since its owner had taken the contents with him on the ships, while several stools had been scrounged from somewhere, and both Octavian and Agrippa were seated on two of them. Standing behind them were three scribes, with Octavian dictating to one of them. I strode to stand at *intente* in front of the pair, saluting Octavian first before turning to render the same to Agrippa. Octavian gave a wave in return while Agrippa was more formal, giving me a parade ground salute in return, which I appreciated. I stood waiting, but thankfully Octavian was almost done and did not make me stand there, perhaps sensing that it would not do either of us any good; my temper, and presumably his, still a bit raw. Balbinus was not present and I assumed that since he had to go himself to get his Legion, he would be showing up shortly. Octavian turned to me, looking at me for a moment before favoring me with a smile so reminiscent of Caesar that I felt weak in the knees.

"Pullus, I want to apologize for the way I treated you earlier," he began, and I fought to keep my jaw from dropping as he continued. "You caught me at a bad moment, as I had just learned that our squadron was given the slip by Antonius, and I took my bad temper out on you. I fully understand why you acted the way you did, as I'm sure these last few days have been very trying."

"No apology is necessary, Caesar. I acted poorly as well, and you are of course correct. The trials of the last days have made me very raw."

I did not really feel that way, but I knew a peace offering when I saw it and it would have been boorish, not to mention foolish, of me to spurn such a gesture. With this out of the way, Octavian immediately turned to business.

"Tell me," he began, "will Canidius, and more importantly his army, put up a fight?"

I considered for a moment, then slowly shook my head.

"I don't believe so," I replied cautiously, and I saw a flash of irritation cross his face. Evidently, he wanted a strong assurance, but I was going to err on the side of caution. "A large part of the army with Canidius is Eastern and any loyalty they felt was to Antonius. The rest are veterans and a good number of them were with us at Philippi. I don't believe they relish the idea of fighting one of their former commanders. Now that Antonius deserted them, I don't believe that they have much fight in them."

He said nothing, just glanced at Agrippa, who nodded in acceptance of my judgment.

"That makes sense, and that agrees with the information I have from other sources," Octavian said.

Now it was my turn to be irritated, since it was clear that I was not telling him anything he did not already know. As usual, I did not do a good job of hiding my emotions, because Octavian gave a short laugh when he looked at my face.

"Pullus, I like to be thorough. Just because I have other ways to get information doesn't mean that what you tell me isn't valuable."

This mollified me a bit, and he turned to other matters.

"What about Antonius? And Cleopatra? How are things between them? What frame of mind was Antonius in going into this battle? Tell me everything."

This was what I had been waiting for, since this was the other reason that Octavian had called in his debt at this moment. He wanted and needed the 10th, but he also wanted as much information on Antonius and Cleopatra, gleaned from people who had access to the both of them. As he himself had just stated, Octavian was and is a very thorough fellow, particularly when it comes to understanding the mind of his enemy. I also knew that Octavian's apology was not to Titus Pullus, but to the Primus Pilus of the 10th Legion, although I did not mind all that much. At that point, most of my outward respect to Octavian was due to his status and not to the man that he was, mainly because I did not know this version of Octavian all that well. I could see that much about him had changed in the time I had been serving with Antonius, but it was still too early to tell exactly what type of man he had become in the process. Now I was able to tell the young Caesar all that took place between Cleopatra and me, along with all that I had seen between the queen and Antonius. Probably unsurprisingly to you, gentle reader, I held nothing back. Midway through my tale, Balbinus showed up and he reinforced some of the points I was making about Antonius and his relationship with Cleopatra. Octavian only interrupted to ask an occasional question or to have me expand on some point that interested him, while Agrippa said nothing, just listening to everything. By the time I finished, I had grown hoarse from speaking, so Octavian ordered one of the scribes to go get me some water.

"You're a lucky man, Pullus," Agrippa said suddenly. "Not many men that Cleopatra wanted dead have escaped, especially someone that's so close by."

"Luck is just the favor of the gods," Octavian said. "And Titus Pullus has always been one of the gods' favorites."

As he smiled at me again, I caught just a glimpse of the eager boy who had wanted so badly to have dinner with me. When he spoke, it became clear that our minds were running in the same direction.

"I still owe you a dinner, Pullus, and while I'm afraid I can't spare the time right now, I promise it will be very soon. I have some ideas about what to do with the army that I want to discuss with you."

Intrigued, I assured him that I looked forward to it, wondering what his ideas were.

"How soon will your Legions be ready to march?"

Agrippa, always the general first, had asked the question.

"I'll have to check, but I believe we should be ready to go now," I said, judging that the Centurions had kept the men busy while I was talking.

"I still need another third of a watch," Balbinus said, and I felt a smug sense of satisfaction, ignoring the fact that we had had a head start. Agrippa turned to Octavian, who walked to the tent flap to look out at the sun, judging the time.

"We can get in at least a full watch of marching if we leave immediately. We'll push on."

Octavian dismissed us to return to our respective Legions and I was relieved to find that my guess had been correct; the men were ready to march. While we waited for the 12th, I called a meeting of the Centurions, knowing that they were waiting to hear how things went between Octavian and me, and by extension the fate of the Legion. As soon as they gathered, I reassured them that all was well, that we were now part of Octavian's army and that we were setting off in pursuit of Canidius. Somewhat to my surprise, many of the Centurions were clearly unhappy about this so I singled out one, Ovidius, the Princeps Prior of the Fifth, asking him what was wrong.

"I don't much like the idea of fighting men that we've been marching with for so long," he replied, and I saw many heads nodding at this.

"I seriously doubt that Canidius' men are going to fight," I tried to assure them, but there was clear doubt on their faces.

"What if they do?" Ovidius persisted.

"Then we'll do our jobs and kill any bastard who's stupid enough to fight us," I snapped, immediately regretting my words and tone.

Seeing Scribonius wince did not help, but I was not about to soften my words. No matter what, I expected the men to obey, despite my hope that they would not have to lift their swords, mainly since I did not want to face the possibility that they would refuse. There was no outright disagreement, but it was an unhappy group that returned to their men. Scribonius walked over to me, his expression easy to read.

"You could have handled that better," was his only comment.

"I'm tired of having to handle anything," I shot back. "They just need to do what they're told, whenever they're told to do it."

"Just like you did, obeying Octavian." Scribonius was straight-faced when he said this, yet I knew that he was teasing me.

"That was different." I could not help grinning as I said it, knowing that it was absolutely no different than my Centurions' reaction to the idea of fighting Canidius.

"Of course," Scribonius snorted. "It's always different when it's you."

I punched him on the arm. "You know, for such a smart man, it's taken you a long time to figure that out."

Joining with the rest of Octavian's army, for the veterans in our ranks, the men of the second *dilectus* and not the replacements we had salted our ranks with after the Parthian campaign, it was almost like a reunion of families. Men who had not seen each other since after Philippi called to each other, the fact that just days before we faced the prospect of eying each other across a battlefield not lost on anyone.

"I'm glad I didn't have to kill you, Proculus, you old bastard."

"As if you've ever seen the sun rise on such a day, Glabius!"

"Herennius, you still owe me 20 sesterces from dice!"

"I haven't forgotten, you old goat! How could I? With a face that ugly, who could forget anything?"

"Rest easy, boys! The 10th is here to pull your fat from the fire again!"

"The 10th! That bunch of poxed old women? They couldn't find their ass with both hands! It's the other way around! The 7th will save you again, just like we did in Gaul!"

And so on, with each Legion marching by while we waited to take our spot in the column. Since we were new arrivals, we were near the rear of the column, causing some grumbling, but it was to be expected. Octavian set a fast pace, except that unlike his adopted father, he rode instead of walking with the men. Agrippa, on the other hand, got off his horse to walk up and down the column, talking to the men, swapping jokes and stories.

As we marched along the southern edge of the bay, I saw men working on the abandoned ships that had been part of Antonius' fleet, making them ready to be towed to the nearest port. I wondered what was to happen to them, since possessing these massive warships was a blade that cut both ways. They were enormously valuable, but they were also enormously expensive to maintain and, as Antonius learned the hard way, finding experienced and well-trained crews was not an easy task. They were useless as cargo vessels, making it highly unlikely they could be sold, while it was equally unlikely that Octavian would be willing to sell them to nations like Bithynia, which would essentially give them back to Antonius. I was just happy that it was none of my concern. It was easy to follow Canidius, the ground being churned and torn in only the way that the feet of thousands of men and hooves of thousands of animals can accomplish, leaving a trail a blind man could follow. It also made the going rough, men stumbling and tripping across gouges in the ground. While it felt good to be on the march again, it had been quite some time since we last carried our packs for any length of time, making it a blessing that we only had a few thirds of a watch of daylight left, since a full day on the march would have been difficult. There was still moaning and groaning while the men worked on the camp that evening and I must admit that I felt a few aches as well.

Once we were settled in, with the duties for the night assigned, I released the men to go see old friends and relatives in the other Legions, and the other Primi Pili did the same. There were a number of new but still-familiar faces around the fire, so I stopped to greet some of the men who I had known in Gaul or during the first civil war. All in all, it was a pleasant evening catching up with old friends, though never far from anyone's mind was the thought that we were in pursuit of Canidius, and soon might be facing other old friends.

Our pursuit of Canidius lasted almost a week before we finally drew close enough for both armies to see each other plainly. The preceding two or three days we had seen the dust cloud hovering in the sky ahead of us, or caught the occasional glimpse as they crested a hill. Now they were just a couple of miles away and we had been led deep into the interior of Greece, Canidius evidently still trying to make it to Thrace. At the end of the day that marked a week of pursuit, we made our respective camps on the tops of hills, barely a mile away from each other, close enough that the men of both armies were plainly visible to each other as they worked digging the ditch and building the rampart. Being in such close proximity, both sides posted a full Legion on the opposite slopes facing each other to keep an eye on things while the rest of the men worked. It was inevitable that almost immediately after the respective camps were constructed that men would walk down into the small valley between the two to meet and talk.

Naturally, following initial contact, talk soon turned to the situation facing the men of Canidius' army, and representatives of Canidius' army asked for an audience with Octavian. While Canidius was trying to convince his men to fight, his men were talking with Octavian, seeking to come to an accommodation that would allow them to avoid the prospect of facing us in battle. Not surprisingly, this was as popular with the men of Octavian's army as it was with Canidius', so it was not long before an agreement was reached. Seeing that his cause was doomed, Canidius and most of his staff slipped out that night to escape, fleeing to the east, with the goal of taking the long way around Asia to rejoin Antonius, presumably in Alexandria. The men of Antonius' army from the East were given their release from service, without any bonus or bounties being paid. The Italian veterans of Canidius' army who were due were also given their discharge. However, they could not receive any bonuses either, since there was no money in the treasury at the moment to pay them. A fair number of Octavian's Legions were past their discharge dates as well and as with the members of Canidius' army, there was no money to pay them their discharge bonuses, nor land to give them at that time. In order to reduce the likelihood of trouble, these men were not discharged all at once, but in smaller groups to disperse them. Octavian also ordered them to disarm, only allowing them to keep their daggers, which was exceedingly unpopular, so the 10th was called to supervise the handing over of the weapons. Tensions were very high and I could sympathize with the men, since every Legionary talked about having their sword hanging over their fireplace at the farm or tavern they would own when they got out, a symbol to anyone who entered that told of their service. Every day, another group was discharged, the process taking almost two weeks before Octavian was satisfied that the affairs of the army were settled for the time being.

Octavian's next order of business was the city of Corinth, which had gone over to Antonius and was still refusing to surrender. Marching up to the walls, we immediately began an investment the city and that was enough to convince the citizens to surrender. With these matters settled, we marched back to the coast, settling back into Octavian's camp north of the inlet, while he founded the city, now known as Nicopolis, to commemorate his victory over Antonius. The seasons were changing and we were ordered into winter camp, staying in that spot on the coast. Meanwhile, Octavian went to Athens, where he dealt with all the administrative matters left in the aftermath of his victory, while he sent Agrippa back to Rome to deal with matters there. Even after all that he had accomplished, there were still massive problems facing the man who was now the master of Rome. Most importantly, while Antonius was defeated, he and Cleopatra still lived and as long as they did, Octavian would not rest.

Chapter 5- Nicopolis

Nicopolis was settled with the discharged Legionaries, their families, and a number of native Italians who were either bribed or forced to relocate to the new city. Overnight, it sprang up from what had been a military camp, and with the strong backs of not only the retired veterans but the rest of the army, streets were laid down, walls were erected, and buildings constructed. While the men did not particularly like it, the work kept them busy and out of trouble for the most part. Almost as quickly as the boundaries of the city were laid out, the shacks and shanties of the camp followers sprung up on the outer edges, meaning that as usual, the first to arrive and set up business were the scum that always hovers about an army the way blowflies surround a corpse. Wineshops, whorehouses, gambling houses, quacks selling fake cures; these were the first inhabitants of Nicopolis, cheering the men greatly.

After spending almost a year on the marshy plain of Actium, even a tumbledown shack selling wine that was virtually indistinguishable from horse piss, filled with whores missing as many teeth as a thirty-year Legionary, was a welcome sight. Very quickly, the men who had a fondness for drink or a talent for trouble with civilians fell back into old habits, but unlike other times when there was a true civilian population occupying whatever town or city where we were garrisoned, these inhabitants were old soldiers or rough characters who were no strangers to trouble themselves. Very rarely were we accosted by an angry citizen who had been roughed up or whose daughter was insulted, since these men were willing and able to take care of their own troubles. However, that meant that there were times when one of my men was carried in by comrades after being beaten senseless for offending a citizen of the town. If that was as far as it went, it would not have been a concern, and I would have told the men who were bruised and battered that they more likely than not had earned their beating. However, there were some new inhabitants who were not content with inflicting a few bruises along with a broken bone or two, and it was less than a month after the consecration of Nicopolis that the body of one of my men was found with his throat cut ear to ear. And it did not stop there; within another month, five more men joined their unfortunate comrade, all dumped in a rubbish heap just outside the wall on the opposite side from our camp, which was a mile south of the new city. All of them had their throats cut, although half of them had also been beaten, one of them so badly that he was unrecognizable. Their identity tokens had all been taken from them, along with their purses and daggers, which are the only weapons men are allowed to take out of camp. The 10th was not the only Legion to lose men in this manner; after asking the other Primi Pili, I learned that perhaps a total of 20 men had been murdered, all the same way, to be left in the same place. An emergency meeting was called with the Primi Pili and the Centurions to whom the murdered men belonged, in order to try and determine what was happening.

"There has to be some common pattern," Aulus Flaminius, the Primus Pilus of the 8th Legion and the man who called the meeting, declared. "Something that they all have in common that will help us find out who's doing this."

"They liked getting drunk, gambling, and chasing whores," said a Centurion from the 8th whose name I did not know. "That makes them like every other man in the army."

"There has to be more than that," Trebellius, my Quintus Pilus Prior, spoke up.

His was the first man from the 10th to be found dead. Turning to Flaminius, he offered a suggestion that each Centurion give a description of the man they had lost, his habits, his service record, anything they could recall. Realizing that this was a good idea, and would also require more of an organized effort, Flaminius requested each Primus Pilus present to summon their clerk and sufficient writing materials with which to take notes. I sent for Diocles, and once all the clerks arrived and had gotten situated, we began our investigation.

While each Centurion talked about the murdered man, the only other sound was the scratching of stylus on wax, each clerk scribbling away, making a record of the proceedings for each of the affected Legions. Flaminius had called the meeting in the *Praetorium*, meaning that it was not long before we had a crowd, since the other Primi Pili and Centurions heard what was taking place and came to listen. Fairly quickly, it was decided to call for the closest comrade of each of the murdered men, which took a bit of time to arrange, but we felt that they could provide information that the Centurions did not have. When the first man arrived, he was clearly nervous and reluctant to talk. It took some persuasion on our part to convince him that he was not in trouble and nothing he said would be held against him.

"We want to bring justice to those who did this to your close comrade, and we want to keep it from happening again," Flaminius said to the first and all subsequent witnesses, whereupon he finally opened up.

As he talked, I began to despair that we would learn anything valuable, since the Legionary described what could have been any other ranker in the army. The man liked to drink, though not to the point where he had been punished excessively, and while his record showed that he had been striped, this was not uncommon at all for a man who was under the standard for a number of years. When we were satisfied that we had learned all we could, the Centurion for the next murdered man began his testimony, followed by the close comrade, while the clerks continued to write. It was in this manner in which the day dragged by, with a few breaks in between to allow us to stretch our legs and discuss what we had learned. It was frustrating work, since no clear pattern seemed to be emerging from what we were learning. The murdered men were not regular customers of the same gambling houses or whorehouses, the most likely places where a man could get into trouble. The only similarity was that they seemed to be roughly divided into two groups, in terms of the wineshops they visited, but they were located in different parts of the town, almost on opposite sides. It was growing dark by the time we interviewed the last man, still with no clear indication that would give us a direction to continue our investigation. Frustrated, we all agreed to end the meeting, and I walked back to our area with Diocles and Trebellius. Diocles was practically staggering under the weight of the tablets he had filled that day. When we returned to my quarters, I was tempted to tell him to erase them and forget the whole mess. I am glad that I did not, since he sat down at his desk immediately to begin reading through them.

"Why are you doing that? Are you a glutton for punishment?"

He shook his head, not taking his eyes from the first tablet. "I just want to look these over before I go to bed. I feel like we're missing something."

"We're missing who's behind this, but I doubt you'll find any answers in there," I retorted, but I did not stop him from his task.

I retired to my personal quarters to do some reading before I slept, and when I snuffed out my lamp a third of a watch later, I could see the flickering light of Diocles' own lamp still burning.

I was in the midst of a very pleasant dream involving Miriam, but was roused from my sleep when I heard Diocles calling my name. He had long since learned, unfortunately the hard way, that touching me in order to rouse me was not a good idea, choosing instead to stand in the doorway several feet away to waken me. My eyes snapped open, my mind trying to adjust to the different world in which I had just been, as I sat up.

"What is it?"

"I think I found something, master!" Diocles' voice was excited, but I did not share it.

"Can't it wait until morning?"

"I don't think so."

Grumbling, I roused myself to walk out into the outer office, gasping in surprise at the sight before me. Spread across the floor, in three neat rows, were the tablets, arranged side by side across the length of the office.

Looking a bit sheepish at my reaction, Diocles explained. "It helps me think if I can see information side by side, and we filled so many tablets that there was no room on my desk."

"Fine. Just tell me what's so important that you had to wake me up to tell me."

"There are two things," he began. "One that I'm sure of, and one that I suspect. But if what I suspect is correct, I think you'll see why I woke you up."

I had learned to trust Diocles when he had these kinds of notions, so I waved to him to continue and said, "Start with what you know."

"What I know is that there's one thing all these men had in common."

"You mean other than being dead?"

He flushed at my jibe, but continued. "All these men won money gambling within a week of their murder."

I shook my head impatiently, interrupting him. "We know that. But it was hardly like it was a fortune. If I remember, the most one of them won was 50 sesterces. And they won in different gambling houses."

"True," Diocles granted. "Individually, it wasn't much. However, altogether it added up to almost 500 sesterces."

That got my attention; I knew how many men would kill for 500 sesterces, and the list was very long indeed.

I began thinking about it, then shook my head again. "That would mean that whoever killed these men would have had to have a spy in each gambling house. That means they would have to pay for that kind of information. By the time they got through with bribes, there wouldn't be much left over."

Diocles nodded as if agreeing with me, but he was one step ahead. "Which leads to the next point—that which I suspect. You're of course correct; having a spy in each house would be expensive, so what else do they have in common? That's where I started looking."

I indicated that he should continue. He looked down at one of the tablets, frowning as he searched for something. I could see the redness in his eyes and the lines of fatigue furrowing his brow, but he was clearly determined and I counted myself lucky to have him.

"Let's see, where was it? I think it was in this one, the testimony from Attius, the close comrade of Minucius, who was the man from the 8th who was murdered. Ah, here it is." He reached down to pick up the tablet, pointing to a line he had written. "Attius mentioned that the owner of the wineshop they liked to attend was a former Centurion who claimed to have marched with Caesar."

I recalled that point, but did not see the relevance, so I just shrugged. "And?"

"He also mentioned something about having a cousin who had been a Centurion as well."

Without waiting for me to respond, he dropped the tablet, then trotted over to another one. "This one is from the testimony of Trebellius, talking about Furius. He said that Furius had mentioned the same thing, that he frequented a wineshop that was run by a Centurion who had marched for Caesar."

"So they both frequented the same wineshop," I was beginning to get irritated. "What does that mean?"

"Except that they didn't go to the same wineshop," Diocles said quietly. "Remember that the only thing in common was that the men all frequented one of two different wineshops, but they were on opposite sides of the town. One is called," he looked down at the tablet, "The Rudis. And the other," he picked the first tablet back up, "is called The Happy Legionary."

"Which tells the men that they cater to the army, and they're likely run by a former soldier," I said slowly.

Diocles nodded. "Exactly."

I had to admit that this was interesting, but I still did not see the connection. However, I was now convinced that Diocles had indeed found something, so rather than have him continue in this manner, I just told him to give me his idea.

He looked vaguely disappointed at not being able to build his case, yet he said readily enough, "I think that these two wineshops are where the information is being gathered about the men winning money, and I think that these two owners are indeed cousins and are working together."

I thought about it, and while it was intriguing, I was still doubtful. "That's awfully thin gruel. But it's definitely something to look into. I think I'll pay a visit to these places tomorrow."

I patted him on the back, thanking him for his work, then told him to try and get some sleep. With that, we both retired for the evening. I confess I was not hopeful that this would amount to anything, and I certainly was not prepared for what I was about to learn the next day.

Deciding to take Trebellius, Diocles, and Scribonius, whom I had filled in over breakfast, we left to visit The Rudis and The Happy Legionary the next afternoon. We chose the shop nearest to the camp first, located one street away from the southern wall. Despite the newness of the city, trash had already begun to pile up on the corners and in the alleys, the gutters running with effluvium since the sewer system was still under construction. Even at this relatively early time, there were men already staggering about, old veterans spending the last of their money in an attempt to drink themselves to death. A few whores were about as well, the early risers among them, looking for men who had an itch to scratch that could not wait until the sun set. Alternately ignoring their calls, or bantering back with them, we found The Happy Legionary easily enough, located side by side with an identical-looking shop, just with a different name. The sign above the door was a crude painting of a Legionary in full uniform buggering what looked like a Gallic woman, with protruding eyes and tongue hanging out.

"That's tasteful," Scribonius commented dryly.

"But it's guaranteed to draw a crowd of idiots who think that there's a gaggle of women just on the other side of the door, waiting to be fucked," Trebellius said, drawing a laugh from all of us, knowing he was exactly right.

Even veterans who should know better would be seduced by the prospect of what the sign portrayed, and I had to salute the owner for knowing his customer so well.

We paused outside the door, and Scribonius asked me, "How are you going to play this Titus? With honey or vinegar?"

"I'll play it as it comes, and act accordingly," I told him, but he rolled his eyes.

Turning to Trebellius, he said, "I bet there's some furniture broken, at the very least."

Trebellius laughed. "I'm not taking that bet."

Ignoring them, I stepped inside, not surprised to see that there were already a couple of tables with men and a woman seated there. We stopped to let our eyes adjust to the dimly lit interior while studying the terrain, so to speak. High on the far wall hung a sword and a *vitus*, the sign that the proprietor had indeed been a Centurion, or at least claimed to be. The counter where the drinks were served was immediately underneath the ornaments, behind which stood a thickset man of average height, with his back turned to us. Hearing the door open, he turned to greet his new customers, the fake smile that all proprietors of such establishments seemed to wear plastered on a face where it clearly did not belong. Seeing us standing there in uniform, the smile froze, his eyes narrowing in clear suspicion and wariness. Then, when I looked into the man's eyes and saw his face, I was struck by a nagging thought that I knew this man from somewhere, but could not immediately place him. He was a few years older than I was, with hair that was still black, but thinning and unkempt, the seams in his face matching his voice. I will say that he recovered quickly, calling out to us in a gravelly voice that belied many years of bellowing at the top of his lungs.

"*Salve* Centurions! Welcome to the Happy Legionary, the best place in this new city for men like yourselves to come and relax and have a drop!"

He swept a meaty forearm in the direction of an empty table. "Please, have a seat and the first round is on the house, from a fellow Centurion. Retired of course." He gave a chuckle at his own joke. "Since it wouldn't be legal for me to run a business while still on the rolls."

I gave him a smile as false as the one he had given us, but shook my head. "We appreciate the offer, but we're actually here on official business. I assume you're the owner of this fine shop?"

"The owner, chief server, cup washer, and security, all rolled up in one. That's me."

"I'm Primus Pilus . . ." I began to introduce myself, but he held up a hand.

"There's no need to introduce yourself, Primus Pilus Pullus. I know who you are. And it's my honor to have the Primus Pilus of Caesar's 10th, the Equestrians themselves, here in my humble shop."

It had been some time since we were referred to as Caesar's Equestrians, and I felt a flush of pleasure, wondering if he also knew that I was one of those men on horseback who faced Ariovistus. At the same time, a quiet voice in the back of my mind warned me not to be taken in, and for once, I listened to it. Still, I responded in a warm tone, thanking him for his kind words. For a moment, we all stood there in awkward silence before he laughed out loud, breaking the tension.

"You know me," I told him, still with a smile and what I hoped was a friendly tone. "But I'm afraid that I'm at a loss, though you do look familiar."

"Forgive me, Primus Pilus Pullus, where are my manners?" he said. "I'm Aulus Suetonius Censorius, formerly the Tertius Pilus Posterior of the 9th Legion, Spaniards like yourself and honored to have marched with Divus Julius and the 10th."

We clasped arms all around, then Censorius said, "You said you were here on official business, Primus Pilus. Might I inquire as to what it is exactly?"

I explained to him the purpose in our visit, at least partially. I left out Diocles' suspicions, instead just telling Censorius that we were gathering information. He listened and responded to our questions readily enough, although what information he provided was not particularly helpful. According to Censorius, the murdered men were just a few of dozens of Legionaries who were regular customers, and he could not recall any altercation or incident involving any of the men that might give us an indication that someone held a grudge against them. He did not seem evasive, at least to my eyes, and he did not hesitate in answering any of our questions. When we had exhausted every possibility, I thanked Censorius, accepting his offered hand, noticing that his grip on my forearm was clammy, leaving a residue of moisture behind as we left the shop. That nagged at me, although I had to admit to myself that I had known men with sweaty hands who had nothing to hide, so I shook the thought away.

Once outside, we paused for a moment to compare our impressions, and Scribonius spoke first. "I should have taken that bet," he said ruefully. "I must admit that Titus was on his best behavior." He turned to look at me. "Did he look familiar to you?"

I nodded. "Yes, but that's to be expected. I'm sure he's telling the truth about being in the 9th, and no doubt we ran into each other at some point."

Scribonius frowned, shaking his head. "It's more than that. He reminds me of someone, but I can't think of whom."

I shrugged it off, then we headed for The Rudis. We had to stop to ask directions, but it did not take long to find once pointed in the right direction. Located on almost exactly the opposite side of the city from The Happy Legionary, if I had been blindfolded then had it removed when standing in front of the second wineshop, I would have sworn that it was a trick, that I had just been led around the block and back to where we started. That is how similar the two shops were, both in appearance and location, along a street that had the same smell of raw wood and plaster, the newness still not worn off. The only real difference was in the painting above the door, this one of a little better quality, depicting four Legionaries sitting at a table toasting each other, all of them smiling happily. I noticed that there were dice on the table, and they of course were Venus, while on one of the Legionary's knees sat a buxom girl with bare breasts, one of which was cupped in the hand of the Legionary. As it went, I could see how this would appeal to the men, not just rankers but Centurions and Optios, many of whom, if not most, still being happy to pursue the life that the painting depicted.

We entered the shop, where I fully expected to see a repeat of The Happy Legionary, and for the most part, it met my expectations, almost down to the number and type of customer. What I was not prepared for was who was standing behind the counter. When the proprietor of the shop looked up to greet us, the same false smile on his face, our eyes met, and it felt as if Zeus had thrown a lightning bolt directly at me to strike my body. He had gained a great deal of weight since I had last seen him, and time had not been kind to him, his mouth now missing more teeth than it possessed. His nose was still a misshapen lump, in fact looking as if it had been broken at least once more since I had seen him last. Scribonius was the last to enter, and I heard him gasp in surprise when he looked over my shoulder. The air hung thick with a sudden tension that even the seated customers could sense, and they began shifting uncomfortably in their chairs, looking from me to the owner. It took a moment for me to find my voice, but when I did, I made no attempt to hide both my surprise and disgust, because suddenly things made more sense as I spoke the name of the man behind the counter.

"Gaius Domitius Celer."

"*Salve* Pullus." Celer looked as surprised and discomfited to see me as I him, while he did not seem to know what to do.

For that, I could not much blame him, given that I felt the same way, but when it came to forgiveness, I held very little in my heart for my former Secundus Pilus Posterior. Gaius Celer had fully expected, as did at least one of his minions, the Princeps Posterior Marcus Niger, to be promoted to the slot of Pilus Prior of the Second Cohort, except that Caesar selected me instead. I was young to lead a Cohort, but I did not, nor do I, bow my head to any man when it came to my record to that point. While the rest of the Centurions of the Second responded well, performing accordingly under my command, Celer did whatever he could to make me look bad, although he was always sly about it. In the same way that we tunnel under a wall to make it collapse under its own weight, so too did Celer work to try and undermine my authority to make me look bad, not just in front of the men and Centurions, but to Caesar and the other officers of the Legion. Thankfully, I was able to overcome every attempt on Celer's part to usurp my authority, but it was not without effort and constant vigilance. So when I stood facing my former enemy, it was with a certain amount of satisfaction.

"Still like your food, I see."

It was a malicious thing to say, and I must say that I felt equal parts satisfaction and shame when he flushed at the insult, despite giving me a forced laugh.

"That was always a weakness of mine," he admitted, patting his stomach.

"That and wine, as I remember."

Now he made no attempt to hide his anger, and I felt Scribonius give me a nudge from behind.

"Remember why we're here," he whispered. I gave a slight nod, holding my hands out towards Celer.

"*Pax*, Celer. I meant no harm, and I apologize for giving offense. I'm just surprised to see you."

"And I you," he said frankly. "I didn't realize you were still with the 10th."

I knew he was lying, but I let it pass. Walking to the counter, I offered my hand. For a moment, I thought Celer would not accept it, then he held his own out. When I felt the dampness on my forearm, I was reminded of Censorius, which in turn reminded me of what Diocles had said the night before about the owners of The Happy Legionary and The Rudis being cousins. It was as if a piece of a puzzle fell into place, and I was afraid that Celer could hear the clicking sound that of course was only in my own mind. I thought back to the mutiny of the 9th Legion, how Celer had approached me with information from a cousin who was a Centurion in that Legion, and I realized that it had to be Censorius, despite the fact that Celer never provided his name.

"Hello, Scribonius." Celer nodded to my friend, offering his hand much more willingly, I could not help noticing.

That made sense, since his relationship with Scribonius had never been strained the way it was with me, and although Scribonius had taken over the Second Cohort, it was after Celer had opted to retire at the end of our first enlistment, still embittered and convinced he had been wronged. I suspected that this belief as much as anything else had led to his obvious physical decline. The two clasped arms before Celer turned his attention back to me.

"So what is it that I can help you with, Pullus? I take it from your uniforms that you're not here to sample some of the best wine in this new city of ours."

Celer was many things, but he was not stupid, so I reminded myself to keep that in mind when dealing with him.

"No, we're not," I acknowledged. "Perhaps another time. We're here to ask you some questions about some of our men."

I indicated the others as I went on to explain the circumstances of our visit. Now that I was aware of the connection between Celer and Censorius, I watched Celer much more closely than I had during our interview with Censorius. By unspoken agreement, and without any prior planning, Scribonius was the one to ask the bulk of the questions, while I stood by, listening, only interjecting when I wanted Celer to elaborate on some point. While Celer answered the questions readily enough, I saw tiny beads of sweat forming on his upper lip, and while I could not swear to it, I thought I saw a slight tremor in the hand he laid on the counter. It could very well have been due to his drinking, but I suspected otherwise.

Scribonius was up to his usual form, asking hard questions in such a way that it did not cause Celer to either take offense or become overtly suspicious, making me fairly sure that by the time he was finished answering, he was convinced that this was a routine matter and that he was not under any suspicion. That was fine with me, and in fact was exactly the kind of frame of mind that I wanted him in. Trebellius asked a few more questions, then I signaled to the others that it was time to leave. Promising that we would return to enjoy his hospitality, something that I knew neither of us wanted, we turned to leave, with me behind the others. Diocles had opened the door and was just stepping out when I turned, slapping my forehead as if I had forgotten something. Celer had been glaring at my back, but recovered quickly enough, pretending to look interested in what I had to say.

"Forgive me, Celer, but I almost forgot," I lied.

"Yes, Pullus?"

"Is Censorius really your cousin?"

His face froze, and I could almost see his mind working as he tried to decide what to do.

"Yes," he said finally, trying very much to make it sound of little consequence, but I was not through.

"Is that the same cousin who was a Centurion in the 9th and was part of the mutiny against Caesar all those years ago?"

Blood shot up into the broken veins of Celer's face. I could see he was both furious and alarmed.

"He was in the 9th, yes, but he wasn't one of the mutineers!"

"Oh," I said in mock surprise. "I thought I remembered that he was and he was one of the men forced to draw lots."

This was a complete and total guess on my part, since Celer had never said any such thing, yet it was plain to see that I hit the mark, his jaw dropping, the blood that had flooded his face rushing out just as quickly.

"That's just a rumor, and it's not true," he protested.

"Ah. I must have been mistaken," I said pleasantly. "But why didn't you bring that up? Scribonius mentioned The Happy Legionary, and your cousin is the owner."

"I didn't think it was important. What does it matter who owns another wineshop? There's already about 30 in the city, and that's undoubtedly going to grow. You're looking for whoever is murdering your men, not keeping track of who owns which wineshop."

"That's true," I acknowledged, then waved it away. "You're right, of course. It's of no consequence."

I turned and left with the others, leaving Celer staring at our retreating backs.

"He's lying," I said flatly.

Scribonius eyed me for a moment, then asked, "About what, exactly?"

"Everything. He's in this up to his neck. I can feel it."

"I'll admit that it's suspicious," Scribonius replied. "But I'm not as convinced as you are."

I looked at him in astonishment, not understanding how my friend, who I considered the smartest man I knew, could miss something so obvious.

"How could you not see it? It's as plain as day!"

"Because I don't hate the man the way you do," he said evenly. "And I think your feelings about him are clouding your judgment."

"I have every reason to hate the man. He made my life miserable for years," I shot back.

"As you did right back to him," Scribonius continued while I stopped, staring at him in disbelief.

"What are you talking about?" I demanded. "I was completely fair with that man, and he repaid me by stabbing me in the back every chance he got."

Now Scribonius stopped, turning slowly to look me directly in the eye. Meanwhile, Diocles and Trebellius looked at the ground as if they wished it could swallow them up.

"Do you really believe that?" he asked quietly. "Titus, you're my oldest and best friend, and you're a great leader, and I'd follow you to Hades should you ask it of me. But you're not perfect. You have your blind spots and petty jealousies just like any man."

I swallowed hard, not liking what I was hearing, but willing to let Scribonius speak, simply because of all the people in my life, he had earned that right more than any other.

Seeing that I was willing to let him continue, he said gently, "It's true that Celer did things to make your life miserable, but look at it from his perspective. He was sure that he was going to be made Pilus Prior, then you showed up, ten years younger and barely through your first enlistment. If the situation was reversed, how would you have felt?"

"I wouldn't have liked it one bit," I admitted, if a little grudgingly. "But I would have done everything I could to prove that the wrong choice had been made, and not by trying to make my superior look bad."

"Yes, that is how you would do it," Scribonius agreed. "But you're different. You've always been different. Just ask Cleopatra. Ask Lepidus. Ask Octavian, and they'd all say the same thing, that Titus Pullus is made of a different metal than most men. Which is why you are where you are. But more people are like Celer than they are like you, and Celer did what most people would have done."

"You would do the same," I pointed out, but I was surprised when Scribonius only shrugged.

"Perhaps, although I'm not as sure as you are about what I'd do."

"So why don't you think he is not involved in this?"

"I didn't say I don't think he's involved, but I'm not as sure about it as you are, and I think we should proceed with caution."

"Maybe now that he knows we're nosing about, he and his cousin will stop, if they are involved," interjected Trebellius. Both Scribonius and I shook our heads.

"If he is, he's not going to stop," Scribonius replied. "Because he's greedy, and he's unable to control himself."

"And he thinks that he's smarter than me," I added.

Scribonius considered, then agreed. "I think you're right about that, but not just you. Celer is the type of man who thinks he's smarter than everyone."

We returned to camp to report what we had learned, and discuss what the next step should be.

After talking it over with Flaminius and the other Centurions involved, it was decided that at the moment there was not enough evidence to take any action against either Celer or Censorius, and that we would be forced to wait and see if Celer was as arrogant as I thought he was. We also discussed shutting the camp down, making Nicopolis off-limits, but we knew from bitter experience that in all likelihood we would end up with more dead bodies than we already had at that point, since men would inevitably take their frustrations out on each other. A week passed, then another, the men continuing to carouse, gamble and debauch, only to return alive and essentially unharmed. I was beginning to think that perhaps Celer and Censorius had become more cautious with age when another body turned up, albeit only after being reported missing a few days earlier. Instead of the trash heap, the man's body was found stuffed in one of the privies that were still being used while the baths were being constructed. After questioning his close comrade, we were faced with another mystery; according to his friend, he had never frequented either The Rudis or The Happy Legionary. However, the name of one of the whorehouses that had been mentioned before came up, this incident now enough to put Venus' Gates under our scrutiny. My suspicion was that Celer and Censorius were connected to Venus' Gates, despite never having been seen there and were not commonly known to own the house, either totally or in part. Knowing that either I or one of the other Centurions poking around Venus' Gate would do more harm than good to our cause of finding and stopping the murders of our men, I called Gaius to my quarters.

"I have a mission for you," I began, and he looked instantly alert, sitting on the edge of his stool.

I had to suppress a grin, knowing that what I was about to ask him to do would be the farthest thing from his mind.

"Are you familiar with Venus' Gates?"

He nodded, but added quickly, "I've never been. To that one, anyway."

I laughed. "Then you're in luck. I want you to go visit tonight."

He said nothing, just stared at me in clear puzzlement. I went on to explain why, telling him everything that I thought he needed to know. I even told him about my history with Celer, and when I was finished, his face was hard.

"Why don't we just go and snatch the bastard like we did Deukalos?"

"Because he's a former Centurion, a citizen, and I could be wrong, though I'm sure I'm not."

"It sounds like he should pay for all that he did to you when he was with the 10th. Just give me the word, Uncle, and I'll make sure that he's taken care of."

Now it was my turn to stare at Gaius, and I could see by his face that he was completely serious. I was both touched and concerned at the same time. When I asked him why he felt that way, his reply threatened to bring tears to my eyes, which would have horrified the both of us.

"Any enemy of yours is an enemy of mine, and any man who would try to usurp your authority isn't worthy of being called a Centurion of Rome. Especially when it was Divus Julius who awarded you that authority. I think he should die just for that affront to his memory."

He was so sincere and passionate, and I remembered what it felt like to have the fire of such certainty burning in your body. I did not know what to say, other than to thank him, assuring him that killing Celer was not something with which he needed to concern himself.

"I want you to go to Venus' Gates, and just keep your eyes and ears open. Don't be obvious about it, just try and learn if either Celer or Censorius has anything to do with the place, and if so, what their role is. I suspect that one or both of them own the place, because it's the only other place that's been mentioned almost as much as their two taverns."

With these instructions, I handed him some coins, while he needed no urging to be sent on his way.

Like I suspected, Gaius did not learn anything that night, nor the next. He rapidly became a regular at Venus' Gates, much to the distress of my purse. However, I did not begrudge the boy having some fun while he was working, and he did report in every day with a smile on his face. It was beginning to get expensive, yet I was determined to see an end to the murders, and was convinced that we were on the right track. The other Centurions were not as convinced, but they had no better ideas, meaning they were content to let me pursue things in my own way. It began to look as if neither Censorius nor Celer were involved with Venus' Gates, and I was about to tell Gaius that the most enjoyable job he would likely ever have during his time in the Legions was done, when two things happened. Another body turned up, this time it being one of my men, and when Gaius came to give his usual morning report, his excitement was clear to see before he spoke a word.

"Celer came into Venus' Gates last night, roaring drunk and clearly happy about something."

That got my attention, but my nephew was not through. "And he's clearly at the very least a regular at the house, and I didn't see him give Parthenia, that's the woman who runs things, any coin."

"Which would make sense, if he's an owner," I said slowly, trying to hide my excitement. "Did you have a conversation with him?"

Gaius nodded. "I told him that I was in the Eighth of the 10th. He told me that he had been a Centurion in the 10th under Caesar."

I could not help asking, "Did he mention me?"

"I did," Gaius said. "I thought it might strike him as strange that I didn't ask if he'd served with you, so I asked him if he knew you."

"And?"

"He said that he served in the same Cohort, but that's as far as he went, and he clearly didn't want to talk about it."

"That makes sense," I agreed, "for a number of reasons. If he had told you about our history, or had said something about me that caused you to relay it back to me, that would cause him more problems than he wants."

"So that's enough, isn't it? We know that he's probably the owner of the whorehouse, and between that and the wineshops, he should be hauled before the *Praetor* and prosecuted."

"It's enough for me. I'll tell Flaminius and the others about it, and I think this should be enough for them as well."

I was wrong. Much to my anger and annoyance, the other Centurions were not swayed by this new piece of information, refusing to do anything. Returning to my quarters, I sat down to think about what more could be done, and the thought that came to me, I did not like. Nonetheless, try as I might, I could not come up with a better alternative, so I reluctantly called for Gaius again.

"Do you want me to go back to Venus' Gates?"

I had to laugh at his eagerness, but what I was going to discuss with him was extremely serious. I had asked Scribonius, Balbus, and Diocles to attend as well, both to hear what they had to say and to serve as witness to what I was going to ask Gaius to do. I had little doubt that he would be willing, so I suppose I was protecting myself by making sure that others saw that willingness should things go wrong.

"Well, you may not be so eager to go after you hear what I'm asking you to do."

That got his attention, and he took a seat across from my desk. The others were arranged around it as well, and I had Diocles offer wine before we started. I was trying to gather my thoughts, knowing in my heart that I was really buying time because of the danger I was about to put Gaius in.

Finally, I began, "The other Centurions involved aren't convinced by what we found at Venus' Gates, so we're faced with a couple of alternatives to try and stop these killings. The first would be to have you become a regular at Venus' Gate and The Rudis, and over time hope that you'd see or hear something that would be strong enough to convince everyone involved in this mess that Celer and Censorius are involved."

I paused, hoping that Scribonius or Balbus would point out the flaws in this idea, but neither of them spoke.

Swallowing my irritation, I continued. "The problem with that is that it would take too long, and in the meantime more men are likely to die, and there's no guarantee that you would learn anything." I took a sip of wine before plunging on to the meat of the matter. "So I have an idea, but it's dangerous, and I won't hold it against you in any way should you choose not to go through with what I'm proposing. In fact," I added, "a part of me is hoping that you say no."

"What's the idea?"

"Did I ever tell you about the time I spent with the 6th? When we cruised the Nile with Caesar and that bitch Cleopatra?"

Gaius looked confused, but nodded. "I remember."

"Did I tell you about how the Egyptians hunt crocodiles?"

"I don't think so."

"Crocodiles are mean bastards, but they're also sneaky. They lie submerged just below the surface of the water, where the animals that come to drink can't see them, then as soon as the poor beast lowers his head to drink, they spring out of the water, quick as Pan. I saw them swallow good-sized goats in one gulp. So to hunt them, that's exactly what the hunters do, they put a goat on the riverbank, tie him down, and wait for the crocodile." I made sure he was looking at me as I finished. "That's what I want you to be: the goat tied down for the crocodile. You're going to go into the city, and let anyone who will listen know that you just won a year's pay at dice, and want to celebrate. You're going to go to The Rudis, buy everyone there a round of drink, have a couple of drinks, then stagger off to Venus' Gates." I held up a wax tablet that I had worked on earlier, containing a sketch of the layout of the city streets. "I want you to follow this route that I've drawn out here. You're going to be followed by me, Balbus, Scribonius, Trebellius, Vellusius, and your friend Lupus."

Gaius took the tablet to study it. I saw Scribonius with his frown, and while I was sure I knew what he was going to say, I waited for him to speak.

"Do you really think that's wise, Titus? You, and I for that matter, will stick out like a whore among the Vestals. Celer is sure to spot us."

"That's why I selected this route," I replied, feeling a bit smug. "If you look, you'll see that most of the way, Gaius will be taking alleys and not the main streets, which are narrower. I scouted it today, and we'll be following on the rooftops, jumping from one building to the next."

I took the tablet from Gaius to point out two different spots on it to Scribonius.

"These two places he'll have to cross one of the main streets, and those would be too far to jump. But I took two planks and put them on the roof at those points. When we get there, all we have to do is lift the plank and drop it across, then we can cross over and keep an eye on Gaius."

Scribonius let out a low whistle, which made me feel proud of myself. "I have to say that I'm impressed. But it will still be dangerous for you, Gaius."

Gaius nodded his understanding. "I know, but unless we do something, more men are going to end up with their throats cut. I don't see where there's much choice, and I'm the logical one to do it. He knows me by sight now, and I'm sure he'll believe that I won. I was bragging about how good a gambler I am when we met."

That was a surprise to me, and I looked at Gaius carefully, thinking that he was much shrewder than I had given him credit for. It was almost like he knew that I would come up with this plan, but I did not voice my suspicions. Scribonius spoke up again, turning my attention away from Gaius. "Are you sure that Gaius should say he won so much money? If anything, that might scare Celer and Censorius off. They've been very careful only to go after men who have won a decent amount, but nothing as large as what you want Gaius to claim."

"That's true," Balbus interjected. "There was a man in the 7th who won a thousand sesterces, but he was untouched."

"I know, and it is a risk," I acknowledged. "But I'm gambling on two things, if you'll pardon the pun. The first is that while it's larger than they've normally taken, I think it's just large enough to tempt them but not too large to scare them off. And that's because of Gaius. I think they'll look at him, see how young he is, and think he's green and easy pickings." I gave Gaius a smile. "But they'll find out the hard way that looks are deceiving, right, nephew? You're a veteran of two campaigns in Parthia."

"That I am, Uncle. Just make sure that you don't lose sight of me, regardless."

The trick was to get in place overlooking The Rudis without being seen. In order to do that, we left after dark, splitting up a short distance away from the wineshop. I had described the building that appeared to be a warehouse of some sort, with a stack of boxes lined against a wall that would allow us to climb to the roof. From that spot, we could lie on our stomachs to peer down on the front of the wineshop. Gaius was going to come to the shop, acting as if he already had ingested a good bit of wine, then make his boast about his winnings. He would spend perhaps a third of a watch in The Rudis; not long after he arrived, he would also let it be known that he planned on spending some of his winnings at his new favorite place, Venus' Gates. Hopefully, this would give Celer time to either slip out or send men to a dark spot and wait for Gaius to emerge from the shop. We each made it to the spot without any incident, settling in to wait.

Not long after, Gaius came down the street, weaving so convincingly that it prompted Scribonius to ask, "Are you sure he didn't drink more than he was supposed to?"

"I told him to rinse his mouth out with wine, but to take no more than a swallow," I whispered back. "I'm sure he did exactly that."

Still, Scribonius had planted a seed of worry in my mind, but there was nothing to be done about it at that point, so we just watched as he entered the shop. Even through the closed door, we could hear him shout something, which was met by cheers by the other customers. As we lay on our stomachs, I could clearly feel Balbus next to me, chewing on something in his mind.

"What's bothering you?"

"I haven't said a word," he said, sounding defensive even with a whisper.

"I know, but you're not saying it very loudly," I replied.

I was rewarded with a quiet snort that I knew was Balbus' version of a laugh. "If it's not Celer that tries to take Gaius, how are we going to know that he's behind it?"

I considered for a moment, then said, "Because if it's not Celer, I'll rely on you to make whoever it is to talk. I know you're still disappointed you didn't get to do what you wanted with Deukalos, so I promise that this time I won't stop you, even if he tells everything."

I could tell this made him happy, his teeth shining in the darkness as he smiled.

"But I hate to tell you, I'm sure that it will be Celer."

"Why?"

"Because Gaius knows him, and Celer will be sure that he wouldn't suspect him of any treachery. In fact, I expect Celer to offer to walk with Gaius over to Venus' Gates, then wait for a dark spot before he makes his move. If Gaius were to run into a stranger, it would be natural to assume that he'll be on his guard. Celer will think walking with Gaius will put him at ease."

"Then why did you get my hopes up?" Balbus grumbled, and I stifled a laugh.

I shot a glance over at Scribonius, who was lying on the other side of me and gave me a wry shake of his head.

"Balbus, I truly hope that you get to turn someone's ball sac into a coin purse before you die, or you will be a very unhappy man," was all Scribonius said before we quieted back down to wait.

Just to be safe, I sent Vellusius, Herennius, and Gaius' tentmate, Lupus, to watch the back door of the wineshop, in the event that Celer or whoever he had selected for this job slipped out the back. Despite thinking it unlikely, I had to account for the possibility that Celer would opt to find his own spot for ambushing Gaius, although I did not see how Celer could be sure that he had selected the right spot. While there was an obvious path to Venus' Gates, drunken men are anything but logical, so Celer would run a risk that he picked the wrong place if he opted to lie in wait. We could hear raucous laughter coming from within the shop, and men and a few women made their way to see what was causing such merriment. Almost all of the arriving customers were off-duty Legionaries, the sight of them striking me with a sudden worry. What if another man came in with the same or similar story as Gaius, and Celer selected him instead, for whatever reason? I knew that this was the only chance we had at this; it would undoubtedly arouse Celer's suspicions if Gaius were to show up again making the same claim. I supposed that we could have him start over again with Censorius, except the risk would be much higher. I offered up a prayer to the gods that no such thing happened, but it preyed on my mind the rest of the time we waited. Men left the shop, each of them in varying stages of inebriation; some with their choice of woman for the evening on their arm. Then, shortly before the time we were expecting Gaius to make his announcement that he was heading for Venus' Gates, two men approached the shop. Squinting because of the darkness, I saw that one of them looked familiar, more by the shape of his body than his face, which could barely be seen in the gloom.

"Is that Censorius?" Scribonius asked, and my heart skipped a beat as I recognized that it was indeed Celer's cousin, accompanied by a man who looked vaguely familiar, but who was clearly a former Legionary.

"Yes it is," I whispered grimly, realizing that somehow Celer had gotten a message to his cousin that they had a fat hen for the plucking, although it would not have been hard.

Obviously, one of the men we saw leaving had gone to fetch Censorius and, as they entered The Rudis, I remembered that I had seen the man with Censorius leaving the shop shortly before, except that he had done so with a couple other men. This was going to make things more difficult, but it could not be helped.

"Get ready to move," I whispered to the others, then gave a soft whistle to alert the men who were watching the back door.

As I felt the tension mounting, for the first time I thought of Gaius' mother, my sister Valeria, wondering what she would do to me if she knew the danger I was putting her son in. I shook my head, trying to clear the thought from my mind, knowing that it would do no good to dwell on such things. Moments passed, during which my heart, and I suspected the others' as well, would start hammering whenever the door opened, but it was never Gaius. Neither was it Celer, nor Censorius for that matter, making the tension mount with every breath. The time we had arranged for Gaius to leave had long since passed, and I was beginning to think that something had actually happened inside the shop.

"What do we do?" I asked Scribonius. "Should we go down and see what's happening?"

He did not answer for a moment, then shook his head. "We need to trust him. If we go down now and show up, it will ruin everything that we've planned."

"It's not that I don't trust him." I must admit I was a bit irritated. "I just am worried that maybe Celer and Censorius did something to him inside."

My friend gave me a long look, then sighed. "If that's the case, then it will prove that Celer and Censorius are behind these killings."

"That's not going to help Gaius any," I whispered angrily.

He opened his mouth to reply, but then Balbus gave me an elbow in the ribs, and I turned to see that the door had opened, with Gaius stepping outside, the light from inside the shop clearly illuminating him weaving, seemingly about to fall. A hand reached out to steady him, but we could not see who it belonged to at first, since Gaius' body blocked our vision. Gaius took a step out of the doorway, then we could see that the hand helping to keep Gaius upright belonged to Celer. Following close behind was Censorius, with the third man who had accompanied Censorius back to the shop there as well. Staggering arm in arm, with Celer on one side, then Censorius moving to support Gaius from the other, the four of them began making their way to Venus' Gates. Or at least, that was what Celer and Censorius wanted Gaius to believe.

The four men turned down the first street, like I had instructed Gaius, and once they turned the corner we rose, crossing over the roof to jump across to the next building several feet from the edge, facing the street in order to remain undetected. We could hear Gaius talking, his voice slurred and high-pitched as he talked about one of the women at Venus' Gates. At first, I wondered why he was talking so loud, then I understood that he was trying to cover the sound of our movement across the roofs. Paralleling their line of travel, we came to the next point where Gaius was to turn, and I heard Celer's voice.

"Let's go this way; it's shorter."

"But I always go this way," Gaius said, the slur in his voice so pronounced that I was beginning to wonder if he might be truly drunk and not pretending.

"This way is better," Celer insisted.

I gave Scribonius an alarmed look, because the way he was indicating would take them on the far side of a wide street, not where I had a plank waiting and would be much too far to jump. It was at this point my nephew showed how quickly he could think on his feet.

"Why do you want me to go that way?" There was no mistaking the belligerence in Gaius' tone, with the added inflection of the drunk who was not getting his way and was about to become combative. "I said I always go this way. If you're my friend, you'll let me go this way. If not, you can go fuck yourself."

"Easy there, young Porcinus." Celer's voice was smooth, but he had been in my Cohort for a long enough time that I could detect the anger lying just below the surface. "We meant no harm. If you want to go this way, go this way. We'll go with you to make sure that nothing happens to you."

"You're a good man, Celer. I'm sorry for my harsh words."

"That's quite all right, Porcinus. No offense taken."

With that crisis resolved, the men continued on, while I breathed a bit easier. We reached the spot where a plank was waiting. After letting them pass by, I lifted it into place and we crossed over one at a time. It creaked under my weight; for a moment, I was scared that it would collapse, but we all made it across. We were now approaching a corner, where Gaius was to turn down the narrowest, darkest, most deserted alley on the route, and my guess was that this would be the place that Celer would try something. I whispered to Scribonius and Balbus to be alert while we crept diagonally across the roof, positioning us partway down the alley, and waiting for Gaius and the others to make the turn. Crouching down, I slowly peered over the edge of the roof so that I could see them approach. We had not worn our helmets, meaning I did not have to worry about the silhouette of my crest, and their eyes were not turned upwards anyway.

Censorius and the other man had dropped behind Gaius, while Celer was walking alongside my nephew, telling him some story about our time in Dyrrhachium during the civil war. I had just enough time to hear what he was saying, realizing that what he was recounting was actually something that had happened to me, when we took the fort from Quintus Albinus, the same Quintus Albinus who was now a Hastatus Prior in the Tenth Cohort of my Legion. To hear him tell it, he was the one to lead the attack and accept the surrender of Albinus, forcing me to bite back a curse. While he talked, Celer draped his left arm about Gaius' shoulders, a seemingly innocent gesture, yet it was an obvious signal to Censorius and the other man, who suddenly leaped forward, each of them grabbing Gaius by the arm.

"Now!"

I roared the command, then using the men as a softer spot to land than on the ground, we fell on top of them. I aimed for Celer, knowing that I might land on Gaius as well, but it could not be helped. However, my nephew had reacted just as quickly, wrenching free while turning swiftly, pulling his dagger. We had brought our swords, but this was not the time to use them, counting on surprise and the crashing weight of our bodies. I struck Celer just as he was beginning to react to the sense of imminent danger, my boots striking him squarely in the back, my weight driving him to the ground. Celer was lucky in that the alley was unpaved, making the ground soft, except that from the stench it was clear that the moisture came from people urinating there. I heard the breath whoosh from his body when he slammed into the dirt, then he lay there motionless, stunned from the shock of my more than 200 pounds falling on him. Turning about, I saw Balbus and Scribonius in much the same position, pinning their men down, and while Censorius was squirming, trying to free himself from the weight of Scribonius' body, the third man was completely motionless. I saw the glint of a wet blade in Balbus' hand when he wiped it on the man's tunic. I frowned; it had not been part of the plan to kill them unless absolutely necessary, but as I thought about it, I shrugged it off, since Balbus' man was not important. It was Censorius and Celer that mattered. Celer moaned, beginning to twist under my knees, trying to get his face out of the muck, so I eased some of my weight off his back, but I kept one hand firmly on his neck. With the pressure reduced, Celer was able to turn his head. His face was covered with stinking mud, his eyes two white orbs while he struggled to focus on the face of the man sitting on top of him.

"Pullus," he gasped. "By all the gods, what do you think you're doing? Get off me!"

"That was my nephew you were about to murder," I said quietly.

I did not think it possible, but his eyes widened even further, and even in the dark, I could see the shock written on his face. Or perhaps I was imagining it because I wanted it to be true.

"I don't know what you're talking about," he spluttered. "I was just helping the young lad because he drank too much."

"Then why did you have your dagger out?"

I pointed to the weapon that had been knocked out of his hand when I landed on him and was lying just inches away from his outstretched hand.

Before he could say anything, I added, "And we were watching from above and we saw your cousin and your other man grab him from behind. Were they trying to help him too?"

"Yes! I swear it, Pullus! I meant him no harm!"

"You can tell that to the *Praetor*. Maybe he'll believe you, but I doubt it. Not after his torture detachment gets the truth out of you."

"What are you talking about?"

"You know damn well what I'm talking about. You and your cocksucking cousin here have murdered more than 20 men over the last three months."

"That's not true," he protested. "I had nothing to do with those deaths!"

"Like I said, you can tell it to the *Praetor*." I grabbed a handful of cloth, hauling him to his feet, which was a chore because of his weight, but I was determined I would not show that it was a strain. Balbus was now helping Scribonius and they pulled Censorius to his feet as he spat gobs of filthy muck out of his mouth, cursing as he did so. Gaius was still holding his dagger, and I looked over to him.

"Well done, nephew."

His teeth showed in the darkness as he smiled. "Uncle, didn't you say that the *Praetor* told you that he was so desperate to stop these killings that he would give clemency to any of the conspirators who testified against the others?"

The *Praetor* had said no such thing; in fact, I doubted that the *Praetor* had been fully informed about what was happening. However, I instantly understood what Gaius was doing, and I answered quickly, not wanting to hesitate and make either man suspicious.

"That's true, Gaius. He did indeed tell Flaminius that very thing. We were about to post a reward for information in the morning as well."

"It was his idea," Censorius shouted instantly, and I felt Celer's body stiffen.

"Shut up, you fool," he hissed, his face twisted into a mask of hatred and rage. "The *Praetor* said no such thing. That's just a trick that this little bastard played, and you fell for it! You're an idiot!"

My fist slammed hard into his stomach, knocking him to his knees. "You just called my sister a whore, Celer," I told him coolly. "And I don't like it when my sister is called a whore."

"Fuck you," he snarled, all hint of the confusion of the innocent man gone now that his cousin had betrayed him. "You always did think your *cac* didn't stink! You should never have been made Pilus Prior! It's only because you sucked Caesar's cock . . ."

I don't know what else he was going to say because by the time I finished, he was in no shape to speak.

Vellusius, Herennius, and Lupus joined us, and we tied Celer and Censorius up while I ordered Vellusius to dispose of the body of the third man. Neither Celer nor Censorius spoke a word after the outburst, although I imagine that they both realized that there was nothing left to say. We bound their hands behind them, during which Censorius did put up a brief struggle, but it ended quickly with the help of Balbus' fists. We marched back to camp, and when we arrived at the front gates, naturally the duty Centurion was not eager to let us in with two bound men. I had him send for Flaminius, who was evidently asleep and not in a very good mood when he showed up, wearing just his tunic and carrying his *vitus*.

"Pullus, what by Pluto's cock are you doing? And who are these men?"

"We just caught these men trying to murder Sergeant Porcinus, in the same manner as the murdered men."

Flaminius' surliness evaporated as he gaped at the two men, still covered in mud, their heads hanging, both men refusing to meet his gaze, but I was not finished.

"And we have a confession from that one," I pointed to Censorius, "that it was this one," I pointed at Celer, "who was behind the whole thing."

"I want to speak to the *Praetor*," Censorius spoke suddenly. "He's promising clemency to anyone who cooperates, and I want to cooperate."

He nodded his head in the direction of Celer, who had turned to glare at his cousin. "It was all his idea, I swear it by all the gods!"

Now Flaminius was looking extremely confused, glancing from Censorius to me in hopes of hearing some explanation. "What's he talking about? We've kept this from the *Praetor* until we had it cleared up, which appears to have happened."

Censorius' jaw dropped, the realization of the truth hitting him hard. He turned to stare at first Gaius, then me.

"You lied to me," he bleated, and I could not help laughing at his pathetic state.

"You always were stupid, Censorius. Now you've killed us both," Celer said bitterly.

I explained to Flaminius all that we had planned, along with Gaius' ruse, and the other Primus Pilus looked at my nephew with marked respect.

"That was very clever of you, Sergeant. And very brave to put yourself in danger that way."

Gaius shrugged, but I could see that he was pleased. "I wasn't worried, Primus Pilus. I knew that I was as safe as a babe in his mother's arms."

"Still, that was very commendable."

Flaminius turned back to the two prisoners. "You'll be taken to the *quaestorium* and the holding cells there until you can be turned over to the *Praetor*."

He called to the duty Centurion to make arrangements to provide an armed escort. Before Celer was taken away, he turned to me, his eyes blazing with hatred.

"I piss on you and all of your ancestors, Titus Pullus. I curse the day you ever showed up in my life."

He turned to Gaius, his lips peeled back in a snarl, and in that moment we all saw the true *animus* of Gaius Domitius Celer. "I should have cut your throat when I had the chance, you miserable little bastard."

"You've never seen the day when you could best him," I snapped before Gaius could answer. "You were a piss-poor Centurion, and you're a piss-poor excuse for a man, Celer. You always thought you were smarter and better than everyone else, and look where that belief got you. I'll be sure to be there when your head leaves your shoulders, so the last thing you see is my face. I'll piss on your corpse."

Before he could say anything more, Celer was dragged off, along with Censorius. We watched them disappear in the darkness, and I must say I felt a tremendous amount of satisfaction. I wish I could say that my happiness was due to the knowledge that the murders were at an end, with the men responsible for so many deaths caught, but the truth is that I was happy to be proven right more than anything else.

"Pullus, you were right. Now we can put this matter to rest." Flaminius came to stand beside me, offering his hand, which I accepted.

"At least the men won't have to worry about having their throats cut when they go into town."

"Not by those two anyway." Flaminius laughed. "But there will always be someone out there waiting to shear the sheep."

The announcement of the capture of Celer and Censorius, and their subsequent confessions at the hands of the *Praetorian* torture detachment gave the men of the army a great deal of relief, and allowed things to settle down. The events in Nicopolis and camp had occupied everyone's minds to the point that we were not paying much attention to what was going on elsewhere.

Octavian had moved to the island of Samos and was making preparations for the invasion of Egypt, which would in all likelihood be the last operation for more than half of the 10th Legion, the men of the second *dilectus,* their discharge now a little more than a year away. The men added as replacements after the first invasion of Parthia still had more than ten years to go, while men like Albinus were salted through their ranks, making them almost as veteran as the originals. There was another momentous event, at least as far as I and a few others were concerned, and that was the promotion of Gaius Porcinus to Optio. After his performance in the apprehension of Celer and Censorius, which Flaminius was sure to let other Primi Pili know about, there was very little resistance to the idea from any quarter. There was a vacancy in the Century of the Quartus Princeps

Posterior, Marcus Didius, whose Optio had died of a fever. I thought briefly of shifting things around so that Gaius would stay with Scribonius, but then decided against it, knowing that it would be seen as an insult to not only Didius, but his Pilus Prior Nigidius as well. I believe I was as proud as I had ever been for any of my own promotions, and I pulled rank to be the man who awarded him his badges of office, reading the warrant with a voice that threatened to choke with emotion. Gaius stood tall and proud, still youthful, but with all of the baby fat chiseled from his face by wind and rain, looking every inch the part of an officer of the Legion. I was most moved by the reactions of his tentmates and the other members of his Century, some of whom openly wept at the idea of his leaving them behind. I knew he was one of the most popular men, not just in the Second Cohort, but in the entire Legion, yet seeing it demonstrated so vividly was quite moving.

Seeing his promotion as an omen, coupled with the more settled nature of Nicopolis now that Celer and Censorius had been exposed, I decided to send for Miriam and the rest of my household. I was also seriously contemplating what was to happen to me when this enlistment of the 10th was over. I was about to turn 47 years old, and there was now more gray in my hair than the original black, although it did not show much because I kept it so short. Despite the fact that I still exercised vigorously, I could not deny that my waist had grown thicker than I would like. I had lost a tooth, and it felt like there would be another one joining it soon, and I tired more easily, taking longer to recover than even three or four years before. I woke up with aches and pains; most troubling was the old wound I had suffered at Munda, but there were other spots on my body almost as sore. However, more than anything was the mental fatigue I felt, understanding that my war with Cleopatra, the mutiny against Antonius, and just the wearing of time was having a cumulative effect on my desire to stay in the army. My mental outlook was not helped with the news coming from Italia, since it appeared that once again, former Legionaries were threatening to plunge the country back into chaos and murder.

Despite Octavian's best efforts, most of the men that were recently discharged made their way back to Italia, instead of staying in Greece the way Octavian wanted. While it was understandable, given that most of the men in Octavian's army that had been discharged were Italian natives, making the peninsula their home, it did not take long for the malcontents among them to start stirring up trouble. They used the fact that they were not paid their discharge bonuses, ignoring the fact that the Treasury of Rome was bankrupt, as an excuse simply to take what they wanted from other citizens, usually wealthy ones. It was true that Octavian disarmed men before letting them go, then had taken the extra step of requiring each man to swear an oath that they would not do the very thing that was happening, but it was a simple matter for a retired Legionary to buy a sword the moment he landed in Italia. As far as the oath went, it was Vellusius who probably summed up the prevailing attitude, and his explanation was a cause for concern on a number of levels.

"What good is an oath if the other man giving it doesn't make good on his promises?" was how he put it. "I know the boys would never be doing these kinds of things if they had been paid like they were promised."

I knew better than to point out to Vellusius that the money simply was not there. This was an argument that meant absolutely nothing to men like Vellusius, which by extension meant the majority of the army. All they knew was that they were promised, from the first day of their enlistment, that they would receive a fat sum of money at the end of their 16 years, and that when it did not come, any promises they may have made they then viewed being as empty as those made to them. Complicating matters, at least from their viewpoint, was the fact that men like Octavian and Agrippa continued to live in fabulous wealth, not stinting on anything, spending profligately on whatever struck their fancy. This was a view that I could actually sympathize with to a point; despite my head knowing that as much money as patricians and highly born plebeians spent, it was just a small drop in a vast bucket of money, I had a reaction in my gut whenever I saw the excesses of my betters. At the very least, I think that men like Octavian and Agrippa should have been more aware of appearances, particularly at that moment when the situation was so tense between them and their former Legionaries.

Matters on the mainland became so bad that Agrippa was forced to send a message to Octavian, essentially telling him that Octavian's most capable man was unable to control the actions of the retired Legionaries. For his part, Octavian knew that the situation must be extremely dire for a man like Agrippa to send such a message. Despite it being the worst time of year to make such a crossing, Octavian boarded a ship for Brundisium. When he landed, an extraordinary thing happened. The entire Senate, minus those holding a *Praetorship*, or those military Tribunes who were also members of the Senate, but were still with the army, along with several hundred *equites* and thousands of ordinary citizens, were waiting for Octavian when he landed, hailing him as he walked into the city from the docks. While this is not unusual in itself, what made this so memorable in our history was that this demonstration was not held just outside the gates of Rome, which is customary and has been done for literally dozens of men over the years, but 300 miles away in Brundisium. There had never been a show of such support for the man who was now unquestionably the First Man in Rome, although Scribonius and other cynics claimed that it was merely their recognition that they were in fact ruled by Octavian and lived at his pleasure. Clearly alarmed by this outpouring of acclaim, the veterans that were running rampant, out pillaging farms and villas of wealthy Romans in the countryside, banded together to march to Brundisium themselves, seeking an audience with Octavian. He was, and is, no fool, knowing that as much as they needed to see him, he needed to see them as well. There was a series of meetings, and at the end of them, both sides extracted promises that were acceptable. For the veterans, Octavian was forced to name a specific amount that each man would be paid, based on rank and length of service. He also allocated land in Italia, most of it confiscated from supporters of Antonius, who were in turn relocated to Greece without compensation.

The colony of Forum Julii was founded by the veterans of the 8th Legion, with smaller settlements salted along the coast of Italia. The veterans were forced to accept a promise from Octavian that the bounty, in the amount promised, would be paid against the treasury, not of Rome but of Alexandria. For that was the only place left where sufficient wealth was stored, and Octavian knew that not only would it be enough to pay all the veterans, but to replenish Rome's own Treasury. Recognizing that he could not afford to wait, Octavian, after settling matters in Italia, returned to Samos to continue planning the invasion of Egypt.

Miriam, Iras, and Agis, escorted by Flavius, arrived in Nicopolis in mid-Februarius, and the change in the slave girl who had originally tried to kill us was startling. Perhaps most striking was the relationship between Miriam and Iras, now acting more like sisters than mistress and slave. Even Agis seemed to have finally been won over by the girl, although she was clearly nervous when she faced me for the first time. The truth is that I only had eyes for Miriam, who looked even more beautiful than I remembered, and I kissed her long and hard, almost crushing the breath out of her. I had rented an apartment, just another in a long series of temporary homes, and strangely, it was this that bothered me more than anything. I realized that at long last, I was ready to settle down, in one place, on a piece of land that belonged to me. I had no real interest in farming, but with what I had saved up, I would not have to perform any labor myself. Truthfully, I was more worried about what I would do with myself without the business and routine of the army, and it was the fear of boredom more than anything else that was the major obstacle in my path to retiring. Then I would look at Miriam, and think of giving her children, seeing her happy with them.

I remember the moment I decided that I would retire from the Legion when our enlistment ended. Nothing special happened; we were eating dinner, just a week after Miriam arrived in Nicopolis, and just Gaius, Iras, and Diocles were present. As Miriam and Iras chattered about something, I remember looking across the table at Miriam's face, the reflected glow from the fireplace making her brown skin glow with a pinkish tinge. She was laughing at something Iras had said, throwing her head back and baring her throat, suffusing me with a feeling of warmth and comfort that reminded me of my childhood, when my sisters would talk about boys and clothes while I sat listening. Those were some of the happiest days of my life, even though I had found much joy in the army as well. I realized that the last time I felt this way was with another woman, with hair the color of fiery copper and a baby on her hip. I decided then that I would have that feeling again, with and for Miriam this time. Saying nothing at that moment, I just looked on happily as I did with my sisters, mainly because I did not want to get Miriam excited when it was still a year away. This was my frame of mind as we waited at Nicopolis for the start of the campaign season.

The only other event of note was the execution of Celer and Censorius, which was delayed because Celer appealed to Octavian, citing his past service to Rome in a plea for mercy. What this meant in real terms is that Celer paid the *Praetor* a huge bribe, which was supposed to be passed on to Octavian. Instead, the *Praetor*, one of Octavian's men by the name of Statilius Taurus, who was also acting as the Legate in overall command of the army in Octavian's absence, put the money in his purse, letting Celer think that he was waiting for word from Octavian. I do not know why he delayed; he could have very simply just taken the money, then parted Celer's head from his shoulders the next day, but he did not. So Celer was allowed to linger in false hope for many weeks, rotting in a cell by himself, since he and Censorius had to be kept separate after their falling out the night of their capture.

The only favor I asked of Statilius, through Flaminius, was that I be allowed to be present for the execution. Statilius agreed, but went even further. After learning of the number of men that Celer and Censorius were responsible for murdering, he ordered that the entire army be paraded by to watch. I will say that Censorius at least died well, walking to the punishment square under his own power, although he flinched whenever he was struck by an object thrown at him by someone in the front ranks, angry at losing a friend or relative. Celer, on the other hand, had to be dragged to the square, blubbering like a baby, and even before he was pushed to his knees, he soiled himself. He kept crying out over and over that he had appealed to Octavian, and it was only then that we learned that Statilius had not bothered Octavian with Celer's plea. Personally, that did not trouble me at all, but it did not set well with Scribonius, and I could see that he was not alone. A fair number of men were muttering about Statilius' duplicity, but I do not see how any of them could believe that Octavian would spare Celer's life. As it turned out, the 10th was too far away for Celer to see me clearly. However, I doubt even if he had looked into my eyes he would have recognized me, so gone with fear was he. The life of Gaius Domitius Celer ended with a brutal swipe of the long cavalry sword that the executioners used, except that it took the man three blows before the head came cleanly away. One more enemy of mine had been struck down, yet I did not feel the sense of triumph that I thought I would. I suppose part of it was due to the fact that I had already felt the satisfaction of capturing Celer, while knowing what his fate was beforehand seemed to have been enough to sate my thirst for seeing him vanquished.

"I think I must be getting soft," was how I put it to Balbus, deciding that Scribonius was not the man to talk to about Celer's death. "That didn't feel nearly as good as I thought it would."

Balbus only gave a grunt, a sign that he was not really interested in hearing what I had to say, but I plunged on anyway, as much to irritate him as anything.

"It's not just Celer, either. I'm not looking forward to the coming campaign at all."

This at last got him interested enough to respond, and he looked at me in surprise. "But this is the end, the end of it all. We'll have been part of something that started with Caesar's murder. When Antonius and that bitch Cleopatra are gone, it will all be over. Then we can do some proper soldiering against the Parthians again. Or those Armenian bastards."

Balbus spat to show his contempt for the Armenian Artavasdes, who had taken advantage of the turmoil between Octavian and Antonius to renounce all ties and treaties to Rome, claiming the title of king of an independent Armenia. The sad fact was that at the moment, there was nothing that could be done about this insult to Rome, but I knew that even after Antonius was subdued, the army would be marching without me.

"You can," I said quietly, not daring to look at him as I spoke. "But this will be my last campaign."

We had been walking back to the Legion area, and Balbus stopped suddenly. I felt his eyes boring into my back as I kept walking, yet I refused to look back.

"You can't be serious," he said, his voice tight with some emotion I could not identify.

"I'm very serious."

Seeing that he was still not moving, I stopped, reluctantly turning to face him.

"But why?"

"Because I'm tired, Balbus. I just want to live a quiet and peaceful life, spend the years I have left with Miriam, and perhaps raise a family."

Balbus snorted, his scarred face twisted in a grimace. "You fell in love," he said disgustedly. "That's your problem. There's no room in a Legionary's life for love. You should know better."

"I seem to remember someone who was so much in love that he ruined a friendship over it," I reminded him, recalling the long-ago feud between he and Torquatus, former Primus Pilus of the 10th and the man I had replaced in that post.

Torquatus had died just a few months before, simply from being worn down and out from a lifetime spent under the standard or with the army, since the last few years he had been Evocatus. As far as I knew, he and Balbus never reconciled, but Balbus' face told me that the memory I brought up was still painful for him, causing me to regret my words instantly.

"And more fool I," he shot back bitterly. "Look what I have to show for it. And I learned my lesson, I can tell you that. I haven't been in love since."

I walked back to where Balbus was still standing, putting a hand on his shoulder. "She died, Balbus. That wasn't your fault."

"What does it matter? She left, and that's all that matters." He shook his head, as if shaking off the bad memories. "But don't change the subject. I still don't believe it."

"You should," I replied. "Because I've made my decision. When this enlistment is over, I'm done was well."

"Who's going to run the Legion?"

Now I was surprised. "Why, you of course."

Balbus frowned, looking anything but pleased at the prospect, deepening my confusion. "By the gods, I hope not. I'd rather be a bum boy at the baths than be Primus Pilus."

I was completely dumbfounded; I had always assumed that Balbus would leap at the opportunity to run the Legion.

"Why not?" I demanded, feeling a little cross with him.

"After seeing all that you've been through? Oh, it may have been true at one time, but I've spent the last several years watching you play politics with the generals, butt heads with the other Primi Pili, and try to keep from being killed by queens." He gave me a grin, forcing a laugh from me as well as he continued. "No, it's not for me. I like running a Century, and I'd like to run a Cohort. Just not the First one."

While I admired his honesty, I felt obligated to warn him of a possibility. "Octavian may not give you any choice. You're the logical choice for a Legion that will still have a lot of veterans in it after the full-term boys are out. If it was a raw Legion, starting from scratch, then it's not so important to have someone running the Legion who knows the men, since they're all new."

"Then I'll retire too," Balbus said, prompting me to laugh again.

"You? Retire? What in Hades would you do if you weren't in the army?"

"That's what I thought about you," he grumbled, "and look where that got me."

I told Scribonius of my decision to retire, but unlike Balbus, he did not seem in the least surprised.

"I've seen this coming for some time," was his only comment.

"What about you?" I asked.

"Oh, I decided to retire when you did. The fact is I've been ready for a long time."

It is true that he had been saying for some time that when I left the Legion, he would as well, but I was still surprised that he was serious.

"Really? And you're going back to Rome like you planned?"

He nodded, giving me a mischievous smile. "Yes, even if it's just to see my brother's face when I show up and claim my inheritance."

Scribonius had learned a few years before, when his father died, that he had been forgiven for running off to join the army, so much so that he was to inherit the bulk of his father's estate. His brother had been named manager of the Scribonius affairs in my friend's absence, and we both knew that his father's bequest was made as an enticement to Scribonius to leave the army immediately and return to Rome. He resisted the temptation; in fact, he did not act tempted in the least, partially because he had made his own fortune in the army, but more because he had no real interest in wealth and comfort. Over the years, I have observed that those born into a measure of wealth often have no real interest in the source of what provides them the level of comfort in which they live. Money was always there, so they assumed that it always would be, whereas men like me, born into poverty and never having two coins to rub together, thought of little else. I was somewhere in between these two extremes; money was important, but it was a means to an end, and that end was within sight. I decided that should the dinner with Octavian ever materialize, I would use that opportunity to broach the subject of soliciting his patronage for my elevation to the class of *equites*. With Octavian's backing and approval, I knew that there would be no resistance to my elevation from any quarter, such was his power and influence. I was also determined to try to make that dinner happen, and the opportunity was approaching, since we were informed that Octavian was to join the army within the week.

The army began preparations for breaking camp and starting the campaign, despite the fact we still did not know whether we would be marching or sailing to Egypt. The rumor was circulating that we would be taking the long, overland route, meaning a long, grinding march, something that I for one was not happy about. For one of the few times in my life, I was willing to risk the dangers of crossing by sea rather than face the prospect of mile after mile of endless marching. I saw this as another sign that I was ready to leave the army, since I had always either looked forward to, or at the worst been indifferent about the prospect of a long march. Once again, I put in the long watches that come from preparing a Legion to march, making for long days of lists and inspections. Then I would go home to Miriam and for the rest of the night I would not think about the Legion, or the upcoming campaign.

Octavian arrived, immediately calling a meeting of the Centurions of the army.

"We're going to finish this business once and for all," he began. "And we're going to take the overland route to Egypt so that I can arrange matters with the various client kings along the way."

There was a low chorus of muttering following his announcement, and it was clear that most of the Centurions felt the same way that I did about the prospect of marching thousands of miles.

Ignoring this, Octavian continued. "That's why you are setting out immediately, as soon as you can make preparations. Don't worry about rations; I've made arrangements for stockpiles of supplies to be delivered at points along the way. I'll be joining you in Asia, as I still have matters to settle here on this side of Our Sea."

With these instructions, we were dismissed to continue our work of getting the men ready to march, then later that day, a messenger arrived.

"Caesar requests the pleasure of your company for dinner tonight," the Tribune told me, the look on his face relaying his astonishment that Octavian would want to share a dinner with, as Cleopatra had said, a lowborn brute like me.

"May I bring a guest?" I asked, thinking that it would give Miriam a chance to dress up, not thinking that it would send her into a panic on such short notice. Fortunately, the Tribune apparently had been told to anticipate this request and shook his head.

"Caesar was specific that he wants you to come alone."

The last time he had been that specific was just a few months before, when he ordered Balbinus and me to attend to him by ourselves, and I had disobeyed him then, but I was not going to this time around. Not only was he now my commanding general, I did not think this was a situation where I was in any danger, but I had learned through bitter experience never to take such things for granted, so I would be cautious nonetheless.

"Tell Caesar I would be honored to be his guest."

The Tribune told me the time that I was to be there, and I hurried to the apartment to make myself presentable. That is when I learned how much trouble I would have been in if I had secured an invitation for Miriam.

Arriving at the appointed time, I was dressed in a freshly laundered tunic, my belt freshly varnished, boots cleaned and polished. I carried my *vitus*, though I was not sure why I did so. The same Tribune was sitting at the duty desk, and as soon as I entered the *Praetorium*, he rose to go to the door to the private quarters of the commanding general. When Octavian was absent, Statilius occupied the several rooms, and normally Octavian would have occupied the *Praetor*'s civil office, but it had not been constructed yet, so he had kicked Statilius out to occupy the space. It was not sumptuous by his standards, I was sure, but it was still richly appointed for a military camp, with several pieces of art, including a bust of Divus Julius by Phidias, or at least so I believed. Octavian himself came to greet me, dressed in a richly embroidered tunic of a deep blue, his golden hair gleaming and brushed. His skin glowed from a good scraping, though unlike his adopted father, he did not have a depilatory slave pluck all the hair from his arms and legs.

"*Salve,* Titus Pullus! I apologize that it's taken more than ten years, but we're at last able to have our dinner!"

Octavian offered his hand, and I clasped his forearm, noting that his grip was firm and dry. He had given up wearing the elevated boots that he wore in the years immediately following Caesar's murder so that he would more closely resemble his dead adopted father. I took that as a sign that he had grown secure enough in his own right to do away with such artifice. His smile was still dazzling, and I must admit that every time I saw it, I went a little weak in the knees, it being so reminiscent of Caesar that it almost took me back to the first time I stood before the man. I had been a *tiro,* a raw youth of 16 years, although I looked much older because of my size and musculature. Now I was feeling the same flush, but I forced myself to remain in the moment and not be transported to that day long ago, knowing that was exactly what Octavian wanted.

"It's my honor that you remembered, Caesar," I replied. "I've been looking forward to it for as long as you have."

With those pleasantries out of the way, Octavian led me to a couch, and I saw that we were indeed dining alone. Agrippa was in Italia, while apparently Statilius was not going to be dining with us, meaning there were only the usual slaves hovering about the walls. There was only one couch, and I saw that he was doing me a huge honor of offering to share one couch with him. While I was flattered, it also put me on my guard. Be careful, Titus, he wants something from you and you need to keep your wits about you, I thought, as we both sat, Octavian seated to my left.

For a moment, neither of us spoke, each clearly waiting for the other to begin the conversation.

The awkward silence caused us both to laugh, then Octavian said, "Well, Pullus, it's been a long time, neh?"

"That it has, Caesar," I agreed, saying no more.

"And so much has happened in that time," he said, his eyes taking on a faraway look, and for an instant I saw the youth looking back on a life robbed of the untroubled time of the young man.

Octavian never had the opportunity to be carefree; Caesar's murder had thrust him into a position of huge opportunity, but even more danger, and I wondered if he had any regrets about the path he had taken.

Startling me, since he seemed to read my thoughts, he murmured, "Yet with all that's happened, I wouldn't change anything."

Snapping back to the present, he turned to a slave, signaling that wine be brought. It was Chian, though of a vintage that was beyond my means, or at least as much as I was willing to pay, and it was excellent. He ordered his unwatered, then lifted an eyebrow when I told the slave to add water to my portion.

"Trying to keep a clear head, Pullus? Are you that worried that I'm up to something?"

"Not at all, Caesar," I lied. "I just don't have a head for wine. I never have."

"Well, you should be," he smiled, taking a sip, his eyes never leaving my face, watching my reaction.

Rather than answering, I did the same, so that we regarded each other over the rims of our cups. Finally, he set his down, and I thought I detected a hint of irritation in his manner, though it could have been my imagination, since his tone was still light and friendly.

"I wanted to get your thoughts on some changes I'm planning on making to the army and how it works."

I did not miss how he had put this, and I raised a finger in question.

"Yes?"

"You said you're planning on making changes to the army?"

"Yes," he nodded. "That's correct."

"That implies that you've already made the decision. So I must ask, why are you asking me if you have already made up your mind?"

I was sure that this would offend Octavian, but he seemed to have quite the opposite reaction. "You caught me, Pullus. I must say that I'm impressed. Not many men in your position would have picked up on that."

I had to bite back a tart reply, realizing that Octavian was only displaying the same attitude as most of his peers, and he continued speaking. "But yes, you are correct. These are reforms that must be carried out, or Rome will collapse under its own weight." He paused, as if expecting a response, but I said nothing, so he continued while the slaves brought the first course of the meal. "No doubt you heard of the trouble that the men of the 8th, and the other discharged Legions caused in Italia."

I replied that I had, but did not elaborate, which again seemed to cause him some irritation.

"Really, Pullus," he said crossly. "If I wanted someone to just nod up and down at everything I said, I could find a hundred Senators that would fit the bill. I asked you here because I want to hear what you think about all that I'm saying. I promise you that I'll hold nothing you say against you in any way. I swear it on Jupiter's Stone."

Frankly, I was still not convinced, but I recognized that continuing to guard my tongue would end up offending him. The one time I was careful to watch what I said, I thought to myself, I am getting in trouble for it.

Still, I said, "I know that you don't have the money in the Treasury to pay the bonuses to the men, but I can tell you, Caesar, that such realities don't mean much to rankers. All they know is that they were promised a fat purse after spending the better part of their lives sweating and bleeding for Rome, and they don't give a rotten fig about whether the money is actually there or not."

He considered this, then nodded. "I understand that, and frankly, it's not the money that's the real problem. It's the land. The fact is, we don't have enough good land that's not already occupied to give every man who retires his 40 acres."

"What about all the Antonians?" I asked. "Can't you confiscate their land?"

"Yes, and we've already done so. And the truth is that there will be enough land for the veterans who just retired, and for the next set of Legions, including the 10th. But it's after that that I'm thinking about. Rome would have to continue to conquer new territory, colonize it, and make it sufficiently peaceful enough, just to give retiring Legionaries their plots of land."

I stuffed a piece of bread into my mouth, mainly to stall for time while I thought about what he said. Despite seeing the sense in what he was telling me, I also knew how extremely unpopular it would be, since the grant of land on retirement had become as much of a custom and tradition in the army as the eagle standard itself.

Seeing that Octavian was not going to speak again until I offered my opinion, I took a swallow of wine, then said, "I understand what you're saying, Caesar, but are you prepared for the reaction you're going to get? The men will feel betrayed; there's no other word for it. We've all grown up under the current system, and many of the men have fathers, brothers, cousins, and friends who received land for marching under the standard. Not to mention the number of men who grew up on farms that were their homes precisely because of their father's service to Rome." I shook my head. "I'm sorry, Caesar, but I see that you'll have your hands full."

"Be that as it may, there is no choice, and the men will obey," he said tightly, and I gave him a long look, wondering if he was going to live up to his promise. His eyes met mine; he let out a long breath, then gave a chuckle. "But that's not your doing, and I shouldn't hold it against you for telling me the truth. I know that what you're saying is true. We'll continue to pay out a discharge bonus; that won't change. And if possible, I plan on increasing the amount from what it is today so that the men can buy land if they so choose. That way, whoever owns the land will be compensated and we won't have to perform evictions."

Seeing that his mind was made up on this subject, I simply gave a nod, which he took to be agreement, although I still had my doubts. For the next several moments, we concentrated on our meal, eating in silence, both clearly absorbed in our own thoughts.

Then Octavian seemed to be ready to move on to the next topic. "Another reform I'm making is to reduce the size of the army. Once things are settled with Cleopatra, of course."

That surprised me, but not for the reason of the reduction of the army.

"Cleopatra? What about Antonius? Surely he has to be dealt with as well."

Octavian said nothing for a long moment, as if considering his next words carefully. "I'm not at war with Marcus Antonius," he said finally, and it was all I could do to keep the mouthful of wine from spewing all over him as I gaped in astonishment. Ignoring me, he continued, "I made a vow to Jupiter Optimus Maximus that I wouldn't war against a fellow Roman, and I intend to keep that vow. I'm at war with Cleopatra, not Antonius."

"But how can we fight Cleopatra without fighting Antonius?"

"Precisely," he answered, his face giving away nothing.

I understood what he was saying, but frankly, that was another fine point where the people of my class, and I suspect a lot of the upper classes as well, would not see the distinction. Nevertheless, I decided not to press the point.

Seeing that I was not going to pursue this, he continued. "I haven't completely decided on how many Legions are going to be kept under the standard, but it will be less than half of the current number. The army is the biggest drain on the Treasury, and Rome will never recover until we cut it down to size."

Again, I understood the logic, yet I was unclear on how it was going to be accomplished. "If you're having trouble finding money to pay the Legions that are retiring, how in Hades are you going to find the money to pay all those men? I realize that you're not going to pay men who haven't served the full 16 years their entire bonus, but it's still a huge sum of money."

"Egypt," he said, popping an olive into his mouth.

He seemed convinced that this was a simple answer, but I was not. "I know Egypt is extremely wealthy, but how can you be sure that there's enough money there? And Caesar, remember, I was with the 6th in Alexandria and I know that the location of Egypt's treasury is probably the most closely guarded secret in the world. Even if the money is there, how can you be sure you can find it?"

Octavian leaned back on the couch, giving me a smile that could only be described as smug.

He seemed to be considering something, then said, "Pullus, I'm going to tell you something, and it's as much of a secret as the location of Egypt's wealth. I don't need to tell you how important it is that this remains secret, do I? I'm willing to trust you because my father trusted you, and he spoke very highly of you."

The threat was unspoken, but that made it no less clear. For a moment I was tempted to say that I did not want to hear another secret, that I was tired of them, yet I knew that would be just as dangerous as betraying the confidence.

"No, Caesar, you don't need to tell me how to keep a secret," I said, perhaps a trifle sharply.

"Good. I not only know how much is in Egypt's treasury, I know exactly where it is located."

I stared at him, not sure if I believed him, but he was clearly serious. "How?"

He smiled, replying, "Because my father told me. He was taken to the Treasury by Cleopatra's high priest of that abominable animal religion of theirs, and they were so sure that the maze of tunnels would be so confusing, and the blindfold they made him wear just to make sure, that it would keep him from learning its location. But as usual, they underestimated Caesar, and he memorized the path, counting every step, how many turns he made and in which direction, and as soon as he was able, he wrote it down before he forgot. I have the tablet in my possession, in a very safe place. When they removed his blindfold, he said that he almost fainted, because he had never seen so much wealth. By his estimate, it would be enough to pay every man in the army a full 16 year bonus at least twice over."

I sat there speechless. Octavian leaned back, looking very pleased with himself, and he had every right to be. I could only shake my head in admiration of my old general. It never occurred to me to think that Caesar had made a mistake and Octavian would never find it.

"Well, that certainly solves a lot of problems," was all I could think to say.

"That it does," he agreed. "But that's not all I have planned. That can wait, however."

He turned to face me, studying me with those blue eyes that can be so unsettling, it feeling as if he can peer into your very soul with them.

Finally, he asked, "So what of you, Pullus? The 10th's enlistment is up next year. What are your plans? Surely you've given it some thought."

Here was the moment I had been waiting for, and I took a breath before I plunged in. "In fact I have, Caesar. I've given it a lot of thought and I've decided that I'm going to retire at the end of this enlistment."

He nodded, clearly not surprised. "I thought as much," he replied. "But what are your plans for after retirement? You're not going to run an inn or a wineshop, are you? That would be a huge waste of your talents, I can assure you."

I had not been flattered this much in some time, which was making me extremely wary, but I answered him anyway. "Actually, Caesar, that's what I wanted to talk to you about. Over the years, through my share of booty, sale of slaves and the various bonuses that I've earned," I emphasized that this was not a gift, that I had worked for this money, "I've managed to save enough money to meet the requirements for elevation for myself and my descendants to be elevated to the equestrian class. I'm asking for your patronage and influence in helping me become an *equites*."

He had been about to take a drink of wine, but the cup froze midway to his mouth as he stared at me for several heartbeats. Then, he set the cup down, his face suddenly a mask, giving nothing away.

"Really?" he said carefully. "I wasn't aware that you had such aspirations."

Something in his tone made me tense, and I felt the tingling up the back of my neck that I sometimes got when danger was imminent. Octavian suddenly seemed to be looking everywhere but at me, and I waited for him to continue.

Finally, he said, "Forgive me, Pullus, that just caught me by surprise, and the truth is that I had something else in mind for you."

Ah, I thought, here it is. Contrary to Octavian, I was not surprised, but a part of me was disappointed that he was just like all the others, using men like me as a piece in a game.

"What is that, Caesar?"

I know my tone was very cool. However, I was sure that I was not going to like what it was he had in mind.

"As part of my reforms, I'm creating a new office in the army, similar to Evocatus, but of even a higher rank. It's been used in the past, but it wasn't a formal post, more of an informal thing that a general would use. I would change that. You would hold the rank of Camp Prefect, one of a very, very few. There will be one attached to every army, and you would be second in command to the Legate commanding the army."

I sat listening, and I have to say that it was extremely flattering that I was being asked to fill one of these spots. However, I was not tempted, and I said as much to Octavian.

"The pay will be 25,000 sesterces a year." He acted as if he had not heard me. That was a staggering sum, more than 10,000 sesterces more than a Primus Pilus made, but I was still not interested.

"I'm sorry, Caesar, but I'm ready to retire. I want to settle down, and live a peaceful life."

Octavian heaved a sigh, which I knew meant trouble. "Pullus," he said quietly. "Rome still needs you. It would be selfish of you to leave her when she still does."

Oh, he should not have said that. My anger flared up hot and bright, catching both of us by surprise.

"Selfish?" I snapped, almost not believing that he had used the word. "You call me selfish, Caesar?" I held out my arms so that he could see the scars. Not satisfied, I pulled my tunic aside so that he could see the puckered hole in my chest that was still purple, even these years later.

"This is what I've given to Rome, Caesar. I have bled, I have sweated, and I have watched friends die for Rome. Even worse, I've sent men to their deaths, knowing that they would die, all for Rome! Like Metellus, my Tertius

Pilus Prior, killed by Agrippa, along with all of his men! Agrippa didn't take them prisoner; he killed every last one of them, simply because I ordered them to be on Leucas and because the 10th was forced to march with Antonius after Philippi! Those were my men, and those Centurions were my comrades!"

I had not intended to bring up the fate of the Third Cohort, but I still grieved for the loss of those men, and at that moment I understood that I harbored resentment that neither Octavian nor Agrippa had bothered to acknowledge the loss of so many good Legionaries and friends. Octavian's face reddened, his lips planing down into a thin line as he listened to me.

"So when you say that I'm being selfish, Caesar, I take great offense to that! There are very few men under the standard whose record of service match mine! That is, after all," I finished, "why you're asking me to be this Camp Prefect, is it not?"

We sat there, glaring at each other, and I found that I was breathing as heavily as if I had just sprinted across the forum.

Finally, Octavian's face relaxed and he held up his hands in a placating gesture. "I apologize, Pullus. I shouldn't have used that word. Truly, you're not selfish, and I apologize for giving you offense. It's just that I'm not exaggerating when I say Rome needs you. *I* need you, Pullus. I need you to be a Camp Prefect so that these reforms take effect successfully."

Knowing that he was making a peace offering, I tried to respond in kind. "I apologize as well, Caesar. I shouldn't have spoken so harshly. And I do appreciate the great honor you're doing me. I'm flattered that you think so highly of me that you would think I was so important to your plans." I shook my head. "But I just want to retire, Caesar. And I believe that I'm owed that much, to be allowed to retire with honor in recognition for what I've given to Rome."

Octavian sat there, saying nothing, looking at me with unreadable eyes.

After a moment, he spoke slowly, his voice quiet. "I can't argue with that, Pullus. But I also won't be refused in this matter. I can't stop you from retiring, but a few moments ago, you mentioned something about your elevation to the equestrian class, I believe?" His tone was gentle, yet my blood chilled nonetheless. In that instant, I knew what he would say next. "If you don't accept the honor I'm doing you, Pullus, I can promise you that neither you, nor any of your descendants will ever be an *equites*. However, if you serve as a Camp Prefect, after your retirement as Primus Pilus next year, of course, for a period of five years, I give you my solemn vow that you'll become *equites*. In fact, I'll make you a Senator, should you so desire it."

It is said that every man has his price, and Octavian had found mine. I had no doubt whatsoever that he would do exactly as he said, that he would ensure that I would never become an *equites*, if I did not do as he required. I was just as sure that if I did, he would make it happen as if conjured by magic. I had no wish to be a Senator; the truth is that I wanted to be as far away from the city of Rome as possible when that day finally came that I settled down. This was the dream I held since I was a child and first conceived the idea of bettering myself, to prove to my long-dead father that he had been wrong about me. Now, it was both tantalizingly close and agonizingly far away, all because Octavian had decided I was still useful. From my perspective, I had no choice but to agree, and I did so that night. The surprising thing was that I was not even that angry about it, realizing that I must have known deep down that something like this was bound to happen. I wish I could say that Miriam felt the same; for the second time since I had known her, she was spitting angry, this time at Octavian.

"That man is as bad as Cleopatra! Worse even, because he claims to be helping Rome and he treats you, *you* Titus Pullus, no better than one of his slaves!"

"I wouldn't go that far," I said mildly, but she was not in the mood to be reasonable.

I had made the mistake of surprising her with my plans to retire, putting her in an ecstasy of anticipation, which only served to make me feel worse when I told her.

"I would! And why aren't you as angry as I am, Titus Pullus?"

She glared at me with her hands on her hips, and I knew it was no time to laugh, but it was hard with Iras standing just behind her, giving me the exact same fierce scowl, in the identical position.

"You are happy this happened," she accused me. "You did not want to retire, admit it! You probably hatched this plot with Octavian to get out of your promise to me!"

I did not recall making any kind of promise. However, this was not the time to point that out, or at least so I thought.

"I'm not happy about it, my love. I'm just not that surprised, I suppose," I said, except she evidently did not want to hear anything I had to say, her only reply a snort.

"So you say, but I do not believe you! You love the army more than you love me!"

"Miriam, that may have been true at one time," I told her, seeing her jaw drop, and I winced as I realized that she had not been expecting me to be so honest. "But that's no longer the case." The words rushed out as I tried to keep the tears that I saw welling in her eyes from falling. "That's why I wanted to retire in the first place, Miriam. For you. I want to live the rest of my days with you, in peace and quiet. And we will, I swear it. It will just take longer than I had hoped, but that can't be helped. I don't have to tell you that Octavian isn't someone we want as an enemy, and with one word, he can crush my dreams of becoming an *equites*. So I don't have a choice in the matter. But, I do have one surprise that I hope will make you happy," I finished, and I was rewarded with a hopeful look, though her eyes were still brimming.

"What is it?" she asked cautiously.

"Well, I don't know now. You've accused me of some horrible things," I said doubtfully, but I was just teasing her.

"I was angry, Titus Pullus, and you cannot blame me for that. But I did not mean what I said. I know you did not want this."

"That's better," I relented, pausing for several moments until she looked as if she would burst.

"Well? What is this surprise?"

The surprise was the one concession I had extracted from Octavian in return for my acceptance of his proposal, the specifics of the request clearly surprising him a great deal.

"Pullus, I would never have mistaken you for the type of man who wanted to be in such a state," was his response. "But I'm happy to grant you this dispensation. I'll have the proper paperwork prepared. You can pick it up from the *Praetorium* in the morning."

"You know that even a Primus Pilus can't be married," I began, to which she nodded.

"Yes, I am well aware of that fact," she replied sadly. "But I have grown accustomed to that and I do not complain."

"No, you don't," I agreed, the sudden look of sorrow on her face making what I was about to say that much sweeter. "But while I know that you don't like the idea of me continuing in the army, I hope that this will make it a bit easier to bear. You see, with this new post of Camp Prefect, I'm not bound by the same rules as if I were still under the standard."

Miriam had been looking at the ground as I spoke. Her head slowly raised and I could see the beginning of a new emotion moving across her face.

I smiled at her, continuing to talk. "As Camp Prefect, I'm allowed to be married. Now, if I could only find a woman that would have me as her husband," my voice trailed off, making a great show of being sad at the prospect of being alone.

"So you are saying that when you retire and become this Camp Prefect, we can be married?"

"No," I replied, and I admit that it was a cruel thing to do, but at the time, I wanted to make a joke out of it. When I saw her face, looking as if she had been slapped, I realized that I had made a mistake, so I hurried to finish. "I don't mean no, we can't be married." I held my hands up to her. "I mean that we don't have to wait until I'm Camp Prefect. I received a dispensation from Octavian to allow us to be married now, before I take the post."

"Now?" Miriam looked dazed, and she turned to Iras, whose jaw had dropped at my words.

"Today, if you want it," I told her, then had to jump across the space separating us to catch her as she stumbled.

"I do not know what to say," she murmured.

My heart started pounding when I was struck by a horrible thought. "I would hope that you'd say 'yes.'" I tried to say it jokingly, but I could not shake off the feeling of dread brought on by her seeming hesitance.

My words seemed to snap her out of the daze she was in, and her eyes were shining as she looked up at me.

"Of course I say 'yes,' Titus Pullus. I said 'yes' in my heart the moment I met you."

Miriam and I were married two days later, in a small ceremony officiated by the army priests and witnessed by Scribonius, Gaius, Balbus, Diocles, and Iras. I felt badly that the ceremony had to be rushed, but we were marching two days later, and Miriam did not want to wait for whenever I returned, since that could be a year. She was dressed simply, yet to my eyes she never looked more beautiful, while Iras had made her face up with just the right amount of makeup to enhance her natural beauty. She also had garlands of flowers woven into her hair, and she held a small bouquet, which apparently was a custom of her people. I chose to wear a toga, and I am afraid that as I did not wear it often, Diocles and Agis had to work very hard to make it as sparkling white as a fresh coat of snow. Our ceremonies are very simple, and blessedly short. Afterwards, we had a dinner with our friends that was one of the most enjoyable nights of my life. I invited all the Pili Priores, which made Miriam a little nervous at the idea of so many hard-bitten Centurions making the usual bawdy jokes about our coming wedding night, but they had been warned and were on their best behavior. I spared no expense in either the quality or quantity of food and wine, so it was very late, or early, depending on how you looked at it, before the party broke up, the men staggering away to get a little rest.

"Now you can write Naomi and Hashem and tell them you're an honest woman," I teased her.

She made a face, and I dodged her kick, almost falling out of the bed in the process. "I have always been an honest woman, Titus Pullus."

"Yes, you have. Which is another reason I love you." I gave her a mock frown as I thought of something. "So if you were already an honest woman, why did I marry you?"

"Because I tricked you!" she shouted triumphantly, laughing as she said it. "I made you think what I wanted you to think, that I was so unhappy unless I was married. Now I have you, and I will never let you go!"

"Promise?"

"I swear it to Baal," she said, not laughing now.

The rest of the night passed as happily, which made leaving that much harder.

"Titus Pullus, the married man," Scribonius teased as we marched away from Nicopolis. Normally, I would not have minded the teasing, but I was not in a good mood this day. However, I knew it would not be right to take my ire out on my best friend.

"How does it feel to be married?" he asked me curiously. I shrugged, since it had only been a matter of a couple of days.

"Not much different, really," I began. "It's harder to leave her behind, though I don't know if that's due to being married."

"It's because you're old and married." He laughed. "How many old, married men are there in the Legions?"

"Not many," I admitted, knowing full well that in the 10th alone there were at least a hundred men who had made their unions more official, in secret of course, because their women would not let them rest until they were married.

So they risked the wrath of the army, keeping the unions a poorly kept secret, one that every Centurion turned a blind eye towards, as long as it did not interfere with their official duties. Scribonius was not the only one giving me a good ribbing about my marriage, but I did not care. For the first time in more years than I cared to remember, I was truly happy with the part of my life not connected to the army. I had been so intent on advancing my career for so many years that I had forgotten that there was more to life than what took place under the standard. The first few days, as usual, were the toughest, the men knocking off the rust of a winter in garrison, and I suffered along with them. After a week, however, the men were fit again, and since we stuck to the coastline, we made good time. While we marched towards Egypt, Antonius and Cleopatra were making their final attempts to stop the inevitable.

Chapter 6- The Fall of Antonius and Cleopatra

Much of what transpired in those weeks and months while we made our way to confront Antonius and Cleopatra we only learned later, except that some of it was relayed through a variety of sources shortly after it happened; traveling merchants heading west from Egypt, ships' captains in the port cities that we passed through, or from dispatches sent to Taurus, during the time before Octavian rejoined the army. We learned that Antonius, made desolate by his defeat, built a small house apart from the royal palace in Alexandria, living there for weeks like a hermit. From all accounts, he had given up all hope, despite Cleopatra still possessing enough ambition and drive for the both of them, and she continued to work desperately to salvage something from the situation. To that end, she secretly opened negotiations with Octavian on her own behalf, and if the rumor were true, had offered herself to Octavian while promising to have Antonius dispatched, in exchange for Cleopatra retaining her throne along with Egypt's status as client state of Rome. In order to deceive her citizens, and keep them from rioting and causing her problems, she entered the harbor of Alexandria with the prow of her vessel decorated with garlands, the traditional method of announcing victory, taking her subjects in completely. She wasted no time in removing men of high rank who had returned with her to Alexandria who knew the truth, accusing them of a variety of crimes before putting them to death without benefit of trial. To prove to Octavian her sincerity in her desire to ally herself and Egypt with him, she lured Artavasdes the Armenian to

Alexandria, then had him seized and executed, keeping his embalmed head as proof.

Antonius, after a month-long drunk in his house, rejoined Cleopatra, whereupon he, not knowing that Cleopatra was secretly negotiating with Octavian on her own, sent a joint embassy to Octavian, with the offer of accepting exile as a private citizen in Egypt. He made the grave error of sending a man named Publius Turullus, one of the last of the assassins of Caesar, as his emissary, while for her part, Cleopatra sent her scepter and her golden throne as a token of her submission. In answer, Octavian immediately executed Turullus, yet made no other reply to the couple's plea. These were not their only troubles; four of the Legions left behind by Antonius in Cyrene went over to Octavian, Octavian sending Gaius Cornelius Gallus, an equestrian whose only experience in military affairs to that point had been writing poems about battle, to lead these Legions. The last remaining Triumvir, the First Man in Rome was implacably squeezing Cleopatra and Antonius.

Meanwhile, we continued to march, cutting overland through Bithynia and Galatia. Unlike our expeditions with Antonius, our baggage train carried the most basic essentials, with only each Legion's complement of artillery, along with enough rations and other supplies to keep us marching, making our progress much faster than our invasions of Parthia. The weather cooperated as well, yet another sign to the men that the gods favored Octavian, who joined us in Nicomedia. He spent part of every day circulating among the men, doing his best impersonation of Caesar, despite the fact only a portion of the army had ever seen Divus Julius in the flesh. However, their comrades had regaled them with stories of Caesar's greatness, most of them made up, and of his love for his men, which was not. There was a different air about this march, I suppose because many of the men knew that this was their last campaign. That is certainly what was foremost in my mind, and I took the opportunity to enjoy the moments that I had long taken for granted as just part of life in the army. I spent more time around the fires, particularly with the men like Vellusius, who would be retiring as well, though for him it was more of a necessity. He had lost so many teeth by this point that he had difficulty chewing the hard bread, preferring when the meal consisted of porridge or boiled chickpeas. He was still tougher than old boot leather, but the fatigue and wear of the past 31 years was plain to see in every line of his seamed, brown face. He still had the same irrepressible cheerfulness, as he, Scribonius, and I entertained the men with stories of all that we had seen and done together. Most of the stories were funny, while some were sad, remembering friends lost. It was in those moments I realized how much I would miss all this.

Another interesting thing that I noticed was that when we talked of the past, how rarely it was of the battles and fighting, but of the moments in between, on the march, or in camp. When we did talk of battles, it was almost always about humorous moments that occurred. Between Scribonius and Vellusius, I took my share of ribbing, and perhaps even more, each of them recounting the prideful raw youth who bragged to all who would listen about how he would be the Primus Pilus of the 10th Legion one day. While normally I did not like being made fun of, particularly by a ranker like Vellusius, for some reason this time it did not bother me at all, and in fact I enjoyed it immensely. During the day, with the army marching along singing songs and swapping stories, I found myself thinking of similar moments, remembering the very first campaign of the 10th Legion, in Hispania, when we followed Caesar for the first time. I could still recall, and can to this day, the first man I killed in battle, and how my career almost ended before it ever really got started because I forgot to draw my sword when leaping over a parapet. The fight on the hilltop, where Scribonius, Vibius, and I fought side by side after being surrounded by Gallaeci, where we saw Spurius Didius, who had earned the nickname Achilles, faking an injury to get out of the fight. Calienus, our first Sergeant, a veteran of Pompey's 1st, and the first to act as my guide and mentor in understanding the intricacies of leading other men. His death at Gergovia was one of the most painful memories of my life, despite the fact that it led me to Gisela, and I suppose that part of the pain I felt when I thought of Calienus was the guilt I felt at ending up with his woman. Thoughts of Calienus naturally took me to Gisela, yet behind that door was a world of hurting and loss that I rarely ever opened. I found it easier just not to think of Gisela, Vibi, and little Livia, now long dead but never really forgotten. The one thing I will say is that all of these memories helped the days of marching pass quickly, and there were many, many days, because we were going all the way to Egypt.

Gallus the poet took the four Legions to Paraetonium, which is roughly halfway between Cyrene and Alexandria. Meanwhile, we reached Syria in mid-summer, our two armies forming a set of jaws about to snap shut on Alexandria. Antonius finally roused himself enough to make an attempt to win back the Cyrene Legions, now commanded by Gallus, and he headed west to confront them. Meanwhile, Cleopatra built another fleet, except this one was to head for Arabia; some said it was to open up an escape route to India. Whatever her motive, Octavian's governor of Syria, Quintus Didius, sent a force to burn the fleet before it could sail. A small army of gladiators had formed in Syria as well, and were marching to join Antonius, but Didius intercepted these men as well and they were massacred. Herod, so firmly in the purse of Antonius in the past, despite his hatred of Cleopatra, now presented himself to Octavian, and once again, the oily toad managed to wriggle out of his predicament by switching sides. He did not come empty-handed, presenting Octavian with, among other things, a Legion of men trained in the Roman fashion, by Centurions he had bribed away from Antonius, which from all accounts was not hard to do at this point. The men of Antonius' army, those who remained with him and were on the ships that had escaped, along with those Legions left behind when we went to Actium, now knew their cause was doomed, meaning that desertions and defections were occurring daily. Canidius had managed to make his way back to Antonius, informing him of the wholesale defection of the portion of the army that had escaped, while I imagined that Balbinus and I came up for special mention. I knew that if somehow the gods turned their back on Octavian, or on me, and I fell into the hands of Antonius and Cleopatra, the last moments of my life would be my most painful. I cannot say that I was particularly worried about that; it was just something that I was aware of nonetheless, mainly because Scribonius and Balbus never let me forget.

"What they would do to us is nothing compared to what they would do to you," was how Balbus put it, clearly enjoying bringing it up.

"Then we both better make sure that we don't lose," I countered.

Scribonius and I spent time on the march together as well, both of us talking about our futures. "Has Caesar given you any idea about where you'll be stationed?"

"No," I said. "I don't think he's thought that far ahead."

"I wouldn't bet on that," Scribonius warned. "I get the feeling that he has the next 30 years planned down to the last detail."

All I could do was shrug at that, knowing he was probably right. "There's nothing I can do about it. He has me in a corner and he knows it."

"I must say that you've been taking it extremely well," was his comment, prompting another shrug.

"I guess I figured out pretty quickly that there wasn't much I could do about it, so there's not much point in getting angry."

"Why, Titus Pullus, that sounds very much like you've finally grown up," Scribonius teased.

"It was bound to happen sometime."

"It must be married life."

That was probably more true than I wanted to admit, but I was not about to tell him that, so for once I remained silent.

The hardest part of the march was crossing the desert of the Sinai, at the end of which we assumed that we would have to fight to take Pelusium. However, Octavian had beguiled Cleopatra through his freedman Thrysus, who convinced the queen that her overtures of love were favorably received, and on her orders, the city's gates were thrown open to us. It was an astonishing development, and I am still not sure how a woman as cunning and intelligent as Cleopatra could have been so easily fooled into believing that Octavian would ever have any congress with her, sexual or otherwise. After all, it was he who had constantly whipped the mob into a frenzy of hatred with his Queen of Beasts rhetoric, and it was only Cleopatra that he had declared war on, not

Antonius. Somehow, that did not stop her from accepting the fiction that Octavian was just the latest in the line of Romans seduced by the queen of Egypt, with the result that the gates of Pelusium were open to receive us the moment we marched within view.

"Symbolic, don't you think?" Scribonius asked, and I did not immediately understand his meaning.

"Cleopatra ordered the gates opened, in much the same way she wants to open her gates to Caesar."

I laughed, but there was certainly truth in what he was saying. "All I can say is that she must know some tricks that a Suburan whore would give a year's pay to know," I replied. "Because she's certainly turned the heads and captured the hearts of Rome's most powerful men."

"It's not their hearts that she captured, and I seem to remember someone not quite as well-born as Caesar and Antonius who panted after her as well." He gave me a poke in the shoulder, just to make sure I knew who he was talking about. I was sorely tempted to punch him right in his grinning face.

"It wasn't like that," I grumbled. "She was nice to me, that's all. And trust me, I don't feel that way anymore."

Scribonius shook his head in mock sadness, infuriating me even more. "Just because a woman tries to kill you, that doesn't mean you should hold it against her."

"For some reason, I tend to hold a grudge against people who try to kill me. I know it's a flaw in my character, but I can't help it."

"Well," he replied, turning serious. "I'm just glad that she didn't succeed."

"So am I," I said fervently, though I was thinking more of Miriam than myself.

We settled in at Pelusium for just a few days, more to recover from the rigors of the desert crossing than for any other reason, while Octavian was still working behind the scenes to further erode the will of the remaining Antonian troops to continue fighting. There was a brief flurry of excitement and activity when our cavalry contingent, ranging a few miles east of Pelusium, ran into Antonius, who was heading west, trying to reach Pelusium before we did. There was a battle in which our forces were routed, but Antonius broke off his pursuit when he came within sight of Pelusium, only to spy us ranged on the city walls. Turning about, he scampered back to Alexandria to prepare himself for our coming assault on the Egyptian capital.

From Pelusium, we crossed the desert between there and Alexandria, except it was not nearly as barren as the Sinai, making the march easier. We arrived at the outskirts of Alexandria to find the outlying neighborhoods deserted of people, with no sign of Antonian troops in the vicinity. Advancing through the Canopus, we stopped at the hippodrome just outside the city, the outer walls of which provided protection from attack, since it was made of stone. Facing outward from the highest row of stone benches, the retaining wall served as a parapet, and it did not take long to get our defenses situated. We built wooden platforms on which we could place our artillery, giving the pieces a clear field of fire. The floor of the hippodrome was not large enough to hold all of the tents of the army, so we built a camp on the far side with one side against the hippodrome, and a trench was dug that allowed men to move under cover into the hippodrome in case of attack. Our remaining cavalry began patrolling through the streets of Canopus and the surrounding neighborhoods, the rest of the army settling in to wait for what happened next.

Once more, Antonius sallied forth with his own personal bodyguard, surprising our cavalry commander in the streets outside the walls. There was a sharp fight, with Antonius' men routing ours, inflicting heavy losses. We learned the next day that Antonius returned to Cleopatra, rushing into the palace in full armor to declare that he had won a great victory. Bringing with him one of his cavalrymen who had shown great valor in the engagement, he introduced the man to Cleopatra, who rewarded him with her golden breastplate and helmet. The way we learned of this was from the man himself, who turned up outside the walls of the hippodrome the very next morning to desert to Octavian, still carrying his trophies.

Later that day, another lone figure on horseback approached the walls of the hippodrome, carrying a flag of truce. Turbo, the Pilus Posterior of the Eighth, and his Century had the duty for that section of the wall, and he sent a runner to find me while sending another to Octavian. The runner informed me of the identity of the man on horseback; it was Spurius, who had chosen to go with Antonius when they sailed from Actium, leaving the youths of the 3rd Gallica under the command of Canidius. Those men had been discharged and scattered, but I was sure that Antonius had given him another Legion to command. When I hurried up the steps, I found him sitting on a horse. I saw that his free hand was out to the side, the other holding a white square of linen on a stick. Even from a distance, the fatigue and despair was clear to see in Spurius' face and body, although he tried to keep his shoulders back and his demeanor confident

. He spotted me, raising his hand in greeting. "*Salve,* Pullus," he called to me.

"*Salve,* Spurius," I replied. "How go things?"

It was all I could think to say. The absurdity of the question struck us both immediately, and we simultaneously burst out laughing.

After a moment, he said, "Oh, well enough. Kind of boring, actually. We lounge about all day, fuck whores, and get drunk. It's the best duty I ever had."

"Sounds like it." I grinned at him, trying to put out of my mind the possibility that we would be crossing swords in the coming days. Changing the subject, I asked him, "Did Antonius send you to ask after my well-being? I imagine he's concerned that I'm getting enough to eat and adequate rest."

This evoked another laugh, yet even from this distance, there was no mistaking the bitter edge, even if it was not aimed at me so much. "Your name has come up a time or two," he admitted. "But I don't remember him asking that, exactly." In a lower voice, he said, "I just wish I had been smart enough to do the same thing you did."

"That bad?" I asked, to which he answered with a grim nod.

"Worse than you can imagine. Antonius goes from exuberance to despair, almost moment by moment. Cleopatra is even worse, though in truth I haven't seen much of her the last few days. The rumor is that she's working on her and Antonius' tomb. You know how these Egyptians are about that stuff."

Hearing a commotion behind us, I turned to see Octavian coming, with Statilius and some Tribunes.

Before he arrived, I called to Spurius, "May the gods protect you, Vibius Spurius."

"And you, Titus Pullus. Keep an eye out for me, will you?"

"I will," I agreed, then stepped aside.

Octavian came to stand beside me, looking down coldly at Spurius. "Who are you and what do you want?"

His tone was abrupt, but if Spurius were surprised or offended, he knew better than to show it. "I'm Vibius Spurius, Caesar, bringing greetings and a message from Triumvir Marcus Antonius."

"I knew of a Vibius Spurius that was the Primus Pilus of the 3rd Gallica, and a man loyal to Rome at one time. You're surely not him, since the Spurius I knew of would have fallen on his sword rather than betray Rome by fighting for the Queen of Beasts."

Spurius stiffened as if he had been slapped, while I could hear the gasps of the men standing on the parapet at the insult, but if Octavian heard, he gave no sign.

Before Spurius could respond, he pressed on, "And there is no such man as Triumvir Marcus Antonius. That office was abolished, and the man known as Antonius, the *Roman* Marcus Antonius no longer exists. In his place is a *numen* that looks like Antonius, and may sound like Antonius, but is a minion of Cleopatra's and is no more Roman than that abomination of a god of the Egyptians with the head of a dog."

"Minion he may be, Caesar," Spurius said, tight-lipped, his voice harsh with the fury that he clearly felt. "But that minion has sent me to challenge you to single combat, in the manner of the ancient heroes, to decide this question that lies between you once and for all. The victor will be First Man in Rome, and the vanquished will be carried from the field and will be interred with the highest honor."

"Is he still going on about that?" I heard Statilius murmur. "I thought he would have given up on this by now since the answer has always been the same."

This was the first that men in the ranks had heard that Antonius had challenged Octavian to single combat, despite most of the Centurions knowing, and Octavian was clearly unhappy that Statilius had just made this public, since it would be passing around the fires that night with the speed of a lightning strike.

"Quiet, Statilius," Octavian snapped, his voice low so that only those within a few paces could hear him.

"I'm sorry, Caesar," Statilius mumbled, but Octavian was ignoring him, turning his attention back to Spurius.

"Tell your master that I'll give him his answer in one third of a watch. You'll return then for my reply."

Without waiting for an acknowledgement, Octavian turned on his heel, motioning to Turbo and me. "Come with me," he said, then bounded down the steps of the hippodrome, heading for the *Praetorium*.

"It's unfortunate, but I'm going to have to take steps to ensure that word of this doesn't spread before I'm ready to let it be known," Octavian announced.

"Caesar, too many men heard Spurius give you the challenge. There's no way to keep that from being known by the rest of the army," I said.

"I wasn't talking about today; I was talking about the previous challenges," Octavian replied, shooting Statilius a withering glance, who looked thoroughly miserable. "It doesn't suit my purpose for the men to know that Antonius has been making these ridiculous challenges and I've been refusing them. To that end, I'm afraid that I'm going to have to send Turbo's Century on detached duty, back to Pelusium."

Turbo shot me an alarmed glance, and before I could stop myself, I blurted out, "Caesar, you can't do that!"

Octavian gave me a look that chilled my blood, but his tone was even. "I most certainly can, Pullus. And I'm doing just that. There's a supply convoy that needs to be guarded, and Turbo's Century is going to provide the escort." Softening a bit, he continued, "This isn't a punishment, Pullus. But you know as well as I do how men talk, and we're at a very, very delicate point in this whole drama, and I can't afford to have any muttering about the fires right now. Surely you can understand that."

He was right, and I could not deny it. I looked over at Turbo, whose mouth was hanging open.

I could only give him a shrug. "Caesar's right, Turbo. You're going to have to go, but it's only for the period of time it takes to escort the convoy and come back. Isn't that right, Caesar?"

I turned to Octavian, but he was clearly reluctant to commit himself. "Perhaps," he allowed. "I believe that this matter between Cleopatra and me will be resolved in the next two or three days, but only the gods really know what lies ahead of us."

Knowing this was the best I was going to get, I turned back to Turbo, giving him a false smile. "See? You'll be back in plenty of time to share the booty."

I knew that was at the heart of Turbo's consternation at being ordered away, that he and his men would miss the chance of looting the dead and getting a share of the spoils.

Octavian, hearing my words, immediately realized the problem as well, so he said to Turbo, "Pilus Posterior Turbo, I assure you that any spoils your men would be awarded if they were present for the coming battle will still be there for you and your men when you return."

He gave Turbo Caesar's smile, which was all it took to melt the last of Turbo's doubt.

Saluting both of us, he asked, "With Caesar's permission, Primus Pilus, may I go get the men prepared to get started for the journey? They need to get their gear together and get something to eat before they're ready to march."

"Pullus will have the Legion slaves gather their gear and bring it to them," Octavian replied before I could say anything. "And unfortunately, I need to dispatch that convoy immediately, so I'm afraid you'll have to eat on the march."

Octavian was plainly determined to keep Turbo's men segregated from the others, but I knew better than to keep arguing the point. I told Turbo to go to Diocles, telling him what was needed, since Diocles was the unofficial leader of all the slaves attached to the Legion. Turbo was not happy, but made no complaint, saluting again before leaving. Not being dismissed, I remained there, waiting for Octavian to give me leave to go, but he had other things in mind.

Turning his attention back to Spurius' message, he drummed his fingers on his desk in irritation. "Will that man ever stop in this foolishness?" he asked, though it did not seem to be aimed at anyone in particular. "I, of course, am not going to accede to his demands. That would just be idiocy, with nothing to be gained on my part."

Except the undying devotion and respect of your men, I thought, somehow managing to bite my tongue. I suppose Octavian was right, except that I could not help wondering what his adopted father would have done under the circumstances, although when it came to swordsmanship, there was no comparison between Caesar and Octavian. I had seen Octavian working the stakes; even a middling swordsman would have made short work of him. With someone of my abilities and experience, his life would have been measured by the span of a handful of heartbeats. Antonius, while not nearly as good as I was, would have chopped Octavian into bloody bits, making it understandable why Octavian had no intention of agreeing to meet Antonius. What I did not understand was why he delayed in giving Spurius an answer.

As if reading my thoughts, he looked up at me, asking suddenly, "You do know why I'm not answering his challenge immediately, don't you Pullus?"

"No, I don't, Caesar," I replied frankly.

"Because while it's not overly important to me that the men think of me as a brave man, neither do I want to appear to be a craven coward to them. The rankers are simple creatures," I bristled at this, but he was oblivious to my taking offense, "and to them it matters that I at least appear to think about taking this challenge. If I had declined immediately, oh how those tongues would be wagging about the fires tonight! That's the main reason I have to send Turbo and his Century away after Statilius' unfortunate blunder."

"I apologize, Caesar. I didn't think," Statilius interrupted, but whatever rancor Octavian had held evidently evaporated, because he gave a careless wave.

"Don't worry about it, Statilius, and forgive my harsh words. The jug is broken; it can't be mended now and I know you didn't say it with any malice or thought. It's your nature to blurt whatever comes into your mind. It's almost as if there isn't a brain in between your ears to stop words from coming out," he joked, even if it was a barbed one indeed.

Statilius gave a dutiful laugh, the redness of his ears belying his real feelings. For my part, it made me feel a little better seeing Octavian belittle one of his peers in the same manner he spoke of men like myself.

Octavian, oblivious of all this, continued. "No, I have to make it appear like I'm giving his challenge due consideration, but we all know that it makes no sense for me to accept the challenge. Not to mention the fact that Antonius would skewer me like a pig," he finished frankly.

I was still not sure why I was still there. Octavian solved that mystery when he turned to me. "We'll wait a bit longer, then you're going to go back to the wall and telling Spurius when he comes back that I decline the challenge. You'll tell him that I call on Marcus Antonius to do the honorable thing and fall on his sword now, although I'm not opposed to him committing suicide by other means. There are many ways for Antonius to die, and I leave to him the choice. As far as his wife, I call for Cleopatra to surrender herself and submit to my authority, as the duly elected representative of Rome. Now, repeat it back to me."

I repeated back the gist of his message, not realizing that he had chosen his words very specifically, so that before I finished, he waved me to a stop. "No, Pullus, exactly as I spoke them."

"You mean you want to include the part about Antonius having many ways to die?" I was confused, but he was adamant.

"That's the most important part of the message," he replied, and while I did not understand why, I did as he commanded.

Satisfied, he offered me a cup of wine, then we chatted for a few moments, mostly about the weather and the quality of the wine, until Octavian was satisfied that enough time had passed. Then he sent me on my way to give his reply to Vibius Spurius.

Antonius was now out of options, and his time had come. He made the decision to make an all-out attack, combining the remnants of his navy that was penned up in the royal enclosure with the rest of his land forces. The night before the attack, on the last day of what is now named Julius, he held a feast, toasting his comrades and announcing that he did not expect to live through the next day. Sometime late, around midnight, there was a huge ruckus that we could clearly hear from the hippodrome, but to this day, nobody knows for sure what caused it. It was a cacophony of noise, music playing, men and women shouting as if at a great revel, the sound moving through the streets of Alexandria, making us think there was some impromptu parade. Just as quickly, and mysteriously, the noise stopped, not fading away but just coming to an abrupt silence as if on some unseen signal. It was not until days later that the story that is now the accepted version was uttered, that the sound was the result of Dionysus, the god whom Antonius claimed to be an incarnation of, with Cleopatra playing Aphrodite, deserting not only the city of Alexandria, but Antonius as well. I do not know exactly where it came from, except that I can assure you, gentle reader, that it almost undoubtedly started at some Legionary fire one evening. Whether or not it was the god deserting the city, Antonius' cause, along with the man himself, were doomed.

The battle the next morning, if that is what it can be called, was merely confirmation of that fact. We were roused before dawn, deserters having warned us that Antonius was planning on his final attack that morning, and the men needed no urging to make their preparations. All through the hippodrome and camp, there was a feeling of anticipation, every man knowing that this was the final battle that would decide all. For men like Vellusius, Scribonius, and for me, this was an even longer road, one that started with Caesar crossing the Rubicon. My first trip to Egypt with Caesar and the 6th, the subsequent fight against the Pontics, and the forays with Antonius into Parthia and Armenia aside, the last 19 years, more than half of the time we had spent in the army, had been facing fellow Romans in one form or another. This upcoming battle would end all of that, for there were no other rivals to Octavian left standing. Looking back, I believe that it was this idea, that peace was finally at hand, that contributed to my desire to retire and live out the rest of my days without a sword in my hand. I still went through my normal pre-battle rituals, just like all the men did, then we were ready to march out of the hippodrome. Filing out in Legion order, we formed up in the clear space between the hippodrome and the houses hard up against the city wall. The 10th, in what I was told by Octavian was in homage to Caesar, formed up on the right, the spot that we almost always occupied in battle. We could hear the *bucina* of Antonius' army sounding the various calls that signaled their approach, while our Centurions walked up and down in front of their respective Centuries, reminding the men of all the various things they would have to remember when it is not so easy to do.

"Remember to push off when you hear the whistle for the relief! Plautus, that means you, you stupid bastard!"

"Keep your spacing, boys! Don't be the one who leaves a gap that gets your comrade killed!"

"A gold denarius to the first man to kill five of the enemy!"

These were the things being said up and down the line. Octavian had ordered us into a *triplex acies,* perhaps because his adoptive father had favored this above all other formations. This was awkward for the 10th, since we were now one Cohort short because of the loss of the Third, and I hoped that the men of the third line, which would be just the Eighth and Ninth, instead of the Seventh along with them, would not be needed. Trebellius' Fifth was now on the far left of the first line of the 10th, but I had every confidence in the Quintus Pilus Prior and his men. Scribonius and his Second were in their normal spot next to us, and I looked over at my friend, giving him a wave and a grin, which he returned before facing back to the front. My only source of nervousness came from the knowledge that this would Gaius' first time as Optio of a Cohort in the first line. While he had been in the Second for his time in the Legion up until his promotion, being a ranker with nothing to worry about other than listening for the whistle and staying alive is completely different from being an Optio. I would have been much more worried if the men of the 10th had been raw boys, but I still offered up a prayer for his safety.

"There they are, boys!"

The shout rang across the ranks, and I turned to see the leading files of Antonius' men finally emerge from the clutter and shadows of the buildings next to the wall. I watched them advance, their spacing what it was supposed to be, in perfect step as they closed with us. Yet there was something about them that told me that their hearts were not in it. Perhaps it was in the slight slump in their shoulders, or the way the some men dragged their feet more than normal, churning up more dust than was usual for this number of men. I glanced over at Scribonius, who turned to look at me, a slight smile on his face.

"I don't think this is going to take long," he called to me, and I nodded in response, sure that he was right.

We waited for them to get aligned on a small rise of ground, which took them a bit of time, another sign that the men under Antonius were less than eager to cross swords with us. Men were beginning to shift nervously about, fingers tapping on shields while they waited for the *cornu* call that would unleash them into a frenzied assault. As it usually happens in such encounters, Antonius being the aggressor, we waited on him to make the first move yet there was no such on the part of Antonius. We could see him clearly, wearing his gold and silver armor, his *paludamentum* swirling in the air as he galloped his horse along the line, heading towards the end closest to the harbor, where he pulled up. Watching him, I could see that he was not facing us, instead staring out to the harbor. I turned to look, but my vision was blocked so I could not see what he was waiting for. What we learned later was that he was watching for the beginning of the naval portion of his planned attack, intending to coordinate his assault with his ships. Because of our position, what we could not see were his ships rowing out to face those of Octavian, who had lined up to face them. However, before they closed, on some signal, they raised their oars in a signal of surrender. Instead of fighting, the two sides then joined forces, after a shouted discussion by the ranking *navarch* from each side. Turning about, the now-combined fleet went sweeping into the larger harbor, heading for the city. Seeing this, the Antonian cavalry immediately turned about, frantically whipping their mounts to flee back into the city. We did not know why it happened; all we saw were the fleeing horsemen, and knew that we could not wait for a command at that point. This was the moment to attack, so I turned to Valerius and ordered him to sound the charge.

I drew my sword, roaring to the men, "Let's end this now! Follow me!"

Without looking back, I went running at the line of Antonian infantry.

This last gasp of Marcus Antonius was the most farcical, lopsided, and anticlimactic battle I, or any of the men of the 10th Legion, ever participated in. Even before we reached the first rank of Antonians, the rearmost men began melting away, turning to run before we even impacted. The men in front, sensing their comrades deserting them, were already beginning their own flight when we slammed into them. At first, our men did as they would have against any enemy, cutting men down, most of them with thrusts to the back, but after just a few moments, they lost their stomach for killing men who were making no real attempt to fight back. Instead, they started using the flat side of their swords, knocking men down or perhaps giving them a kick to sweep them off their feet. Antonius, seeing the utter collapse happening around him, did not stay long either, turning to gallop off with a few of his bodyguards and other retainers. The confusion and chaos was total, both sides intermingling, the cohesion breaking down when men spied friends in the mass of Antonians, breaking ranks to run to their aid. Some men, their bloodlust unleashed, were heedless to the cries of their comrades to spare friends on the other side, prompting blows, and in a couple cases, worse between Legionaries on the same side. Centurions and Optios were running about, blowing their whistles or shouting as they grabbed men by the back of the harness to pull them apart. I spotted Spurius, and like I had promised, I made my way to him where we clasped arms briefly.

"This is a fucking mess!" He had to shout to be heard as some of the more stubborn Antonians were trying to put up a fight, while others cried out for mercy, making it extremely confusing to tell who was willing to fight and who wasn't.

"Stick with me," I told him. "I need to get this sorted out."

I called to Silva, ordering him to take the standard back to our original position, then had Valerius sound the recall, and he blasted the signal over and over, but to no avail. Men were either too carried away engaging with the diehards, or looking for friends, ignoring both the *cornu* and the shouts of their Centurions and Optios. I watched for several moments, my anger growing at the lack of discipline, frustrated with the Centurions for clearly being unable to rein the men in.

"Pluto's cock," I snarled.

Turning to Spurius, I pointed to the rear. "Go on back, and tell whoever asks you that you're under my protection. Tell them I'm holding you for ransom; that way they'll leave you alone."

A look of alarm crossed his face. "You're not planning on doing that, are you?"

"Maybe." I grinned. "It depends on what kind of mood I'm in after I sort this out."

Ignoring his spluttered protests, I headed for the swirling dust and mass of men, and then just began grabbing those that I recognized as belonging to the 10th.

"Get to the standard!" I would tell them, seeing their eyes widen at the sight of their Primus Pilus snarling at them.

Heading for the First Cohort, I found Balbus thrashing a man with his *vitus,* the man whimpering, trying to dodge and get out of the way.

"You stupid bastard, get on the standard or I'll flay you," Balbus was roaring.

"I'm trying, Pilus Posterior, but you keep hitting me," the man wailed.

Balbus then relented in his thrashing, allowing the man to scamper back to our position, his arms and one side of his face striped from the blows.

"Get your *signifer* out of here and back to the line. Maybe they'll follow him," I ordered Balbus, who seemed at as much of a loss as I was.

I went to find Laetus, Celadus, and the other Centurions of the First to give the same orders. I passed by a small group, probably one tent section, of Antonians, their backs to each other and their shields up, looking over the rim at my men, who had surrounded them. Nobody was fighting; they were just standing there looking at each other, both sides waiting for the other to make a move. Seeing a Sergeant from Macrianus' Century, apparently the ranking man, I called to him.

"Fulvius, either fuck those men or fight them, but either way, do something. You need to get back on the standard."

"You heard the Primus Pilus, boys," Fulvius called to the Antonians. "We don't want to kill you, but we will if we have to because he's telling us we have to get back on the standard. So what's it going to be?"

I saw the eyes of the men shifting to each other behind their shields, and I understood that this was a situation where no man wanted to be the first to throw down his sword. This could last for some time, so not wanting to waste any more time, I strode over, pushed my way through my men to walk up to one of the men, who stared at me wide-eyed at my approach. I had sheathed my sword, but still carried my *vitus*, not having to drop it to pick up a shield since there was no real fighting going on, and I used it to rap on the rim of the man's shield.

"You and I both know that you don't want to die here," I told the man, speaking loudly enough so they all could hear. "And you can see that the only men being hurt or killed are the ones putting up a fight. So do us all a favor, drop your weapons, and make your way to the rear." I jerked my thumb over my shoulder, but still nobody moved.

"Now!" I roared.

Just as I suspected, the habit of obedience overcame whatever fear they had, the clanging of their swords as they dropped them and their shields together all I needed to hear. Without waiting, I resumed my original chore of finding the Centurions. As I walked, I continued to grab men by whatever purchase I could make, yanking them from what they were doing. In one case, one of my men was engaged with what I assumed to be an Antonian, but on getting closer, I saw that it was two of my own men, from the same section of the Second Century. They were not fighting with swords; they had sheathed them and dropped their shields to bash each other with their fists. One had blood streaming from his nose, the other clearly was going to have a black eye. Dropping my *vitus,* I reached out, grabbed both of them by the necks of their mail shirts, then bashed their heads together, shaking both of them like a dog shakes a rat.

I was still strong enough to lift both men off the ground, and I did so as I yelled at them, "What are you two idiots doing?"

Shaking their heads clear, they both began babbling while pointing at each other, making it difficult to tell exactly what, but I gathered that it had something to do with a woman, and that the feud had been simmering for some time. Shaking my head in disgust, I growled at them to stop the nonsense and get back to their spot in line. Moving on, I found other Centurions, and slowly order began to be restored. However, it was not before one man, thinking that I was another ranker trying to cut in on his looting of a dead Antonian body, one of the few men who had put up a fight, reacted to my grabbing of his harness by lashing out with a fist. I was quick enough to dodge the blow, while he was not so lucky, and I essentially kicked him all the way back to our lines. Finally, the men were formed back up in their original spots, the Antonians having fled or surrendered, leaving a surprisingly small number of dead and wounded behind. The final battle between Marcus Antonius and Octavian was over. All that was left was the capture of Antonius, and more importantly to Octavian, Cleopatra, but they had other plans.

We spent the rest of the day taking the parole of the men of Antonius' army, which is essentially a nightmare of paperwork, since two copies of each man's parole had to be recorded. That first day, however, paroles were taken by Century, with each Centurion being the only man actually to sign a document. After that, the men were disarmed before they were allowed to return to their own camp, having no room for them at the hippodrome. While this was being done, men from our army were going about the ranks of the Antonians looking for friends or relatives, checking to see whether they were safe. For the men of the second *dilectus*, they had seen this played out before, but for men of the replacement draft after the first Parthian campaign, this was a new experience. It was brought home to me again how much time we had spent fighting each other, yet I truly believed that this was going to be the last time we would do so, at least during my career. There was no real rival to Octavian among the Romans of his, or any class for that matter, with the possible exception of Marcus Agrippa. However, Agrippa was as loyal to Octavian as it is possible for a man to be, so Rome lay before Octavian like a beckoning virgin, to be enjoyed at his pleasure.

Meanwhile, Antonius had retreated back to the royal palace. It would be learned from questioning the palace slaves afterward, he strode in shouting that he had been betrayed by Cleopatra. The queen, hearing the commotion and fearing that somehow Antonius had learned of her secret dealings with Octavian, ran to hide herself inside the tomb she was preparing before sending one of her servants out to face Antonius, who informed him that Cleopatra had already killed herself. It was at that moment I believe the *numen* that had inhabited the body of Marcus Antonius fled as well, leaving Antonius the Roman behind. Knowing that all was lost, and learning that his only reason for living was now dead, or so he believed, Antonius finally became Roman again by falling on his sword. Unfortunately, he botched the job, piercing his bowels instead of his heart, and was in horrible agony, begging anyone who ventured near the couch where he had fallen to put him out of his misery. Rats that they were, they scurried away rather than do the right thing and help ease him on his way. Cleopatra, hearing the commotion, sent one of her maids to investigate, learning what happened from the maid. Stricken with remorse, she ordered her maids to bring Antonius to her, since the eunuchs and male palace servants were making themselves scarce. The two women somehow managed to drag the wounded man to the crypt, which must have been excruciating for him, then tied a rope around his chest. They heaved his body up through the small hole that was left in the crypt to allow passage, and the terrified slaves later told how

Antonius' agonized screams could be heard almost the entire length of the palace. It was during this process that Cleopatra finally seemed to realize that she truly loved Antonius, leaning down out of the hole with outstretched arms, while Antonius did likewise, both of them reaching for each other in their last thirds of a watch.

The women managed to get Antonius into the crypt, where they tried to make him comfortable, then waited for what was to come next. While they hid inside the crypt, one of the few Antonians of the Brundisium Cohorts remaining, a man by the name of Dercetaeus, brought the bloody sword that had pierced Antonius' bowels to Octavian as proof that he was dead. From one of Diocles' contacts in the *Praetorium,* we learned that Octavian locked himself away in his quarters, crying for a full third of a watch. I was shocked when I heard it, and in fact did not believe, but Diocles insisted that his source was extremely reliable and would not exaggerate. I talked about it with Scribonius, who unlike me, not only found it easy to believe, but he was sure that it happened as had been described.

"He and Antonius have been intertwined for more than ten years. They're related both by marriage and blood. Octavian's sister was married to the man, and she loved him deeply from everything I've heard."

I understood that, but I could only recall all the acrimony and hatred they had shown each other, making it seem to me that the fall of such a bitter enemy would be cause for celebration, not anguish.

"Think about it this way," Scribonius continued. "For almost as long as any of us can remember, Octavian has been striving to come out on top over Antonius, and now that moment has arrived. It has to be very strange now to be done with it all."

I answered with a shrug, still not seeing why Octavian was so worked up, but I did not feel like arguing. When he regained his composure, Octavian sent one of his aides, an *equites* named Proculeius to treat with Cleopatra, who was still stuffed in her crypt. The problem was that nobody who was questioned knew exactly where the tomb was located in the palace, and it took Proculeius a fair amount of time to find the spot. When he did discover it, he saw immediately that there was no way to get in a position to be face to face with Cleopatra, since the hole in the wall was too high for him to jump and pull himself through, besides which Cleopatra warned him that if his head popped through the hole it would be chopped off. This convinced Proculeius to conduct his negotiations with the wall of the tomb between him and Cleopatra, whereupon he told the queen all the gentle lies that he had been instructed to by Octavian. Octavian's goal was straightforward; take Cleopatra captive to display in his triumphal parade in Rome. If he was right about knowing the location of the treasury, and I believed that he did, he did not need her to disclose it. What he wanted, and in fact needed, was her humiliation, the sight of her draped in chains just like so many of Rome's enemies in the past, in front of a jeering mob of people. I for one would have liked nothing better, but Cleopatra was as wily an enemy as had ever faced Rome, with the possible exception of Mithridates, at least from the stories I was told. Proculeius and Cleopatra talked for more than another third of a watch, but the queen did not show any inclination to put herself into Octavian's hands. Frustrated, Proculeius left to return to Octavian, taking careful note on how to get back to the tomb. After discussing matters, Octavian sent both Gallus and

Proculeius, but as usual, Octavian had something devious in mind.

Proculeius carried with him a scaling ladder, and did not announce his presence to Cleopatra when he and Gallius arrived at the tomb. Gallius began talking to Cleopatra, making the same false promises that Proculeius had, but while he did so, Proculeius quietly set the ladder against the wall underneath the hole. While the queen was distracted, Proculeius scaled the ladder, then dropped through the hole, running over to where Cleopatra was standing with her ear to the door, listening to Gallius talk. Her two women saw him, shouting a warning, whereupon she tried to draw her dagger to plunge it into her breast, but Proculeius was too quick for her, seizing her wrist. Admonishing her for trying to kill herself before Octavian could show his clemency and kindness, he searched her thoroughly, while her maids wailed and shrieked in despair.

With Cleopatra secured, Octavian turned his attention to the city of Alexandria, and we were ordered to form up late in the afternoon. We entered through the Canopus Gate, in a procession designed to awe the natives, which judging from their expressions, is exactly what we did. Octavian, however, did not want to completely terrify the inhabitants, so he had the philosopher Areius, one of Alexandria's most notable inhabitants, accompany him at the head of the procession. Marching down the Canopic Way, headed for the gymnasium, I took a good look around. The people were clearly terrified, waiting to see whether Octavian would unleash us to ravage the city, but we had already been told beforehand that this would not be happening.

I was more interested in the city itself, and I was happy to see no sign of the damage we had inflicted with

Caesar 18 years before. I had always felt badly about what we had done, although at the time there was little choice, because Alexandria is a truly beautiful city. I know that for a Roman to say such a thing is almost blasphemy, but I consider Alexandria more pleasing to the eye than Rome. The boulevard was as wide as I remembered it, still well swept and clean, the curbs lined with people eying us silently while we marched by, the only real sound the slapping of the hobnails of our boots against the paving stones.

The faces of the people, some brown, some black, but most of them the olive hue that bespoke their Macedonian blood, were neither hostile nor were they welcoming and there were no cheers greeting our passage. They were waiting and watching to see what happened, but I knew from bitter experience how dangerous these people could be when roused, and I hoped that Octavian kept the lessons that Caesar had learned in mind. Octavian certainly seemed to be thinking the same thing, explaining the presence of Areius, and when we arrived at the gymnasium, the men were ordered to wait in formation while Octavian entered, along with all of the Primi Pili. We filed in behind him and Areius, seeing that the building was packed with people sitting in the wooden tiers of seats. These Alexandrians were visibly afraid, and on Octavian's entrance, they prostrated themselves in the same manner that they did before Cleopatra. Mounting the rostra to face the audience, he said nothing for several moments. When he spoke, it was in flawless Greek, and he spoke so rapidly that it was hard to keep up, though I picked up the essentials. He assured the people that there would be no reprisals against the citizens of the city, immediately causing a stir of exhaled breath that sounded like a small wind had whipped up. Going further, he promised that the men assembled outside would not go on a rampage to sack the city. At this, their relief was even more expressive, some of the citizens even letting out a cheer for Octavian. He did this, he said, for the memory of Alexander, and because he was moved by the beauty of the city itself. Areius stepped closer to him, whispered something in his ear, to which Octavian listened before gravely nodding his head. Returning his attention back to the crowd, Octavian called out the names of a number of Macedonian nobles. I watched the stirring in the crowd, their fellow citizens betraying their presence among them by turning to look at the man whose name had just been called, whether they wanted them to or not. One by one the men stood then came forward, some clearly very reluctant. I could tell from their clothing and the peculiar objects adorning their bodies, in the form of a hat, or tunic with large sleeves that they were badges of office. Once the men were assembled before Octavian, some trying not to show any fear while others visibly quaked, the young Caesar surveyed them, his face giving nothing away. Then, with a sudden smile, he announced in a loud voice that thanks to the intercession of Areius, he was pardoning these men for their work for Cleopatra. The gymnasium erupted in cheers, while one of the men fainted dead away, causing snickers from the Primi Pili, myself included. After a few more remarks about what the next few days would hold, Octavian turned, signaling to us to follow him out of the gymnasium.

"What about Cleopatra?" Someone shouted the question, which was clearly picked up by others, but Octavian ignored the cries and continued to exit.

It was the smart thing to do, since I did not think that the people would take too well to what Octavian had in store for the captive queen, but Octavian was not the only one with conjurer's tricks.

The queen was allowed to stay inside her crypt, after the space was thoroughly searched for any tools that could be used to take her life. She was also under guard, of course, while she and her two maids prepared Antonius' body for her version of the underworld. The process that Egyptians use to prepare a corpse, which they call embalming, is a gruesome and disgusting process, and in my opinion was no fit way for Marcus Antonius to end. My feeling was shared by a number of the Centurions, some going as far as to bring it up with Octavian. His explanation was that he wanted to keep Cleopatra calm, and giving in to her on this was simply the most expedient way to ensure her cooperation. On the surface, I could see this made sense, but I suspect that Octavian had a deeper motive than just soothing Cleopatra. I think that by allowing Marcus Antonius' body to be defiled in such a manner, Octavian was reinforcing the belief that Antonius the Roman no longer existed, further securing his own status as First Man in Rome. Whatever his reasons, Cleopatra was secure in her crypt, while Octavian went on tying up loose ends. One of those ends was Antyllus, Antonius' oldest son by Fulvia, who had just reached his majority in a ceremony conducted jointly for he and Caesarion, who at that point was missing. Antyllus' tutor, Theodorus was his name, betrayed the youth for a paltry sum of money and the boy was seized by the provosts. He was immediately put to death, his head being chopped off, but during his execution, a fair-sized ruby that had hung on a chain around his neck disappeared. It was discovered on the person of none other than Theodorus, for which he was crucified, but that was a few days later.

Once Antonius' body was prepared, Cleopatra was allowed to inter her husband and father of her children, which she did with all the pomp and ceremony that the Egyptian throne can produce. She went into mourning, in the Egyptian style, which calls for the beating of the breasts until the blood flows, along with the pulling of hair and tearing of garments, and from all reports, her grief appeared to be genuine. I was not convinced, however; I had seen too much with Cleopatra to believe that her tears were for anyone but herself. She played Antonius for a fool for more than ten years, and as far as I was concerned was using his corpse as a prop to try to soften Octavian's heart. Finally, Octavian went to visit the queen herself, intent on soothing her fears and convincing her that her best interests lay in going along with what Octavian had planned for her and Egypt. All of which was a lie, of course. He was going to strip Egypt as clean as any vulture would strip a carcass in the desert, while she would end up being strangled in the Tullianum, though only after enduring the most public humiliation possible. I do not know what was said exactly, since Octavian went alone to see her. She had been allowed at this point to leave her crypt and had retired to her own personal chambers, attended only by her closest slaves and only after they were thoroughly searched. The men assigned to guard her all relayed how horrific she looked by this time, having lost even more weight, the wounds on her breasts suppurating and having to be bound, with patches of hair missing from where she pulled it out. This was what greeted Octavian when he went to visit her, and I have no doubt that she tried every trick she knew to pull Octavian under her spell. However, Octavian was made of a different metal than Antonius; of all the people she could have chosen to try and seduce, even at her best Octavian would have been the last one to succumb. Where Antonius was ruled by his passions, Octavian, from everything I had seen, was ruled by his head. Where Antonius was fire, Octavian was ice, and not even the queen of Egypt could melt that ice. Given all that transpired from that meeting, I believe that despite his best efforts to disguise his coldness, Cleopatra saw through his veneer of kindness and sympathy, only after that meeting realizing that she was truly doomed. However, while Cleopatra was not fooled by Octavian, the guileful queen succeeded in tricking Octavian into thinking that she had put all thoughts of suicide from her mind. He left the interview convinced that she accepted his fiction that he intended no harm to her, that she would be treated as an honored guest of Rome, and that her treasure and son were safe from harm. He was about to learn just how wrong he had been.

We received word that the bulk of the army, including the 10th, would be marching again, back through Syria to Greece, where we would go into winter quarters, the last for the men of the second *dilectus*. One of Octavian's staff, Cornelius Dolabella, like many men, had a soft spot in his heart for the queen, so he warned her that a few days after Octavian and the army departed, she and her small children were to be transported to Rome. Knowing that the time was at hand, she somehow smuggled in an asp, a deadly snake whose venom is always fatal, although it can take some time to die. Reconstructing matters later, there was a rumor that a farmer who often brought supplies to the queen smuggled the serpent inside a basket of figs, but I saw the basket and there is no way that a snake the size of that asp could have fit inside. I believe that this version started because an overturned basket of figs was found next to the queen afterwards, but however it happened, she was successful. I happened to be in the *Praetorium* getting orders from Octavian and Statilius when a messenger arrived, bearing a scroll. Walking straight to Octavian, he announced that he bore a message from the queen.

Taking the message, Octavian, looking very pleased with himself, heaved a sigh. "I wonder what she wants this time? To make sure that she has the same house she occupied the last time she was in Rome, I'll bet."

"Fat chance of that," Statilius laughed, while Octavian began to read the contents of the scroll.

I was watching his face as his eyes scanned the words, the smile melting off of his face, followed by all the blood draining away, looking as if some invisible creature had just sucked every drop out of his body. His fingers went nerveless, dropping the scroll on the ground, causing Statilius to start in surprise.

"Caesar, you're getting clumsy," he began as he reached down to pick up the scroll.

It was only when he had straightened that he looked into Octavian's face, and a look of alarm passed over his own.

"What is it?"

Ignoring Statilius, Octavian shook his head as if trying to waken from a dream, then snapped at the messenger, "How long ago did you receive this message?"

"Just a few moments ago, Caesar."

Without saying another word, he whirled, then ran out the door, leaving everyone standing gaping in astonishment. Statilius, having retrieved the scroll, opened it and read it.

"Pluto's cock," he gasped. "No wonder he bolted out of here. This," he waved the scroll, "is a suicide note."

And so it was; Cleopatra was still alive when Octavian came rushing to her, but was too far gone for anything to be done except watch her die. For perhaps the first and only time in his life, Octavian had been outfoxed, by a woman at that. Not surprisingly, he was furious at being thwarted. He took his anger out on Caesarion, whose whereabouts were betrayed by his tutor, much in the same manner as Antyllus. The poor boy was secretly executed, far away from the eyes of the army, who might have revolted if they had seen the spitting image of Caesar treated in such a manner. I was told of this development by Octavian himself, which I suspect was a test of loyalty as much as anything else. It also turned out that Caesar had been extremely accurate in his description of the location of the treasury of Egypt, as in a stroke, all of the money problems, not just of the army, but of the Republic itself were solved. We went from a cash-strapped Republic to being awash in funds, and before we left on our return march, Octavian announced to the army that all bonuses would be paid in the amounts previously promised, to both current and former Legionaries who had yet to receive their payments. Not surprisingly, this cheered the men immensely, making up for their disgruntlement at not having an opportunity to plunder Alexandria. The paroled Antonian men were allowed to go home, and were even allowed to take their swords with them, along with a sum of 250 sesterces, in exchange for their oath to cause no further trouble. I did not ransom Spurius; I had never intended to, but I did have some fun at his expense for a few days. Other men of the upper classes were not so lucky, many of their captors taking the opportunity to squeeze the hapless men for every sesterce possible.

In the few days that we had before we returned, I took Scribonius, Balbus, and Gaius about the city, pointing out the places where we had fought, despite it being hard sometimes to find the spots, since the Alexandrians had completely rebuilt the area, except for the great library, one wing of which was still a blackened ruin. We walked the Heptastadion, while I recounted the bitter fighting that had taken place, and how Caesar had been forced to swim for his life, with his *paludamentum* clenched between his teeth as he did so. These were all tales they had heard before, but I like to think that hearing it from someone who was there, who could describe the day, how the weather had been, the things men had said, made it come alive to them. I described the wells that we had dug, when the men of the 28th Legion had almost mutinied, and how Gaius Tetarfenus and his brother took matters into their own hands to help quell the mutiny by removing one of the ringleaders. I was reminded by Scribonius that Tetarfenus, who I had brought into the 10th during the second *dilectus*, had done the same on the Campus Martius, which had cost him his life, and Nasica's honor.

"He always was hard-headed," I agreed. "But he was a good man nonetheless."

The royal palace and enclosure was off-limits to most of the men, but I had received special dispensation from Octavian, so I took my friends about, showing them where we spent nine months before taking them to the throne room, taking pleasure in seeing their jaws drop at the opulence. Despite being stripped of many of the more valuable items, it was still a stunning sight.

"No wonder we don't have money troubles anymore," Scribonius said, while Gaius whistled.

"If this is just one room, I can't imagine how much there all is."

"And we couldn't get our hands on any of it," Balbus said, his tone resentful as he fingered a chair inlaid with gold and ivory.

"What do you call the bonuses we're going to be paid?"

I wanted to steer this conversation away from dangerous waters.

"That's just what we're owed," Balbus grunted. "I'm talking about the extra gravy."

I rapped his knuckles hard with my *vitus* when he tried to filch what looked like a small gem-encrusted thimble, causing him to yelp in pain.

"What did you do that for?" He rubbed his knuckles as he glared at me.

"You know damn well why," I countered. "And you're going to keep your hands to yourself. I don't want to explain to Caesar how one of my Centurions ended up with a bauble that was last seen in Cleopatra's palace."

"Who would miss it?" he grumbled. "She's dead. She's not going to complain."

"Do you have any doubt that Caesar has counted every bauble in this palace?" Scribonius asked Balbus. "He leaves this stuff out and about precisely because he knows it will be tempting and he wants to know if he can trust his men."

He looked directly at me as he finished, "Particularly those who he plans on giving more responsibility to."

Balbus' mouth tightened, and he did not reply, but he kept his hands to himself the rest of the tour. Deciding that it would not be smart to linger and continue putting his willpower to the test, we returned to the camp at the hippodrome.

Leaving Alexandria behind with a garrison of two Legions, we retraced our steps back to the east, following the coast as it turned north through Syria. Crossing the barren Sinai, even in early autumn, was still a trying ordeal, but we managed to make it through with just a few mules lost. Every step brought me closer to Miriam, the thought giving me an energy that I thought was lost to me forever. The men were in high spirits as well, buoyed by their own thoughts of the bonuses that were now less than a year away. We would arrive back at Nicopolis in early November, if all went well, then we would have the routine of winter quarters, our final lustration ceremony, followed by our mustering out in April of the next year. The days passed, blurring one into the other, the gods once more blessing our march with perfect weather and no obstacles over and above those that normally occur in such an endeavor. Sometimes a wheel would crack, or a mule would go lame. Occasionally, a man would suddenly be stricken with some illness, and we even had two men come down with a fever that proved fatal, but none of that was out of the ordinary. There were only two days of storms bad enough to halt our progress, forcing us to make camp early.

Rolling down the Via Egnatia, we cut across the Peloponnese, to arrive in Nicopolis on the Kalends of November, a bit earlier than expected. Our winter quarters were in good repair, other than needing to be swept out and the mice chased away. I hurried the men through the process of unpacking the mules and transferring their baggage to their huts, while sending Diocles to let Miriam know that I had arrived. My reunion with Miriam was as pleasant as I had dreamed, and I was happy to see that she seemed to have finally accepted the idea that we would be with the army for the next five years, albeit in a different capacity. Iras was extremely happy as well, which I found puzzling, since I could not imagine that she was as happy to see me as Miriam had been. It was not until the next morning that I discovered the cause, when I was awakened by a whispered conversation just outside the door to our bedroom. Rising carefully in order to avoid disturbing Miriam, I tiptoed to the door, freezing when I heard the sound of a man's voice. It was not the high-pitched whisper of Agis, but a lower tone that caused me to grab my sword hanging from the end of the bed. Crossing to the door, I took a breath before I whipped the door open, catching a flurry of movement in the dim pre-dawn light. I saw two figures moving quickly apart, recognizing by the shape and size that one of them was Iras, while the other was much taller and broader through the shoulders than Agis. As I stepped into the outer room, the larger figure moved towards the front door, clearly trying to escape.

"Stop!" I roared, though I am not sure why, since letting him go would have been the smart thing to do.

Much to my surprise, the figure froze in place, and I stood there for a moment, unsure what to do next. Glancing over at Iras, who was standing a few feet away, I ordered her to light a lamp.

"Master, it's not what you think," she whispered, as I heard a commotion behind me in the bedroom. Miriam had obviously been awakened by my shout, which did not help my mood.

"I don't know what I think right now," I snapped. "But I will, as soon as you light that lamp."

The figure made a move, so I pointed my sword at him, but I kept my voice low. "You'd be much safer if you don't shift about like that. It's liable to make me nervous, and I'm pretty handy with this thing."

"I know; you've taught me everything I know about how to use one." I froze at the sound of the voice, scarcely believing my ears, and my confusion could not have been any greater.

"Gaius?" I gasped. "What by the balls of Cerberus are you doing in my house before dawn?"

"What do you think he is doing?"

Whirling about, I saw Miriam with a shawl wrapped about her shoulders, just as the flame on the lamp flickered to life.

"I don't know. That's why I asked," I replied, more bewildered than angry now.

"I was . . . visiting," Gaius said lamely.

"Visiting?" I echoed, still not understanding. "Then why did you come so early? And why didn't you wait until we were awake at least instead of trying to sneak out?"

There was a long silence as Gaius suddenly became interested in the floor, while Iras studied the lamp, neither looking in a direction that could be construed as anywhere near each other. That is when it all fell into place.

"Because you weren't coming to visit us," I said slowly.

In answer, Gaius slowly shook his head, giving a shrug that seemed to say more than any words he could have uttered. I whirled about to glare at Miriam, who was giving me an innocent look.

"You knew about this?"

To her credit, she did not shrink, just gave a slight nod. "Yes, I knew," was all she said.

"How long has this been going on?"

"Since they arrived in Nicopolis," Gaius spoke up, but he was not through with the surprises. "But I've been in love with her since the night we met."

"*What*?" I was flabbergasted, my jaw feeling like it would drop to the floor. "But the first night you met, she was trying to kill us!"

"Because she had to," he said defensively, but my mind was still struggling to comprehend all that was happening.

"Love? *Love*?" I repeated the word, looking over to Iras, who nodded shyly.

Now that the secret was out, she only had eyes for Gaius, and when I turned my attention back to Gaius, I saw him gazing back at her like a moonstruck calf.

"Love," I said disgustedly, shaking my head.

"Yes, love." Miriam spoke, her voice firm. "You supposedly know the meaning of the word, Titus Pullus, since you tell me that you love me all the time."

"But that's different," I protested, knowing as the words came out of my mouth the reaction it would get.

"Why is it different?" Gaius demanded. "I love Iras, and she loves me. What more matters?"

"You mean, other than the fact that she's a slave? That you can't be married?"

"I'm well aware of that, Uncle," Gaius replied sharply. "But that doesn't mean we can't be happy."

"That's exactly what it means, boy," I sighed, but I also knew a hopeless cause when I saw it. We stood there in awkward silence for several moments before I finally spoke. "Well," I grumbled. "You might as well kiss her goodbye. Then we can all go back to bed and get some sleep before it's time to get up. We'll talk about this more in the morning."

Gaius opened his mouth, looking like he wanted to protest, but he took a look at my face, and just gave an abrupt nod. Not waiting to see the young couple embrace, I turned to stalk back into the bedroom, feeling foolish now with a sword in my hand.

"Why didn't you tell me about this?" I asked Miriam the next morning, but if I was expecting her to act repentant in any way, she was not showing it.

"Because I knew you would not take it well," she replied.

"How am I supposed to take it? The girl is my property, and he's my nephew."

"What can it hurt? They are young, Titus Pullus, and they are in love."

"What can it hurt?" I echoed. "It can hurt plenty, and it can hurt both of them. What end does Gaius see for this . . . distraction?"

"Distraction? It is no distraction! They say they are in love and I believe them. He is even talking of marriage."

This was even worse than I thought. "He can't marry her! She's a slave, and he's in the army." I made no attempt to hide my alarm at this development.

"It seems to me that he can marry whoever he wants," she said mildly.

I shook my head in irritation. "You don't understand our ways. Gaius could only marry Iras if his father, as *paterfamilias,* gives his consent."

"And you are not his father; you are his uncle. So I suggest that you let this be or you will just drive them together."

It was only then that an idea that had been slowly forming in my mind became clear.

I blurted it out, as usual without thinking it through. "But I plan on adopting Gaius and making him my heir so that he will be an *equites*."

Miriam looked like she had been slapped, which puzzled me, at least until she spoke. "And what of our children? If you have a son, then what of him?"

I had not been expecting that, although looking back I do not know why it should have been a surprise. I had given up on the idea of having children, simply because after Miriam's loss of our baby, she had not become pregnant again, through no lack of trying. Even with all of my frequent absences, it seemed to me that if she could have gotten pregnant, she would have.

"I hadn't thought about that," I said slowly, and she looked even more hurt.

"You have given no thought to having children?"

"It's not that," I said hastily. "It's just that, since you lost the baby . . ." My voice trailed off, since it was a painful memory, although not nearly as hurtful to me as it was to her.

Still, her voice was steady as she replied, "I plan on having children with you, Titus Pullus. I make offerings every day, not just to my gods, but to yours as well. So I have not given up hope. But," she turned her mind back to the matter at hand. "You did not answer my question. If we have a son, and you have named Gaius your heir, what happens to our son?"

"I'll have to think about that," I admitted.

"And what of Gaius' father? Surely he would not consent to having his son taken away from him in such a manner."

I started to explain the Roman view on adoption, how it is a very common thing, and how men were happy to allow sons to be adopted if it would advance the son's status and fortunes, but there was no time. Promising to explain later, I made myself ready to go to camp.

We settled into the winter routine, checking gear back into stores, carefully greasing and wrapping the artillery pieces, exchanging unserviceable pieces of equipment, all of which had a wax tablet or scroll that had to accompany it. Little did I know that as much paperwork as there was in the army at that point, under Octavian's reforms this was minuscule compared to what was to come. Speaking of Octavian, he had returned to Rome to a hero's welcome, the accolades heaped upon his brow exceeding even his adopted father's in number and accrued glory. The most important action he took was the closing of the doors to the temple of Janus, signaling the end of war, at long last. Those doors had been open for the last twenty-plus years, telling all of Rome's citizens that the Republic was at war, and it must have been quite a moment for Octavian finally to be able to close the doors at long last. The members of the Senate fell all over themselves getting into line to see who could proclaim the most loudly and eloquently all of the great deeds of the man now known as Caesar, although in my mind he was always Octavian. I had at least learned not to slip up and refer to him in this manner, and I suppose that now he is secure enough that he will let an old man have his one small act of defiance in referring to him by the name under which he was born.

In his usual manner, he wasted no time in basking in the adoration of the people and the upper classes, instead starting on his reforms almost immediately. He announced his plans for the Legions, causing quite a stir throughout the ranks, and not a little fear among the citizens. At the height of the war, there were 59 Legions on both sides, with Octavian's plan calling for that number to be reduced to less than half that number, 28 in all, but that reduction had already been taking place for some time. Some Legions would be allowed to finish their enlistments, while others, unsurprisingly most of Antony's Eastern Legions, had either already been discharged or would be immediately. The last of Antonius' loyal lieutenants were dealt with, and here Octavian's policy of clemency was not quite so all encompassing. Sosius was forgiven; in fact, he was given a governorship, but Canidius was not, and was executed by Octavian. However, it was for the memory of Antonius himself that Octavian reserved his most vicious treatment. His name was stricken from the Fasti, where all events pertaining to the Republic are recorded, while all statues of Antonius were removed, his name stricken from all bronze tablets. Not content with that, Octavian also prompted the Senate to pass a resolution that made the naming of any member of the Antonii with the *praenomen* Marcus against the law, then had the date of his birth declared *nefas*. It was as if Marcus Antonius never existed, but removing the memory of the man from the minds of Romans everywhere was not as easily done; even today, people still talk of his exploits as if they witnessed them personally. Despite Octavian's best efforts to erase all trace of Marcus Antonius, his memory still lives today, and I believe that it will only grow as time passes. For all his flaws, and all of his failures, Marcus Antonius walked like a giant among his fellow Romans, larger than life but fatally flawed, and most surprisingly to me, his relationship with Cleopatra has become as important to his story as anything else he did.

I had been giving much thought to what to do about Gaius, now that I had learned of his affair with Iras. He avoided me for a couple of days afterward, but soon enough the pull of whatever it was that he was feeling for Iras became too strong to overcome. I dealt with the situation by ignoring it for the most part, despite being concerned that he was seriously considering doing something stupid like making their arrangement permanent. While I had not completely made up my mind to do so, I was giving much thought to adopting Gaius and making him my sole heir, so that he would have the bulk of my estate and most importantly my status as *equites* when I died. I was so sure that his father, the elder Gaius Porcinus, would not object that it did not even occur to me to write to him or Valeria to tell him of my plans. There were sweeping changes taking place at all levels of the Republic, in both the army and in the civilian world, of which I planned on taking advantage, knowing that it was rare for such opportunities to present themselves. I also began spending time with some of the oldest men, men of my *dilectus* like Vellusius, trying to make sure that their affairs were in order, and to find out what plans they had made. The system of banking by the *tesseraurius*, while not started by Caesar, had been more stringently enforced under his command, so all of the men had something set aside, some more than others. I was most concerned about Vellusius, Herennius, and a few of the other old veterans who were essentially unfit for any other type of work. The toll of 32 years of marching, making camps, and fighting was severe, so that these men hobbled about, crippled by wounds, their hands gnarled from gripping spades and turfcutters. Their backs were bent from the weight of their *furca*, and even when they did not carry their packs, they leaned slightly to one side like they did. They were covered with scars, they cursed horribly, and they were more or less unfit for any other company besides themselves. If they did not have sufficient means to provide for themselves, they would end up begging in the streets of Rome, or worse, and I for one did not want to see any of my men resort to banditry. Most of them had accepted the idea that their days under the standard were coming to an end, but for a few the prospect of life as a civilian was more terrifying than any foe they ever faced. Vellusius was one of these, and when I called him to my office, I learned that he was harboring the idea that he would be allowed to continue marching.

"Vellusius," I said as gently as I could. "What do you think the prospects are of you finishing another enlistment?"

He blinked rapidly, a habit of his that showed he was nervous. "I haven't given it much thought, Primus Pilus. I just know that I can still outmarch and outfight any man in this Legion, I don't care how much younger they are!"

That might have been true just two or three years before, but it was no longer the case.

I had no desire to hurt Vellusius by pointing out the truth, so I agreed with him. "You're one of the best in this Legion, Vellusius. But all of us old warriors have to hang up their sword at some point. I'm going to do it myself, you know that."

"I know, Pullus, but you'll still be with the army. And I can't be Evocatus, can I?"

"No," I acknowledged, since the position of Evocatus was open only to those in the Centurionate, and Vellusius, while a good Legionary, was no Centurion.

"But haven't you always wanted to open a wineshop, or farm?"

He looked confused by the question. "Why would I want to do that? It's too much work."

He gave me a grin that was almost completely toothless.

"Vellusius, do you really think that marching every day, then digging the ditches and chopping the wood for towers and building roads is less work than running a wineshop?"

That got him blinking even more rapidly while he considered the question.

At last, he just shrugged. "It's not work that I'm used to, I guess. I never really wanted to do anything more than be under the standard. I'm happy here, Pullus. I just don't see why I can't keep doing what I like doing."

How does one respond to that? I wondered. With all the complaining, the men trying to shirk their duties at every turn, or outright deserting their comrades, here was a man who loved all of it, and all he asked was to be allowed to continue. But I had to think of the Legion first, and the brutal truth was that Vellusius was not fit for full duty any longer. He had forgotten, or refused to accept the fact that he had struggled mightily on this last march, which had been one of the easiest we had ever done. He did not straggle, finishing with the Legion every day, yet had retired early, and as each day progressed, had looked worse for wear. It caused me great pain to tell Vellusius the truth, and I struggled to find the words. The gods chose that moment to give me an inspiration in the form of an idea popping into my head that caused the words to come tumbling out before I had a chance to think things through.

"That's too bad," I began, "because I was hoping that I could convince you to give up marching under the standard for a chance at some easy duty that will allow you to remain in the army."

That got his attention, and he leaned forward, his face a picture of avid curiosity. As hard a worker as Vellusius was, and as willing as he was to do whatever job he was given, he was a Legionary through and through, and there are no more magic words to a man's ears than "easy duty."

I said nothing for a long moment, savoring Vellusius' anticipation. "You know that I am assuming a new post, don't you?"

Vellusius nodded.

"And with this new post of Camp Prefect, I'm authorized to have a bodyguard. I've given it a lot of thought, and there's no man I'd rather have watching my back than you, Vellusius."

He stared at me for several heartbeats, his expression confused. This was not the reaction I was expecting, and my heart sank as it seemed that he would spurn my offer.

However, the source of his consternation became clear when he asked, "Why in Hades would you need a bodyguard, Pullus? You're the best man with a sword that I ever saw, and you're stronger than two men put together."

I relaxed, knowing that this was an objection that I could handle with relative ease.

"But I don't have eyes in the back of my head," I explained. "And I don't have ears everywhere. I won't be leading a Legion, which means I won't be as close to the men as I'd like, and I need someone who's respected by the rankers. That's you, Vellusius."

His face flushed, clearly pleased by my words, as he rubbed his chin thoughtfully. "What does it pay?"

"Twice what you're making now," I said instantly.

His eyes lit up at the prospect of making more than a thousand sesterces a year, along with all the wine and whores that would buy.

He stood up, offering his hand. "Primus Pilus Pullus," he said formally. "I'm yours until death."

"Hopefully it won't come to that," I replied, taking his arm in return.

Vellusius left a happy man, while I sat down to try and figure out a way to make what I had just offered happen, since I made it all up on the spot.

The beginning of the year that was the occasion of the fifth Consulship of Octavian started auspiciously for me, when Miriam came to tell me that she was pregnant. Despite being extremely happy, there was a fair amount of nervousness because of what happened the last time she was pregnant. I immediately sent Iras to pay for a white kid goat to sacrifice to Bona Dea, and I was careful not to hug her too hard, which Miriam laughed about. Aside from my personal life, most of my time was devoted to the business of the retirement of this *dilectus* of the 10th. I decided that in my last weeks as Primus Pilus, I would take the opportunity to remove all of the dead wood from the ranks, culling those men of the replacement draft that had proven to be slackers, malingerers, or cowards. Despite this not being a particularly large number, it was enough that between the retiring veterans and them, the 10th as a Legion would essentially exist no more, at least until the youths that would fill its ranks got some experience. Even more damaging to the prospects of the Legion would be the loss of Centurions, since more than two-thirds had announced that they would be retiring as well. From the First Cohort, only Laetus and Macrianus were staying on, and I knew that there was little chance of either of them being named Primus Pilus. Octavian would undoubtedly take this opportunity to put a Primus Pilus in place that was of his choosing, someone he could control and would be predictable in his actions. It was understandable, and if I had been in his place, I would have done the same, like I did when I became Primus Pilus with the Centurions under me. That did not mean it would be easy, and that those Centurions who were staying would like it, or even have a spot available for them. With the size of the entire army being reduced, there would be a glut of Centurions to fill the available slots, so the competition would be fierce. And lucrative, I thought, if whoever was making the choices was so inclined. As part of his reforms, Octavian was raising the pay of Centurions substantially, partly in an effort to curb many Centurions' habit of squeezing their men by various means. I had serious doubts about how effective that would be, but I agreed that something needed to be done. There is nothing wrong with men paying their Centurions to switch guard shifts, or miss a fatigue, as long as it is not for punishment, but too many were going much, much farther.

Scribonius, Balbus, and I had resumed our evenings together, with Gaius a frequent guest, regardless of my mixed feelings about seeming to approve of his relationship with Iras. However, for once in my life I listened to Miriam and did not put any pressure on Gaius to break things off, accepting that it would only make matters worse. Most of the time we spent reminiscing, or discussing our respective plans for the future. Balbus had decided to try for status as Evocatus, with my patronage, while Scribonius seemed to be wavering in that direction, instead of returning to Rome. Balbus and I teamed up on Scribonius at every opportunity, working on him to make the decision to stay with the army. The idea of keeping Balbus and Scribonius nearby was incredibly appealing to me, for purely selfish reasons. Miriam was growing visibly larger, almost with every passing day, taking on that glow that pregnant women seem to have. Iras did everything she could to make her mistress' life more comfortable, but I did not like the look of envy in her eyes whenever she thought I was not looking, watching Miriam walk by. I thought about warning Gaius to take precautions, but I quickly recognized that it would only make matters worse. He was an excellent Optio, at least according to Didius, his Princeps Posterior, and Nigidius, his Pilus Prior. Gaius had a bright future ahead of him, if he chose to stay in the army, but my hope was that I would be able to provide an option for him should he decide to leave the army. No matter how much I loved the army, and as well as Gaius was doing, it was never far from my mind that it is a dangerous profession. I had also never forgotten that I had been exceedingly blessed by the gods, and that what I had attained was available only to a very select few men. Gaius had many valuable and admirable attributes, but the one thing I had seen that he was missing was the gift of fury, that sense of rage that is unleashed when it is needed to win a fight, giving one the ability to do anything that is necessary to come out victorious. Because of that, I had great fear about what was in store for Gaius if he chose to remain in the army, and I wanted to give him another way to improve himself.

April arrived, and along with it the wagons containing the money with which to pay the men, rumbling through the gates under heavy guard. Its arrival was supposed to be secret, but it did not surprise me in the slightest to see the men lined up at the gate, chattering excitedly to each other about who was going to spend their money the fastest. The atmosphere was almost exactly that of a festival day, and to commemorate the occasion, the Centurions pooled their money to pay for a feast for the Legion. This was for the men only, no guests allowed, not even for the Centurions, including me, a meeting of warriors one last time. We spent as much money on wine as we did on the food, and we rented extra slaves, including cooking slaves who were supposed to be the best in the region, although Nicopolis still being such a young city that was not saying all that much. Fortunately, it does not take much to satisfy a soldier; quantity is valued over quality, meaning a few hundred pigs were slaughtered in anticipation of the coming event. We also paid for an extra milling of the flour to make it even finer, making the bread soft and golden. As one last surprise, we hired every whore in Nicopolis, even sending for women as far away as Athens, which we planned on announcing at some point in the feast, before the men were too inebriated to do anything about it. It was going to be a night to remember, even if most of the men would be unable to at the end of it. Tables were laid out in the forum, and I gave the provosts a hefty bribe, both to make sure that men from the other Legions did not try and sneak in, but also to look the other way when the inevitable high spirits brought out the equally inevitable violence. The evening of the feast came, and while Miriam did her best to hide it, I could tell that she was not happy. Finally, just before I left, she could contain herself no longer.

"You are going to find a woman that you like better than me," she burst out, causing me to freeze in mid-stride as I headed for the door.

I could not help gaping at her, taken aback that this was her fear. I was expecting some sort of admonishment about drinking too much, despite resolving in front of her that this night I would not moderate myself like I usually did. I was unprepared for this, but I instantly knew that I was on very dangerous ground, on which I would have to tread carefully.

"Why would you say that?" I asked carefully.

"Because I am fat and disgusting, and why would you want to lay with me when you can have one of those thin, beautiful women?"

The tears started to flow, and I moved to comfort and hold her, which had become awkward because of her size.

Patting her on the back, I said in as soothing a voice as I could, "There's no other woman I'd rather have than you, no matter what size they are." Thinking to lighten the mood with a joke, I gave her a swat on the behind then teased, "Besides, I like my women a little plump."

That was the wrong thing to say, and it took some time before I was able to get things sufficiently calmed down before I could leave, with Iras glaring daggers at me. I stopped by Scribonius' quarters, then met Balbus and Macrianus on the way. The forum was decorated, but in a very martial manner, with the standards of every Cohort and Century arranged around the edge of the forum. Behind the table set on the rostra, where the Pili Priores and I would be sitting, was the Legion eagle, flanked on either side by a pair of shields embossed with the Legion emblem. Crossed behind each shield were two javelins, while underneath the standard was a stand on which we placed our armor and helmet, with a highly polished helmet and matching mail shirt placed on it. Similar touches abounded, the legs of the tables wrapped in ivy in a symbol of our many victories. Those men who were decorated wore their decorations, including those of us who won Coronae Civica, Coronae Muralis or Coronae Vallaris, though in my case and of one or two others, we had to select which crown to wear. I chose the Corona Civica, because it meant the most to me since it was Scribonius that I had saved to win it. We wore just our tunics and belts, while no weapons of any kind were allowed, but we did not go as far as to search the men before they were seated. The men of the 10th Legion began to arrive, all of them in high spirits as they took their seats. Placards were placed on each table with the Section, Century and Cohort of the men assigned there, knowing that as the evening progressed there would be much shuffling about.

Taking their places, we waited for all the men to arrive, and I was pleased to see that there were no empty spots, this being the one duty that nobody wanted out of. Seeing that the entire Legion was assembled, I nodded to Valerius, who put the *cornu* to his lips, blowing the call to *intente.* As one, the men of the 10th Legion jumped up to snap to the position, the forum thunderously silent once the notes fell away. I waited several moments, savoring the sight of these men, my men standing in perfectly aligned rows, none of them moving or fidgeting in any way.

Satisfied, I filled my lungs to bellow, "SEATS!"

Again, as one unit, the men immediately sat down on their benches, but since they had not been given leave to talk, they remained silent. I believe that because they all knew that this was one of the last occasions the entire Legion would be together, and would be among the last orders that they would receive, this made it easier for the men to obey, as I had never seen them so quiet. I gave the signal to the serving slaves to fill every man's cup with unwatered wine, although as the evening wore on I would have them cut it. Once all cups were filled, I stood on the dais, climbing onto my bench so that I could clearly be seen, my own cup in hand. Raising it, I spoke loudly but without yelling, not wanting to spoil the dignity of the moment, relying on the Centurions seated further back to relay my words.

"Comrades of the 10th Legion, Caesar's Equestrians . . . " This brought an appreciative chuckle, if only from those relatively few men who were part of the original *dilectus* and had witnessed the event firsthand.

"Most of us have come to the end of a long road together. For some men like me, most of your Pili Priores and a select few in your ranks, that road has been longer, as this is our second enlistment. All of us sitting here have been blessed by the gods to have survived hard fighting, hard marching, and even harder playing."

Like I expected, the men roared their appreciation at my acknowledgment that they were essentially incorrigible wine drinkers and woman chasers.

"But let us not forget those of our friends and comrades who do not fill their seats. You will notice the section of empty tables," I pointed to the area that I had ordered to be roped off, taking almost a third part of the forum.

"Those tables are for the comrades and kin that are no longer with us, men who fell at Philippi, in the bitter winter of Parthia and Armenia, and in all the battles we have fought for Rome. Let us not forget them, and let us always honor their memories."

All of the men had fallen silent, many of them turning to look at the empty tables, each of them lost in the memory of a friend no longer there. I did not want to dwell on all that we had lost, but neither did I want to minimize the price we had paid.

"For you men of the second *dilectus*, and for those of the replacement draft, I have been your Primus Pilus for all of your time in this Legion. That means that most of you have known no other Primus Pilus, and it is my hope that you are as proud and honored to have been led by me as I am to have led you through all that we have been through together. To those comrades who started with me, now 32 years ago, you are brothers to me, and your deeds have been so glorious, so awe-inspiring that you set an almost impossible example for the men of the second *dilectus* to follow."

I paused, happy to see that most of the men were leaning forward on their benches, listening intently.

"But it is with equal parts pride and regret that I must tell you that, from the viewpoint of your Primus Pilus, the men of the second *dilectus* have acquitted themselves with every bit as much courage, honor and professionalism as I could have hoped for, and their deeds have added to the glory of the 10th Legion. The 10th, more than any other Legion, has achieved a record that has made it famous throughout the world, and when our enemies learn they are facing the 10th, they know they are facing their doom! All that we have achieved will live forever, and the name of the 10th Legion, of Caesar's Favorites, will be on the lips of men for as long as they walk the Earth."

I raised my cup higher.

"To the 10th!"

To a man, the Legion rose, hoisting their own cups in the direction of the dais and the eagle.

"The 10th!" they all roared as one, causing a burning in my eyes and a tightening in my chest, the swell of emotion threatening to overwhelm me.

That night I got the drunkest I had been since I was a young man in Gaul, with the wine flowing in a series of toasts made by one Centurion after another. Some of the men in the ranks, men like Vellusius for example, were even allowed to speak some words, though by the time his turn came around I am afraid I do not remember much of what he said. The evening was spent in regaling each other with stories, and I could not help noticing that Scribonius, Balbus, and a few others seemed to have decided to team up to tell stories that would be extremely embarrassing to me. However, I did not mind in the least; the way I saw it, my time as Primus Pilus was at an end so there was no need to preserve my *dignitas* in front of men who were leaving themselves. Scribonius, naturally, had the most tales to tell, and he had men roaring when he described one of the few times I sneaked out of camp with he and a few other men when we were *tiros*, the resulting night spent huddled in a ditch as we tried to evade the provost, who had chosen that evening to conduct a sweep of the very establishment we were frequenting. Frankly, I had forgotten about that until Scribonius brought it up, but once he did, I vividly recalled the feeling of terror at the thought that my career would be irreparably damaged because I wanted to be considered one of the boys. Many of my misdeeds and misadventures were brought up; thankfully, some of them both Scribonius and Balbus were involved in and none of us had any desire to make those known. I gave as good as I got; for as many tales Scribonius had to tell about me, I had as many to tell about my former Optio and best friend. Balbus fared little better, since I exposed his bizarre fascination with the idea of taking someone's ball sac and turning it into a coin purse. The food was good, but most importantly it was plentiful, and I saw men loosening their belts a notch, always a good sign. The wine continued to flow, and I must confess that I forgot to tell the serving slaves to start cutting the wine, and it was not that long before things became raucous. As I, and the other Centurions expected, long-simmering feuds erupted, first with shouted words, followed quickly by a flying fist. Fortunately, no man tried to sneak in a weapon, or if they did, it was not used, making the worst damage some missing teeth and a broken nose or two. All in all, it was one of the most peaceful and enjoyable gatherings of this type we ever had. The evening began to wind down, mainly because men were becoming incoherent, but before I could officially adjourn the banquet, Scribonius and Balbus came from their respective spots to stand side by side on the dais, facing the men. They held their hands up for silence, which I thought was unrealistic of them at that point. Eventually the men took notice and began to settle down, except that it was not nearly as silent as at the beginning.

"Before we finish," Scribonius cried out, waiting for those Centurions still sober enough to relay his words, "there is one thing that must be done, here and now."

That quieted the men down more, while I eyed my two friends curiously, not having any idea what was in store.

"As all of you know, the Primus Pilus is not leaving the army, he is assuming a new post that is part of Caesar's reforms of the army."

Despite my bleary vision, I saw men nod their heads up and down.

Evidently so did Scribonius, for he continued. "He is being honored by Caesar by being one of the first of these new officeholders called the Camp Prefect. He will be the second in command of the army where he is stationed, only behind the Legate himself."

Some men cheered this, while others started gazing about, clearly getting bored.

Scribonius clearly sensed or saw this, quickly getting to the point. "As a token of our esteem and our best wishes, the Centurions of the 10th Legion have selected these gifts to help him in his new post."

I was completely bewildered, since I had never heard a whisper of any kind of gift. Balbus turned, waving his arm over his head, clearly signaling, and I strained to see a man on the far side of the forum, who turned to trot off in the general direction of the *Praetorium*. Meanwhile, Scribonius bent down to uncover a bundle that he had apparently tucked away underneath the dais, which I could not see until he pulled it up onto the platform. Pulling the cloth covering it out of the way, he lofted a cuirass, similar to the type worn by Marcus Antonius and

Caesar, except it was not as ornate as theirs. Still, the workmanship was exquisite, and when he turned to allow me to examine it, I saw that it had two bulls facing each other, symbol of the 10th Legion. Centered underneath it was a prancing horse, while around all of it were garlands of ivy in filigreed silver. Although it was highly decorated, it was plain to see that it was also designed for function, made of a thin sheet of highly tempered metal, with the edges hammered and curled. It had clearly been made with my specifications in mind, because the chest was much wider than normal, and was longer as well to accommodate my torso.

"As you can see, this cuirass is decorated with the symbol of the 10th, and the horse is to commemorate the day that Titus Pullus was one of Caesar's equestrians when they rode to face Ariovistus."

Scribonius handed me the cuirass, the men cheering while I examined it, but they were not through. Balbus now stepped forward, waving again. I looked to the back of the forum to see the man he had signaled earlier, only this time he was leading a horse. The horse was gray, with dapples and when it drew closer, I could see that it was a magnificent beast. Its mane was black, outlining the line of its neck, thick muscles rippling underneath its skin with every step. It tossed its head, eyes rolling nervously when the man I could now see was Vellusius, brought the animal to the foot of the dais.

The men murmured appreciatively while Balbus began talking. "With his new post of Camp Prefect, the Primus Pilus is entitled to a horse, paid for by the people of Rome. Well, we are the people of Rome, aren't we?" The men roared their answer, then Balbus continued. "And since the people of Rome don't know how big the Primus Pilus is, we didn't want him riding some swaybacked nag that could barely carry his fat ass."

Only Balbus could have gotten away with this, while I was still too flabbergasted to take any offense even if I had been of a mind to, and he turned to shoot me a wide grin. I replied by way of an obscene gesture, which some of the men saw, causing them to laugh harder.

"So we present the Primus Pilus with this magnificent animal, from one of the best breeders in Cisalpine Gaul. And we will make sacrifice to the god Apollo Atepomarus that he never go lame and always carries you safely in and out of battle."

Balbus waved to me to come examine the horse. I rose on wobbly legs, trying to focus and not do something horrible like trip over my own feet. Stepping down from the dais, I approached the horse, marveling at its size and the promise of power in its hindquarters, where the dapples were the most prominent. The horse nickered nervously, tossing its head and blowing at my approach, taking in my smell, the both of us sizing each other up. I reached out my hand, allowing the animal to sniff me and get my scent before putting it on his neck. He flinched but did not step away and I felt the warmth transfer from his body to mine.

"He hasn't been named yet," Balbus told me.

I did not know what to say, almost overwhelmed by emotion. Even having ridden many horses by this point, starting with that steed on which I rode to face Ariovistus with the rest of the Equestrians, I had never owned a horse, let alone one of this quality. I thought about vaulting onto the beast's back but quickly realized I was too drunk and the horse was not familiar with me, making the chances of him flipping me off his back or me just missing him altogether very high, so I refrained. Instead, I took the lead rope from Vellusius, and holding the end I climbed back onto the dais. The men were standing and cheering now, making the horse even more nervous, and he began prancing about, almost pulling the rope from my hands. Rather than have a stampeding animal tearing through the packed forum, I handed the rope back to Vellusius, telling him to lead the horse away. While he did, I gave my thanks to Balbus, Scribonius, and all of the Centurions, but I cannot remember exactly what I said, still too choked by the sentiment they were showing me. The men were still standing, clapping their hands, cheering or calling my name, and I could not stop the flood of tears, forcing me to turn away from them so they could not see my weakness. Balbus and Scribonius came to me, both embracing me, then each man kissing me on both cheeks.

"You bastards," I managed to say, and they both laughed.

"This is for you, Titus. It's our way of thanking you for all you've done for us and the Legion."

"You had just as much to do with it as I did," I told Scribonius. "You and all the Centurions."

"But you set the example, Titus. We followed you," Balbus put in.

I could not think of anything more to say, instead just shook my head while trying to dry my eyes.

While I was occupied, Scribonius turned back to the Legion. "10th Legion, *intente*!"

I have to say I was impressed; I did not know that Scribonius could create such volume with his voice. Despite their inebriation, the men snapped to the position smartly enough, facing the dais. Scribonius turned to render a salute, the men following suit, it taking a moment for my fogged brain to understand that they were saluting me, and that I should return it. It may not have been the most perfect salute I ever rendered, but it was the most heartfelt.

When the salute was finished, Balbus turned back to the men and called out, "Enough of the seriousness. It's time to get drunk!"

That received the loudest cheer of the night.

I vaguely remember being carried back to the apartment, but I do not know who it was that did so. I felt hands stripping my belt and tunic off, that being the last conscious thought until the next day, when I became aware that Vulcan had decided to use my head as an anvil, while it felt like a Legion was marching through my stomach. I barely had enough time to roll over and vomit over the edge of the bed. Hearing a pitiful moan that I assumed came from me, I saw a pair of feet approach the bed, except that it hurt too much to lift my head to see who it was. From the size and shape, I knew it was Miriam. Hoping for a sympathetic voice and perhaps a cool rag for my head, I waited to feel her comforting touch. However, none of that was forthcoming.

Instead, she spoke in a tone that could not be described under the best of circumstances as sympathetic. "You made a mess on the floor. I hope you are satisfied with yourself."

Tilting my head slightly, wincing at the pain it caused, I squinted to see a pregnant woman that looked like Miriam, except that the scowl on her face along with the hands on her hips were unfamiliar to me.

"I'm dying," I croaked, hoping that my clear misery would soften her heart.

"You are not dying," she scoffed. "You are just a miserable drunkard. And you are making a mess on my floor."

"Woman, I said I'm dying," I tried to roar, yet the pain was too great, and I am afraid it came out more of a squeak.

"Then hurry up and die so I can clean up," she shot back, then turned to walk out of the room.

"If I had known you were this cruel, I would never have married you."

It was the best I could come up with under the circumstances.

"If I had known you were such a drunk, I would never have said 'yes,'" she scoffed, taking the final honors in the exchange.

I settled back down into my misery, and I am not sure how much time passed before I revived enough to swing my legs out of the bed, holding my head in my hands. Naturally, my feet landed in the puddle of vomit, causing another revolt in my stomach, making me heave but nothing came up. Staggering into the main room, I had to squint to see Iras sitting at the table sewing, with Miriam nowhere to be seen.

"Water," I gasped. For a moment, she did not move, her expression mirroring that of her mistress, or at least so I assumed.

"Don't make me beat you, Iras," I warned her. "I may not be able to do it right now, but I won't forget. Now get me some water."

She rose then, going to the bucket, dipping a cup into it and bringing it to me. Her nose wrinkled at my sour smell, but I ignored her, grabbing the cup and draining it.

"Where's your mistress?"

"She went to the market."

"Alone?" I asked, alarmed that she would be out in her condition by herself, but Iras shook her head.

"Diocles is with her."

"Good," I grunted.

I bid her to get another cup of water, and when I finished it, I felt slightly better. Iras examined me for a moment, saying nothing. Finally, shaking her head, she went to the cupboard by her bed where she kept her belongings. Rummaging around, she retrieved a couple of vials and a jar, bringing them back to the table. Without saying a word, she took the cup from me, filled it back up with water, then taking a small spoon, began scooping contents from the vials and jar, dumping them into the cup. Stirring it vigorously for several heartbeats, she took a sip, making a face before adding a bit more from one of the vials. Tasting it again, she seemed satisfied and she brought the cup to me.

Thrusting it at me, she ordered, "Drink this."

I examined the cup for a moment, seeing the vile green concoction in it, then shook my head. "You already tried to poison me once," I said. "I'm not about to give you the chance again."

"If I had wanted to poison you," she said patiently, "you would have been dead a long time ago. I thought we were past that."

"Maybe you think you're doing me a favor by putting me out of my misery," I suggested.

Iras shook her head again, but I could see that her forbearance was wearing thin. "This will help with the hangover. It's what my father used when he drank too much. And he drank a lot."

This was the first Iras had ever mentioned anything about her family, at least in my hearing. I think it was that more than anything that prompted me to take the cup. Drawing a deep breath, I drank the concoction down in one gulp, almost gagging at the taste, feeling the particles of whatever was in it passing down my throat. Slamming the cup down on the table, I staggered a step, suddenly lightheaded, having to sit down at the table to let my head clear. Iras stood watching me, an expectant look on her face, and for a horrifying moment, I thought that she had indeed poisoned me and was waiting to see me keel over dead. However, the opposite happened, because within a few moments I started feeling better.

"It seems to be working," I said cautiously, to which she just gave a matter-of-fact nod.

"I told you," she replied, turning back to her sewing.

"Who was your father? What did he do?"

I did not plan on asking the question, it just came out. Her needle stopped, hovering over the fabric, but her face was turned away, and I could not see her expression. Her shoulders rose as she heaved a great sigh, then she set the fabric down.

Without turning to face me, she replied in a very small voice, "My father was Ptolemy Auletes."

"Ptolemy Chickpea?" I gasped.

"Yes, that is what you Romans called him," she replied, her tone defensive. "But he was Pharaoh of the Two Kingdoms, King of Sedge and Bee, son of Ptah and Isis."

"So who was your mother?"

"She was one of his slaves," she said flatly. "He was bored one day, and he took her."

A thought suddenly occurred to me, and I am glad I was sitting down.

"That means Cleopatra was your sister," I gasped.

"Half-sister," she corrected, then gave a bitter laugh. "Me and half of the palace slaves around my age were related to her."

"Did she know?" I asked her.

"Yes, she knew."

Iras turned to look at me squarely, the very last piece of the puzzle of why it was Iras she had sent after me falling into place.

"That is why she sent me to kill you, and why she wanted Deukalos to kill me afterward."

I struggled to absorb this, not helped by my hangover, yet I had to admit that the concoction she had made me drink was making me feel better. "Does Miriam know this?"

Iras shrugged. "I never told her, but your wife is very smart. I would not be surprised if she figured it out."

"But she never told me," I said, more to myself than to her.

"Husbands and wives always keep secrets from each other," Iras told me, giving me a look that I could not interpret. "Are you saying that there is nothing you keep from my mistress?"

I was about to answer her, then stopped to think for a moment. "No," I conceded. "I don't tell her everything, but when I don't, it's to protect her."

"Maybe she did not tell you what she suspected to be true in order to protect you," she suggested.

"No, I think if she did that, it was to protect you, not me," I told her frankly.

Because the fact is that if I had known that Iras was related to Cleopatra by blood in those early days of our acquaintance, I would have undoubtedly killed her, and it was then I understood that is exactly why Miriam had not told me. Iras bowed her head, closing her eyes, then I saw her lips move, and I recognized that she was saying a prayer of thanks. I supposed I should have done the same, given the way Iras had become part of our lives and was so important to Gaius by this time, but frankly I was still not feeling that well.

Miriam returned, clearly still angry with me, while Diocles gave me a sympathetic look. I assumed that Miriam had been unloading her feelings about my night of debauchery on him, but she studiously ignored me. Frankly, I was grateful for the peace and quiet, hoping that the storm in the house would blow itself out. My stomach was still too queasy for any solid food, but after cleaning up my mess, Diocles slipped me some broth.

"Don't let the mistress know I helped you," he whispered.

"You belong to me, not her," I grumbled.

"True, but she runs the house, and we both know it. Besides, I learned from watching my mother and father that upsetting a pregnant woman isn't a good idea."

"Fine," I muttered. "Let's just get out of here and get to camp. I have work to do."

The sun was blinding, making me sure my head would split while I used Diocles' shoulder for support. The poor man looked like he would collapse under the weight, so we were both miserable for the walk to camp. I was perversely happy to see that most of the men and Centurions were in much the same state I was, stumbling about holding their heads while they tried to attend to their duties. Some of the whores that had been rented were still about, and I told Diocles that they had to be dispersed immediately. In reality, it was a farce, and if there had been an attack on us from some enemy, the 10th Legion would have been slaughtered. Thankfully, there was no prospect of that happening, and Statilius, still left in Nicopolis as both the commander and with *Propraetor imperium,* had given his consent to the banquet in the first place. Entering my office, I fell into the chair behind my desk while trying to gather my wits through the headache. A few moments later, I heard a knock, immediately after which both Balbus and Scribonius entered, the former looking obscenely fresh while Scribonius looked like I felt, making me feel better.

"Don't speak above a whisper," I warned them, to which Balbus gave a mocking laugh.

"You have the head of a woman when it comes to wine," he jeered.

"I can't even think of something to say back to that, so I guess you're right," I admitted. Turning my attention to other matters, I asked Balbus, "You said something last night, at least I think you did, about the post of Camp Prefect rating a Public Horse. How do you possibly know that? Or were you just making it up?"

In answer, Balbus turned to Scribonius, who explained, "No, it's true. Camp Prefects are entitled to a Public Horse, though I don't know if they're going to call it that. But the funds come from the treasury, so it's the same thing."

"How did you know about it? I didn't know that Octavian had announced the position, let alone put out any details."

"He didn't," Scribonius confirmed. "That's why I asked him."

"You what?" I could not hide my surprise at Scribonius' boldness.

"Not in person," he added hastily. "I wrote to him, told him what we planned as far as honoring you in some way. He's the one who came up with the armor and the horse."

"Really?"

Scribonius nodded. "Yes, really. In fact, he thanked me for making him think more about the position, and that he was going to make this standard for every Camp Prefect."

I must say that I was a little disappointed; I would have liked it better if I were the only one to be honored in this way.

"Did he say how many Camp Prefects there will be?" I asked curiously.

"Actually, he wrote that at first there would be no more than four, maybe five, with each army that's stationed throughout the Republic, but he didn't go into any more detail than that."

Thinking about it, I realized that I had no idea where Octavian would place these armies around the Republic. I wondered if I would be given any choice in the matter of where Miriam and I were placed.

"Thank you for all of that," I said.

"You thanked us already," Balbus replied.

"Did I? I don't remember doing it."

"I don't remember ever seeing you that drunk." Scribonius grinned at me painfully. "And I haven't been this bad off myself in some time."

"So what are you going to name the horse?" Balbus asked. I confess I had not given it any thought to that point, barely remembering that the beast existed.

"Bucephalus," I blurted out the first name that came to mind.

"That's a bit presumptuous, don't you think?" Scribonius offered. "Naming him after Alexander's horse is a lot to live up to, even for an animal as fine as this one."

"Then what do you suggest?"

He frowned, obviously not liking having the burden of coming up with the name on his shoulders.

"Mars?"

"Mars!" I scoffed. "Bucephalus might be presumptuous, but don't you think Mars is a bit . . . predictable?"

"Well, it's not my horse! You name it then."

"I tried to but you pissed all over the name."

"What about Ocelus?"

I looked at Balbus, who had offered the suggestion, trying to place the name.

"Isn't that one of the Gaul's names for Mars?" asked Scribonius, and Balbus nodded.

"He is from Gaul, after all. And he is a war horse," he added.

"I like it," I announced. "Ocelus is his name."

I stood and told the two, "Now let's go get acquainted with Ocelus."

Fortunately, Ocelus was already broken to the saddle, making it more a case of getting acquainted with him, and him getting accustomed to my weight on his back, which at first he was not happy about. After a few days, however, he and I seemed to have established a bond that sometimes happens between man and animal. It was not something I had ever experienced before, this feeling of attachment to an animal, even when I was a boy on the farm back in Astigi, but I welcomed it. We developed a routine where I would hide an apple or carrot on me, which he would nose about for, sometimes even grabbing the fabric of my tunic with his teeth in his search, more than once getting more than fabric in his mouth, giving me quite a bruise. I took to spending more and more time with Ocelus, saying as the reason that I needed to become proficient at riding, since Octavian expected it of me. The truth was that in the last months of her pregnancy, Miriam was becoming increasingly hard to live with, and I grew tired of being snapped at for things I did and did not do. At first, I did not remember Gisela being so irritable, until I recalled that I had not been around for either of her pregnancies, making me feel a stab of guilt at my anger at Miriam. She was clearly uncomfortable, and I did not need the midwife to tell me that it was a difficult pregnancy. I sent Iras to the temples of Bona Dea and Juno Lucina every day to make an offering, even incorporating one of Miriam's gods, Malakbel who protected pregnant women, into my household gods. In short, I was doing everything I could think of to help Miriam, both with the gods and for her physical comfort, except spend time with her. The plain truth was that I was extremely uncomfortable being around Miriam, not due to any lack of love for her, but because I felt so helpless seeing her in such distress. I am afraid that the only comfort I could offer her she did not want, which did not put me in a good temper, and for the first time in our marriage, I was actually tempted to seek release with one of the whores in town. The only thing that stopped me was the knowledge that it would hurt Miriam. I had learned to accept that her people did not view sex outside of the union of marriage the same way that Romans did, meaning that the only time I sought female company outside of her was when we were separated for long periods of time. Normally this was not a hardship, since I truly loved Miriam, and when we were together, I had no desire to stray, but because of her condition, this was more difficult. We were a week away from the final dismissal of the bulk of the 10th, with most of those days spent in the men turning in their gear, which was then inspected for serviceability. Those pieces that were still usable were put back into stores, with the rest either sold as scrap, or the pieces used as parts for repair. Worn metal bits like spades and turfcutting blades were melted down to make new ones, while the links of chain mail shirts were kept to use as spares. The only things that were not sold, even if they were worn were weapons, including javelin shafts, since we did not want them to fall into the hands of possible enemies. Helmets and shields were also items that would not be sold; helmets were generally not melted down, but hammered back into shape, while the wood from the shields was stripped down to be used for other purposes. Grinders, wicker baskets, pots, and the various leather bits were the pieces that merchants lined up to buy, sold in lots to the highest bidder. Men also packed their personal belongings while they made their plans for where they would go. Most of them were going to at least make an attempt at farming the plots of land that they would be given, despite the fact that experience told me that a large number of them would fail for one reason or another. Usually it was due to boredom, once the reality of the grinding hard work that it would take to make a farm work set in, even one in Italia that was confiscated from Antonian supporters, where the most senior men of the first *dilectus* would go. The rest, those men of the second *dilectus* would be settled in Pannonia, recently conquered as part of Octavian's campaign in Illyricum. This was most of the men, and they would find it much harder going in a country that was conquered just six years earlier and was still largely uncivilized. Granted, their tracts were along the river bottoms, where the land was more fertile, but there were stories of the Panonnii and their warlike nature still causing problems for those Legionaries that had already been retired there by Octavian. Speaking of Vellusius, there had been no opportunity to discuss keeping him on as my bodyguard with Octavian, not that I tried very hard, telling myself that he would not like being bothered by such a petty matter when he was back at Rome, essentially rebuilding the Republic. Then, Diocles came back from the *Praetorium* one day, just days away from the retirement with a look that was equal parts excitement and anxiety.

Without waiting for me to ask him, he blurted out, "I just heard that we're going to have an important visitor from Rome to oversee the payout of the Legion."

"Not Caesar, surely."

I could not imagine him taking the time to attend to such a matter, expecting that it would be a Senator of some sort. I was not prepared to hear Diocles' answer.

"Not Caesar," he acknowledged. "But close enough. Marcus Agrippa is coming. He's supposed to be here in two or three days."

It took Agrippa four days to show up, arriving late in the day in his usual style, which is to say with just a handful of men, some of them bodyguards, some military Tribunes, and a pair of scribes. He wasted no time sending a runner to find me with an invitation to dine with him that evening. Arriving at the *Praetorium,* I found Agrippa busy with Balbinus. Once he was through, he beckoned me to follow him into his private quarters, and I was surprised to see that Balbinus did not follow, since I expected that he would also be joining us, but he just gave a wave to me while he headed out the door. Whenever I was alone with a member of the upper classes, particularly someone as powerful as Marcus Agrippa, I got very nervous. However, there was nothing devious in Agrippa's nature, although I had no doubt that if Octavian had sent him to do some dirty work he would not hesitate. Agrippa was renowned not only for his military abilities, but for his absolute unswerving devotion and loyalty to Octavian. Agrippa was reported to have been the first to call Octavian "Caesar," rather than by his given name, and what was inarguably true was that Agrippa's rise was due as much to his relationship with Octavian as it was to his abilities, which were prodigious. He was waiting for me in the room that served as both *triclinium* and meeting room, but I was happy to see that instead of couches, there was a plain table with chairs.

Before we took our seats, he offered me his hand, and I clasped his arm. "Congratulations on your promotion to Camp Prefect, Pullus."

"Thank you, sir," was all I could think to say.

"It's well deserved," he added, then motioned to a chair, which I took.

Seating himself across the table from me, we made small talk, mostly about the anticipation of the men for what was coming. Wine arrived, and we were silent, both of us sipping from our cups, while I waited for him to bring up his purpose for this meeting. Food arrived; very simple fare of bread, chickpeas, and pork, which I appreciated, and somewhat to my surprise, he indicated we would eat first.

Only after we were finished did he begin. "There are two or three things that Caesar has asked me to discuss with you and the other new Camp Prefects about the changes being made to the Legions."

"That suits me, sir. I have some questions of my own."

He lifted an eyebrow at this. "Questions?"

"Er," I stumbled, "to be more accurate, they're more requests than questions."

He sat back in his chair, face unreadable. "Why don't we start with what's on your mind first, then."

"First," I began, "I wanted to ask if Caesar would authorize the use of a bodyguard for me."

Like I expected, Agrippa's expression was a combination of amusement and puzzlement. "I must say that you surprised me. I wasn't expecting Titus Pullus of the 10th Legion to feel the need for a bodyguard."

"I don't," I replied, probably a bit too sharply.

Ignoring his look of irritation, I explained the situation with Vellusius.

"He's one of the only men left from my original tent section," I finished. "And although I don't need help in protecting myself, I trust him with my life."

He said nothing for a moment, then gave a shrug. "I don't see that it will be a problem. I'll check with Caesar, but actually, I think it's a good idea for every Camp Prefect to have one. What else?"

This request I was more comfortable with asking, since I assumed it would be little more than a formality. "I wanted to make an endorsement for Primus Pilus Posterior Balbus and Secundus Pilus Prior Scribonius as Evocati." I was very happy that Scribonius had decided to join the ranks of the Evocati, and before he could say anything, I added what was essentially the meat of the request. "And that they be part of the Evocati that are with whatever part of the army that I'm with."

Agrippa suddenly looked down, and I thought that he was going to tell me that putting us together would be a problem. When he spoke, he seemed to confirm my fears.

"Actually, it's the Evocati I wanted to talk to you about. Among some other things." He seemed to gather his thoughts before he continued. "Caesar has decided to do away with the Evocati."

I looked at him in shock, and it took me a moment to speak. "But the Evocati have been part of the army since even before the Marian reforms!"

"And Caesar believes they've outlived their usefulness," Agrippa replied, making me wonder at his choice of words. Did that mean that he personally disapproved of their disbandment? "He believes that they're a drain on the resources of the treasury in return for little value," he continued. "Being frank, during the civil war, they turned out to be more trouble than they were worth."

That I could not argue. In more than one case, some of the Evocati had been the most vocal among the troublemakers, not only for Caesar but for Antonius as well.

"True," I granted. "But now that Antonius is dead, Caesar has no other rivals for the foreseeable future." I fought a sense of desperation at the thought of Balbus and Scribonius not being at my side in some way. "And you can promise Caesar that the Evocati who are with my part of the army will stay loyal to him, especially with Balbus and Scribonius there."

"That's something you can promise, but no mortal can tell the future, not even Caesar, and he's not one to take a chance like that."

I struggled to keep my composure, deciding to drop the matter for the moment. "What other changes is Caesar making?"

Visibly relieved that this was going no further, Agrippa said, "To start with, the size of the Legions. We're going back to the traditional Century and Cohort size, except for the First Cohort."

It had been Divus Julius who started the practice of hundred man Centuries, notably enough with my Legion with the first *dilectus* in Hispania. Every one of the Legions he personally enlisted after that had that number, but Pompey had stayed with the traditional number of eighty-man Centuries.

"What's going to happen to the First?" I asked.

"Well, since it's the First Cohort in every Legion that sees the most fighting, it traditionally takes the most casualties. The number of the First Cohort is going to be doubled, to 160 men."

"Will it have the same number of Centuries?"

"Yes," he nodded. "But that's not all. We're going to put the best men in the First Cohort, the cream of the

Legion. With the reduction of the size of the army, as we consolidate we'll be able to find enough men to fill the ranks of a new Legion with experienced men."

What he was describing, other than the numbers, was already taking place, except that it was more by happenstance than design. I had thought about this in the past, and my conclusion was that the reason that the First Cohort of almost every Legion I had seen was the best in that Legion, except for some of those conscripted during the civil war that were filled with either raw youths or foreigners, was because of the situation that Agrippa had described. He was absolutely right that the First Cohort saw more action, and because of that, got more experience, which naturally increased their proficiency. While the Cohorts were rotated in the line of battle in the second and third lines, or the Second, Third, or Fourth was sometimes switched out, I had never seen a First Cohort not be in the front ranks. It was also true that the First usually took more casualties, except in the case of catastrophes like what had happened with the Tenth in Parthia or the Third on Leukas Island.

"That makes sense," I said, if a little grudgingly, still smarting from the rebuff on the Evocati, though an idea was slowly forming in my head. "What else?"

"We're going to make it standard practice that when losses get to a certain level that those men will be replaced. No more of a Legion marching into battle at half-strength because they've been whittled down over the years."

That was not much of a surprise, and in my mind was long overdue, having already been done by generals like Antonius, after the disaster of the first Parthian campaign.

"You already know from Caesar that land will no longer be part of a man's retirement, correct?"

"Yes, he already told me."

Agrippa took a deep breath, seeming to gather himself and when he uttered his next words, I could understand why. "Finally, the term of enlistment is being raised to 20 years."

For the second time in the conversation, I found myself almost too shocked to speak. "Twenty years?" I gasped, but before I could say anything more, he put up a hand.

"Pullus, think about it. The truth is that most of the men ended up serving more than 16 years because their generals could not spare them. Caesar is just recognizing that as a reality," he said, to my ears sounding a trifle defensive.

"And look at the trouble it caused those generals, even Divus Julius," I pointed out.

"Be that as it may, Caesar has decided, and on this point he's made up his mind."

I took that as a sign that perhaps there was still hope for the Evocati yet.

I spoke slowly, my mind racing as I tried to form the argument that I would use to change his mind. "Enlistments used to last for just a campaign season," I began. "Then when Gaius Marius made his reforms, that was changed, first to four years, then to six. Then it was ten, and Divus Julius made it sixteen. Starting with the 10th," I felt compelled to add. Agrippa nodded but said nothing, which I took as a sign to continue. "Now, in my lifetime, this will be double what it used to be. I understand the need for changes in the army, and for the most part, I agree with what Caesar has decided. However, Marcus Agrippa, you and I both know that the class of men who fill the ranks of the Legions are almost as afraid of change as the patricians. And you also know as well as I do that the way the lower classes express their discontent will make the streets run red with blood. I'm not saying it will happen," I held up my hand to stop whatever Agrippa was about to say, "but you can't deny that it's a strong possibility. The people love their traditions, and the men of the ranks are no different. Thrust too much change too quickly on them, and there's no telling what will happen."

"I know," Agrippa said quietly, which I was not expecting at all. "I told Caesar that myself, but he's determined to make these reforms."

"Which is why I think doing away with the Evocati at this point is a mistake."

That is when the idea hit me, and I suddenly leaned forward. "Why not keep the Evocati as they are, but don't add to their ranks and just let it die a natural death?"

He studied me for a moment, pursing his lips thoughtfully. "That might work."

"There are two exceptions that I'd ask for, and you know who they are already."

He gave a small smile, tilting his head as he did. "I was expecting that. And what do you have to offer in exchange?"

Is he asking for money, I wondered? I dismissed the thought immediately. Marcus Agrippa had become one of the wealthiest men in Rome, and whatever I could pay was a pittance when compared to his fortune.

"What did you have in mind?" I asked cautiously.

"Your service as Camp Prefect for ten years instead of five," he answered instantly.

It was then I knew that I had walked right into a trap.

I swallowed hard, but I answered as quickly as he had. "Fine, as long as Balbus and Scribonius serve with me, for however long they care to."

His brow furrowed, not the reaction I was hoping for. "Not the whole time you're Camp Prefect?" he asked sharply, shaking his head, clearly not liking the condition.

"I'm not going to bind them in that way, and that's my final condition. And it's nonnegotiable."

"Very well," he said crossly, folding his arms.

I reached across the table to offer my hand to seal the bargain, and for a moment, I thought he was having second thoughts and would not accept, but then he extended his own.

With that matter settled, I assumed that we had concluded our business, and it was more out of curiosity than anything else that led me to ask him, "Where will the *dilectus* for the new men of the 10th be held? In Hispania, I assume."

His hesitation caused me to look up from my plate, where I had been finishing up the candied figs provided as a dessert. One glance at his face told me that something was afoot, and I sat back to listen, not sure that I was going to like what I heard.

"Actually, there's not going to be a *dilectus*."

"I don't understand." A thrill of alarm shot through me. "The 10th isn't going to be disbanded, surely?" I gasped, and my relief was intense when he shook his head. It was equally short-lived.

"No, it's not going to be disbanded," he allowed, then seemed to search for words. "You're aware that when the 10th chose to march with Antonius, Caesar was forced to raise another 10th Legion?"

"We chose to march with Antonius?" I was incredulous, this being the first I had heard that choice of words used to describe what had happened to the 10th. "We had no choice in the matter. He was the legally appointed Triumvir, and we were ordered to go with him. How is that choosing?"

"In the beginning, that's true," he replied evenly. "But when the . . . difficulties began, the 10th chose to remain loyal to Antonius."

"We were on the other side of Our Sea, with a dozen other Legions, and we were in Parthia," I shot back. "Caesar didn't truly expect us to suddenly declare for him in the middle of a campaign, did he? How long do you think it would have taken Marcus Antonius to give the other Legions the order to fall on us and wipe us out? There would be no 10th Legion left if that had happened."

I was getting very angry, which Agrippa could see in my face, but he did not back down. While I did not like it, it only raised my respect for him.

"You had other opportunities after that," he shot back. "But you chose to stay with Antonius, and because of that Caesar has decided to combine the men of his 10th Legion with yours."

I was about to continue the argument by asking Agrippa exactly how we could have done as he clearly believed we should have, then decided to let it drop, recognizing that I was wasting my breath. Octavian had obviously made up his mind on the matter and arguing with Agrippa about it would solve nothing, but I resolved to bring it up with the man himself the next opportunity I got.

As if reading my mind, Agrippa warned, "And, Pullus, this isn't a subject I would bring up with Caesar. He's made up his mind on this, and his feelings about what happened with your 10th aren't going to change. In fact, it's a very sore subject and you'd make him very angry."

"Well, that at least explains why he was the way he was the day after Actium." I remembered how abrupt and unwelcoming he had been when I had shown up with the First Cohort, contrary to his instructions. If he truly suspected the 10th of being disloyal, I could see why he was so adamant that I come alone. Turning back to the original topic, I asked Agrippa to continue.

"Your men," he corrected himself, "your *former* men will be sent to Syria to join the rest of the 10th, where they're on garrison duty."

I considered this for a moment, then a thought struck me that was so horrible I could barely stand asking about it. "The 10th will still be the 10th Equestris, won't it?"

For the first time, Agrippa looked genuinely regretful. He slowly shook his head. "No, Pullus. Caesar has decided that since we're combining the two Legions, the 10th will be known as the 10th Gemina, the Twins."

"The Twins?" I could not hide my scorn. "What kind of name is that? Men aren't going to want to fight for a Legion named for the Twins, and neither are our enemies going to be afraid of them. The 10th Equestris is known throughout the world, and the very name strikes fear in our enemies' hearts. How can Caesar throw that away?"

"If it makes you feel any better, the men of the other 10th aren't any happier. They were the 10th Veneria, because of Caesar's descent from Venus, and they're just as proud of their name as you are of the Equestrians."

"Perhaps, but who ever heard of them? How many battles have they won? Did they conquer Gaul? Were they at Pharsalus? They were guarding the baggage at Philippi if I remember."

"They were a raw Legion then, and they were guarding the camp," Agrippa said stiffly, clearly offended, but I did not care.

Of all the insults done to the 10th, this was the worst. I sat back, fuming, Agrippa no less disturbed than I was as we sat staring at each other.

Finally, Agrippa said in a calm tone, "Pullus, I can understand why you're upset. But must I remind you that after tomorrow it will no longer be your concern? Your time as Primus Pilus is over, and the 10th is Caesar's to do with as he wills."

There was certainly no arguing that, yet it did not make me feel better; in fact, it made me feel worse, reminding me of my powerlessness. It took some effort, but I turned my attention back to more pressing matters, at least as far as I was personally concerned.

"So where am I going? Has Caesar decided that yet? Will I be going to Syria with the 10th?"

That idea did not distress me, thinking of Miriam and how happy she would be to be returning to her home. However, my hope was immediately dashed when Agrippa shook his head.

"No, Caesar has decided that you're going to be the Camp Prefect of the army in Pannonia."

"Pannonia?" I considered this for a moment, and I cannot say that I was pleased.

My first thought was that I would be taking my wife and infant to a wilderness, a rough land that was still not completely pacified.

"What Legions are going to be there?"

"The 8th, the 11th, a new enlistment of the 13th, the 14th and 15th."

"At least there's one Spanish Legion," I said a bit grudgingly.

"The area isn't as peaceful as we'd like," Agrippa allowed. "The Legions won't be all together in one place, you understand."

"I wouldn't expect them to be. Where are the other armies going to be stationed?"

Agrippa counted out on his fingers. "Syria, which I already mentioned. Pannonia, Macedonia, Hispania, northern Gaul along the Rhenus, and Egypt, which is a special case."

"How so?"

He hesitated for a moment before answering. "Because of Egypt's importance to Rome, Caesar has decreed that nobody of Senatorial rank may govern there, nor hold the post of Legate. In fact, at least in the beginning the Camp Prefect will be the ranking Roman military commander."

That seemed to me to be the most important post, and I was a bit offended that I was not considered for it.

"Who's going to be in Egypt?"

"Balbinus," he replied.

Ah, I thought, that confirms just how much of Octavian's man the Primus Pilus of the 12th actually had been, and continued to be. Octavian would clearly not entrust Egypt to just anyone, unless he was absolutely convinced of the man's loyalty. Neither of us spoke after that, since it was clear that our business was concluded. I stood to leave, thanking him for the meal, then we clasped arms once more, and I left with my mind full of all that I had learned that night.

"Ten years?"

I stood watching Miriam's eyes fill with tears at the thought, and I had yet to tell her where we would be living. I decided to delay that, taking the coward's way out but not wanting to distress her even more.

"It was the only way I could get Scribonius and Balbus into the Evocati," I explained, then told her of Octavian's decision to do away with the Evocati altogether.

"And Balbus and Scribonius mean more to you than your wife?" she asked accusingly.

"No," I protested. "Don't you want them there with me to protect me?"

I thought it was the smart thing to say, but this only deepened her anxiety.

"I thought you were done with the dangerous work." Now the tears began to fall freely, so I moved to her to try and offer her some comfort, but she was having none of it, pulling away instead.

"I won't be in the front line of battle, but being in the army is not without risk," I said as gently as I could, fighting my own irritation. How could she not understand that as long as I carried a sword there would be danger of some sort?

"You're happy about that," she accused. "You want to risk your life. You're like a man who loves his wine too much and cannot live without it or you will become sick."

I opened my mouth to protest, then recognized that it would do no good. Arguing with a pregnant woman is a hazard, not only to one's peace of mind but to their health.

Thinking to change the subject, I asked, "How are you feeling today?"

"How do you think I feel? I can barely move about, the baby is kicking me night and day, and I cannot get comfortable no matter what I try. And now my husband is telling me that he lied to me about how much longer he has to stay with this cursed army."

It could be worse, I thought to myself. I could tell you that you'll be in the wilds of Pannonia for at least the first part of those ten years, but for once, I wisely held my tongue. Instead, I called for Iras, who came into the room with an almost identical expression of a man afraid of walking into an ambush, peering cautiously at the two of us standing across from each other.

"Your mistress is unhappy and uncomfortable," I said sternly. "Why aren't you attending to her needs instead of off mooning about Gaius?"

"Don't be mean to her. She isn't the one who is causing me grief and anguish, you are! Why don't you just leave and go back to your precious army? You love it more than you love me!"

She and Iras stood there glaring at me. I knew that I was beaten and that it was time for me to make my retreat.

"Fine," I said over my shoulder as I left. "If that's what you want, I'll go. But don't get angry at me for being gone."

"Don't tell me how to feel," she yelled as I walked out the door.

If this was what Gisela had been like, I thought, I did not regret missing out on any of it.

"Ten years?"

For the second time I was asked the question, this time by Scribonius and Balbus, sitting across from me in my quarters in camp. They looked at each other, then Scribonius spoke, presumably for the both of them.

"I don't know that I like the idea of being responsible for you being tied to the army for five more years. How does Miriam feel about it?"

I gave him a rueful grimace. "How do you think she feels?"

"I can't say that I blame her all that much," he replied.

I sat looking at the both of them, the thought suddenly blossoming in my mind that they would turn the offer to join the Evocati down.

"You aren't thinking of turning it down, are you?"

Balbus spoke for the first time. "Scribonius is right. I'm not any happier at the idea of you doing ten years than he is, but mainly because I think that means we'll be doing ten years too." He gave a slight shrug before continuing. "And as much as I love you as a brother, Titus, I don't want to spend the rest of my life in the army. Five years is one thing, but ten is another. I'll be more than sixty by then."

I always tended to forget that as old as I was, men like Balbus and Scribonius were older. Scribonius was just three years older than I was, but Balbus had been in Pompey's 1st Legion when he was selected to fill the ranks of the 10th during the first *dilectus*, and he had been 22 then. Granted, he was still in excellent condition, and like me had never been seriously ill during his time under the standard, but I could not argue his overall point.

"Caesar wants to do away with the Evocati altogether," I pointed out. "The truth is that I doubt that he's going to want an Evocatus around ten years from now, or even five years from now. And we all know that what Caesar wants he gets."

"But why agree to the ten years if you think that's the case?" Scribonius asked.

"Because I'm about as sure as I can be that it was always going to be ten years no matter what," I answered, for that was the conclusion I had come to, given Agrippa's quickness in bringing it up. It became clear to me that whether or not it had always been in his plans, Octavian had determined that the post of Camp Prefect should be at least ten years in duration, and I was convinced that allowing Scribonius and Balbus into the Evocati was just a ruse on his part. They considered this, while I waited for their decision.

"Fair enough," Scribonius finally said, looking at Balbus, who nodded his agreement.

"We'll do it. Personally, I don't much care if it is ten years. I know that I'd be bored if I went back to Rome and became a man of leisure. But I understand Balbus' concern. He's already an old man," he grinned at our friend, who gave a mock scowl, punching Scribonius in the arm, not lightly either.

Turning to me, Balbus said, "I'm in. But if you're wrong and I find myself doddering around in uniform ten years from now, I'll kill you."

"If Miriam doesn't do it first," Scribonius added helpfully.

The retirement ceremony took place the next day, with the rest of the army on parade to watch as each section was called forward, while a brief account of their service record was recited, including the decorations earned, the campaigns and battles they participated in, and finishing with the wounds received in battle. Then they moved as a group to the paymaster's table, where each man was given his retirement bonus, minus of course any amounts still owed to the army. This should have been an occasion of great joy, but more often than not left men cursing bitterly as amounts for lost and broken gear added up, proving once and for all that the army never forgot. It was at moments like this that one could see exactly where all those myriad forms and pieces of paperwork went, while it was especially vexing because some of the gear was destroyed through no fault of the men. What seemed to anger the men the most was the deductions for gear that was lost when our baggage train was destroyed during the first Parthian campaign, which was through no fault of any man in the Legion. That did not matter to the army, however, since the money was still deducted over the protests of almost every Legionary. Fortunately, there was still a lot of money left over, so it was more grumbling than anything more incendiary or dangerous. Regardless, it cast a pall over the process, which was trying enough because it took the entire day. Once paid, the men returned to their spot in the ranks to wait for their comrades to go through the ordeal. Since the men were retiring, we allowed them to stand in loose formation or walk about within their Centuries and Cohorts, which helped pass the time.

Agrippa was seated on a curule chair, underneath a canopy, face impassive as he oversaw the proceedings, and he had told me that he wanted to say some words once all the men were paid. The other Legions were not so fortunate, required to stand easy but unmoving while they watched the 10th perform their last duties. The men of the 10th who would be staying behind looked on as well, yet they seemed to share in some of the joy at seeing their friends receive their reward at long last. I knew that foremost in every onlooker's mind was the thought that one day, if the gods willed it, this would be them as well, which helped keep them settled down as they watched. The sun was hanging low in the sky by the time the last men were paid off and had returned to their spot in formation. Agrippa rose from his chair, walking to the rostra of the forum, as I turned and called the Legion to *intente.*

"Veterans of the 10th Legion," Agrippa began, pausing to allow his words to be relayed by the Centurions. "I come on behalf of Caesar Divus Filius, Princeps of the Republic, and father to you all."

This was the first time I heard Octavian referred to as Princeps, but was certainly not the last.

"He has sent me, Marcus Vipsanius Agrippa, to thank you personally for the service you have rendered Rome, and to oversee the payment of your well-deserved bonus and plots of land. All that you are receiving is in recognition of your sacrifice, but I am also required to remind you that your duty to Rome does not stop. For those of you settling in Pannonia, I call on you to be vigilant, to show the natives of the region the proper respect, but never forget that you are Legionaries of Rome, and she may yet call on you in the event of an emergency."

The men remained silent, their faces registering their barely concealed boredom and impatience. However, his next words got their attention, except I do not think it was in the way they were expecting.

"I remind you of Caesar's clemency, which he granted to the 10th for their choosing to march for the deceased Marcus Antonius, for which each of you should be eternally grateful. Caesar, as father of the Legions, is a loving and forgiving father, but his forgiveness is not infinite, so I offer this warning to you that such actions as have been taken by other veterans will not be tolerated with veterans of the 10th by Caesar."

The angry buzzing started immediately, my own jaw tightening in anger at his words. I had hoped he would drop this insistence on casting the 10th as mutineers because of their service with Antonius, but clearly he had not. He appeared unmoved by the obvious outrage of the men at being characterized in this manner, staring back at us without blinking.

Continuing as if he did not hear the muttering in the ranks, he said, "Remember these words, and heed them. There has been enough unrest and bloodshed, and the citizens of Rome have grown tired of seeing its veterans being the cause of the trouble. I call on each of you to refrain from falling into those habits, and to keep faith with your father, and with Rome. I wish each of you the best of health and fortune for however long each of you has in this world of the living, and offer up this final prayer."

Lifting his hands skyward, he tilted his face up, uttering the prayer that was always said before going into battle.

"Jupiter Optimus Maximus, protect this Legion, soldiers all."

Agrippa was wise enough to know that there would be no applause for his stark warning disguised as a parting farewell. Mercifully, it had been much shorter than I, or anyone for that matter had expected. Without saying a word, he abruptly turned to walk off the rostra, heading to the *Praetorium*, his scarlet *paludamentum* swirling behind him. I thought briefly of going after him to confront him about his words, but quickly dismissed the idea, knowing it would only make matters worse. Instead, I turned back towards the Legion, and seeing the looks of hurt and anger on their faces, made a quick decision. Striding from my spot, I mounted the rostra. The other Legions were in the process of being dismissed but most of the men, seeing me and curious about what I would say, did not leave the area, choosing to stay and listen.

"Comrades of the 10th Legion," I cried out. "And you will always be my comrades, for as long as we live. You heard Marcus Agrippa, and if you are like me, you do not like the taste his words left in our mouths."

Men nodded, shouting their agreement, while I calculated on how far I could go.

"But Agrippa is wrong," I continued. "You did nothing to deserve the scorn or censure of any man, even a man as wise and powerful as Caesar, or Marcus Agrippa. At the time we left Philippi under Marcus Antonius, he was the legally appointed Triumvir, named as such by the Senate and People of Rome. We were given no choice in the matter, but neither did we complain, and we did our duty, and we did it well. Your friends, your relatives who died in the cold of Parthia, or in the fighting in Armenia, or who took sick, neither did they do anything to be ashamed of, and they did NOT die as rebels against Rome!"

There was no way that Agrippa did not hear the roar of the men shouting their defiance, and I looked over to see that even men of the other Legions were cheering. I held my hands up, waiting for the men to quiet down.

"That does not make everything he said unwarranted. Whether we want to admit it or not, many of our brothers have been the source of much of the trouble during these last years. So I am asking you, as your Primus Pilus, a man who knows you and your hearts, to do as Agrippa asks and become productive and peaceful citizens. It would cause me a great deal of pain and anger to learn that any of my men have become bandits, or are causing problems with their actions in other ways. This is not an order; it is a request."

I stood there, surveying the men, then I filled my lungs for the last command I would give as Primus Pilus of the 10th Legion.

"10th Legion, you are dismissed."

The men were allowed to remain in the camp overnight. However, the next day, they had to leave immediately, naturally making that last night a riotous affair, men saying their final goodbyes, not only to the men of the replacement draft but to those friends and relatives in other Legions as well. I spent the night in the camp, giving Miriam the excuse that men would be coming to say farewell and I did not want her being disturbed, except the reality was that I did not want to get my head bitten off. Miriam was a month away from when the child was due, and I did not relish the thought of spending that time without any distractions. I had been given two months to make my way to Pannonia, except there was no way that Miriam would be able to travel so soon after the birth of our child. I had arranged for Vellusius and Agis to accompany Miriam, and Iras of course to Pannonia. We would be living in the town of Siscia, which had been what passed for the capital of the region, being taken by Octavian five years before. The camp was located on the outskirts of the town, but according to men who had seen it, the camp had actually been connected to its walls for added protection. This would present a challenge in keeping the men from spending too much time in town, and as Camp Prefect, I supposed that solving this problem would fall on my shoulders. Now that I had learned the identities of the Legions that would be in Pannonia, there was one more task to complete, which would be getting young Gaius transferred out of the 10th as soon as possible.

But I have said enough for now; both Diocles and I need a rest. It has been several days since my old friend Ocelus and I have enjoyed each other's company as well, because when I am absorbed in a task, I tend to forget everything else. Only the gods know how many days we will have together, yet I need to refresh myself, for there is still so much to tell, of more fighting, killing and dying, and of the rise of the man who assumed Caesar's mantle, taking Rome into a new era. And I am still one of the only men left who can tell the world of the role my comrades and I played in changing our Republic into the new form we see today, Titus Pullus, Legionary of Rome.

Author's Note

What would become the second part of this portion of Titus' story was essentially just the second half of what is now Marching With Caesar-Antony and Cleopatra: Part I-Antony, until neither my editor nor my group of advance readers could find a part of the book they thought could be excluded, except for one minor episode in Parthia. Naturally, as the author I'm not very objective in such matters, so I had to disqualify myself. Consequently, it's somewhat difficult for me to view these Historical Notes as a separate piece and not just a continuation of the notes I wrote for what is now Part I-Antony.

However, this second part is much more focused on Cleopatra, and her influence on Marcus Antonius, so there are a couple of points I would like to make concerning how historically accurate this might be.

In terms of the events that the star-crossed lovers engineered, participated in or were victims of circumstance, there is a substantial record that has been accepted as historical fact. As in all cases such as this, it's less that we absolutely believe the events occurred as the surviving record indicates than it is that to date nothing has been found that would refute the commonly accepted view. For the most part, Cleopatra's physical presence at the various locations in the book hews as close to the record as I can get. Where matters get complicated is in trying to discern fact from fiction about Cleopatra, the woman and queen. It's a truism that history is written by the winners, but I'm inclined to argue that Octavian's smear campaign against Cleopatra still ranks as the most successful in history. The Cleopatra of the "historical record" is a figure that is viewed through the lens that was ground by Octavian and his supporters, and I don't think any facet of her life was left untouched.

That makes my goal of historical accuracy somewhat difficult, and I confess that I might have chosen the easy way out in Titus' adoption of at least a partial view of Cleopatra as orchestrated by the Princeps. But I do have some sympathy for Cleopatra's plight as the ruler of a much weaker country, trying desperately to maintain at least a semblance of autonomy from Rome, and how incredibly demanding and dangerous such a balancing act might have been. Perhaps it's also because I was raised by a single mom that I hold a soft spot in my heart for the Egyptian queen and Pharaoh, looking for a way to protect her child. Of all the fascinating "what-ifs", one that intrigues me a great deal is what a world with a fully grown son of Caesar would have looked like. Ultimately, however, I do believe that Cleopatra wasn't content with coexistence with Rome, and that she harbored her own ambitions in regards to seeing Egypt in the ascendance again. Because of that, she is ultimately going to be viewed as an enemy by a man like Titus Pullus, who is Roman through and through.

Finally, there is the topic of the 10th Legion's "betrayal" of Octavian by supposedly choosing to march for Antonius. And just looking at the historical record, it would certainly seem that the 10th betrayed Octavian, if only because of his attitude and treatment of the Legion after Actium. At that point in time, the 10th Legion was arguably the best known and most celebrated of the Legions of Rome, and the name of the 10th Equestris was undoubtedly worth some sort of advantage against any potential enemies. Yet Octavian disbanded the 10th Equestris, and it was never referred to in this manner again, at least in the records that we have found. So clearly they did something to deserve his censure? I don't believe this, for the simple reason that the more I have learned about Octavian, particularly in this, the early stages of a long career, the less I admire the man. He clearly had a vindictive, petty streak that he indulged on numerous occasions, and I believe that timing also had something to do with his actions. He had just returned from Egypt, where he had been outsmarted by Cleopatra, who he clearly despised. For someone with as much pride as Octavian, who always believed, because he usually was, that he was the smartest guy in the room, that had to enrage him. More than anything, however, is that it would be next to impossible to convince me that when the 10th, along with all the other Legions, were divided up between the victors of Philippi, the men of the Legions were asked their opinion about who they wanted to serve with and where they wanted to go. No, I am convinced that the respective Primi Pili of each Legion were given orders, that they saluted and replied to with the only response that would have been acceptable, a simple "Yes sir."

When conducting my research, I never found any real description or explanation of what happened at Actium as far as which Legions boarded ships and which didn't. Titus' leadership of the 10th Legion into a mutiny against Marcus Antonius is, of course, fictional. However, I would like to think that if it's not likely to be similar to what actually took place, it is at the very least plausible. For whatever reason, the evidence suggests that the 10th Equestris that had been part of Antonius' army didn't board those ships that escaped Actium and ultimately sailed to Alexandria for the final showdown. Hopefully you like my version of how it happened as much as I do!

Made in the USA
San Bernardino, CA
21 March 2014